COMPANY OF FOOLS

Selling For Love & Life,
Is A Tricky Business

By

J. W. Nelson

Copyright © J. W. Nelson 2020
This book is sold subject to the condition that it shall not, by way of trade or otherwise, be lent, resold, hired out, or otherwise circulated without the publisher's prior consent in any form of binding or cover other than that in which it is published and without a similar condition including this condition being imposed on the subsequent publisher.
The moral right of J. W. Nelson has been asserted.
ISBN-13: 9798677697968

This is a work of fiction. Names, characters, businesses, organizations, places, events and incidents either are the product of the author's imagination or are used fictitiously. Any resemblance to actual persons, living or dead, events, or locales is entirely coincidental.

For John Allen & the beloved memory of Alec Caesar.

ACKNOWLEDGEMENTS

I'd like to acknowledge the many companies within the IT computer and software sales world that I have worked in over the years since 1991. Particularly DEC (Digital Equipment Company) during the mid 90's into the early noughties, (it became Compaq and is now HP – Hewlett Packard).

The inspiration from my tenure there has helped in writing this book and a trilogy/thriller (Crime of the Century) about the infamous 'Millennium Bug'.

There are too many to thank here. However, special mentions go to my sales team at DEC, managed by John Allen that included Lynda, Karen, Pamela, Angela, Jeff, Joycelin, Paul, Anne & Helen (to name but a few).

A final thanks to Claire Johnson, daughter to Alec Caesar, he and John Allen are the main thrust behind many of Justin Whalley's 'incidents', throughout this book, with more to come (I hope) in the follow up book - Journey into History.

Thank you all.

CONTENTS

PROLOGUE 1
THE SALES CONFERENCE 5
KEEPING FOCUSED 45
FAMILY AFFAIRS 119
WORK HARD, PLAY HARD 178
ALL GOOD THINGS… 202
FOOLS 256
STORMY WEATHER 311
ABOUT THE AUTHOR 357

PROLOGUE

I was a boy born into an already-large family. I had two sisters and two brothers. All of my parents' offspring were older than I; that made no odds to me. I believed I was a bright, intelligent, adept man.

In chronological order, my parents, Donald and Shirley, had Jennifer, followed by Oliver, then came Mark, penultimately Emily and finally, me (Justin).

I knew deep down that I was not absolutely gorgeous to look at, yet easy enough on any female's wandering eye. That's what I always liked to believe. As I developed, so did my personality and my emotional state.

As a child I would cry very easily at things, such as being smacked by my mother. The threat of punishment also brought the same results though; an embarrassing time in front of my other older siblings.

I felt as though I couldn't control my emotions. Worse still, I thought I would never be able to. That was far more frightening. Eventually I did learn to master them. In fact, I seemed to go the other way, showing no emotions whatsoever. I obviously overcompensated.

Yet I look at my family, who are close, but in a distant, unspoken way. As a youngster, I recall very few hugs. There were not many times I heard the words 'I love you' and 'you be careful'. Yet intrinsically, that language of love was always quietly spoken. I always knew it was there. Just because something wasn't said, it didn't mean no one was thinking it.

I must make it clear, that I do love my family, unequivocally. No doubts. I understand that everyone handles and displays emotions differently.

Oliver and Mark work in so-called brilliant jobs. Whatever that meant. Both still live at home. Jennifer, the eldest, has a different father. She works as lawyer or a barrister, I think. Then Emily followed, born just a year before me and does some kind of office work.

I wondered if mum and dad made up Jennifer's job to feel proud, I was never too sure, as she was so many years older than I. The barrister thing was probably just a dream.

From what I can remember, she is very attractive. Maybe her beauty emanated from her father's genes. I never asked my mum about *her* father or about what happened. She always displayed a wounded, sorry expression, when I – or one of my brothers – asked about him.

Our house was always overcrowded, although I do remember my time there with some glee and humour. I recall Mark's first kiss on the doorstep with Vanessa Trindel. As we watched from the bedroom window, he burped in her face, just before that most crucial moment when their lips touched. He heard us laughing. I'm afraid my laugh can be raucous and easily identified. He never forgave us; he certainly never forgave me. Maybe that's why he's still living at home with Daddy.

I looked at my two older brothers, Oliver who was thirty-five and Mark who was thirty-two. I was determined to not end up like them. Content with very little, and had no freedom, no place to call their own. Then again, there were reasons for that.

Well, I found my liberty to a certain degree and escaped the loving home life. The sanctity and safety my dear mother provided.

I began to wear glasses when I turned eighteen. I had reached six feet one inch in height. I took care of my jet-black hair, washing it regularly. Styling it with gels and sprays recommended by hairdressers. Wore aftershave and dressed in suits, something I'd always liked doing.

My school friends would think I originated from a wealthy family, simply because I was always turned out crisply, looking the part, whatever the occasion. The real truth was we had very little, but my mother's paternal pride kept all of us looking better off than we really were.

This simple trait paid dividends for me. My attitude reflected how I looked and came across. Confident, calming, loyal, enthusiastic. Unknown to anyone seeing me, I was like a swan. Serene, austere, gliding on top of the water, everyone admiring you. Yet underneath the water, the swan's legs are working like fuck to move itself supremely along. That's me, Justin Whalley.

On the outside and to the outer world, a confident slick operator. Inside, my heart thumps so hard, I think I'm going to fall over. My hand shakes so much, if people saw, they'd think I was Elvis. Thankfully my ability to withhold urine is legendary. Otherwise, there'd be a lot of changing trousers, and some explanations that wouldn't make anyone proud.

I'd done well, so I thought, at twenty-eight years old, getting the job I now do. I've been there just over a year and I really do like it. However, some of the procedures and processes are nothing short of idiocy. But then again, who am I? A young twenty-something upstart, from a dodgy area of the city. They certainly wouldn't give a shit what I think.

Anyway, there are three major tangibles I want from life. I don't think it's asking much.

1. A wife (or at least a long-term girlfriend to start with).
2. Children (the patter of tiny Justin's makes me go all giddy inside).
3. A good job (one out of three isn't bad).

This is my story of obtaining and keeping these three major life-changing factors. I know life is a learning process, but for friggin' hell's sake, I didn't think it would be this difficult.

THE SALES CONFERENCE

1

I had finished my presentation in front of a buoyant, ebullient audience. Three hundred pairs of eyes bore into my frail, medium-sized frame.

A drip of perspiration ran from high on my forehead into the crevice created for my eyes, and under my thin-rimmed designer spectacles. The vision of the 'swan scenario' floated in and out of my mind. This increased as the audience erupted into riotous applause.

I stepped two paces back from the podium, and smiled at the applauding audience.

'Thank you, thank you,' I called out over the noise.

Even though my mic that I had pinned to my jacket lapel was on, I doubt if anyone heard me. They were enjoying this. Admittedly, so was I.

My nerves began to turn into adrenalin as I lapped up the praise. Was I really that good? Damn, I must have been. That's what I kept telling myself, until I could get down, which I desperately wanted to do.

Turning to three senior executives on my right, seated behind me on stage, I beckoned the chairperson to step forward to introduce the next speaker. I was glad I didn't have to follow me.

Usually the sales audience were either boisterous, but listening to you, or they were quiet as a mouse whispering in a library; in other words, they were fast asleep and paying no attention whatsoever.

Relief flooded my whole body as I finally took the five steps down off the 'pop star'-like stage. Each step was extra carefully taken, as the cameramen videoed my every movement. This would always be played back at a later date in each of the twenty offices around the world.

I stepped off without a hitch, striding confidently down the left-hand side of the enormous auditorium that all the Eiron Plc (pronounced 'eye-ron') sales execs were sat in. The host made some witty remark about the applause I received, but I wasn't listening and I didn't care either way.

With an aisle in the middle and down each side, the 'Lincoln Suite' would easily have catered for three or four times the number of execs that were there.

The high ceilings had intricately decorated chandeliers hanging ostensibly from them. Thick plush carpeting covered the part-wooden-panelled floor. The air conditioning, attempted to keep everyone cool and awake.

It was no different to any other similar hotel business function room, that I had been to.

The host, however, was an absolute arsehole. That's not like me to bitch, but he was. One hundred per cent tosser. I didn't know someone could be as awful a person as he was. Unfortunately he was the UK Managing and Sales Director. We had to answer to him. Not everyone did, but that's another story.

He stood proud and haughty looking out across the audience. Lapping up the remainder of my adulation. His eighties curtain hairstyle swayed forward and back as he nodded his head to accept the applause. At six foot five, with a stern, straight face and piercing ice-blue eyes, Walter Baker smiled smugly, as was his trademark.

Towards the back of the hall, I fixed my eyes on a few guys from my team. My immediate manager, Errol Hughes. A clever, shrewd black guy, with a style that reminded me of Huggy Bear, from an eighties cop show. The exception was the hair. Errol hardly had any. And of course the clothes.

He was getting out of his seat, signalling me with his right hand. I think he was going to congratulate me. I hoped so. As he struggled to get by the legs of the other execs, I saluted Tom and Shaun, who smiled back and bowed their heads, mouthing, 'We are not worthy.' I got the joke.

Errol finally stepped over his underlings and reached out his right hand. I stood beaming from ear to ear, grasping his hand in a firm handshake.

'So you did it, you old bastard. Well done, my man. How's your underwear?' Errol asked me confidently, with an assured toothy grin.

We had to speak quietly, and continue walking, ready to exit the hall. The nob-head on the stage built up the next speaker.

By now Errol had his left arm around me. He knew I was nervous, that's why he asked me about my underwear.

'You know me too well. Where'd you think I'm heading now? The loo. I'm gonna have to go. You know the score,' I explained to Errol.

'Hey, you can talk to me,' Errol responded, laughing quietly as we pushed open the heavy oak wooded double doors, to exit the 'theatre'.

'Don't worry, Justin, I'll be right by your side.'

I gave Errol a strange look, which he ignored and continued to smile.

I had known Errol a long time but I never knew him wanting to go to the toilet with me before. I was obviously being paranoid.

When we reached the toilets, Errol told me why he wanted to come along. I was glad he did.

Inside, there were four urinals. One exec, I had seen around from our London office, stood at an angle with his tiny bit firing out his liquid waste substance. Errol and I gave him a quick once over. He finished and moved toward the basins to wash his hands. When he'd gone Errol began telling me what had grabbed my interest.

We stood with one urinal in between us. It was a man thing. Nothing was more awkward than when a third man entered and had to decide which urinal to use. You keep your head straight ahead, never turning left or right. Every man should be allowed his privacy.

So Errol began.

'Yeah, Just.' Nearly everyone shortened my name to this, when I allowed them. 'I overhead the big man on stage tell the European MD to look out for you.'

'What do you mean?' I replied just as I my urine was making its way out of my cylindrical orifice.

'Don't worry, it's all good. Good for you, I mean.' I broke the rule and glanced to my right, but keeping my head erect and in level eye contact with Errol. I had a 'tell me some more' look on my face.

'Walter actually singled you out, you know, for greatness and shit.' Errol chuckled in a deepish, throaty roar as he said the words. I couldn't believe it either.

'So I could be moving up in the world,' as I turned back to face the sterling white-tiled wall.

'Uh huh.' Errol finished and zipped himself up.

'You know I was never quite sure whether Walter liked me. He's one of those people you can't really judge. He doesn't give much away.' I tried to explain something, but the words coming out sounded as though they came from someone else.

I finished, nervously looking down at my light-grey-coloured trousers, hoping there were no splash marks. This time I was lucky.

Turning to the basins, I washed my hands when in walked Len Ferris. A mid-forty-year-old jackass in my book. Lived in the past, thought he'd done it all, always said too much and at the wrong time; this opportunity was no different.

Errol and I had dried our hands, when Len stood at the second urinal.

'Alright lads. Great conference again, eh? Usual bullshit speeches and pats on our back, while that slimy Walter bastard does fuck all and gets nearly half a mil a year.'

I had to step in, even though Errol held my arm.

'Look Len, these conferences are a third business, a third geeing up the troops, and the last third is a piss-up. It's never been any different. You of all people should know that.' I told him straight. No messin' around. I think Errol was mildly impressed.

But Len wasn't.

'What the hell do you know? You're a young whipper-snapper, still wet behind the ears no doubt.' I raised my eyebrows and noticed Errol about to make a move. This time I stopped him. I let Len continue.

'This company has its arse in its hand. Doesn't have a fucking clue what it's doing. I'm telling you now, I'll be the first to speak up when it comes to issues and Q & A.'

We both nodded and heard Len let out a string of consecutive farts, saying that's what he thought of Walter Baker, the UK Sales Managing Director.

I had to warn Len about something, before he went shouting his mouth off. Potentially making every salesperson's life a misery – including his wife, who was in the audience.

'Len,' I said in a calm, psychiatrist-style voice. 'Look, before you dish any shit, make sure no one else does the same to you.'

Len looked at me as innocent as a new-born baby.

'What? Me, dirty! I'm the cleanest motherf—'

I didn't let him finish.

By now Errol and I sat leaning against the basins. My arms folded. Errol had his hands in his trouser pockets, shaking his head at Len.

'What about Barbara, in sales admin? The sales conference in Paris. It was the only time they were allowed to come along, because we had a fantastic year, my first as I recall.' I paused. Len interjected.

'So, and?'

'So you shagged her silly, her words not mine. Said you were like a tiger, starved of food for weeks. You couldn't get enough. You cut her on her left breast, you were biting that hard. Should I go on?'

Len was actually quiet for a whole minute. Errol looked at me. I returned his gaze. Len looked at the floor, rubbing his chin with his free right hand.

'How the friggin' hell do you know about it?'

'Whoa, so you admit it happened, no denial. That will help you with Sarah. She'll probably forgive you for shagging her best friend.'

I had a smile on my face, but I didn't know why. Errol said we'd better get back, otherwise people would talk about us being in the gents' for so long together. I think it was more to do with getting out of the same room as Len. As we headed for the door, I turned to Len.

'Remember Len, no company is perfect. Neither are any of us. Think about who else might know what I've just told you, they may try and use it against you. You can trust me that I won't. Let's hope no one heard us.'

'Look son, thanks, it was one of those irresistible urges that we men get. You know the score, she virtually laid on a plate, and boy oh boy, I lapped it up. It was the best screw I've ever had. I can't complain.'

Len had this ability to be supremely crass, or crude at any opportunity. He did it effortlessly. Almost as though it were a gift. It seemed to be his way. His version of the spoken word.

Errol was now outside the gents'.

I'd had enough of listening to Len trying to justify his one moment of passion. I knew that he was lying. He'd been having an affair with Barbara before I started at Eiron. His poor wife did not have a clue.

'Let's hope Sarah doesn't hear you say that.'

Len laughed as I let the door close behind me.

Meeting Errol, we headed back towards the hall. A strange, eerie feeling came over me. We couldn't hear anyone speaking in the hall. It was far too quiet as we approached. There were four huge sets of double doors. We were heading to the fourth, aiming to enter at the back, where we'd exited.

Standing outside the second huge set of doors was Len's wife Sarah. She looked as if she could kill someone with her bare hands.

She was to all intents and purposes a calm woman. But provoked, I heard she could be a nightmare, worse than anyone could dream up. Right then and there, I was glad that I was not in Len's size six shoes.

Yet I wondered why she was upset. There was no way she could have heard us. Then I saw the way Errol looked at my jacket and shook his head.

I watched Errol's lips move. They mouthed, 'Oh shit.' I raised my arms as if to say, 'What's up?'

There on my left lapel, was the mic. It was still switched on. We both knew they were waiting, the whole sales force for EMEA (Europe, Middle East and Africa), for us to enter. I had no idea what kind of reaction we would get.

Thankfully Errol was brave. He volunteered to go in first.

Using hand gestures he told me to turn off the mic. Pointing toward the door, mouthing he was going to push it open. Errol then mouthed, 'One, two, three,' and he pushed open the door. Approximately five seconds later I followed him. The reaction was something I'll never forget.

2

If I thought the rapturous applause after my presentation was anything to go by, it paled into insignificance. It was Mardi Gras with all the fireworks. Errol and I stood at the back, facing over three hundred salespeople and senior executives, by taking a bow.

Errol whispered to me to keep smiling and lap it up. He was sure heads were going to roll. Everyone in the auditorium heard everything. Luckily, they all saw the funny side, including the chief Mr Walter Baker.

Right there and then I needed the toilet again. This time for different reasons.

I did as Errol said, kept smiling as the standing ovation lasted a whole five minutes. I removed my spectacles, rubbing my eyes as though I was crying with laughter. When really I was dying with utter and total embarrassment. I'm positive it was a whole lot more demeaning for Sarah Ferris.

Most of the salesmen in the office knew about Len. So did some of the women that Sarah worked with. No one decided to tell her. Until I did. Now who had the big mouth?

We endured the what must have been the longest ever standing ovation in Eiron's twenty-three-year history. Finally, and at last the vibrant audience settled down.

Walter Baker was on stage telling his over-excited sales force to simmer down. They did and Errol and I waited for the pithy comment that Walter was guaranteed to make.

'Ladies and gentlemen, you've heard it first here. Yes, that's right. What one of our experienced salesmen thinks of me and this company. However, on reflection it seems as if he made a right tit of himself. Don't you?'

The audience rumbled into quiet laughter. Some weren't sure that Walter's joke was ill-timed and insensitive. Walter didn't seem to care.

'Oh, sorry, it was the left tit wasn't it?' Most of the females did not laugh at that. The men did, saving Walter any embarrassment.

Walter realised his last joke was crap so moved on swiftly.

He gave me and Errol permission to resume our seats. Informing me in front of the whole audience, that I should be careful what I say in future – 'You never who could be listening.'

The next couple of hours passed quickly thankfully. A few country managers rambled on about how good their country was, and how they'd nearly reached their targets.

During those riveting speeches, Errol, myself and Shaun O'Dwyer, whispered throughout, discussing what might happen to me and Errol after the conference.

Walter made jokes, or attempted to, to hide whatever scheme he was conjuring.

As much as he'd praised me, I still did not trust the magnanimous prick.

What did make our whisperings interesting was when Shaun informed Errol and I what the reaction was 'live' when they'd heard our voices. Apparently Walter asked for complete quiet when he realised what was happening. The mumbling and giggling in the crowd halted in the flicker of an eyelid, when Len and I revealed his extra-marital shenanigans. All eyes focused on Len's wife Sarah. She was four rows from the front, in the huge auditorium, that made our three hundred attendees seem like ants.

At first, she stayed rooted to her seat, her eyes filling up. She held back the tears and calmly stood up, walking out of the second of the large doors.

Shaun spoke in his lilting mild Irish accent. A little too quick for my liking, but I caught the gist of what he was saying.

'That wasn't it, lads. When we heard Barbara's name, there was a huge gasp. Someone shouted, "Fuckin' hell, how did the old fart manage that?" We all laughed again.'

I thought about what it must feel like. To be publicly humiliated like that. Not just for the UK staff, but everyone in Europe and beyond will remember this one incident. There was always one thing to carry away from these events, and I created one for everyone to tell all their friends and colleagues, wherever they worked.

At least now the mind-numbing speeches were over. I looked up at Walter Baker who had returned to the podium. I reluctantly joined in the weak applause given to the German country manager, as he returned to his seat on the front row.

Now for the interesting part. The nominations for successful salespeople from last year. To my utter surprise and delusion, there was an award for the worst salesperson. Whoever recorded the least amount of sales by value got the award. Errol tried to explain it to me once, but I didn't really pay much attention. It seemed ridiculous and a complete waste of time and effort.

As the names were read out, I forced myself to look in front, behind and across the room, only when a female name was read out. I wanted to see if there was any potential talent for the dinner dance later that night.

Hopefully now I didn't need any promotion, or 'building up'. My stunt with the microphone had hopefully made me into a mini-star. It would certainly be a conversation opener.

Each person whose name was read out had to stand up. This gave my sharp, sniper-like, trained blue eyes the opportunity to go to work. My rectangular-shaped spectacles also helped.

I watched Errol perform the same ritual, although he was supposedly happily engaged to his long-time live-in girlfriend. He was window shopping. So was I. But I could actually buy something. In fact I was getting on the desperate side to buy the whole bloody shop. Anything within reason to start with. Looking at the candidates, there was plenty to go on. I hoped they put me on a good table, that way I could begin my plan, to try and start something.

And there was someone. Her name was read out. She wasn't the type I would usually go for (like I had all the choice in the world), yet there was something about her.

She was no more than five and a half feet tall. Shapely figure (from where I was sitting), all curves in the rights places, with relevant body parts protruding from a silky, mauve-coloured blouse. Her hair was a lively shade of brown. Layered at the front, cut by a professional, who left the length resting on her rounded shoulders. I wondered whether she wore make-up. Hopefully not like a significant majority of saleswomen. Some of whom obviously believed they worked on a cosmetics counter in a department store. Or in the circus.

I began to stare as salacious thoughts began permeating my corrupted mind. I capitulated far too easily. The feeling, however, was a lovely warm, fuzzy one. Embarrassingly I became excited and crossed my legs, hoping no one would see the bulge in my light-coloured trousers. More importantly, Errol caught me staring.

I quickly turned away. But he'd seen that look on my face. Not the look of love, more like lust. He smiled, raising his eyebrows.

'What are youse two smiling at?' Shaun piped upon my left.

'Oh, nothing. Just admiring the view,' I replied as nonchalantly as I could muster.

'Oh, I see. Spotted a little something for tonight, eh? …Ha ha, don't worry, me ol' mate, Errol and me will make sure you get off tonight, if you get my meanin'.'

I understood perfectly.

I was already dreading the dinner dance. Two minutes ago I couldn't wait to go. Something else that I'd tried to circumvent all day continued to festoon itself in my head. I couldn't shake it.

3

The hotel rooms were spacious, ostentatious and oozed luxury. Errol and I shared room 304. Only the senior management team had large double rooms to themselves. We all knew why that was. Dirty bastards.

We were dutifully instructed that we should be in the 'Kensington Suite' by 7pm. On entering the suite, there would be a large blackboard showing the seating plan.

Between 7pm and 7.45pm Walter Baker would be handing out the 'Achieving Rewards for Sales Executives' (otherwise known as the A.R.S.E. awards). On this occasion only, would any of us accept being called an ARSE.

I was dressed first, allowing Errol, my manager and friend, to take longer than any of my sisters in the bath. I had hardly uttered a word once we were in our room. Errol figured there was something on my mind, but out of politeness, he didn't ask. He didn't have to.

At ten minutes to seven Errol finally emerged, emitting some new aftershave. He was always leaving things to the last minute.

'Don't worry, Just, I'll be a few mins, okay.'

'Yeah, right,' I replied.

Walking in front of a full-length mirror bolted onto the front of a huge wardrobe, I checked myself over. Ticked off each point in my mind.

1. Exhaled into my cupped hand which covered my mouth and nose. Breath was okay.

2. Straightened my bow tie and jacket, undid one button, leaving one open across my slender girth.
3. Another quick spray of my eau de toilette (damn, I smelt good).
4. Hair check – my jet-black mop was spiked up with gel, but not too much, in a modern messy style.
5. Second breath check. I had two packs of minty chewing gum in my left trouser pocket, and some loose change.
6. Tissues. Two or three man-size tissues in my right trouser pocket.
7. Keys to the room (I did wonder whether I might need them).

I was set. Ready to rumble.

To my pleasant surprise, I turned my head ninety degrees to see Errol suited and booted.

'Mr Whalley, are we ready to do some damage?' Errol's tone was effusive, confident.

'You lead the way, Casanova, the Pied Piper is right behind you…'

I didn't have a clue what I was saying. Neither did Errol. I loved saying stuff like that.

We left our room, meeting Shaun O'Dwyer and Tom Greenfield-Crown, in the widest corridor I'd ever been in.

Tom was the complete opposite to Shaun. I was interested as to how they had got on whilst at the conference. I was sure to find out later.

The four of us headed to the lift, each saying how much we were looking forward to the night-time activities.

'Hey Tom, press the button, or we'll be here all night,' Shaun quipped.

Tom didn't reply, shrugging his shoulders.

The doors opened and the lift revealed three other salespeople from Eiron. One of them was that girl I had seen. She looked fantastic.

Sparkling green eyes, no make-up, a natural beauty, in a sequined black, strappy dress. I was obviously staring again, as Errol elbowed me in the ribs. The others laughed out loud. She smiled, coyly.

We moved into the lift, saying polite 'hellos'. Shaun began making a few crude jokes which everyone laughed at. He was a funny guy. Naturally.

I stood nervously beside Victoria Shepard. She was with two other women. One possibly in her early forties, and she looked damn good too. Apart from her armpits, which she obviously forgot to shave.

The other girl was younger. She seemed like the coquettish type. I could be wrong.

As the lift began to descend from the fourth floor, I used my peripheral vision to see if Victoria had a wedding ring on. She didn't. But I also checked to see if there was any ring mark on her finger, as though she'd taken it off, which a lot women (or men) do.

We all were making small talk, asking the girls which office they worked in, when they started and what they thought of the tosser, Walter Baker. Then Shaun (or it could have been one of women) allowed the unforgivable to happen. One of them surreptitiously let an unforgettable, despicable odour fill the large thirteen-person lift. The smell was determined to linger and would not dissipate. Eyes searched from one to the other. Guilty expressions on at least three faces. I won't say which ones.

'Justin Whalley, that's the last time I go anywhere with you,' Shaun shouted. 'How could you, in front of these fine upstanding women? Uh, it's disgraceful.'

In response, I simply pointed my index finger at him. The women were not impressed. And the smell came from where I was standing. If I didn't have the hots for Victoria Shepard, I would swear that it was she was the guilty party.

As we exited the lift, heading down various corridors, I was left at the rear with Victoria. She touched me on my arm.

'Is everything okay?' I asked, with concern.

'Yeah, fine.'

She had a slight Birmingham accent. Not too heavy.

'I just wanted to say, sorry.' She had me confused.

'What for? You've done nothing. Have you?' My eyebrows arched. I was trying to be debonair, and hoped it was working.

She stopped walking and looked up at me.

'It was me,' she whispered.

It only took me about a minute to calculate what she was talking about. It *was* her in the lift. We laughed together. The rest of them turned around and saw us. I didn't care. The ice had been broken.

4

My confidence was up. Maybe a little bit of arrogance was creeping in. I had heard one or two comments come via Errol saying that I was an arrogant so-and-so. I never saw it myself. I viewed it as sheer unwavering confidence. Nothing wrong in that.

At the entrance to the Kensington Suite, there stood the large blackboard with several eager salespeople vying to see where and who they were seated with.

As we approached, Tom spoke up in his accentless, monotone voice.

'I bet you we're on a shit table.'

It was unlike Tom to use any semblance of foul language.

'That's what usually happens,' Errol responded.

Actually, they were both wrong. Errol, Shaun and Tom were all on different tables. They didn't recognise the names, but soon calculated that at least half of the names belonged to females. That was enough to activate their tense, pent-up adrenalin.

I, on the other hand, had the good fortune of being seated on Victoria's table. So I thought.

'It looks like we're seated together,' she said brightly. Those green eyes were glistening.

I smiled back, displaying my bleached ultra-white teeth.

'Looks like you're a lucky lady,' I boasted.

'We'll see, cowboy.' She walked off. The guys laughed and we all entered the room.

Immediately to our right was a photographer, taking photos of salespeople together. Some in couples, some in groups. The four of us had our photo taken. It reminded me of the Untouchables, after Elliot Ness had made his first major bust.

Behind the porn-star-looking photographer, were three large tables with glasses of red, white, and rosé wine. We made our choices and stood over the far side of the room, where Walter Baker was about to speak.

A microphone had been rigged up, which Walter spoke into.

'Good evening, everyone. Hope you're ready for cracking good night. And it has nothing to do with eggs!' Walter roared with laughter at his own piss-poor attempt at weak humour, at best.

'We've already had a fantastic day, one that I'm sure I'll never forget.' Walter could not let go of what had occurred earlier in the day.

He talked briefly through the usual pleasantries, before beginning announcing the winners of the A.R.S.E. awards.

Twenty minutes or so later, he read out Victoria's name. She had wandered off with her other two friends, in the opposite direction. As she strode up to collect her brass-edged award, she turned to smile in my direction. I'm not sure whether she was smiling at me.

She faced Walter, smiled and shook his hand, accepting the award with her left. The porn-star photographer was down on one knee recording the posthumous moment.

And my oh my, did she look heavenly up there. For first time in years, I felt my stomach churn. My heart thump inside my chest. My hands, clammy with nerves. My mouth dry like the Sahara on a summer's day. This was not like the Justin Whalley I knew.

She stepped down and walked down an aisle created by all the execs split in two. As she neared I noticed again that she wore the smallest amount of cosmetics. Demure-coloured lipstick and matching nail polish. She didn't look in my direction, and I was disappointed.

With the awards being read out in alphabetical order I knew I would be one of the last. Walter announced me without using my name, but everyone did laugh this time. Again, at Sarah's expense. Not surprisingly, Sarah did not turn up. In fact she probably went home. Who could blame her?

Yes, Walter loved it. Calling me the 'superstar of secret conversations', and 'early edition', telling everyone not to tell me any of their secrets, as they'd be front page the next day. However, Shaun, Errol and to my surprise Tom, whooped and hollered as I collected my award. The noise was food for my adrenalin and ego. That needed to be served. So far I'd had a three-course meal.

Once seated the meal was served and the nineteen other guests around the table made pleasant and sometimes, inextricably tedious conversation.

I watched in envy, as Errol, Shaun and Tom, seemed to be getting on too well with the salespeople on their table. Just my luck.

Victoria hardly said two words to me during the meal, although I did notice, that she had a lot to drink. One drink followed the other, and it was obvious that she was getting pissed very quickly.

I visited the men's toilet at least three times, as my only means of escape. All within ninety minutes. Funnily enough, I'd only had the one glass of the free wine.

On my return the Kensington Suite I witnessed a very attractive foreign-looking girl, slap a man across the face. She stormed off, leaving him visibly red-faced. I could not hold back my smile. From the atmosphere that pervaded the evening so far, I imagined that incident would be the first of many.

When I entered, Walter Baker was back up on stage. The excruciating squeal of feedback from the microphone permeated the room and everyone's ears.

Shaun approached me, and we stood in the middle of the room looking forward up at the edifice known as Walter Baker.

'You gettin' on with that Victoria lass?' Shaun asked me positively.

I paused before replying. When I did I kept my head pointing straight ahead.

'No,' was my short, laconic answer. Shaun gathered more from my tone, than from what I'd said.

'That's cool. Plenty more fish in the sea. In fact there's a couple on my table.'

'Sounds good to me.' I half smiled, trying withhold my keenness. Not for anything heavy, just to get to the getting to know you, having a laugh stage.

Our attention was diverted to the sound of Walter's orotund voice.

'Ladies and gentlemen, please put your hands together for someone who has worked tirelessly for the last few months, helping the organise these horrendous events. Please thank, and applaud my personal assistant, Miss Fiona Watson.'

We all clapped, genuinely.

Fiona was brilliant, a true right-arm woman. Hardworking, a little old-fashioned in her style, but pleasant, quiet, and very, very, funny. A dour-looking woman in general, but not tonight. Her light brown hair was down, usually always up. Some make-up, I think in the right places, new oval-shaped specs, hiding happy hazel eyes.

She collected a bouquet of flowers, her defined cheeks flushed red with embarrassment. We all cheered her down of the stage. She wiped a tear from her left eye. She almost got me going.

5

Now it was time for the real enjoyment part.

First, a comedian called Frank Carlos appeared on stage. He was sizable man, sullied complexion, thick caterpillar-style eyebrows, and a girth that would require at least two measuring tapes, to determine his waist circumference.

Shaun and I listened to a few of his average and some awful jokes. He picked on people who were standing up or moving around. He wanted to hold the audience and assume control.

Shaun put his arm around my shoulder, and led me over to his table. He had met Theresa, from the Dublin branch, and Thelma from Eiron's South African office.

After the introductions, which went well, I was left with Thelma.

Shaun skulked off, giving me a wink from his left eye, as he strode away with his arms around the anorexically shaped Theresa.

Thelma, however, was a tall, straight-figured girl, who I swear should have been a model of some sort.

As we talked, the aberration on stage managed to raise a few raucous laughs from the audience. Which I thought would be easy enough, considering the mass populous had been intravenously fed alcohol for about two and half hours. And it was still early.

Ignoring Mr Carlos, and the subsequent live band 'The Monkey Men', I preferred to get to know Thelma.

'You been working here long?' I shouted over the live band now playing.

'About four years now. I really enjoy working for them. And the people are lovely too.'

'Thank you.'

She laughed, well more like giggled, as I expected after Shaun had probably convinced her to drink more and more.

'You're welcome,' she responded. Her words ever so slightly slurred. 'So you're the one no women should trust, eh?'

I wondered when my phoenix was going to rise from the ashes.

'Oh yes, that's me alright. Anything you tell me will not be taken in the strictest confidence.' I forced a laugh, looking around to see where Errol was. Going out of the door with his arm around a woman, was Errol disappearing for the rest of the evening?

'So should I trust you, Justin?'

'Well that depends…' I turned to face Thelma.

'On what?'

'On everything and nothing.'

'Trying to play head games, eh?' Thelma was still smiling. Her face bright, lucid, energetic.

'Me? No way.' I raised my hands in surrender. 'Okay, I'm going to trust you.' I sat forward on my cushioned chair. My face inches from Thelma's. Her odour entered my nostrils and I floated off into a brief lascivious dream. Forgetting everything around me, except Thelma.

The clanking of wines glasses disturbed my stupor; there directly in front of me was Thelma's slightly worried-looking face.

She repelled a little, leaving an equidistant gap between our faces.

'You were going to trust me…'

'Yes, I'm sorry, I tuned out there for second. Umm, yes, what I'm going to tell you nobody knows about.'

'Go on.' Thelma leaned forward again, closing the gap. Our faces inches apart. Her eyes seemed too big. Her lips, slender, shapely, kissable, uncommonly smooth.

'Well, I haven't had a girlfriend for nearly two whole years. There,

I've said it.'

There was no immediate response. She stared at me with those big, hypnotic eyes, saying absolutely nothing.

Then she smiled. She reached over with her left hand and placed it on my left shoulder. Moving her face to my left, she whispered in my left ear.

'If it's true, then you're a very brave man. And not bad looking either.' She kissed my left cheek, softly as though it were a feather (if a feather had lips).

With my heart thumping, I told Thelma she looked beautiful.

'You're far too polite, Justin. I cannot imagine why you haven't had a girlfriend.'

'It's a long story.'

'I understand.'

I believed she did. Genuinely.

Thelma was an interesting girl. Gorgeous even. Yet my mind was occupied. Shaun had disappeared. I was not surprised as the live band was shite. I'm positive at one point that I heard booing from all quarters.

It seemed to happen every year, apparently. The company would squander hundreds of pounds on a dodgy rock band, who cleared the dance floor quicker than a dose of Senokot clears your stomach.

Following thirty more atrocious minutes the band finished their set.

When the DJ started playing some good R&B and dancy pop tunes, Thelma dragged me onto the dance floor.

The dance floor area was packed. Bodies moving, gyrating, swaying here and there. Errol should have been here, he could dance. Got the crowd going.

There, across the other side of the dance floor was Tom Green-Ass (I changed his nickname whenever I liked) dancing with Victoria. I had to admit to a slight bout of childish jealousy. I didn't let Victoria see me, but I was glad she couldn't as she was far too drunk to notice.

The DJ put Kylie's 'Can't Get You Out Of My Head' on and Victoria went wild. She embarrassed Tom, which made me and new friend Thelma laugh, 'til our stomachs hurt.

To keep all the variety of people happy, the DJ had to let my ears suffer some awful, trashy music. I watched Victoria try to dance with Tom and with Walter, by linking arms to some crappy song that was on. She fell over on her arse, her dress fell down her legs, ending up around her waist. She revealed more than she would have liked.

I observed Walter, who I'd heard was a sexually starved male, take a good long look, before coming to her rescue. Tom walked away in disgust, even though he was pissed. The dance floor erupted. The DJ announced her name over the microphone so everyone knew.

They began chanting her name. 'Go Vicky, go Vicky!' and 'Whe-hey!' as more of the crowd enrolled in her act of sheer humiliation.

Thelma could dance all night, that was my honest belief. She had an unwavering, insatiable energy. From her athletic figure, it was clear she loved taking part in various sports.

By now my bow tie was loosened, my top button undone. My heart beating, thumping inside my ribcage. My feet beginning to ache a little. We took a five-minute break back at our table.

'What are the men like in South Africa?' I asked, panting a little.

'Like everywhere else… only after one thing.'

'Oh, I see.' She smiled at me, to show that she was teasing me.

I smiled back and nodded my head to show I got the joke.

'But I can tell you're different to most of the others in here. You're not just out for the one-nighter, are you?'

For someone so inebriated, Thelma had an uncanny clarity about her.

'How do you know for sure?' I tried to tease her back, raising my eyebrows.

'It's a feeling I get. You know, like a sixth sense. I'm rarely wrong.'

'Impressive, very impressive.'

She laughed, touching my hand on top of the table.

'Oh come on, just let me dance with you, for this song,' she pleaded.

Without being given the opportunity to refuse or accept Thelma pulled me up and we walked over to a quiet spot in the huge auditoria.

Forgetting what happened earlier today and everyone else, Thelma and I danced slowly together in a corner, away from everyone. The DJ played 'If You Don't Know Me', the Simply Red version. It was a great slow song to smooch to. My body needed a smooch. And I needed to get Victoria Shepard out of my head. Thelma De Groot provided the solution. A solution any man could be proud of.

6

Tom saw me smooching as he left the main hall. I watched him watch me, out of my peripheral vision. I didn't care who he told.

He was known as Green-Grass, as you couldn't trust him not to spill the beans, or snitch on you. Hell, he must have been great fun to be with at school.

Whilst smooching with Thelma, I realised how shapely she was. Like an athlete. I became aroused as she held me oh so tightly, and she seemed to like it. Gyrating her midriff against mine. She didn't pull away.

Her breathing began to labour. Her hands gripped my backside. My heart raced. My breathing became shallow. Maybe it was time to leave. Together? Oh shit, maybe that was what she was thinking. She lay her head on my left shoulder, moaning in what sounded like ecstasy. Pleasure.

My knowledge of women, told me she was aroused. Her moaning became louder, she gripped my body in a WWF-style hold. I thought my trouser zip was about to burst. I hoped no one could see or hear us. Thelma was working herself into an ecstatic sexual frenzy. She started licking my left ear. Lightly chewing on it. I couldn't control my breathing or my heart rate. Nor could I control my internal juices. Neither could Thelma.

Her voice seemed to leap in octaves. Thankfully the music was too loud. At least that I was hoping for.

'Oh, yes, oh yes, ooh, ooh, yes, yes, oh my…' Thelma had satisfied herself. The audible moaning, reduced in decibels.

My quick scan around the immediate vicinity, gladly revealed that no one had seen or heard her.

Pulling her head from my left shoulder, she kissed me, fully on the lips. I couldn't deny that I loved it. Wanted more. She was a damn good kisser.

I told her I needed to visit the loo. Thelma smiled broadly. Sensually. I needed to go to the men's room, desperately, for two reasons. The second reason was a little more scary. And I hoped I had some loose change in my pocket.

Thelma linked arms with me and gave me that sensual smile again. What did it really mean?

'Are we ready?' she asked me as we walked arm-in-arm out of the Kensington Suite.

I couldn't think of the answer fast enough. If I said yes, that would mean sleeping with her. If I said no, then she'd probably be offended and embarrassed. So I found something in between.

'I er...' I coughed nervously, 'need the gents'. I'll be back in a sec.'

'Don't go running off now, I'll be waiting...' Thelma stood outside the second door to the Kensington Suite, waving at me.

I smiled back, my broadest smile, emitting a message, that I couldn't wait. She probably also thought I was going to buy some protection. If she was thinking that, then it possibly turned her on even more.

Outside the gents' were some of the salesmen, laughing loudly in a drunken stupor.

'Oh, here he is!' they shouted in unison. I didn't recognise any of them. I needed some support.

But two my immediate friends were probably already in a variety positions, upright, flat or otherwise, that I was not entirely comfortable getting into.

I looked at the three salesmen, pondering on their cryptic

comments. So I played dumb.

'What you guys on about?'

'Oh come on, don't be shy, I know I wouldn't be. Hell, you should get a medal. The goddess. How'd you do it?' The salesman was short, wide, and obnoxious. It was in his face. In his expression. His other two mates forced out a laugh.

I wondered if they were talking about my earlier performance with the mic. They weren't.

Needing to use the loo, I cut things short.

'What the hell are you people on about?' I raised my voice slightly, letting them know I was not in the mood for guessing games.

'I see you gave Thelma a 'Harry Met Sally' moment in there.'

It went quiet. I went quiet. All three men stared at me for my reaction. Someone had seen us. Heard *her*. Not wanting to capitulate under the pressure, I attacked as my form of defence.

'At least I got her going. More than what I can say about you guys.' This time they went quiet. So I finished them off. 'I guess you'll be sorting each other out tonight then, in a threesome.'

This time I forced out a laugh, not giving them time to respond. I pushed by them and into the gents' toilets. They all mumbled something under their breath, but I didn't care what they uttered.

Whilst drying my hands my memory of Thelma came rushing back. The sounds of moaning could be heard from one of the toilets. I began to suspect that everyone at Eiron was sex mad. What made this thinking worse, was that I was sober. Everyone else was pissed as farts.

In my right pocket I found change and took a long, hard look at the condom machine. Should I or shouldn't I?

A variety of scenarios clouded my mind. So should I go ahead and then claim the vainglorious plaudits the next morning, with all the other men? Or do I decline what seems a tempting and possible earth moving experience, in favour of valour?

There was one very important question I hadn't asked Thelma. That was, whether she had a partner or husband. I had rules. Never with a married woman. However gorgeous she may be. No matter how fantastic her body may be. I had kept to that rule so far, I wanted keep my record clean.

Nevertheless, I was horny that night. I felt the adrenalin switch on when we danced. And even though I was having doubts, I could not switch it off.

I met Thelma immediately outside the gents'.

'I thought you going to leave me, Justin,' she said softly, throwing her long arms around my neck.

We kissed, in public view. That got me going again.

'I'd never leave you, Thelma. I'll always be right by your side,' I told her confidently.

Thelma smiled and ushered me towards the lifts, with her right arm around my waist. She was giggling uncontrollably.

'My room is free tonight, just for me and you.' She told me this looking deep into my transfixed eyes. Those seductive eyes of hers and that entrancing kiss. It was all I could think about.

'Lead the way.'

I walked her to her room and did not see a soul. Thank goodness. No revelations in the morning – I hoped.

Inside the room, Thelma told me she was getting undressed and I could watch her if I wanted. She told me she liked being watched. I began to worry. How could I extricate myself from this predicament?

She put some music on from the television, from one of the radio channels. Then she commenced her strip show. She'd obviously done this before. And maybe, she was doing it in the evenings and weekends. She was too good. Then it the hit me. How many men had she done this with before? How did those the sales guys now her name? Maybe Thelma was a goddess. But just maybe she was the annual bike, who each salesman took it in turn to ride. Well, it'd be bad enough on a tandem, but was sure as hell not riding on a bike with that much mileage.

Thelma was now completely naked. She stood posing against a wall, her right arm on her right hip.

'So come on, big boy.' Believe me, all the wild horses were needed to restrain me. Even with what I knew and what I was feeling about something far more important, I could have so easily eaten what was on my plate.

'Okay Thelma.' I was thinking on my feet. An exit strategy. 'I have something for you.' My speech was in staccato mode. I wanted legato to come out.

'Yes, what is it Justin?'

'Well, I need you to go into the bathroom and count to twenty. Count out the numbers so I can hear. For my surprise to work, you cannot cheat.'

I witnessed excitement caress her face all over.

'Ooh, I like the sound of this. Okay, in the bathroom, count to twenty.'

'Yep. That's it.'

Great, I thought. Foxy lady. Fantastic body. But easily fooled by little ol' me.

Thelma closed the door to the bathroom. In a flash I leapt off the chair I was sitting on. I heard Thelma reach nine, ten. My hand was already on the handle and opening the door to her hotel room.

She reached fourteen when I closed the door quietly behind me.

Without delay I ran to the nearest exit to the stairs. Pushed open the doors and exhaled a huge sigh of relief.

Surprisingly when I returned to my shared room, Errol was fast asleep. But I was not surprised when I distinctly smelt the odour of a women's perfume in the room. Underneath that smell, was the fragrance that can only be left when two people have had sex. And the women's nether regions were a bit sweaty. The dirty, cheating little so-and-so.

Thankfully, I was now in my own single bed. In my boxer shorts, running my hands through my jet-black hair. Tired, confused, and frustrated.

7

I was up early. Fully dressed.

The conference was due to finish by 11.30am. On my right, Errol stumbled out of bed, wearing women's knickers. I had no energy to smile or laugh.

My expression, explained what I thought of Errol's actions. Elisa was a miserable bitch, but a faithful one to Errol. And loyal. Rare qualities these days.

However, sitting in the grandeur of our hotel room, only painful, regurgitating flashbacks, remained permanently in my mind.

A few years ago on this very day, my mother was killed. In effect murdered. However, it was deemed a reckless blip by an otherwise gentle and caring family man.

On a night, not any different to last night, Vernon Peters had consumed massive amounts of alcohol. So had most of his friends. He was four times over the limit, when he was driving home from a sales conference. Vernon truly believed he was okay to drive. What he didn't realise was, he didn't stop drinking until 5am that morning. I can never forget the events prior to my mother losing her life so frivolously.

- At 0800, he had a few glasses of orange juice, apparently because he was thirsty. He had no breakfast, other than two slices of dry toast.
- At 0845, Vernon gets into his 4x4. His overnight bags are securely in his boot.

- At 0932 Vernon is driving through Birmingham. His eyes are tiring. As he isn't far from home, he makes the fateful decision to keep going.
- The music is loud in his car. Another trick to help him stay awake at the wheel.
- At 0944, is driving down the usually busy Hagley Road. There are two narrow lanes going both ways. His car swerves between the two. Other drives are blowing their horns at him. He keeps on coming.
- At 0948, Vernon Peters loses control of his huge 4x4, plunging head-on into my mother's supermini.
- She died at the scene. Paramedics did everything they could.
- At 1005, after the confusion had abated, Vernon Peters was breathalysed. The officer said he was four times over the limit.
- He got two and half years. Banned for ten years from driving. He'd be out now. No scars on him. Only a few cuts and bruises. I'll never forget that day.

In my own world, sitting on the edge of the bed, Errol was calling me.

'Justin, Justin!' He raised his voice the second time.

I jumped up, coming out of my reverie.

'Look, Just, I know how you feel about, you know, all of us drinking and that. I haven't forgotten, never will.'

Errol placed his right on hand on my left shoulder and squeezed it gently.

'I know. It just gets to me sometimes. You understand.'

Errol nodded. He probably was the only one, outside my family, who genuinely had some semblance of what had happened. He helped me alleviate some of the pain. Supported me mentally to get through it. I'll always thank him for that. And certainly will never forget what he's done.

At breakfast, the usual banter proliferated around the room. Who screwed who. Whether it was good, bad or indifferent. Who made a total arse of themselves. Who threw up down someone's top.

I heard a story from behind our table. Shaun had a big grin on his face whilst he ate. Tom seemed a little more reserved. A noncommittal expression on his face. He kept quiet over breakfast. Errol and I guessed why Tom had remained almost mute.

The story was being whispered by two women and two men. There were from the Netherlands I think. Spoke good English, but their accents gave it away.

No sooner than they had commenced with their exciting story, I fully understood who they were talking about. Their vernacular traits did not conceal, that the topic of conversation was Thelma and that man with the mic.

By laughing out loud on my table I hoped none of my immediate sales team would hear the revelations being made. They did, however, look at me strangely, wondering why I had laughed out loud. Tom at that moment was revealing what a shit night he had had. He gave me a stern 'fuck off' look with those pale green eyes of his. I didn't care. I had to protect against any potential embarrassment.

I needed something to dissipate the story being told. I then asked Errol to fetch me another glass of orange juice. He was sitting like I was with my back to the whispering table. Errol obliged and I was relieved.

*

Once the breakfast revelations had come to their natural end, most of us ventured quickly back to our rooms for a quick clean up. We returned fifteen minutes later to the hall where I announced myself to the Eiron world.

The conference ended with rapturous applause with Walter Baker and the EMEA CEO holding each other's hand aloft. They promised bigger rewards for all those who achieved the tough targets set. The applauding added to the painful headaches suffered by most.

In the applauding crowd, was Thelma. A fugacious glance was all I was willing to give her. Nothing more. That was yesterday. In the past. Thankfully I managed to circumvent any interaction with her. It could have only been to my detriment if we had to cross paths.

On the plus side I won't see her again for another year. By then she'd have forgotten about me, and me about her. Amen.

I was ready to go home. Back to Nottingham and my comfortable two-bed bachelor pad house. I was hoping to dispense with the bachelor part, but I was prepared to wait.

Due to my mother's death, I always try and drive Errol to these kind of events, as he knows I won't drink at all, or very little, if it's the previous night.

We said our valedictions to the UK crowd. The EMEA salespeople had to leave immediately to catch flights back their home countries.

To my utter shock and complete horror, a voice from behind me said goodbye. I was besieged with nerves, hoping no one could see me trembling. It was Thelma.

Was she going to be angry? No. She walked up to me and kissed me on the cheek, in full view of Shaun, Errol and Tom. *Shit*, I thought, *I'll never hear the end of this.*

She whispered in my left ear.

'You were a real gentleman last night. I apologise if I scared you off. But tell your friend Tom, that I won't forget last night, and I'll email him when I get back home.

Those few words were music to my ears. Tom Green-Grass, doing my impression of the swan. Holding it all back, playing it cool. I'm sure his neurotic ex-wife wouldn't mind. Neither would their seven-year-old son.

'You take care, Thelma. Nice to meet you.'

We all waved, and I turned to Tom and gave him my most cryptic smile, winking at him. He knew exactly what I was getting at.

Going our separate ways, we agreed to see each other on Monday at work, in the Nottingham office. It was Friday morning, brunch time. The M1 or the M25 motorways did not offer any simple or quick route northwards.

The weekend was near; I was ready to sleep on my own, in my own bed. Errol had Elisa to look forward to.

An above average woman, in terms of height, with long strawberry-blonde hair, florid complexion, and grey-green eyes. She didn't smile as often as she should. She always seemed to be sour-faced, and in my humble opinion, she was far too attractive for that. Yet her attitude was her downfall. In some ways I can see why Errol was reluctant to go home. So we took our time.

8

The journey seemed to fly by. Traffic was steady, yet flowing seamlessly. I chose the A1 north out of London and then the M1, from Junction 2, heading down to junction 25 of the M1 on the Nottingham/Derby border.

Errol reclined his seat slightly and made himself comfortable. I hoped he wasn't going to sleep and leave me to drive home with little or no conversation.

I flicked through the radio stations, but nothing took my fancy. The CD player in the boot, had six discs. All jazz albums. My favourites. I made my choice and watched Errol perk up.

'Good choice, Just. Something to keep us both awake, hey?'

'You could say so.'

Errol pulled his seat upright and yawned, stretching out his arms in front of him.

He turned to me asked me a question I didn't expect, but welcomed.

'How's your little sister Emily getting on? Baby due yet?'

'No, well, yes I think she is due soon. Not sure when. She's nervous though, you know, with it being her first.'

'Yeah, I can bet. My mum had six of us in ten years. Don't know how she coped.'

'Well I hope Emily does, I know the last time we spoke she was scared. It doesn't help when her supposed boyfriend and father does a runner.'

'Shit, has he? – You never said…' Errol's voice trailed off. He was disappointed I hadn't told him. Emily asked me not to tell anyone outside our family. I had to respect her wishes.

Errol picked up the conversation.

'So what about the Child Support Agency? Have you thought about nailing the bastard to a wall with them?'

Errol, when I ever I gave him the opportunity, always wanted to protect me and my sisters, especially Emily. I think he had a soft spot for her, but would never make a move because of our friendship. It was a male bonding thing, that drew a line which he would never cross.

'Not yet, no. Haven't had time to think it through. Emily's been in and out of hospital with the pregnancy, so the CSA was the last thing on her mind. But I won't forget – don't you worry.'

Errol read the concerned and determined expression on my tired-looking face. He smiled, realising I would not let this go. So he switched the topic.

'I meant to ask you,' Errol began and then paused. He turned to face me at an angle, his arms folded. I was doing eighty-five miles an hour on cruise control. 'Are you going to see your mum, you know at the, er, er…' I finished his sentence.

'Cemetery.'

Errol nodded.

'Yes, I think I will. I try to every year. Don't know how long I'll be able to though.'

'As long as you never forget her, which I know you never will, that's all she would have asked of you. Nothing more, Just. Nothing more.'

I kept my head straight and let the cruise control take over the car and let my right foot relax.

Errol eased back to a slightly reclined position and gradually acquiesced under the warm air emitting from the air-conditioning system.

I wasn't long before I pulled up outside Errol's large four-bedroom house in Bramcote, Nottingham. He did snore and had gone the whole journey without asking for a cigarette. He was an awful passenger. Preferred to be in control. A fag usually calms him down. But not in my car.

Nudging him with my left elbow, Errol opened his eyes and let out an audible yawn.

'Oh great, back already.' He rubbed his eyes and he saw me gave him a wicked delinquent grin.

'Piss off, Whalley. You wait till you're in a relationship like mine. That's how they all get eventually!'

'Ah that's where you're wrong, Mr Hughes. I'll never get in your situation.' I continued to smile and eventually chuckled.

'You wait and see, my young apprentice. You just wait and see.'

'Whatever. Look, the boot's open, get your stuff and get back to that lovely, welcoming girlfriend of yours…'

Errol collected his luggage from the boot and headed up the driveway. I let the driver's window slide down.

'See you Monday… if you survive that long!'

Errol dropped his luggage and gave me the middle finger sign. I laughed out loud so he could hear me and drove off.

Ten minutes later I was home, and dumped all my luggage in the living room. For the first time in nearly twenty-four hours, I switched my mobile phone on.

Still standing up, I ventured to the kitchen to see what was available to drink. Luckily I had a few cans of fizzy stuff. I heard my phone beeping, realising I had received a text message.

When I read what was sent, it made my day turn black. I crashed to the sofa and began to cry.

KEEPING FOCUSED

9

It was Sunday morning. It was very early, maybe 6.30am.

I had called the hospital last night but Emily didn't want to have any visitors. She didn't want to see anyone. I told myself to muster the inner strength and I would go later today, regardless. That text message sent shivers done my spine. And it made me cry, like I haven't done since I was in Primary School.

Emily had lost her baby. An ectopic pregnancy, they called it. Whatever that was. It would have been a girl. I could not begin to fathom what she was going through, so I tried to kill my own miserable pain.

I sat up for most of the night drinking the remains of some brandy and vodka I'd had in the cupboards for months.

After breakfast, I put on my thick duffle coat and scarf and gloves. I walked the usually short ten-minute journey to the cemetery, where my dear mum Shirley was laid to rest. This time the journey lingered. Time itself, ran at half normal speed. I hoped the walk would cure my thumping hangover and head. I was in no fit state to drive.

My mum had requested that she be buried in Nottingham, next to my grandmother, who was born and raised in Arnold. It made any journey by my sisters and brothers a trek. We had to grant her one of her last wishes.

Walking through the cemetery at this early hour frightened me a little. It was winter and still dark, but the liquid spirit made me feel brave.

Stumbling through the graveyard, I could not navigate where my mother's grave stone could be. Going once a month still left me confused, feeling that I never knew where to look, when so many headstones looked familiar. The cemetery always seemed different to me. Maybe the drink was having an effect.

The wind calmly whistled through the dense tress, that surrounded the cemetery. I walked, following a narrow path and then cut across the grass. This was ridiculous, I couldn't see a damn thing.

Taking each step slowly, my step found no solid ground. My whole body careered forward and downward. I screamed at the top of my voice.

There I was falling into what must be a newly dug eight-foot-deep grave. I landed hands first then body. Flat out. Once I regained my senses I turned to face and look upward out of the grave. The darkness seemed to be swirling, moving as though some creature had just thrown me in.

I stood up and dusted myself down and immediately started to call for help.

'Help! Help! Can anybody hear me?' Of course no one replied.

I tried one or two attempts to leap upward but the depth was too steep. Well that's what I thought. Without warning, down there in the depths of this new grave a voice spoke to me. 'Don't bother, mate, I've been here all night and can't get out.'

You've never heard a scream or yell like it. My throat was sore from that yelling and screaming and boy, oh boy, when I thought eight feet was too high, I could have jumped three or four times that if I had to.

I don't know how but I found a spring that allowed me to escape what could only be described as spiritual experience, in some way. I know some people have the power to talk to the dead, but this was too close a call.

In the furore I forgot why I had gone to the cemetery. I had to go back at a later stage, and I had promised myself that I would go and visit Emily in hospital.

The only benefit of my graveyard experience was that it sobered me up pretty quick.

After going to home to get changed, calm down and have a strong cup of tea, I took to the road and walked from Wollaton to the Queens Medical Centre.

Using interrogation questioning skills learnt on various sales courses, the nurses eventually told me where my sister was.

The maternity ward was a strange place, not having been in one for a long time, since my older brother Mark had his two girls. Mothers, women with their breasts out all over the place. Babies crying, being fed, being comforted. So many natural human attributes being displayed, all the things that my Emily was missing right now. I was hoping she'd welcome my surprise visit.

I approached the room she was in. She had her own room and I could see a reflection on a television set playing inside her room. A small smile came to my face when I recognised her. She was talking to another woman. She had jet-black hair, which was short and scraped back. I knew who it was. Mary Leadbetter. She was Elisa's best friend. Elisa was Errol's happy-go-lucky girlfriend.

Not wanting to interrupt, I took a seat outside the room and decided to wait. It had been an anticlimactic weekend already. I tried in my own way to alleviate what was happening. It didn't feel like my attempts were having any positive effects. Pushing my own inadequacies to one side, I had to be strong for Emily. So did her sister and two other brothers. They would be here too. Of that I was sure. My mum would always espouse that 'someone is always in a more dire situation than you. Be thankful for what you have'. Smart, wise words.

Next to me was a girl probably about eleven years old. She reminded me of Mark's eldest daughter. She sat with her hands under her, swinging her legs.

'Are you waiting for your Mummy?'

She nodded her head.

'Where is she?'

'She's in the next room,' a high-pitched voice said.

'Is your mummy not well then?' I asked, trying to make her feel at ease. Knowing too that the world is dangerous place for any young person, especially talking to strangers.

'Yeah, she's very sick. I think we were going to have a baby brother, but I think he's died inside Mummy. But they think I don't know, but I'm not stupid, just because I'm twelve.'

I couldn't believe what I was hearing. And I couldn't believe what happened to me next. Tears began falling from my eyes. I wiped them away quickly and was justifiably embarrassed.

'It's okay, Mister. I was crying last night too. My dad cries too you know.' She tried to reassure me.

It hit me that this twelve-year-old girl had sat there and talked to a stranger about one of nature's most horrendous occurrences. One day I wanted to have a son or daughter like that.

Just then, her dad came out of the room. He had being crying. I nodded to him, and he reciprocated. He could tell I'd been doing the same. I guess my eyes were still watery and my face withdrawn.

He took his daughter by the hand and she turned to me. 'See you, Mister. I hope your wife gets better soon. She can always try again you know, I heard the doctors talking.' I nearly burst into tears again, but held it back.

She waved goodbye to me, and her father, mouthed 'thank you' to me.

Taking a deep breath, I stood and approached Emily's door. I knocked and her looked up at the window in the door. She recognised me and my heart tore in two when she smiled and beckoned me to come in.

Mary said hello and left us alone. I hugged my sister gently and she looked radiant, considering what she'd just been through. More than ever before she reminded me of our mother. Not in looks alone, but in character, strength of mind and the ability to make situations such as these, easier for people like me.

We talked for what seemed like hours, I made her smile and laugh, but not too much. In between, two nurses paid her a visit to take samples of blood and to give her medication, which she reluctantly took.

Eventually the medication wore her down and she capitulated under its effects and fell asleep. I left my sister hopefully in a better frame of mind and on the slow road to recovery.

10

Tossing and turning all Sunday night, counteracted me getting any decent sleep or well-needed rest. Mentally and physically, my body and mind had just about enough for the year, never mind a few days.

I met Errol at the office in Nottingham on Monday morning, my focus and concentration on selling.

Sitting at my desk at 0845, somehow I managed to be one of first ones in. Errol said his good mornings to a few female saleswomen and secretaries who got in early just to please their managers. They were hoping for some return. I had other ways of brown-nosing.

My concentration had switched back to work mode when Walter Baker's email hit everyone's inbox.

Ladies, men and all salespeople, we are ready and set for another successful year. We know that the economic climate is tough, but that is not an excuse for ANYBODY to fail this year. The targets set are achievable. Everyone should make their numbers – remember this – WE WANT TO PAY OUT LOADS OF MONEY – so if you want it EARN IT!

My mind and Errol's, as he glanced above my shoulder at my computer to get his initial reaction, knew this was typical Walter bullshit. Yes, that's what his surname should be. Not Baker. He'd no idea what the market conditions were like or what the customers' issues were. He was only concerned with one thing. Success and money. He wanted us to get him both. Lazy bastard. The email continued.

Anyone slacking in any way will be let go. I for one will not put my job at risk if one of my salespeople does not want to pull together. It's up to all of you how much you earn this year. When you see your goals and targets you should be genuinely surprised.

Good luck to all of you. I'm expecting great things this year – don't let me down – and above all, DON'T LET YOURSELVES DOWN!

Regards
Walter Baker
UK Sales & Managing Director
Eiron Plc

'What do you think, Errol?' I arched my head backward to him, as a few other people came into the office.

'Same old shit again and again.'

'What about our targets for this year, then? Any chance of making some real money?'

'Ooh, that's a tough one, Just. I'm waiting final approval but we should know later today. And as for making money, you're in sales, aren't ya? Course the you'll make money.' Errol laughed, turned and walked towards his office.

Sometimes, he sounded like a real manager or more like a politician. He knew the answer but wouldn't tell you. Or he'd give us a cryptic statement that actually meant nothing to no one, but deflected from the real issue. I suppose that's the kind of ability I'll need to develop if I'm going to get into sales management. A sobering thought.

Tom and Shaun came in later that morning and Errol reprimanded them both for taking the piss. He printed off Walter's email and shoved it in front of them. That was a warning in Errol's books. He had to watch his back and try to protect the salespeople he managed.

I watched Tom take his seat and gave me a cold, hard stare. I knew what he did with Thelma at the sales conference. After my look I think he realised too.

With my mind continually wandering, I asked Errol via an email to have a couple of days off. I ignored the email policy to only ask for days off by completing a holiday request form.

Errol ignored this part and granted me my two days to get my 'shit' together, as he called it. He granted it after I explained what had happened to Emily.

Later that afternoon I left work early, to Tom and Shaun's surprise. I could hear their heavy brains cranking into some sort of motion, to calculate where I was going. I could trust Errol not to tell them. Especially not Mr Greenfield-Crown.

Arriving home, I realised that I had not done any shopping. It was the last thing on my mind.

11

Sarah Parker had been with my brother Mark for over a decade. They had decided to never get married.

She was young when they met, eighteen years old I think. Mark, a keep-fit fanatic, pulled her at the gym, after pretending to pull a leg muscle. It was a weak attempt, and somehow it did the job. They'd been together ever since.

Now they have two of the smartest and loveliest children, that I am proud to be uncle to. Lucy had recently turned ten years of age, and Lillie had just turned seven.

Both had light brown hair, always spotlessly clean and immaculately groomed. It was always a pleasure to baby-sit for Mark and Sarah, for my two favourite nieces.

Over those next two days, that's what I did. Sarah and Mark lived in Birmingham, near our family home.

Mark came to Nottingham to see Emily, and some friends he had here. So did Sarah, who had a night out planned with some girlfriends in Nottingham. Lucy and Lillie stayed with Uncle Justin.

It was the best tonic for me to try and clear my head a little. Having two young, bright, carefree children around made me see the world in a better light. Even if it was only for a short time.

The night came around and Lucy and Lillie gave me big hugs when Mark dropped them off.

'Hello Uncle Justin, got a new girlfriend yet?' Lucy asked out loud. Mark winked at me, and I pointed my finger at him, giving him a wry smile.

'Well not quite yet, but I'm still looking… You can help me find one if you like,' I responded calmly.

'Okay Uncle Justin, if you have a modern television we can look at the dating channel for you,' Lucy told me.

I was shocked. Mark laughed. I was embarrassed. Lucy had grown up, big time. Lillie chuckled quietly, covering her mouth with her hands.

'Okay Mark, you can go now, I can take it from here.' I tried to ease him away to save any further outbursts from Lucy.

I ushered them both inside.

'I'll be back around elevenish, Just. Put Lillie to bed between eight and eight thirty. Lucy at around nine. You might need to read Lillie a story, she's not quite out of that phase yet.'

'Okay Mark, you say hi to Emily and give her my love, yeah?'

'Will do. See you later.'

The girls pulled back the curtain in the lounge and waved at their father as he drove away.

Inside, we watched a video of a computer-animated adventure, which Lillie had brought with her. I sat with both girls at either side and felt a warm flush of happiness pass over and through me.

Sitting eating microwavable popcorn, which wasn't as bad as I'd thought, I didn't have any trouble with them. Some people have all the luck. What I'd give right now, to have what my brother had. Not out of envy, but sheer and utter pride.

Lillie went upstairs, brushed her teeth and put on her 'jimmy jams' as she liked to call them. I left Lucy looking through the dating channel, in her honest bid to find me a girlfriend. As soon as I finished reading Lillie her story she was sound asleep.

As I made my way downstairs I heard Lucy's voice call my name.

'Uncle Justin, look at this one.' Lucy tugged at my jogging top for me to sit down. 'Look, she's pretty, isn't she? And she's from

Nottingham. Even my mum says that you're handsome.' She was determined. I was surprised.

'Oh, yeah… yeah, she seems okay, but do you know something, Lucy, I don't have to have a girlfriend you know. I'm okay on my own, honestly.' I had just uttered the world's biggest lie. Worst of all I told it to my ten-year-old niece. I'd bottled it in favour of not having to face or reveal to Lucy the real, abominable truth of how it was getting to me. Being single.

I consoled myself by knowing full well that Lucy would not understand what that was it like.

'Can you get ready for bed now, Lucy?'

'Do I have to, Uncle Just?' She gave me her cutest puppy dog face. I acquiesced.

'Alright, for half an hour more, then bed – deal?'

'Deal.' We shook hands.

At ten thirty I checked on the girls and they both were sound asleep.

I returned downstairs and refilled my glass with a small shot of French brandy. It was my second. Conscious of being 'the father' for the night, I was reminded of my responsibilities. As an uncle, as a 'good citizen' and of course as a practising decent bloke. As relaxed as I was, my heart jumped when there was a sudden, unexpected knock at the door.

I peeped through the curtains as my nieces did earlier and watched a taxi driver pull away. It was Sarah.

'Hello, Sarah.' I kissed her on her cheek and immediately smelt the booze on her.

She stumbled into the hallway and I closed the door.

'Ooh, hellooo, Justin, you sexy beast!' Sarah was pissed.

'I take it was a good night, then.'

'The best one in years,' she told me, slurring most of her words.

She managed to make it to the sofa in the lounge and predictably she stumbled and fell onto the three-seater sofa.

I moved swiftly into the kitchen and made some coffee. I had to ask Sarah twice to keep her voice down, and not to wake her children.

She told me how good the night was. How many men chatted her up. How good it felt to be noticed by men. Handsome men, who wanted her, for more than her not-so-bad looks.

'I hope you didn't—' Sarah cut me off.

'Didn't do what, Justin? Shag someone. Snog loads of men. Let them fumble my breasts,' she blasted back.

'Shit, calm down, I was only joking,' I told her. Then there was that awkward silence. Then she started to sob. Then it all came out.

How her and Mark were not getting on. Sleeping apart. He works late and never says he loves her anymore. I had no experience to draw on, except to tell her that it was a phase that married couples go through. Flimsy. He'll get back to how he was. I assumed every relationship does not stay as passionate and 'new' as when couples first meet. It couldn't be easy.

'Look, I grew up with Mark, and I know that you are the best thing that has ever happened to him.' I passed her some tissues from a box on my coffee table. 'You've talked to him, I take it.'

'He won't listen. Says he's too busy. I'm going to leave him, Justin.' She turned to face me on the sofa. I put my arm around her and she nuzzled her head against my chest. I had already baby-sat two girls tonight, now I was doing it again. Their mother.

Sarah wiped her rivulet of tears and pulled head up from me.

'Why he can't he be more like you?' she asked, in a whisper.

'Look Sarah, whatever you need, you need to talk to Mark.' Her eyes glistened with the drying teardrops. She had stunning hazel eyes and a body to match. I didn't understand what my brother was doing. Maybe he had someone else.

I was about to tell her something when she moved quickly forward and pressed her soft lips against mine. I let it linger longer than I should have, yet I fully understood this was a violation of the highest order. That line I knew Errol would never cross, maybe I just did.

Also her children, my nieces, were upstairs. I pushed her away, gently. My conscience wasn't totally clear. I enjoyed it, and began to wonder about the ten commandments – *'though shall not covet another man's wife'* .

'Sarah,' I whispered. 'This is not the way,' I interjected.

'I'm sorry, Justin, I know I shouldn't say this, but I've always… you know.'

My heart raced like never before. I couldn't believe what was happening. Here I was having two days off work to get my head straight. Now everything had been fucked into a cocked hat.

We agreed never to mention what had just happened. Regardless of Sarah's problems with Mark. She was an adult and she had to sort it out one way or the other. Without any assistance from me. I made that perfectly clear.

'Can I ask why you came here, Sarah? You're staying at the Westminster Hotel, aren't you?'

Once I'd asked the question, I already knew the answer. She wanted to stay well away from Mark. And from what she'd told me, he preferred it that way.

'You can't stay here, Sarah. Not now. It's not fair on you, on me, or Lucy or Lillie. There'll be an atmosphere and Lucy will sniff it out. You cannot afford that. Can you?'

'No. I know you're right. I'll go back to the hotel. I'll see you in the morning. Okay.'

I called another taxi and kissed her on her cheek, with my body being held back by a control mechanism I was oh so glad was working. Watching her get into the taxi gave me the biggest exhalation of relief. I had passed that test. Mentally I kicked myself for crossing 'that line', because admittedly I wanted my brother's partner. It was not my proudest moment, even if he was screwing around.

A selfish thought occurred to me, that I had to look after what I was doing, or could do. Not anyone else. I was only responsible for my actions.

Thankfully the brandy helped me sleep through lingering ideas and notions. It would not, however, allow me to forget.

12

The next morning went without a hitch. I said nothing to my brother when he and Sarah arrived to collect their two daughters.

Acting as normally as possible, I used Lucy and Lillie as the necessary distraction, to keep my mind off what had happened.

We all waved goodbye to each other displaying happy smiles. Underneath that current of goodness was a stream of potential deceit.

To keep busy, I used my second day off to clean my two-bedroom house. Lovely.

I made a few calls to Shaun and Errol at work, just to keep me up to date on any changes, whilst I was on leave. There was one. A graduate had started, as part of Eiron's graduate sales programme. He was young, apparently good looking and had already turned a few female heads on his first day. *Jammy bastard,* I was already thinking. Internally my main concern was camouflaging my initial feelings developing into hatred for someone I hadn't met. I'd soon sort him out though, if the situation required that expertise.

My spirits were somewhat dampened when Shaun of all people told me, this graduate was an affable chap. No heirs or graces, he seemed a straight-as-they-come bloke. I was despondent. No matter, more important tasks required my attention and focus.

As the second day flew by, and before it ended I made my second journey, this time successfully to visit my mother.

Locating where she had been laid to rest, for some strange reason, appeared like an epiphany. Complete clarity. Straight to the spot, unlike my first ill-judged attempt, fumbling in the darkness.

I knelt by her gravestone, saying a short prayer for her. I always hoped she'd be watching me, somehow. Transcending her wise, rational advice through an invisible translucent force, like a Jedi.

The wind picked up and surrounded me. The leaves whipped up in a twister-like fashion. Standing up, the chill of the afternoon air seem to bite that bit more. I pulled up my hood on my parker coat and covered my head, walking away slowly. This ritual of mine allowed balance for me. Secretly this process impressed upon me the necessity for family, for friendships in general, utilising the advice of others for my own growing and learning.

Once home, I ate a pre-packaged dinner of southern fried chicken and chunky chips. Drank a can of five percent beer and went to bed early. It was the best way for me to end the day.

*

My first day back didn't start well at all. I thought I was relaxed and composed. I had a customer meeting which I was late for. The rain lashed down, from the moment I got into my car, and continued until I reached my location.

The motorways were heavily congested, and you could guarantee an accident on any day when it rained like that.

Back in the office, by just after two in the afternoon, slightly wet, and pissed off. I saw Victoria give me the once over with those piercing green eyes of hers. In return I hoped the smile I responded with showed her my innermost feelings. She returned my gaze with a curt professional grin. I was warmed immediately.

Reaching my desk, Shaun approached me first, before I could dump my laptop bag and briefcase.

'Hey, it's Mr Whalley. Back in business,' Shaun said, loud enough for everyone in the open-plan department to hear.

I heard laughter and someone saying, 'Wally by name – probably wally by nature.' I hadn't heard that voice before. It incensed me.

Turning round, and dropping my bags on the floor, my eyes observed this young, tall, model-looking person.

'And you are?' I asked with the straightest of faces and a firm tone.

'I'm Phil, the graduate.'

I watched his eyes; he put out his hand for me to shake. By way of introduction. I let his hand hang there. I wouldn't shake it.

'So you think I'm a wally, do you? Huh?' He didn't move a muscle and an audience was starting to build. I carried on.

'You think you can start here for a couple of days and that earns you the right to take the fucking piss out my family name. Who the fuck do you think are?' My voice must have risen and carried over the dividers. Conversely I didn't care; this tall, lanky tosser was gonna get it big style.

'Hey, take it easy I was…' I refused to let him defend what he'd said.

Errol moved to toward me and held my arm. I ignored him.

'Was what? Making a fool of someone you don't know. Taking the piss because it's easy, clever. What, did they teach that at Oxford!' That got a few chuckles. Errol by now was not impressed. He stepped in.

'Everyone back to work. Phil, in my office now! Justin, I'll speak to you later.'

The proverbial was going to hit the fan. The whispers and mutterings continued. I finally set myself up to work and looked up to see Victoria's face. It was one of surprise, maybe shock. I had no clue whether any chance I had of making her like me had increased (brave for standing up), or decreased (overreacting?), I guessed only time would tell.

Errol's voice bore through the walls of his office. He was yelling at Phil. Giving him a verbal blast. Errol was a calm man, however, incensed like I was, he could be quite frightening. I suppose that's what I seemed like to the poor uninitiated graduate. Served him right.

I had more important things to think about and carry out. Victoria Shepard was one of those goals. A target. I'm sure my mother would have approved wholeheartedly.

13

In a foul mood for the remainder of the day, hardly anyone approached or spoke to me. I didn't give a shit what anyone thought. Well, maybe Walter Baker, if he got to hear about the graduate incident, which somehow, I'm positive he would.

Finishing at six fifteen in the evening was a normality. My working hours were nine to five thirty. I didn't know anyone who managed to stick to those times, apart from TGC. The sucker always got away with it.

To relive the stress of the day and to help relax and prepare for a major customer meeting, I agreed to meet Errol at the gym later that evening. It was his clever idea. 'Take out your anger on objects, not people.' Wise words from my long-time friend, confidant and line manager.

The weather had calmed down from earlier in the day. Still cold, with little or no wind in the air. The gymnasium was a modern building, created for customers who had the money and wanted a certain 'kudos'. Not the fundamental reason for keeping fit. From a man's point of view it could make a pleasant surprise in observing the opposite sex. In a completely different light.

At eight thirty Errol began his circuit. I followed his routine, well almost. We began on the bikes, ten minutes to warm up. Errol looked at me, with a resigned expression.

'Have I done something, Errol? You're making me nervous.' I attempted to probe for his innermost thoughts.

'Do you think you should have done what you did today, the way you did it?'

It was a heavy question. My brain worked itself around like my legs on the bicycle. Not fast enough.

'Okay, maybe I was a bit forceful.' Errol, who had turned away, gave another glare from his face that was now only three-quarters turned. 'Alright, too forceful. But do you know what? The more I think about it, that arsehole deserved every flippin' minute of it.'

Errol carried on pedalling hard, facing forward. I continued hoping the half-empty gym clientele would not hear our conversation.

'Errol, you know me. Yeah?' I paused. Errol nodded after a few seconds. 'Emily lost her baby.' That got his attention. His facial expression altered to one of concern, yet cautious, trying not to show too much sympathy for my outburst in the office.

'She had an ectopic pregnancy. She's having a funeral in a day or so. On top of that, I visited my mother's grave. I have had two days off to gather my thoughts and get myself together. I come back to some jumped-up prat, who is still wet behind the friggin' ears...' I left it hanging right there.

Errol, unusually, stopped pedalling. We'd been going for seven and half minutes. He took a sip of water from a bottle and swilled around in his mouth before swallowing it. He was breathing normally. I was not.

'Look, I apologise. I should have remembered. I hope Emily's okay. Give her my regards.'

'Thanks. I will.'

The was a pause whilst we moved to the rowing machines. I hated them.

'Errol, you are like another brother, and I tell you things that I tell no one else. I only do that because I can trust you. I won't use our friendship as an excuse to "get away" with things when we're at work. If I need a rollicking, then do it.'

Errol started his rowing back and forth and gathered a smooth rhythm.

'I'll always treat you the same as everyone else, Just. Always will. Hey, let's not talk about shitty stuff like that, you found a bird yet?' Errol finally had a huge despicable grin on his face.

I let him wait a while before I answered, using the exertion of the rowing machine as the perfect deflection from answering his question. It didn't work.

'Come on, Just, it's me you're talking to. You need any help?' Errol chuckled.

'No one yet, I'm afraid,' as I puffed and panted.

'Not even a kiss? A snog?' I was smiling and didn't know why. Errol raised his eyebrows. 'A fumble?'

'Sssh, will ya? Keep it down.' Two women beside me had smirks on their faces. They must have overheard.

I turned to Errol, who was on my left.

'I did have a kiss, but it shouldn't have happened.'

Errol finished his rowing and watched me end my session immediately afterward.

He pulled out a flannel and wiped the beads of sweat from his face and forehead.

'So who was she? The neighbour's wife, eh? You old devil.'

'Hell no, worse than that,' I whispered.

'Who then?' I had Errol's full concentration.

'Promise first that you will not tell a soul. Especially anyone from work.'

Errol crossed his chest. I could trust him. Damn, I had to tell someone.

'It was Mark's Sarah.'

Errol said nothing. He mouthed 'fuck me'. I nodded my head to agree.

'How the hell did you…' His voice trailed off, as he stroked his chin, trying to decipher the revelation I'd just uttered.

I explained in brief terms what happened and how. Errol said it took a special person, particularly any man, to pull back from crossing that line. I did explain that my mind said one thing, my heart really wanted to do something else.

As we used a few more machines, I revealed what I did with Sarah and what she told me about her relationship.

'I feel so dirty, Errol. I mean nasty, you know? I shouldn't have feelings like that for my "sister-in-law". I'm glad nothing happened.'

'I know this doesn't sound like much, you could do with someone regular. It would take the edge off, if you know what I mean?'

I knew alright.

Next we did ten minutes on the running machines. There I admitted my feelings for Victoria Shepard. Errol said he'd put a good word in for me, which I dutifully declined.

When Errol asked me what type of woman I was looking for I pointed a few out in the gym. They were tallish, in good shape and they noticed that I was watching, or ogling at them. At least I made them laugh a little when I missed my step on the treadmill and had to grab onto the rails for dear life.

I stood erect and waved at two of the female audience, and to my surprise they waved back.

In fact more than two people were looking, as everyone heard Errol laughing, so I saluted everyone, whilst running, doing my utmost to remain composed. Smiling broadly, I received an ovation of applause.

'Well done, mate, it's good to see you laughing again,' Errol commented.

'Anytime.'

Dripping in perspiration, and after lifting a few weights we showered and sat in the spacious, modern-designed relaxation lounge.

'What about you, Errol, how's Elisa and you?'

'We're okay.' He spoke in staccato fashion.

'You're always okay. Nothing more in it?' I quizzed, reciprocating in like mode.

'What do you wanna know, Just? Come out with it and don't beat around the bush.'

'Does Elisa know about Nikki?' Errol's act of seeming surprised almost worked. 'From the sales conference. I saw you disappear upstairs and could smell the odour of female perfume in our room. Any comment?'

Not usually stuck for words, Errol Hughes swigged two mouthfuls of his diet cola. Turning his head left and right, he leaned forward, telling me to lean forward too.

'Look, honestly Just, nothing happened. We kissed – yes we did. It was good. She wanted more, I said no. We talked for a bit and I walked her to her room.'

'And that's your story.' I smiled a wry smile. I'd known this cat for far too long.

'Ab-so-lute-ly!' That's how it sounded.

My half of lager tasted good, so I finished it, and completed that with an audible 'aah'.

A minute or passed, when I dropped this into the stagnant conversation pot.

'The only reason I asked about you and Elisa is that, Mary Leadbetter was at Emily's beside for some time the other day.' I witnessed Errol shake his head. I heard him mumble, 'Oh, that nosey bitch.'

'You know what she can be like. And Mary tells Elisa everything – true or false, gossip or not.'

'Too bloody right. Out of all the friends Elisa has, this Mary and I just do not get on.'

Errol reached for his denim jacket pocket and pulled out his mobile phone.

'I don't know what it is. May be she knows what I can be like.'

'I think she does. You be careful. That's why I'm telling you. I'm looking out for you, that's all.'

'Cheers – what are mates for, eh?'

Errol had two text messages from Elisa asking him what time he'd be home. He deleted them both.

'I'd better be off, Errol, got those presentations to I.N.P. in the morning and Memray Computers Plc, in the afternoon. Must finish off the slides.'

'Okay. If you need any help, just call – you get it.'

'Ha ha… yeah…'

His oldest joke was still as poor as it was when I first heard it over a decade and half ago.

We left, going our separate ways. I left with a smile and wave from one of the female audience. It was encouragement enough to keep going back. Errol left with a worried look and nervously slow walk back to his car.

14

It took only forty-five minutes to get ready. My light grey suit, dark blue shirt and silver-coloured tie should do the job.

Reviewing my presentation for the twenty-first time at breakfast, my confidence continued to strengthen. My nerves were steadying, not because of who I had to present to, but because Errol would be there. As well as that, I knew that Walter Baker would be asking for an update on how the meeting went.

I.N.P. Plc, were our third-largest customer. Eiron had been in a six-month sales cycle to win a £2.2 million order for product and services. These were to be the final presentations from Eiron and two other competitors.

Leaving at 0815 would give me plenty of time to collect Errol and for us to get to the customer on time. On the way there, Errol reminded me of a few things. What to say, how to say it. Made sure I had copies of the presentation printed out and in neat binders for each of the attendees.

We were on last. At 11.30. It was usually a two-hour drive. Errol and I stopped off at services near the customers site near the Wirral. I had to use the toilet.

'Remember, Just, keep it simple,' Errol told me as we walked back to the car. 'Our presentation is short and to the point. This customer is a real quick decision maker, he doesn't want a long one-hour pitch that's going to send him and his board of directors to sleep.'

'I gotcha.' I exhaled heavily.

'Do you want to drive the rest of the way?' Errol asked.

'Yeah, go on then, I'll go through my pitch one last time and check I've got everything I need.'

I tossed Errol my keys. He caught them and opened the doors.

It seemed only minutes later, as I was reading my eighth slide, that we pulled into the I.N.P. car park.

Upstairs, in the I.N.P. boardroom, one of Eiron's competitors were taking questions and answers. It was ten minutes after eleven. Errol and I signed in at reception. The entrance to reception reminded me of a hotel lobby. It was huge. The receptionist wasn't bad looking either. In fact, she was stunning.

Tall, slim, straight as an arrow dark brown hair, and the most happy, smiling hazel eyes. Maybe it was the diversion I needed, away from this boring business stuff, I was about to get into.

'Come on, Justin, we'll wait upstairs.'

Errol summoned me onward and upward.

Outside the boardroom, we were greeted with large, sumptuous leather armchairs and a second receptionist. This time older, not like Clara downstairs. Errol kept my mind in focus.

'Okay, Just, like we prepared, keep it simple. Aim any financial benefits toward the FD, the technical benefits to the IT Director, and of course the big benefits to the company to the MD and chairman. Remember, this solution is going to make them money and save them money.'

Hopefully that was Errol's last speech before we had to face the lion's den. However, I should be okay, I kept telling myself. I'd rehearsed, practised and gone over the dialogue enough times. I'd done the presentation at Eiron's sales conference and that went down well. Yes, I had nothing to worry about.

At 11.32 Kevin Johnson the IT Director came out to meet us. The other company were let out by another door, so we wouldn't see them. We shook hands, firm grips, as Kevin apologised for running late, but we said it was okay.

He explained briefly what was going to happen. We had ten minutes to set up our laptop and get anything we needed ready. Then he would lead the decision makers back into the boardroom. Shit, I could have used more waiting time. It was too late. I had to deliver the goods.

I got what I wished for. Kevin came back to the room and Errol and I stood up looking professional as possible in our best 'bib and tucker'.

Then the introductions started and this is when it all started to go downhill.

Kevin stepped to the side and said, 'This is Bevan Cole, our FD.'

I stepped forward to shake his hand and said, 'Hi Justin, I'm Bevan.' There was a split-second silence as everything went ultimately quiet. My already warm face metamorphosed into something resembling a dying tomato.

Once that split second had passed, I quickly made a joke of it.

'My apologies, you're Bevan and I'm Justin.' I tried to laugh it off. I didn't look back at Errol's face or expression, that would have made things worse.

Bevan smiled although I could tell he was sort of offended.

The rest of the introductions went without hiccup. Everyone sat down and had coffees in front of them.

Errol introduced Eiron, for about five minutes, telling the three-man-and-one-woman audience what kind of company we were. Kevin, Bevan, Roy Roland, the chairman and Susie Killner, the MD, sat attentively listening to Errol's spoutings. They looked genuinely interested. Then again, they had to. They were good at this. They did this all the time. In fact I'm supremely confident these buggers rehearsed these sessions, in some secret 'buyer' tips training they all go through.

Then, that time arrived when Errol passed the mantle over to me.

'What you'll hear next, for about the next twenty minutes or so, is Eiron's proposed solution for I.N.P.'s database requirements. Justin will take you through this now. Justin.'

Standing up and facing Susie Killner, I didn't realised how attractive the female MD looked. She was to be in her late forties (shouldn't make any odds to me), but damn, she looked fine. I never noticed it earlier after my embarrassment with the FD, so I rushed through the other intros to ensure no repeat. We'd all given out our business cards across the table to each other. Like some card game in Vegas, our business cards whizzed from side to the other. As I collected each card I laid them in front of me so I would not forget anyone's name.

I switched my focus and concentration back to the presentation.

I'd gone through the first three slides and everyone looked to be awake and keen. I had already answered two questions from Susie. She was my ally, I could tell. Bevan looked distant, but it was a customer/supplier meeting trick. Trying to unnerve me, or see what I would do.

As I pressed the return key on my laptop for the fourth slide to appear, the laptop went blank.

'Excuse me, ladies and gentlemen, I won't be minute.'

Errol leapt to his feet and moved around to the front of the room, where I was presenting from.

We whispered to each other, checking cables, tapping keys on my laptop, checking the projector. But nothing. It was dead. I was dead. My presentation was dead. The opportunity to win £2.2 million was dead. Walter would do the killing. And just maybe, Errol would too.

I looked at the faces of the decision makers and wasn't sure how to read them. They understood something like this could happen, but it never looked good if it did. We were going to ask this company to spend over two million pounds on IT and telephony equipment, services and software. One of the same hardware models had just broken down. It did not say a lot for reliability of our so-called 'robust' products.

As an olive branch I had printed copies of the presentation, which I had to hand out.

'I do apologise for this inconvenience, but if you could follow me through from slide four, we'll take from there.'

Susie and Kevin said not to worry and at least I came with a backup plan, which I did have to use. It was something positive. Errol was silently fuming. He remained calm and erudite in front of our important customers.

Still standing, I completed the presentation and Errol and I waited for the volley of questions. Especially ones about reliability, and stability of Eiron's hardware products.

As questions were being asked, I kept noticing Susie staring toward me. Really, really staring at me. She smiled at one point, leaving me to display a somewhat embarrassed smile. Kevin did the same, as he noticed Susie's eyeline trajectory.

For a moment of sheer panic I hoped with all that had happened, I hadn't risen to the occasion and Susie had seen. By now I didn't know what was happening and wanted to get out of there ASAP.

The room was warm; the projector added additional and unwanted heat. The windows were closed and we were on the fourth floor.

They finally finished asking questions and we agreed that the meeting was over. Thank goodness.

Kevin said he'd be in touch with us within the next two weeks or so with a decision. The other members in the room rose to leave and we shook hands and then Errol and I disconnected our equipment.

As Susie shook my hand to say, 'Thanks for your presentation, I enjoyed it,' she also whispered in my ear, 'Your trouser zip is undone,' and walked out. I finally got the joke. At my expense. I surreptitiously zipped up.

Kevin walked us to reception, where I got to have another look and the gorgeous receptionist. We said our goodbyes and hoped for the best.

Errol drove back to the Nottingham office. We didn't stop on the way back and Errol hardly said two words to me.

15

It was a cloudy afternoon as we got back to the office. And that's how I felt. Errol was disappointed in me, and that's what was really niggling me. I hated letting anyone down, especially a friend or a manager.

Errol had loosened up a little as he offered to buy me lunch from our small canteen/tuck shop downstairs.

We sat opposite each other both munching on a chicken salad sandwich with a bag of flavoured crisps.

'Look, Just, a few things to remember.' Errol started his meeting revision and summary, looking at me straight in the eyes. 'Remember.' He paused again, letting me sweat, suffer. He did not take his eyes off mine. He continued to eat.

'Remember to always, I mean always, ensure that your zipper is securely fastened at all times.'

I waited a few seconds and there it was, Errol was smiling, then began to laugh. The bastard had me going. He knew I'd be expecting a blasting after the meeting, he had calmed down. Either way, I was sufficiently glad that Errol's demeanour had altered.

'You had me then, you little shit,' I responded confidently.

'Anyway, on a more serious note,' Errol bounced back.

I thought, *Here it comes, the teaching bit.*

'Your laptop, did you check it before you came out?'

'Yes I did.'

'Checked the AC adaptor, the laptop battery?' Errol raised his eyebrows, whilst consuming the last mouthful of his chicken salad sandwich.

'Yes. I powered it on and it all worked. I've never had any problems before.' I tried to retain a calm monotone voice.

'Well Just, do you know why your laptop died?'

'No.'

'When you stepped on the power cable, you pulled it out of the socket. It wasn't in firmly enough in the first place.'

I wasn't sure whether Errol could determine my fear-filled face. He continued to look straight at me the whole time, and I didn't know where to look, or how to reconfigure my facial expression to one of someone accepting advice and welcoming it. I'm not sure it worked.

'Did you notice this, Errol, and not say anything?' I had to ask.

'All part of your training, Just. I actually gave you my AC power cable, which is faulty. I wanted to see how you had prepared, for example, you had an alternate version of the presentation. Also if your laptop failed, we need to know how you would continue to present without detriment to the customer. I must say you passed with flying colours.'

I finally took my eyes away from Errol's and buried my head in my arms. I leant on the table in front of me, groaning quietly. Looking up, Errol was smiling again, a successful happy smile, which I supposed meant I did okay. I didn't feel successful. Only time would tell, if I.N.P. selected Eiron for the project.

'Justin, when we go back upstairs, ensure that you create a brief email to Kevin at I.N.P. thanking him for the opportunity and for the meeting. You know, the usual buttering-up stuff.'

I nodded and understood.

Errol had more to say as I burped after taking my last sip of fizzy soft drink.

'Also, you may have noticed, and this may be in our favour to win the deal.' At this point after remaining calm, and neutral, I began to worry once again. It was Errol's tone that did it. 'I realised during the meeting and more so when we'd finished that the MD, what was her name again…?' Errol let me finish.

'Susie Killner.'

'Somehow Just, I guessed you'd remember.' Errol burst into a chuckle. He stopped when I asked him a question that obviously surprised him.

'What would you like me to do?'

Errol rubbed his chin, motioning me with his free left hand to stand up and start walking out of the canteen. He put his left arm around my shoulders and commenced whispering in my ear.

'I'm not asking you to do anything you don't want to. However, as you are single and believe Susie is divorced and hot.' Errol gave me his 'ooh I would love to' eyes and shook his head, as though he was missing out.

He told me to experience women. Try a few before you buy. Errol almost convinced me it was okay to sleep around but to be mindful of certain types of women. His arguments we reasonable, and I suppose as long as no one got hurt, and everyone involved knew what the rules were, everybody wins, so to speak.

Back at my desk, I logged on and deliberated over what to write in what supposed to be a 'standard' reply to having a customer meeting. I also had to complete meeting notes on what was discussed in the in our sixty-or-so-minute session.

I had developed my own folder, where all my information on every meeting I went to was kept. To my knowledge only two other salespeople did this. This gave the management an excellent precis of any customer I had as an account. If I was off ill or on holiday, Shaun or Tom, in my team, could easily pick up where I had left things. No such policy exists in a company that prides itself on professionalism.

It should be a basic statute.

Once I completed my email, I looked up from my computer to see Shaun O'Dwyer staring at me.

'Good meetin', Justin?'

'You know me. Always good.' I laughed nervously and dropped my eye level back to my monitor.

'Don't worry, I'll ask Errol for the truth.' Shaun laughed wickedly and walked over to his desk.

I ignored him and reread my email twice before sending it. I received a read receipt five minutes later, which was good sign. At least Kevin from I.N.P. had got my email and read it.

By now the clock had spun around sufficiently to make it nearly twenty minutes after five. I logged off and wanted to get home. It had been an okay day, when all things considered. I stood up, ready to say my goodbyes when Errol called out to me from his office, his door slightly open.

'You can't go yet, Just, got a phone call for you.'

Great bloody timing.

'Okay. Put them through.' I waited and heard clicks and tones as Errol's voice came on the line.

'Justin, it's I.N.P., good news I think. Don't mess this up.' Errol left those last few words ringing in my ear.

'Hello, Justin Whalley speaking.'

'Oh, hello Justin,' a sultry female voice said. 'It's Susie. Susie Killner, from the meeting earlier today.'

'Yes, hello, how are you?'

'I'm fine.' There was one of those awkward silences. I wasn't sure whether I was supposed to fill it or her.

'Justin…'

'Susie…'

'Oops.' We both spoke simultaneously. I leapt in.

'You go first,' I said, heart beating; the swan was alive again. Susie chuckled nervously, almost in teenage girlie fashion. I hoped none of the snooping bastards were listening.

'Okay, Justin, I not used to this, but I'll come straight to the point. I actually live in Nottinghamshire. And what I'm trying to say is, that, erm, that if you fancy going for a drink sometime… maybe.' She was as brave as a gladiator for doing what she did. So I felt guilty and had to make it easy, for me and her.

'Yes, I'd love to. Tell you what, Susie, I've got your business card and your mobile number, how about we arrange something for the next couple of days, maybe Friday?'

'Yes, that would be great. We can get to know each other a bit better. You never know what you might learn about the project…' I could hear her smile and relief was in her voice.

We finished talking and I must have seemed happy. Shaun sat on the corner of my desk waiting for me to finish.

'You jammy bastard, Friday night for a bit of rumpy pumpy!! Hey, hey!'

I said nothing to him or Errol, who put his thumb up to me. Leaving the building, I pondered on what I had just started.

16

Errol called me later that night to tell me or rather advise me on what to do. I did my best to explain that I wanted a wife, children and to be a good husband and father. Errol explained that I was still young and had more than enough time to do all those things. Although, in the meantime I should get as much practice as possible and build up my experience.

It didn't seem such a bad plan of attack.

Why not? I told myself.

It was Friday night and Susie booked herself into a local hotel to stay over in. I didn't know what signal or sign that was meant to be. Maybe a secret clandestine one. Something the CIA or MI6 would be interested in.

We met at Joney's Bar & Restaurant in Nottingham at seven thirty. She wore a thin shoulder-strapped dress, which fell just below her knees. Her searing pale blue eyes were beautifully round and hypnotic. Covering her shoulders was a lime green throw-over cardigan, to match her stunning dress. Very little cosmetics were employed apart from an unusual-smelling perfume. I couldn't fault her.

When we met I didn't know whether to shake her hand or kiss her on her cheek. I did both. I think she was pleasantly surprised.

We went inside and gave our names to the restaurant manager who took us to our seats. I had a reoccurring nightmare that Shaun and Errol and maybe Tom were in here.

'So you wanted to see me then?' I asked Susie, cheekily.

'Indeed I did, Mr Whalley.'

We ordered drinks. Susie asked for a sweet martini and lemonade.

I ordered an vodka martini, but I didn't ask for the shaken and stirred bit. The waitress taking the order smiled. So did Susie. She seemed relaxed, comfortable.

We talked freely over two or three drinks before our starters came. Chicken liver pâté for us both.

Susie had been married for twelve years and had three children. She didn't tell me what a despicable cheating bastard he was, well not in so many words. Her children sounded lovely, all doing well at school.

'You know…' She began to open up. I was happy to listen. This was an experience for me, to learn about women. All different types and with differing backgrounds and 'luggage'. 'I always suspected something was wrong with our marriage. You can generally tell when, your husband doesn't like you touching him anymore. Or there is no lovemaking for weeks or months on end. Always tired. No little hugs or holding hands. The small things, in isolation stand out like a sore thumb.'

'I'm sorry to hear that. It must be tough having three children and a highly responsible job, as an MD. How the hell do you to keep looking so fantastic?'

She smiled, a tad embarrassed by my compliment. It was, however, very true. I had to ask her a question that wouldn't go away.

'Can I ask you…?' I paused and she responded.

'Anything you like.' Susie took another sip from her glass of red wine. Our third bottle.

'For someone like you, attractive, good looking, financially stable, how is it you don't have a trail of men after you?'

'It's a fair question. The answer simply is – I don't have the time or the generally the inclination to go through all the usual games you have to play. And normally once I say I have three children, most men run like Linford on a warm sunny day.'

'Understood.'

'And what about you, Mr Whalley, what's your story?'

Scratching my head and raising my eyebrows, I stuttered out an explanation of my brief and actionless life.

'Not much, really. Part of a big family. Mum died some years ago. Did okay at school, nothing fantastic mind you, but good enough. Studied IT in various ways and here I am today.'

'Short but sweet. Yet I'm sure you missed out all the good bits.' Susie was no fool and I was no good at acting or disguising the parts of the story that she probably wanted to hear from me.

The impish waitress glided over to our table with the dessert menu. We took one each and made our selections.

'Another glass, Susie, you may as well finish this off.' She smirked and her stunning eyes rolled over; she was seventy-five percent drunk, and serenely so.

Who would have thought that I was the one who only had two glasses? Whilst pouring her a glass, my aim deviated and plunged wide of the mark. Susie yelped out.

'Oh! Oh, Justin... what have you done?'

Leaping upward and over to her side of the table, I tried to mop up the spillage. Everyone in the packed restaurant was looking over.

'I'm sorry, don't worry I'll er, get it to the dry cleaners, I'm...'

My words were fruitless. Susie rushed by the restaurant manager and into the ladies' toilets. I was left holding and soaking up all the eyes that deemed to linger on me.

The manager assigned one of his staff to do the cleaning up, whilst I settled the bill. I cancelled the desserts.

I knew seeing Susie was a mistake and this incident just made things doubly bad. On a personal and professional level.

Ten minutes later Susie came outside Joney's where I'd been

waiting patiently.

'Look Susie, I know whatever I say isn't going to change what's happened or cure the damage to your clothes.'

She faced me in her three-inch heels and looked up at me, not angry and not pissed off.

After a deep breath she spoke. 'Justin.' She seemed to have sobered up a little. 'Can I make a suggestion?' I nodded to concur.

'Can I ask you that we stay friends? Can I also ask that you accompany me back to the hotel? I'm saying I forgive you.'

I managed a reply. 'Thanks.'

We linked arms and walked toward a taxi rank.

'I'm not usually this clumsy, it's because you were so beautiful, it, you know, made me tremble and I…'

Susie smiled. She laughed her stuttering laugh, which made me relax. She held my arm and we stopped near the taxi rank. She faced me again and unexpectedly kissed me full on the lips. I responded slowly, as visions of Shaun or Errol seeing this would have destroyed the moment. And what a moment it was.

Maybe because she was older, more mature and she'd had loads of practice, but that kiss, sparked a tingling sensation like I'd never felt before. My stomach filled with what I can only call butterflies. My legs weak, ready to buckle. My strength ebbed away like Samson, after a haircut.

If anyone was watching I had no reason to care.

We separated, and looked at each other, smiling, as if we'd been partners for much longer than a few hours. We hugged, her head buried in my chest. My bodily fluids doing all sorts, and my brain in overload mode in an attempt to control everything physically and emotionally. I was just holding steady. Thankfully the taxi arrived and we got in.

The ride was short, yet pleasant.

'I like you, Justin Whalley, and er, you're not too bad a kisser either!' Susie pecked me on the cheek and left me alone in the taxi. Her hotel on Mansfield Road, looked rather nice.

I couldn't think of being with her. She'd already said what our status should be. Maybe that would be a good thing. I had to think of the other business relationship we could possibly have as well. She'd obviously done that thinking well ahead of me. The kiss must have been a bonus. I sat in the taxi, as it trundled along, thinking of Susie Killner's kiss.

That night I actually allowed myself to feel content and happy. I had every reason to.

17

For the next few days at work, Errol and particularly Shaun, pestered me about my date with Susie Killner. I told them the same words every single time.

'No comment.'

Eventually they became bored and my interrogation ceased.

Susie had, however, contacted me twice since our dinner date. The first occasion was regarding the presentation and Eiron's chances to win. She had asked for some additional information from me, which was always a good sign.

On the second occasion Susie talked about us. It was personal. She did tell me on the night what our personal relationship would be. At least to start with, if anything was going to start. She reiterated those sentiments over the phone, telling me it was best to see what happened with the project and then consider what we should do.

Not that experienced around women, her tone made it sound as though she had my best interests at heart. Her words equalled to what I had come to know as a 'brush off'. It was good whilst it lasted.

I tried to forget what happened, everything except that kiss. I had targets to meet and loads of other customers to visit and get money from. I still needed a distraction. Errol and Shaun provided it. Tom watched from afar.

It was after four in the afternoon, when Errol asked me into his office.

He had an oblong desk, with his computer, docking station, two telephones and a handheld IPAQ computer device all linked into the building's IVPN network system. A few papers covered one corner and a desk blotter sat tidily in the middle.

Errol took his seat and told me to sit opposite him in the spare chair provided.

'Look, Just, whatever happened with Susie has nothing to do with this project we're working on.'

'I know.'

'Good.'

'So what's up, boss? Have I been coming late?' I attempted to add some dire humour.

'Nothing... Well, actually Justin, I want to make you happy. Not just at work, but in your personal life.' Errol leant back in his chair and placed his feet on his odd-shaped table.

'Sounds interesting. What do you have in mind?' The conversation didn't feel like Errol and I. The strangest aura of a twilight zone movie filled the room.

'Did you know, Justin, that employees who are happy in their personal life are twice as likely to work better and harder, than those who aren't?'

I leant back and flashed Errol a quizzical look.

'I s'pose so.'

I let him reveal his words of wisdom.

'Please, listen before you answer to what we, that's myself, Shaun and Tom, have come up with.'

Now my nerves, which were almost dying a death, leapt into life. My blue eyes began dancing in their sockets. Errol continued, whilst playing with a blue biro in his right hand.

'We have come to the conclusion that you need some help in the getting a date department.' I leaned forward and Errol raised the palm of his left hand to stop me from speaking.

'On Saturday we would like you to go to Brown's in Hockley at about seven thirty...'

I had to step in.

'A bloody blind date!' I cried.

Errol pulled his feet off the table and leaned forward on his desk.

'Justin, this is something I wouldn't do for just anyone. Shaun knows a few women and he has arranged for you to meet her on Saturday. We kinda hoped you'd be there...'

I knew deep down they were all trying to help in their own way. I should really thank them. As Errol told me before, I need the practice, and there was no harm in me dating several women whilst I was young, free and single.

'So what's it to be, Just? A chance of some fun, a few drinks and who knows, maybe a quick grope and snog before bedtime!'

I had to chuckle. Errol understood how to appeal to me. What could I do but concur, go along for the ride?

'Okay. Set it up then. Seven thirty it is.'

'Great. You tell me or Shaun what you're going to wear, and we'll do the same so you know who to look for.'

I nodded and stood to go. As I reached the door I turned back.

'Errol, promise me one thing. I'm not looking to get married or have children from the first date. I hope she isn't a desperado who knows time is running short and is clutching at straws.'

'I understand. From what I know she is in her mid-twenties and from Birmingham. Remember Justin, there is no pressure. Have some fun, get to know her and see how the river flows after that.'

I shook my head after hearing the last part and exited his office, closing the door quietly behind me.

I returned to my desk and collected my things. Tom had returned from a customer meeting with a big cheesy grin. He'd obviously got an order. From the inane grin, I'd guess a pretty big one.

'Well lads, this is the way to do it. Four hundred and twenty thousand pounds, booked, signed, sealed and delivered, by yours truly.'

My gut wrenched, but I managed to spew out a congratulatory retort.

'Well done, Tom, I take it this was the deal you've been closing since 1999.'

A few other sales guys were quietly rumbling with laughter, but Tom didn't see the funny side.

'We'll see who ends up on top, Whalley. Maybe you should bring in some deals, if you knew what one was!' Tom hit back. Errol came out of his office.

'Hey Tommo, you did it at last! Make sure you pass the info to admin to get all the paperwork sorted. Walter will be pleased, it's our first biggie of the year.'

Tom lapped up the praise and could not stop smiling.

Without saying goodnight to anyone I left, quietly, knowing I had to bring in a deal soon. The first month of the financial year would be over soon and I'd hardly broken into my four-million-pound target. Tomorrow had to bring better news, at work and at home.

18

Thursdays and Fridays were usually my better days. I'm not sure why but they were.

Two deals from late last year closed and I prodded and subtly nudged the customers to email over their purchase orders ASAP. At last I was off the mark. Just over a hundred grand. That made all the difference. Thursday flew by and my mood percolated all day. A gentle simmer.

Friday was better. Susie called to say she thought we were ahead in the running to get the project. Another 30k deal came in and Tom Greenfield-Crown, began to eat his words.

It was the weekend in four hours' time and I had one more customer meeting for the week to complete.

Errol was off ill, which was rare. Shaun came in on Friday with a hangover and a story of another female conquest. If I had half his charm and Errol's mental strength, panache and savvy, I'm sure I could match them any day. Well, at least in my dreams.

*

Errol called me on Saturday morning to make sure I was not going to back out. I had a cough developing, which was just my luck.

I explained what I would wear. Black jean-like trousers, navy short-sleeve designer shirt and a three-quarter-length black leather jacket.

In my not-so-full cupboards, lay a half-empty bottle of cough syrup. I filled two teaspoons sequentially and hoped it would do the job.

Later in the day, once I'd completed my shopping trip, I returned to do some well needed house work.

Early evening arrived and after some tea and dry toast to eradicate any tummy rumbles, my bath was calling me.

I loaded a Christmas-bought smelling bath and shower gel underneath my running bath tap. The bubbles increased exponentially. I stayed in for thirty minutes. Let the masculine odour soak in.

As soon as I was dry and half dressed, I used the same make of aftershave and body deodorant spray, to allow the scent to last that much longer.

A final few checks in my full-length mirror and I was set. The taxi firm confirmed that they would be at my house by seven fifteen.

Downstairs in the living room, I put my leather jacket on did a final once-over.

1. Money for the taxi and the drinks.
2. The usual breath check, with my hands over my nose and mouth.
3. A full packet of spearmint chewing gum.
4. Backup credit and debit cards, just in case (in my shirt pocket).
5. Check to see if I could smell my aftershave.
6. Took my mobile phone with me to wait for Errol's call on the 'blind date' woman I was going to meet.
7. Checked whether I looked better without my specs on. I didn't.

My cough wouldn't go away regardless of how hard I tried to hold it in. Nevertheless, I had no time think about that, as the taxi horn sounded outside my front window.

Thoughts of why I was doing this and what my mother would say, permeated my mind. Mentally I wanted to be ready for this. Just have fun. Relax, kick back and do something, rather than hoping and waiting. It was time to take decisive action.

Waiting outside Brown's for a few minutes, my mobile vibrated inside my trouser pocket. It was Errol.

'Hey, hey, hey, she's on her way, in fact she might already be inside.'

'Okay, so what's she wearing? And who do I look for?'

Errol sounded too happy. I wasn't sure whether he was with Elisa or someone else.

'Yep, she's tall, got dark hair, and is wearing a bootcut grey trousers, a black blouse and she's carrying a silver-coloured handbag… You can't miss her…' Errol's voice trailed off.

'Errol. Errol. What's her name?'

The line went dead. Just bloody great.

I took a deep breath and went inside. It was busy. I saw one or two faces I recognised from the ground floor of Eiron's office.

Scanning the packed room, my eyes searched out every and any tall dark-haired woman I could see. Some gave me tentative looks in return. Others didn't.

Approaching the bar, I shouted over to the bar girl what I wanted to drink. Wyclef's album the 'Eclectic' was being blasted out of the speakers. I asked for a Michelob bottled beer.

As the girl returned with the bottle, a woman brushed up against me.

'I'll pay for that if you like?'

I turned, remaining calm, displaying the swan scenario, to view a tall, dark-haired, stunning-looking woman.

I leaned into her, moving my mouth towards her left ear.

'I take it you're Shaun's friend?'

She reciprocated.

'Yes, it's me. I'm Charlene.'

'Pleased to meet you, Charlene. What will you have?' We had to move between each other's alternate ear, to be heard above the smooth yet booming soulful sounds being played.

'I'll have a pint of best bitter please.'

I blinked for a second and stood back so she could see my face. She began to laugh. She had me. First blood to Charlene.

She wanted a vodka drink with lime in it. An alcopop, I think.

We moved to a slightly quieter corner of the wine bar and sat down.

Conversation flowed freely, and I observed all her features with a keen eye.

After a few drinks we moved on to Lloyds bar further up the road. It had previously been a bank, converted into a wine bar.

We sat upstairs and Charlene spoke eloquently about being an only child. Having no brother or sister to play with. She was born in Dublin, and came to England when she was three. There was no accent.

'You know when Shaun asked me to go on a blind date, I was dreading what you'd be like. I suppose you felt the same?' I felt totally relaxed and could ask her anything.

'Oh yeah, you can't imagine how scared I was. But you're not so bad. I've seen and been with a lot worse.' She was teasing me I think.

'Oh thank you, flattery will get you a long way,' I responded.

'Will it now?' she giggled, her shoulders moving up and down.

'Well how about we get something to eat?' I asked, coughing violently.

'If you can walk there without collapsing, maybe, yes...' Charlene was tipsy, and so was I.

'Don't you worry, young lady, I'm as strong as an ox.'

Groups of girls and guys were looking at us as we linked arms and stumbled out of Lloyds. Then she surprised me with something she said.

'Justin, you are so easy to talk to. I feel like I've known you for long time.'

'Well thanks, Charlene. I feel the same about you. You're funny, sexy…' She opened her eyes wide when I said that. 'Tall, attractive… should I go on?'

'Oh, please do.'

We both laughed and headed for a cheap restaurant about five minutes away.

I had paella and Charlene ordered a folded pizza dish.

On our table were more drinks. In a window table for two we sat and talked some more about me, my family, my job and Shaun O'Dwyer.

Charlene revealed that she hadn't had a boyfriend in over a year. I couldn't tell her about how long my stay of execution had been. Maybe Shaun had already told her. Shit.

Whilst taking a mouthful of my average-tasting paella, my cough returned with a vengeance. I tried with all my willpower and strength to stop it but it overpowered me. As looked up to talk to Charlene I coughed a mouthful of paella into Charlene's face.

I thought Susie could scream. My gosh. Charlene beat her hands down.

The other patrons must have thought I'd murdered Charlene, or shown her my you-know-what.

She screamed and screamed. The ingredients of the Spanish dish dripped slowly from her face, which she refused to touch. A waiter rushed over and withheld his laugh, as he tended to Charlene and helped her to the ladies'.

Everyone looked over in my direction. Some shaking their head in utter disbelief. People from outside were doubled over in pain from laughing so hard. I was in the middle of a freak show and guess who was the star character? Justin friggin' Whalley.

Maybe there was something in a name.

I sat there, once again quietly paying the waiter for our meal.

However, this time I was going home alone.

I stood up and returned everyone's gaze. In the background I could hear Elton's John's 'Sorry Seems To Be The Hardest Word'. Who says that lighting doesn't strike twice?

19

They had lied to me. Errol and Shaun. I learned that Charlene was hired from an Internet dating agency. I should have known better. This, however, had nothing to do with the outcome. Although I displayed my disappointment toward Errol and Shaun by not speaking to them for a whole day.

It worried me further, when paranoia set in. My mind splintered into multiple possibilities of web cameras watching our every move, as part of some new 'live' minute-by-minute dating show. Thousands of internet users would be logging on and paying a fee to watch how a blind date progresses, without the two stars knowing anything about it. Frightening.

That incident and the fact my so-called colleagues and friends had to help me with acquiring regular female attention, led me to remember what my dear departed mother always told me. 'If you want a job doing, do it yourself.'

Taking her words to heart, I arranged to go out with Tom. I couldn't ask Errol or Shaun, plus there was no way I was going to go on my lonesome.

Strangely, when I had asked Tom to come with me to go clubbing, he said he was going anyway. I looked at him with some surprise.

'We're all going for a few drinks and whatever else for my birthday…' Tom mumbled the last few words.

'Sorry, my apologies Tom, congratulations.' I gave him a warm genuine smile to show my sincerity.

'A few of the sales girls from the Birmingham office are coming up for it. Some of them, are staying over.'

My heart began to beat faster and my face twitched. Victoria Shepard would hopefully be one of them. I dared not ask Tom, as he would smell a rat and ask too many awkward questions. Anyway, she had probably forgotten about me anyway.

The only problem now, was that Errol and Shaun would be there. I was hoping that if enough people were there, I could hide away somewhere and do what I needed to, without an audience. The planned night out was one major task to mull over. I did have other things on my mind.

Planning for the next two customer meetings, I contacted all the relevant people within Eiron to get the pricing I needed. Ensured all the technical staff were available. Wrote the proposal with the help of one of our proposal writers. My presentation would be to three people and Errol may want to come along. At this point in time, I would prefer to go on my own. As I wasn't speaking to Errol, and in a sombre, atrabilious mood, I could take the easy faceless option by emailing him all the information. Asking him to read it and suggest any revision, if required.

As always, I attached a read and delivery receipt on all my emails sent, so I could see when the receiving buggers denied that they'd read or that the email had never reached them. I got Errol on both counts. I awaited his reply.

It was Monday and as usual the office was very busy. Errol had a management meeting every Monday with Walter and three other managers from Professional Services, Customer Services and Service Delivery. I wanted to leave early, but wouldn't do it until Walter had gone. I didn't really care too much about the other managers, although they reminded me of Tom. They liked him as well.

He always received big smiles and handshakes from them. Maybe because he'd been there longer. Or maybe they could tell me where he was half the time. My intuition told me he wasn't the good, clean-living husband and father everyone thought he was. Maybe they knew and he was working on a big deal somewhere quietly. I think they liked Tom because he always followed the rules. Did what was necessary and toed the political Eiron line whenever requested. I had my own way of doing things. That's was one reason why we differed, Tom and I. As well as his age, and his height.

Tom was nearly forty and only five feet two and had been married for quite a few years. A cute round face (according to some of the women…) and a mature moustache. And he smoked.

Somehow he had the whitest of teeth. Not sure how many a day, and he slipped off quietly to have one, but our nostrils were not spared the odour of cigarette smoke which latched onto his clothes. Once women ignore this, his pale green eyes, are apparently another feature that woman talk about. Maybe I should just wear a bloody mask.

For me I'd rather get promotion from hard work, showing my ability to handle people and situations. Rather than, in effect, being a manager's sidekick. His puppet, well almost.

I had made several appointments and it was nearly five in the afternoon. Walter had just left, which was unusual and potentially scary. He never stayed that long. A strange apprehensive thought entered my mind. I knew, however, that Errol would be sworn in by Walter not to say a word. Not even a hint. If it ever leaked, Errol would be collecting his P45 quicker than he could blink.

Errol's face did not display its usual happy smiling expression. It was replaced by a frown and pain-filled eyes, as though he had just received some seriously bad news. Now I was worried and kicked myself, because I couldn't ask him anything now. He'd have no reason to talk to me or tell me anything.

Standing up, Tom and I noticed Errol's expression and we both shrugged our shoulders. Tom, more than I, always seemed to have the inside track. Possibly from one of the other managers. I guessed they'd be there tomorrow for the piss-up in Nottingham. They probably had rooms booked in hotels and Tom would visit beforehand and get the top-secret info. Sneaky bastard. I had to hope that Errol would get drunk and hopefully he'd let something slip.

Returning my concentration to our work, Tom and I sat back down and hearing Errol's door slam behind him, we glanced at each other again and this time I raised my eyebrows.

Checking my watch, it was time to go. Nine to five thirty is my contracted time, although in sales, I've never worked exactly forty hours. More like fifty to sixty, and sometimes more. It was time to go, as I only had tomorrow to finalise my next big presentation for Wednesday morning.

20

Tom was supposedly in Birmingham all day Tuesday. He was there to take some of the girls who were staying over and going out for his birthday. I wondered what his wife would think.

I worked from home in the afternoon after Errol had sent me some revisions to make to the presentation and the proposal. That was sent by courier to the customer once I'd completed a few cosmetic alterations to how it looked as well as how the executive summary sounded. Certain customers still operated in an archaic manner, requiring hard copies sent in the post, plus an electronic copy. More work for me. More cost to Eiron. Oh well…

Whilst at home I finished early, as everyone was going to Tom's party did, to get ready.

Stepping out of the shower, I heard my phone warbling in the hallway.

'Hello.'

'Hi Just, it's Shaun. When are you leaving?' he said hurriedly.

'About seven thirty, why?'

'Do you wanna share a taxi?'

'Yeah, okay, book one for seven fifteen. And don't be late.' I heard Shaun's whispering laugh on the other end.

'Whatever. See you at seven eighteen sharp!' Shaun carried on laughing. He was obviously in a good mood and ready to cast his wizardry again.

'Yeah, yeah… see you later.' I told him in a couldn't-care-less tone.

Following my checking procedure, all steps done, I heard the sound of a car engine rattling outside. It was diesel car and a Hackney Cab. Damn, this was going to be pricey.

I locked my front door and turned around to Shaun's beaming face glaring at me from the rear of the taxi.

'Whoa, Mr Whalley, you're looking rather sexy tonight, if can be so bold to say so.'

I laughed out loud and the taxi driver drove on.

'So you ready for tonight then, Shaun? If you catch my drift?'

He smiled, patting his trouser pocket and saying that 'everything's in hand'.

'So, who is coming from the Birmingham office?' I had to ask. I hoped Shaun couldn't see where I was going with my questioning.

'I'm not sure of exact names or numbers, but I think Victoria, Caroline, Angela are definitely coming. There should be about eight or nine.' Shaun smiled again and rubbed his hands.

Remaining calm, almost complacent, I responded.

'Oh, I see, sounds like a pretty good crowd are turning up. Didn't realise old Tommo was such a popular guy...' I left the sentence hanging for a while, before Shaun said anything.

'You'd be surprised, Justin, very surprised...' Now Shaun left his sentence hanging. I wanted to know more. We were nearly there.

*

Inside the first bar, painful fresh memories reoccurred. We were in Lloyds. Nevertheless, familiar faces from our Nottingham and Birmingham offices helped me push those aside with some ease.

I spoke to Errol, as everyone talked in small groups of four or five each. Tom was surrounded by a bevy of women. He was smiling and lapping it up. Maybe I should have phoned his wife and told her it was a surprise party, asking her to turn up. But that would be cruel and unnecessary.

In amongst the group was Victoria Shepard. In tight black trousers that were wrapped around her arse. Ouch! A silky off-one-shoulder black number, that to be quite honest got me in a hot sweat. Shit, she looked hot. Her hair had grown and was tucked behind her ears, revealing her lovely porcelain skin and radiant cheeks and eyes. I hated being caught staring; this time Shaun nudged me.

I worked my way through the crowd, drink after drink, trying to steady my nerves and build courage.

We moved to three other bars with nearly everyone partaking of far too much alcohol. By this time I'd spoken to all the people I wanted to except Victoria. The last bar didn't close until 1am and they had a dance floor.

Shaun was first on, with some other girl that was already there. She seemed pretty happy to have him dance with. Mind you, the state most people were in no one seemed to care. As the evening wore on, we were all dancing. I showed them what I was made of. Unknown to me, I couldn't dance. Errol strutted his funky stuff and two or three women followed his every move.

Tom had vanished and so had Victoria and a few of the other girls. I found myself swaying, my head thumping and feet doing things my brain could not control. Shaun was the only person I recognised.

'Where's…?' I belched. 'Oops, sorry mate, where's everyone else?' Shaun held me up straight. I couldn't tell if he was pissed or not.

I was laughing, looking at two other girls that Shaun was with.

'Sit down here, mate, I'll get you another drink.'

I smiled at the two girls. They looked like mother and daughter. My vision wasn't as it should be so I could have been wrong.

The R&B, hip-hop and dance music continued the boom and thump out of the speakers. My head felt like a boxer's punch bag. I said hello to the ladies who did look lovely. They were both from the

Birmingham office.

Shaun returned and took the older woman onto the dance floor. She left, smiling broadly. I turned to stand and wobbled. The younger lady leapt to my rescue. I asked her to accompany me onto the dance floor.

We smooched to some slower songs, and to my utter surprise, Tamsin told me she fancied me. I couldn't believe it. It was an unexpected boost. More so as I spotted Victoria dancing with one of the salesmen from Birmingham. I thought she'd already left. I did wonder where she'd gone.

Ignoring her, I turned my full attention and concentration onto the lovely twenty-year-old Tamsin. With long, straight, blonde hair and quiet brown eyes, she stood beautifully at about five foot seven.

We laughed, whispered and kissed whilst smooching on the packed dance floor, not a care in the world. For once I had no inhibitions, about who saw me, particularly Victoria.

My legs were, however, about to give up, as the drink began to take hold. Tamsin held onto me, as we giggled and swirled around wildly, bumping into other couples. We ended up on the floor, in fits of riotous laughter. I could have stayed exactly where I was, lying there prostrate, with a woman I hardly knew. But she knew me. It was that performance at the sales conference nearly two months ago that lingered in the memory.

Attempting to stand, I wobbled and Tamsin managed to keep me upright. I thanked her. A chorus of laughter from all around me could be heard. I guess I put on another performance for everyone else to enjoy. Maybe I should become an actor. I wouldn't need any drama classes.

Heading for the gents', I told Tamsin I'd meet her back at the table where we'd met. I'd never been to the toilet as much as this before.

Meandering through the crowds, my head drummed to the rhythmic beat of Kelis' 'Good Stuff'. Feeling slightly dizzy, woozy I think, somehow my legs carried me to and from the gents' toilets.

Returning to my seat, Tamsin smiled at me and had another drink for me to absorb. A brandy and Coke. I sank in two mouthfuls. It tasted wonderful. I sat there smiling like a village idiot, saying words that I didn't understand to this lovely girl sat opposite me.

We talked, and I doubted whether I was making any sense whatsoever. She was intelligent, quick witted and had a great sense of humour. Completely at her mercy, she looked at me with sultry, lustful eyes.

She leaned forward and whispered in my ear.

'Shall we go now?'

'Yes please,' I managed to slur out.

I was unsure whether it was Errol, but I saluted a black guy, shouting, 'See you in the morning!' Whoever he was, he kindly raised his glass to me.

As we walked arm in arm up some stairs I glanced back to see bodies still gyrating sensually on the dance floor. Men and women dancing so close, only water could possibly seep through.

We left in a taxi but I couldn't hear what address she gave for the taxi to go to. Even in my drunken stupor, a light flickered in my brain, to tell me my luck just might be in. I hoped so. Then again I hoped all the alcohol would not affect my performance and make a hat-trick of disasters. Only time would tell.

21

With a mammoth headache, which I realised as soon as my left eye was open, I attempted to get out of bed. That was my first inclination.

My second was to find out what time it was. My mouth represented a dried sandal that had been rained on, covered in sand and then the sun had shone on it for hours afterward.

As my eyesight cleared and my vision restored, I turned my head to view the room. Minutes later, I began to realise that this was not my bedroom. Wallpaper covered the walls, wood chip I think. I had no wallpaper anywhere in my house.

Shit! Where the hell was I? Rubbing my throbbing, spinning head, I started to cry out, 'No! No! No! Aarrrgggh!'

Holding onto the bedside cabinet, I got to my feet. My specs were neatly placed on the side. I put them on. I had on just my boxer shorts and nothing else. Turning to look at the bed, it was crumpled up, and the pillow beside mine had been used. Fear shot through like an arrow, when my nostrils picked up the scent of sex. The fear would not acquiesce. I needed emancipation, right here, right now.

Worst of all, and there was no dispensation for this, I couldn't remember how I got here. Wherever here was.

Reaching for the bedroom door, it opened before my hand could reach the handle.

'Mornin', or should I say afternoon!' It was Shaun O'Dwyer.

'Bollocks, Shaun, what the fuck's going on?' I hated swearing, but I was genuinely worried about what might have happened to me.

He smiled, brightly. He was suited and booted, looking as if he went to bed at eight in the evening.

'Look, I can explain everything,' he told me calmly. 'First you ought to have a wash, get some clothes on and come with me. Don't worry, Just, this is between you and me, okay…'

He kept his voice monotone, even after the way I'd reacted.

Thirty minutes later I was dressed and tad more refreshed. We sat at the kitchen table and Shaun passed me two paracetamol tablets and a glass of water, which I wasn't sure I should take.

Shaun explained what had happened and where I was. Tamsin took me to her friend's house where she had her wicked way with me. Apparently she was yelling, and moaning into the early hours. Shaun and his lady friend, who happened to be Tamsin's older sister, heard every word.

Every request she asked me. What positions she wanted to perform, and crying in ecstasy when she reached her peak. At least five or six times, Shaun told me with a genuine look of disbelief.

He described what was probably my best ever sexual encounter and I couldn't remember a single bloody thing. Absolutely nothing. How it started, how it finished, the pleasure I must have missed out on. I was crushed. Flattened, like the pancakes I used to enjoy as a child.

'Hey, hey, Justin, don't cry yet, she does really like you. She'll be back.'

Shaking my head and thinking ambiguous thoughts, nothing to stop the fear of not knowing what you've done. Good or bad.

'I'm worried, I cannot remember a thing, Shaun. I feel drugged, you know, like when you under a general anaesthetic.'

He said nothing for a minute. That advocated he knew something and hadn't told me.

'Well…?'

'I don't know for sure. Maybe, just maybe she did use something, whatever it was, in your drink? I'm sorry, mate. She was desperate to get laid.'

Sitting back in the hard plastic chair, justified anger fired through me. Shaun tried to change the subject. No chance. This matter had my unhindered attention.

'Look, that's the least of your worries.' It was the first time in ages that I saw Shaun, looking serious and pensive. 'Your meeting was today wasn't it. At 10.30am? With Errol...'

He didn't have to say any more, the message got through loud and clear. My balls were on the chopping block and Walter Baker had a damn sharp knife. Knowing him, it would be a sharp axe, wielded by a madman.

'Shit, fuck, damn! ...What am I gonna do, Shaun? I'll get fried for this.'

'Justin, it's all in hand. Well, the cover story is anyway. After what had happened to you, I reckoned you weren't going to be up and ready. I called Errol and made up some bullshit story of alcohol poisoning and that you wouldn't make it.'

'Shaun, I owe you the biggest sloppiest kiss ever.' I managed a weak smile.

'No friggin' way, you ugly bastard.'

We smiled some more and Shaun told me to get on home pretty damn quick.

Moving as quickly as I was physically able, Shaun drove me home, telling me he would find out if anything had leaked about my story in the office. He'd instructed Tamsin and her sister to keep quiet. There were never any guarantees, but I couldn't be more grateful to Shaun for his selfless act. Even if he did get a great night of vicarious passion from Tamsin and me.

Just my luck. The time of my life recorded, and someone's taped over it.

Now I had to worry about the story leaking, Tamsin's feelings, although it should be the other way around. And what Errol and

Walter would do if the story did leak. Worse still, we could lose the business, and my absence could be misconstrued as being part of that.

Once at home, I fell back into my own bed dreaming of the dangers of being under the influence of drugs usually used on women, by unsuspecting men. The roles just got reversed.

22

I'd known Errol Hughes for many years, as a straight up bloke. A man's man, whatever that means, I hear people say a lot. Maybe it means a genuine quality, to support other men. Have your back when you may need it. Goodness knows I've had a few of those sticky situations already in my working career.

Errol spoke rarely about his family, although I understood he had a brother and a sister, with Errol being the eldest. A few stories leaked out over our friendship tenure about his mum and dad splitting up, which I never questioned him about. Not after the only occasion many years ago, when my youthful inexperience allowed me to pose a few pertinent questions about this sensitive subject.

Errol's response, although calm, resulted in the realisation of a question that shouldn't asked ever again. It was one of few times I have witnessed Errol incapacitated, frozen. Now years later I have some complete reassurance, empathy for his emotional state at that time. Knowing what it is like to leave the past where it is. Some sleeping dogs, must be left to sleep.

Since our early burgeoning friendship, Errol supported me with job applications, wise words and advice about the world of work. Something I felt my two brothers should have done. Errol's ability to manage multiple tasks, drove him out of sheer determination to ensure the job was done, yet also be inclusive of his workforce, bearing in mind everyone's own variance in skill and expertise.

My interpretations of how my day would develop, commenced when on Wednesday afternoon, Errol summoned me to his office. He had asked that I come in specially for a meeting. He said it was to bring me up to speed on the meeting I had missed.

Eyes from all over my floor, searched me out as I entered. Was this my epitaph?

No one intervened or walked across on route to my desk. I set up my laptop and glanced around with everyone studiously turning away as soon as my sight caught theirs.

A peaceful, library-like silence fell on my sales department, which usually had phones ringing and people talking confidently to the people on the other end.

'Hiya, mate, feeling better now?' Shaun asked, packing away his laptop into his bag.

'Yes thanks, the stomach's better now. Thanks for asking though.'

Those were the only kind words I heard for the rest of the today.

On entering Errol's office, my predicament reached an anticlimactic state, when sitting alongside Errol was Walter Baker. Taking several deep breaths, they both asked me politely to sit down. Their courtesy was frightening. They offered me a choice of hot or cold drinks. On the table they asked me to sit at, there were biscuits to choose from as well. Obviously the softening-up technique.

Accepting a coffee and a chocolate biscuit so as not to offend, Errol began with why they had asked me in.

'Justin, I've known you for a long time now so I'm going to get straight to the point.' I nodded to show that I understood.

'What happened the other night, must never happen again. From what I know it wasn't entirely your fault, nevertheless, you have to be more careful. You have a responsibility to our customers, to me, Walter and to yourself.' Errol paused looking me straight in the eyes. Walter chipped in.

'You see, Justin you're very good at your job and since you've been here, I have been impressed. Your high standard of emailing, letter writing, your presentations, always smart, looking the part. It would be a shame to see such immense talents wasted, or worse still, never get the opportunity to flourish.'

A veiled threat from Walter Baker. If I didn't buck up my ideas, I wouldn't get promotion, or worse still, be considered for it.

'Do you have anything to say?' Walter asked.

'Walter, Errol, I sincerely apologise for missing that customer meeting. I have realised I let my team, the company and myself down. It won't happen again. You have my guarantee on that.'

'That's good to hear. However, it's going to take more than apologies to rectify the deal. We may still lose it,' Walter continued.

There was nothing to say to bring absolution for me. Nothing at all.

'Justin, think very carefully about anything that may affect your work and your ability to do it properly. As we know you can,' Errol advised me.

Then something fundamental occurred. Walter accepted my recourse and what I intended to do to put things right. He then, seemingly forgetting what had just being said previously, gave me the strongest hint that I would be the next to for promotion to Senior Sales Exec. Bewildering it certainly was. My mind dissipated into confusing scenarios of how this was possible.

I should have come to expect this from Eiron and particularly Walter 'I have the power to make you or break you' Baker.

Errol concurred with what Walter had said and I did wonder whether Errol had some dirt on Walter and somehow used it to save my ass not only once but twice, by getting me on the rung in the promotion stakes.

If Tom heard about this, he'd hit the roof, especially after I screwed up big time.

Not being cocky or obnoxious, with my mood boosted, I exited

Errol's office with the widest of grins. Tom looked up at me in total surprise and angst. He was bursting to find out what was said. He could not fathom what and why the hell I was smiling. So I did it even more.

Tom rose from his seat and stormed over to Errol's office. Walter was leaving and saying his goodbyes when Tom approached him.

'Walter can I see you a moment?'

'Erm, I'm afraid not, Mr Greenfield-Crown, I have another appointment, and unless you want to deal with my wife, I think you'll have to postpone.'

Yes, yes, yes, just what I wanted to hear.

Tom was disappointed and Errol said he was too busy to talk then and there. Tom knew they were stonewalling him. Putting him off.

Little did I know then, that he had already got his own back.

23

Without warning over the next two days, my email inbox was full of replies from female employees that worked at Eiron. Some were not ladylike at all.

'You dirty, filthy, pervert, I hope you get the sack,' one read.

'I think it's disgusting that any man should be allowed to send an email like that,' another screamed.

After reading through over forty-two emails, some of which were copied to Walter and Errol, I cowered behind my monitor the day after the mail came out.

I worked from home the day after that.

Whilst in my meeting with Walter and Errol, the son-of-a-bitch, Tom, typed an email from my laptop using my email. We were always being reminded to never leave our email unattended. I thought I was amongst peers and colleagues. Obviously my trust was a futile one.

Searching through my sent items, I located the mail Tom had sent. I had no other suspects. It had to be him. That little shithead.

Opening up the mail my eyes cast over the recipients that he sent it to. The email had gone to our EMEA branch offices as well. How much more ominous could things get? How could I justify or vindicate myself from being framed? I was seething. However, I needed to read the contents. I needed to know why all these women were pissed with me. There was one mail I did not open, when I realised who the sender was. Tom's mail had to come first.

Sitting at home, I moved my mouse over the email and double-clicked. It opened. I began to read. What I noticed immediately was that the email was addressed to Vicky Shepard. Somehow all these other members of staff received the mail. A little guilt seeped through me. Maybe Tom was not as much to blame. Although somehow, something happened to culminate in this embarrassing malaise. The email needed to be read.

Victoria, it's me, Justin. I know the email system is not supposed to be used for this, but I have to tell you this.

You looked fantastic the other night. Your outfit, your boobs, your smile, all bursting out, ready to be…ooh I can't say the words, but you know what I mean. Oh yes, you looked hot, foxy. I can't tell you how horny I felt seeing you look that that. I have dreamed about you and me, you know…doing 'the business'. I hope you feel the same, as I can't wait to…agghh, shit, getting so frustrated, can't wait for you and me to release all my pent up angst and willing.

Shit, look if anyone sees this, I'm dead okay, so don't save it. Print it off and delete it immediately.

Can I ask you out, there I said it. I've fancied you for ages and just love every inch of you. Every curve, and my oh bloody my, what curves you have. Ummm, ummm, ummmm… tasty.

Okay, well, better sign off, getting worked up just writing this and my palms are sweaty and well er…anyway, see you soon hopefully and please say you'll go out with me, I do anything you want..(honest!)

Love you always.
Justin W.
xxx

What a wanker. Tom's crime was writing the email. Somehow the distribution got screwed up.

Rubbing my chin, my mind wandered off into a million potential scenarios. What stories would be flying around each Eiron office in the whole of Europe, the Middle East and Africa? All because Tom

Greenfield-Crown, believed he was a comedian. Well I wasn't laughing and nor were hundreds of Eiron's female employees.

After taking a sip of very strong coffee, I felt brave enough to open Victoria's mail. Before I did that I deleted all the other responses, bad or indifferent or good, there were surprisingly a few of the latter. Mainly from men who saw the lighter or sicker side of this whole Email-gate scandal.

Exhaling heavily, my mouse moved and hovered over Victoria's email. My index finger pressed the mouse button twice in quick succession. The email opened.

My laptop worked slower at home because of the broadband connection. It eventually displayed what Victoria had written.

There wasn't much of it. It only took a few seconds to read and a few seconds to sink in. I was devastated.

In large size font, Times New Roman, in red capital letters, she wrote the words:

FUCK OFF YOU PERVY BASTARD. I HOPE YOU DROP DEAD SOON!
V.S.

Short and sweet. Any hopes, faint or otherwise of getting to know Victoria Shepard better disappeared like a fart in the wind. I had two options. Two chances. Slim and none. A betting man would say I had an outside chance, but no one bets or gambles on guaranteed losers.

Doing my best to put the incident behind me, I sent an email to Errol and Walter telling them what must have happened. Although Tom did delay the email, so no one read it until the day after he wrote it, the Support Desk would be able to determine when the mail was created.

So for ten minutes after reading Victoria's mail, I mounted my defence campaign. I put a call into Joe Ballard on the helpdesk. He searched the network and the email server and told me when it was sent. I asked him to create an email with that evidence and send it to me.

While he did that, I created my email to Errol and Walter, apologising for my lack of security measures, in not sufficiently protecting my email. Although once I received Joe's email, I attached it to mine and forwarded on to the senior managers.

It was almost closing time on a what was a very long day. As usual I attached read and delivery receipts on my emails.

Leaving my laptop in my small bedroom, used as my home office, I ventured downstairs for some dinner. Chicken breast in barbecue sauce with potato wedges, washed down with a can of Stella.

When I'd finished, I returned upstairs and checked my emails. Errol and Walther had read my mail. They hadn't replied, however. Maybe Tom's delinquent behaviour had backfired. Or they were seriously considering what my punishment would be.

There was no point in worrying about it. Whatever would happen, was out of my control. There was no deviation from facing, head on the unexpected.

My schedule, displayed that I had to go into the office anyway. Prepare for three further customer meetings. Then with courage I had to 'face the music and dance'. And I have two left feet.

Maybe my regrets at never watching that Strictly show would hamper me. Protocol meant some tap shoes would be order of the day, and maybe for the foreseeable, if my legitimacy as an Eiron salesperson were to remain constant.

24

Bored at home and nearly nodding off, my sluggish stupor reinvigorated into life when my phone rang.

'Yep,' and I burped immediately afterwards. 'Sorry.'

'Justin.'

'Errol.' My voice dropped. I froze, just for a second.

'Justin, we need to speak to you again,' he said. His voice monotone, steady and professional. No warmth or feeling at all. This was unlike Errol. It meant he was worried for me.

'Make some time in your dairy for Thursday at 11am. Clear anything you've got. And I should tell you that Personnel will be there.'

I said nothing for a minute. I let the silence fill the void. After clearing my throat I calmly responded.

'Errol, you've seen my email, haven't you?'

'Yes I have.'

I was silent again. I expected him to say more. He was being odd, strange. Something was occurring.

'Well, didn't you read it through. Didn't you—' Errol cut me off and interjected.

'Yes we did. I spoke to Walter and ultimately, what you sent us might just save you. However, we need to see you about more than that.'

Now that last statement did frighten the life out of me.

'What do you mean?' I had to ask.

'I'm afraid I can't say, Just. You'll have to—' This time I cut Errol short.

'Bullshit, Errol. For crying out loud, what's happening to you? What the hell's going on!' I was glad I didn't use any stronger language. Although we were friends, he was still my boss. But I hated, despised the secrecy and MI5-style whisperings and clandestine meetings.

On this occasion, Errol remained absolutely quiet. I could faintly hear breathing on the other end of the phone.

'Errol, look, I just want to know what I'm gonna go into. Do I need to prepare anything, bring anyone? Tell me at least that, please,' I implored him.

'Okay, all I can say,' some feeling had returned to his voice, 'is that you'll need to carry that email in hard copy with you and bring some notes from your last few meetings. What I'm trying to say is that, your performance is okay but everyone is being scrutinised by Walter... I can't say any more.'

'Oh, I see. Oh well, I'll see you Thursday then. Thanks for the call, Errol. Maybe we can do this again some other time... if there is one.' I left it there and put the phone down. I heard Errol release a heavy sigh as a closed the phone call.

What a shit day.

Before going to bed I called Shaun for support. He told me he couldn't go in with me, as he had been called in as well. He wouldn't say what for. Whatever was happening, this virus was spreading. It all seemed to centre around the meddling, brown-nosing tosser, Tom Greenfield-Crown. It was a shame he couldn't smoke himself to death. And couldn't wait for Thursday not to come.

My head hit my pillow but my eyes and brain percolated all night. I was unable to sleep.

FAMILY AFFAIRS

25

Shaun O'Dwyer, the Irish charmer and the consummate flirter with most females. Generally Shaun presented an acceptable comedic façade, which circumvented the true steely, competitive nature of the man.

I often pondered at what was truly underneath the O'Dwyer skin, other than the witty sarcasm that pervaded when he was around. Like me, Shaun came from a fairly large family. Three older brothers and three younger sisters kept his mum on her tiptoes for nearly two decades. I could tell he loved his family, however, his older brothers were very serious about their work, something Shaun didn't quite share. He never let on what this work was, so didn't feel I was qualified to press for any further details.

Subsequently for many occasions, I leaned on Shaun's pragmatic understanding of human nature, of women. I guessed he acquired knowledge from his sisters, and many female relatives.

I wouldn't be without that light of Shaun in the cutthroat darkness of the sales world that I had been assimilated into. He helped me slice through the treacle that existed, and in retrospect, I too hoped to recompense him should he ever require a payment from me.

His life in Dublin, seemed a great one from what I had understood. Things altered somewhat when one of his brothers drew the attention of the police, to his family's grievance. In order to liberate himself from the association, Shaun opted to move to the UK. In some way, in his innocent view, he was extricating himself from whatever happened back in Dublin. Standing by his family, was standard protocol. His prerogative to stand by his hard-working mum and dad, who were landlords in a small chain of inns within the Grafton Street area in Dublin.

My interpretations of Shaun rang true when he explained his family connections. Out of everyone at Eiron, my empathic side drew me to Shaun as he intrinsically and in an unspoken manner, dialled into my wavelength. Found the correct wavelength. Something, on certain occasions, not even Errol could do. When those moments arrived, if Shaun had a number to contact him, it would maybe be 111, not quite 999. That analogy came to life sooner than expected.

The ramifications of Thursday's twenty-five minute 'axe' meeting, would only affect me. Well maybe Shaun as well, for trying to cover for me. What a rock.

Walter told me unequivocally, that I should not come back to work for the rest of Thursday and Friday.

'Take these next two days off to fully reassess where you want to be in Eiron and what role you intend to play. Above all we need to know whether you are capable of meeting your numbers.'

Errol hardly said anything during the meeting.

I was stupefied by the whole saga. One minute I was in there seemingly in trouble, yet in the end I was put forward for promotion. The next thing I know I was being asked to revaluate my position. Confused, bruised mentally, there was no compunction on my behalf to defend or fight with Walter or Errol, or Eiron's personnel system. I resolved myself to a defeat, a withdrawal from everything.

Seeking any understanding for the internal bureaucratic process, remained a mystery. Legitimacy, well maybe, somewhere in subsection X, on page four hundred twenty-one. Yes maybe there is an explanation, written in code or a foreign language very few would want to entertain.

Leaving the meeting room, I deliberately left behind the email evidence and Joe Ballard's number on the support desk, for Errol to contact. I cannot believe they didn't ask for it. Here was hard evidence of when the email was sent, and I was in their presence at that time. If that wasn't an iron-clad alibi, then I was completely bemused. Dumbfounded.

Closing Errol's office door quietly, I exited the building immediately, quietly, negating the opportunity for anyone to see me, let alone quiz me on what the outcome was. As always the story would leak out like any Chinese whisper. At that time, as I welcomed the fresh, brisk late February breeze; nothing about Eiron had any importance in my life.

Trying to remain positive, I told myself it was a bad patch in my working life. Just as in relationships, in business, this was one of my troughs; at least I could only go upward, hopefully.

I reached my car, aimed the key fob at it and the lights flashed and the locks shut upward. I sat inside for a few minutes, praying no one was watching, to gather the few thoughts I had spinning aimlessly around in my head. Starting the engine, I looked out toward the office windows and saw the blinds being hurriedly put back into place on the fourth floor. Nosey bastards.

They wanted a good story. A juicy bit of gossip. Everyone did; I was no different, truth be told. However, it never felt the same when I was at the centre of it. The core of all that seemed to be happening. I could trust Shaun not to expunge any details of my performance at Charlene's. If Walter and Errol knew about that, things may have been worse.

As it was, I drove home to my comfortable semi, in Wollaton. Nice house, all alone, pissed off, melancholy, downbeat, it was time to call in my family.

Not seeing them for some time was probably all my fault. My

oldest sister Jennifer had her my nephew Ben, a bright, intelligent brat. Her husband and Ben's father was a builder by trade. They had a plush house in an exclusive, salubrious area of Sutton Coldfield, in the West Midlands. It had multiple bathrooms, en-suites, playrooms and stuff like that. Oddly enough I found it easy to talk to her and to Emily. Oliver and Mark, although older than me, were different men altogether. I needed a female angle anyway. Jennifer would give the wisdom, and Emily would analyse the here and now of what women truly like and what they look for.

When I contacted Emily, I smiled and never felt so happy to hear she was recovering so well and had been out a few times already. I suppose she had enough memories she wanted to erase. A fallacy it might be to try and shake demons like that away, yet it beats sitting around and moping about it. That was my outlook on things. Forget what happened with Walter and Errol. Do something different. Go away, in effect, and come back with a fresh, lively verve and passion.

Emily suggested we both visit Jennifer in Birmingham at the weekend. She promised to help me out in the finding a girlfriend department. Although flicking through my head, had to be why would I torture myself further? Positive mental attitude is an appropriate facet of being in sales. It's also fundamental to get through what I had endured thus far.

Emily informed me that she me would arrange things with Jennifer and call me back. It was just the tonic.

Jennifer called me later that evening and we spent nearly an hour on the phone. She was looking forward to seeing me, and couldn't understand why I was still single. Neither could I. Well actually, I could if was being completely honest and forensic about my approach. Not being totally honest aided any potential recriminations, a protection system if you like. I needed some shielding to keep living, moving on.

'Don't worry, Justin, Jennifer and Emily will sort it out for you. Even if we have to tie them down.' She had a stuttering laugh, which made me laugh.

'Thanks sis, we'll be down there on Saturday morning, hope that's okay.'

'Fine. Roger's away building some film star's house in Cheshire, so I could do with company and Ben wants to see you and his aunty.'

'Sounds great. Take care, Jen.'

'You too, Justin. See you Saturday.'

After I closed the call, I made myself a brandy and orange with ice. Sitting in my favourite armchair, in my comfy pyjamas, I sat watching one of my best films of all time, The Shawshank Redemption.

26

Friday thankfully came and went, very quickly. Apart from one call. No blame can be centred on Shaun, and there he was, looking out for me even though I wasn't there. It was a few minutes after three in the afternoon when the phone in the hallway burst into life. After three rings I picked up the receiver.

'Yep.'

'Justin, it's Shaun,' he whispered.

'Yeah, why are you whispering?' I asked, a little annoyed at first, as I was answering a question on an afternoon quiz show.

'Look, I can't stay on long, but I thought I'd better call you ASAP.'

'Okay, so what's happened?' I relaxed a little, already wondering what the possible news was going to be. The reason for Shaun's call.

'I've heard on the Eiron grapevine that everyone knows what happened to you with Charlene.' Shaun paused, awaiting my reaction. There wasn't one. I was stunned, absolutely mortified. 'Justin, you still there?'

'Yeah, er, yeah.' I exhaled heavily, performing my version of deep breathing for balance. My mind could not focus, could not develop any coherent thought patterns. Or string anything together to make any sense of what Shaun had just revealed.

'Look, Just, it seems as though Charlene spilt the beans and the rest is history. And it gets worse. Twice over.' Those last two words were like a javelin hurtling towards me. I didn't know if I was going to avoid it.

I pulled the long telephone cord into my living room and pulled up the nearest chair. I took a seat.

'Go on. How much worse can it already get?' To make things easy I resigned myself to expect the worst, whatever that was going to be.

'I'll keep this short, Just. That arsehole, Greenfield-Crown, has been spreading all kinds of FUD about you. He is good friends with Vicky Shepard and has an inside track into the Birmingham office. God knows what he's telling Vicky Shepard about you. This guy is putting the knife in, mate. If you still want her, the world's gonna have to reverse its rotation.'

'Anything else?' The words rolled off my tongue and out of my mouth.

'Justin, whatever happens,' Shaun spoke in a more audible tone, 'make sure that twat Tom, doesn't get to you. Vicky will see him for what he is. I have my suspicions about him; he is not as clean as everyone thinks.'

'Shaun, thanks for the call. I appreciate the heads-up on this. I'll face everyone on Monday and the management. It looks like a hat-trick of visits to Errol's office inside a month, can't be bad, hey?'

In a weak attempt at humour to soften the blow, a little laugh surfaced out of me, and Shaun reciprocated on the other end.

'You're a good man, Mr Whalley, don't ever forget that, okay?'

'Shaun, you're a star. See you Monday. Thanks.'

When I briefly analysed why Shaun had called, I quietly forgave him for interrupting my quiz show. To forget about the call I ventured upstairs to think about my weekend.

*

Saturday arrived and I began it by finishing off packing a few things together and ensuring my house was locked up securely, I left home to pick up Emily from her flat in The Park. Apparently, and this was a shock to me, she shared this flat with none other than Mary Leadbetter. Somehow my suspicions about Mary increased. I knew she was good friends with Emily, but not that good.

Then again, I pondered on that fact that I was only worried for Errol's, sake not mine, as Mary and his fiancée Elisa were best friends. Sod him for now. I told myself I wouldn't think about work for a whole weekend. After everything that had happened and that had been said about this week, I was surprised I didn't make the front page of every national newspaper. Maybe one day I will, for the right reasons.

Emily was ready as soon as I arrived. Punctuality at its best. I wasn't sure where she got it from, but not my mum or dad.

Traffic flowed freely along the M1, between junctions twenty-six and twenty-four. The M42 was busier yet moved along nicely.

Playing my favourite jazz CDs quietly, Emily listened to her music on her phone, headphones in. Every now and then she'd look across and me and smile, bopping her head to her music.

As we neared Sutton, Emily turned off her music and pulled out her headphones. She then produced a slip of paper from her handbag with Jennifer's address and some directions.

'Okay, pilot, we need to head towards the Belfry Hotel. Drive by that and we'll come to an island.'

'Understood, co-pilot, heading for the Belfry along the A446.'

Thankfully the instructions were spot on. We reached Jennifer's house and Emily informed me of the plans that were arranged for our going out tonight. When she told me that we might meet up with Mary Leadbetter. I raised my eyebrows and possibly frowned.

'How is it that she's in Birmingham too?' I had to ask.

'Her father lives here now. Her parents divorced and he wanted to get away from Nottingham.'

'Oh, I see.' I looked at Emily conspiratorially. The hairs were beginning stand up on the back of my neck.

'Look, Justin, I know about her, Elisa and Errol, she's is really a nice girl. Even if Errol doesn't like her. Give her a chance and don't cause a scene or anything, please… for me.'

I nodded in response. Again, I wouldn't do it for Errol. I was doing it for me. Mary never sounded or seemed sincere about anything or anyone. I could be wrong.

Jennifer came to her large front door and welcomed Emily and me with big sisterly hugs. I held on for longer than I should have. I needed it more than I cared to admit to anyone. Jennifer realised. I witnessed the recognition in her eyes.

'Come in, come in.'

We entered the long hallway, with a room off it on either side. On the left the room housed a large grand piano, a few old-looking stools and chairs, and a huge fireplace and original hearth.

'Justin, you're in the loft conversion, on the top floor, Emily you're in the room next to Ben's.'

'Where's the little tyke anyway?' I asked fervently.

'He's upstairs on a video game or something.' Immediately Jennifer shouted for Ben to come down and meet his uncle and aunty from Nottingham.

A minute later the sound of footsteps could be heard from the rear bedroom, then onto and down the wide staircase.

Ben ran to Emily and hugged her. She picked him up a little way off the ground. He was bigger and heavier than when we last visited. That was nearly three years ago. Kids grow up fast these days.

'Hello Aunty Em,' his head buried in her stomach.

He pulled loose and turned to me and came over.

'Uncle Justin,' he shook my hand, 'do want play on my video game?'

'Yes, er, okay.' I threw Jennifer a quizzical glance and shrugged my shoulders. She waved me upstairs, instructing me to carry my holdall and Emily's up to the bedrooms at the same time. Now I knew how valets and porters must feel. At least the day got off to a pleasant start.

27

It was quarter past one in the afternoon when Jennifer suggested we should go out and get some lunch. We piled into my Jaguar XF. Ben sat in the front. In fact he demanded it. To save a scene occurring Jennifer acquiesced. Under the circumstances, I concurred. Anything for a quiet life.

Leaving her house in the salubrious surroundings of Four Oaks, Sutton Coldfield, Jennifer directed me towards the A446.

'I like your car, Uncle Justin, was it expensive?'

Jennifer leapt in.

'Ben, don't be so rude. Sorry, Justin.'

'It's okay,' I replied calmly, smiling at Ben who looked a little browbeaten.

I showed Ben how to operate the electric windows and the heated seats. He called out to Jennifer excitedly, telling her how his bum was getting warm.

Emily and Jennifer sat chuckling in the back. nattering to each about some new outfits that Emily had recently purchased, in some designer shop. I heard the words shoes, matching bag, and something about a buy two and get the third free. Goodness only knows what that amounted to.

Approaching a very large traffic island, I was directed to take the third exit and immediately there was a large public house with a play area for children. Strangely enough, adjacent to the pub was one the world's largest fast food chains. Ben didn't bat an eyelid.

The weather was mild and dry. There was no rain, or cold late February breeze to speak of. After ordering our food, we decided to sit outside as there were at least four other families out there.

Sitting on a bench-like table, Jennifer sent Ben off to play on the park with the other children. She looked at me and Emily.

'How are you both? The truth now. No holding back.'

Emily and I glanced at each other. I pointed at Emily, initiating that she should go first.

'Look, Jen, I'm fine really. Mentally I'm getting myself back together, in my own way . Honestly. Thanks for asking though.'

'And what about you, Justin?' Jennifer turned her head in my direction.

'You know about me already. I thought that was one of the reasons for me coming here. To sort me out?' I asked with a smirk.

'Yeah, it'll probably take more than one night, Just. Who knows, we might have to get you a blind date,' Jennifer replied.

We all laughed. But I was laughing in total anguish and nauseating emotional pain. Little did they know about my disastrous 'blind date' back in Nottingham. I prayed Jennifer could recognise the pained expression. Fortunately the food was arriving so the conversation could be diverted.

'Ben, Ben, can you come here please?' Jennifer called out.

Ben looked up and waved at his mother. He swung from the monkey bars and leapt to the ground with ease. He ran towards our table and his eyes opened wide when he saw his favourite dish of fish fingers, beans and chips.

We'd obviously been oblivious, because some of the language used by some of the children on the park was horrific. Particularly one couple's son.

Whilst we were eating, and Ben being an inquisitive eight-year-old, he asked a question that left us all with our mouths open. Jennifer was mortified.

'Uncle Justin, what does wanker mean?'

Jennifer dropped her fork. A piece of scampi that was in her mouth flew out. She looked around at the other parents, who immediately looked across in disgust and abhorrence.

I cleared my throat several times and saw Ben's innocent little face turn red with angst as Jennifer reprimanded him. The chorus of oohs and aahs of shock and surprise quickly dissipated.

'Ben, don't worry, it's not your fault. If you hear words you don't understand, you don't have to repeat them, okay?' I tried to explain how things work in this vast universe of ours, and I wasn't sure whether I was of any help or use.

In record time we finished our meal and neglected the opportunity to try one of the tempting deserts. Jennifer wanted to go. Although Ben was doing what any eight-year-old would do, somehow she felt obligated to anyone else who heard her son swearing.

At home Jennifer called her babysitter and informed her to come over for about six thirty in the evening.

I sat with Ben and watched a video with him for the rest of the afternoon. Every now and then I'd flick over to check the football scores, to Ben's annoyance.

Emily and Jennifer started to get ready for our night out. I could not get excited or in the mood. This didn't alter when Emily confirmed that we would be meeting up with Mary Leadbetter later tonight. At least it would make the evening more interesting.

I'd never spoken to her properly. Got to know her own her own. My view of her had come mostly second-hand from Errol, who was biased. I suppose it couldn't do any harm to be civil and courteous.

Once the babysitter had arrived, who was a very small, short girl about sixteen, Ben was packed off upstairs to have a wash and to get a book from his extensive range. The young girl had short-cropped pink-coloured hair, black nail varnish, but no make-up whatsoever. Unusually big eyes, white porcelain skin and a chubby frame. She seemed competent enough, and I know Jennifer would not trust just anyone to look after her beloved Ben.

It was time for me to hit the shower.

28

We'd been to three bars in Birmingham city centre, when we met Mary at the fourth.

'Hello Em!' she shrieked in her higher than normal pitched voice. They gave each other a massive hug and I looked at Jennifer raising my eyes upward.

Jennifer told me to leave them alone. Nothing wrong with female bonding or friendship for that matter, she told me.

'Hiya Justin. You're looking sexy tonight. Phworrr!'

Emily and Jennifer doubled over with laughter. I was somewhat embarrassed at Mary's unexpected outburst. She'd had to have been drinking for a couple hours prior to us meeting.

'Well, what can I say? It comes natural to some of us, you see.' I played to her tune.

'Ooh, we are confident, aren't we?' Mary answered back.

'How 'bout I buy you a drink to test my confidence?'

She smiled, covering her mouth. She had a lovely smile too. Accurate white tombstone teeth hidden behind full luscious lips. Her eyes were a dull-looking shade of blue. This was offset by jet-black hair. We did have something in common, which was rare for me with any woman, it seemed. I understand I was a little behind the curve, but not that far. For some reason she wore shades on top of her head. Her hair was short, but just had enough length on the sides to be tucked behind her ears.

Emily, Jennifer, followed by Mary and I, approached the bar and I paid for the round. Not that I should have noticed, but Mary had small feet. Maybe size four of five. I also noticed her pulling a cigarette out of her bag. Ugh! I hated smoking, well at least the smell and fumes.

Mary, briefly left the bar to 'consume' her nicotine-filled fix. Kindly she only smoked one, when she realised how much I detested smoking, which lifted her up a little in my estimation of human traits.

The jazz music in the background blended into the surroundings and the humming of multiple conversations with the lounge bar that we were in.

'So why are you here in Birmingham?' I asked Mary. We'd sat in a corner and Emily and Jennifer were in clear view opposite us.

'To see you.'

For the second time I was left with my mouth open and speechless. I stopped my glass of rum and Coke heading for my mouth in mid-flight. Then I saw Mary emit her high-pitched laugh. The bitch had me.

'Don't look so frightened, Justin, I'm not that bad am I?'

I took the sip of my drink that I originally planned, and then another.

Breathing out heavily, I responded. Trying to keep myself together and remembering my eldest and youngest sister were watching.

'No, actually you're quite attractive. I could quite fancy you. Yes I could.' I left my comment to melt into her ears. Mary was now quieter than before as she pondered whether I was being serious or not.

She swigged her bottled beer, keeping her eyes on me simultaneously. Now I was smiling.

'Okay, Justin, let's just be honest with each other from now on. Yeah. Agreed.'

I nodded.

I finally sat there and don't honestly recall how many drinks we'd had, but I learned a lot about Mary Leadbetter. Not the woman that

Errol often told me about. She was a bit quirky, a bit loud at times and an alright girl. She complimented me, genuinely, made me laugh and most of all I forgot all about work. I think I did the same to her. All I hoped for was for friendship. That would do. If something else happened after that, then maybe that would be satisfactory too. I was happy to wait and see.

At ten minutes after eleven at night we decided to dance off all the booze we'd consumed at a night club in the 'Chinatown' area of the city.

Jennifer kept smiling at me and so did Emily. I knew what their smiles meant.

Above the terrible din of loud blasting music, Emily came over to me.

'Where's Mary gone? She hasn't left you already?' she shouted into my left ear.

'Ha, ah, very funny. No she hasn't actually. She gone for a number two!' I grinned wickedly and Emily slapped me on arm.

'Hope you two are getting on alright,' she quizzed.

'We're fine. I'll tell you it all when we get back,' I told Emily as she walked back to the dance floor to join Jennifer.

I was worried that I smelt something on Emily I hadn't smelt in years. The odour was the same and it made me wonder. It was something else to worry about.

Mary and I danced close, cheek to cheek, on the slow songs, especially the song 'Move Closer'. Two men with odd-looking features approached Emily and Jennifer for a dance; Jennifer refused but Emily accepted. That wasn't like her. She was far too relaxed.

Doing my best to keep my emotions in check, I let things slip and became aroused whilst dancing close to Mary. She didn't seem to mind. Instinctively, to rectify this I tried to pull away to save any embarrassment. Mary just held me tighter. It was the kind of thing I hoped she wouldn't tell Emily about, however, I suppose it's the type of subject matter that women do talk about. I threw off any negative thoughts and let go, enjoying myself without feeling guilty.

When the songs finished Mary rolled her eyes at me gleefully. I urged her off the dance floor, returning to a quiet area.

'Whoa, my feet are killing me,' she moaned.

Her three-inch-heeled shoes had two straps across the front and were tied around her ankles. Her feet were small, but ever so cute. She removed her shoes and rubbed her feet. Watching from my seat I jokingly held my nose. Mary threw her shoe at me, which I caught, like a cricketer in the slips.

'My, my, what lovely feet you have,' I commented.

Mary came over to my armchair and sat on my lap, sideways on.

'You taking me home tonight, cowboy?'

'Cowboy?' I gave her a quizzical look.

'Don't you wanna ride tonight?'

Damn it. For what the seemed like the umpteenth occasion time today I'd been stumped. Although Mary had had a skinfull, there was seriousness in those dull-looking blue eyes.

Placing my arms around her, my courage came from a place unknown to me.

'I like you, Mary, and we've had fantastic night. However, let's take one step at a time, if you don't mind.'

She hugged me and kissed me on the cheek. She let that embrace linger, as though she was falling into me, rather than cuddling. I didn't mind; her warmth made me feel cosy, satisfied in some small way. The feeling sent a lovely tingly sensation right through me.

Mary pulled away from her cuddly embrace. She looked at me, our faces inches apart, my heart studiously beating in a rhythmic fashion.

'You're a lovely man, Justin Whalley, and I think you're fucking gorgeous.'

I could only laugh. Now I had to circumvent what my real, selfish, gratifying emotions wanted me to say and more importantly do. Grappling with those sensual thoughts and protracted scenarios, getting completely naked with Mary dispersed utilising my breathing strategy. That coupled with switching mind and thoughts to the mundane, like work or driving to a meeting, poured water on my flames.

As I looked around Mary, who remained on my lap, Emily, supported by Jennifer headed towards us. It was time to go.

Mary and I said our goodbyes with a quick kiss on the lips. She moved in harder and I didn't have time to back out.

Two taxis arrived and Emily could just about speak as Mary told her she'd call her once we all got back to Nottingham.

Jennifer did not look too pleased.

I had a good night for once. Tomorrow looked better already.

29

The babysitter had slept over. We all nursed hangovers the next morning. I awoke with a broad contented smile on my face. Ben was up early, playing an electronic keyboard at eight thirty. Emily and particularly Jennifer were not impressed by the mis-sounding keys.

Following a wonderfully fattening brunch of eggs, beans, sausages, tomatoes, hash browns, washed down with two cups of tea and a glass of orange juice, I was ready to take a power nap and drive home.

Emily slept until ten thirty. She managed to consume a sausage and a few mouthfuls of baked beans.

As our throbbing heads, eased, Ben had no such ideas. He ensured we held onto the deadening pain of a heavy alcohol-induced headache. Jennifer had no strength to tell him to be quiet; luckily the babysitter did her job efficiently and ushered Ben swiftly out of the kitchen.

Emily returned to her sluggish stupor and lay peacefully on the large three-seated sofa. Jennifer and I decided to go for a walk. It was her idea so I went along. The fresh air would do me good.

We discussed what happened to my mum; it brought back unwanted memories. Painful ones. She told me our father, not hers, was living on his own across the city, apparently feeling sorry for himself. That part of my life was numb. His problems had nothing to do with me, Emily, Mark and Oliver. Good riddance.

The wind increased, as we strolled slowly through Sutton Park, swirling around us.

'You'll find someone, you know,' she told me with some assurance. 'When the time the is right. As clichéd as that sounds, it's the way it tends to happen.'

'Hope so, Jen. I mean I'm not asking for much, just what many people seem to have.'

Tired and forlorn I must have looked. Jennifer linked arms with me and told me what a pleasure it was to have her two youngest siblings stay with her. A feeling of warmth flowed through me when I heard that.

'Thanks, sis, I must do this more often. You never know, the next time I visit I may well be bringing two people…' I gave her a cheeky grin.

When we arrived home, it was time to go home. That late night would be waiting to catch up on me, and I could not afford that to happen once I was behind the wheel.

So at just after two in the afternoon, Emily and I hugged Ben and Jennifer and thanked them for letting us staying over. I reminded Ben about his choice of words, particularly when in public, so hopefully there'd be fewer embarrassing instances.

'We'll call you when we arrive back home,' I called out to Jennifer as I placed the luggage into the boot.

They both waved as I drove off, smiling and calling out, 'See you soon!'

Emily managed a few weak smiles in response, but she was still suffering from the after effects of last night. And it wasn't just the drink.

*

With any remnants of my last few days at work eradicated, Monday's projections had to be positive.

Shaun and Tom were out at customers, as was Errol. It was unusually quiet.

Looking out of the fourth-floor window to my right, the sun shone its rays of light across the half-empty car park. It could be sign that things were changing for me. A bright new start.

I said good morning to a few other junior salespeople and Errol's secretary, who flashed a tired, ambiguous smile in return.

An ironic thought passed through my mind, as Errol's secretary reminded me of Mary Leadbetter. I still didn't know what to think about her. More time was needed and certainly more investigation on my part. And maybe on hers too.

Settling down to a swarm of emails, half of which I didn't need to read, I used 'ctrl' and 'D' to erase the unnecessary junk mail. Unfortunately a lot of that mail was from Walter, which Errol had been forwarded on, 'FYI', copying all sales. I continued to delete them.

At eleven thirty, Errol's secretary came over to my desk. I hadn't realised that she'd been standing there waiting for me to raise my head above my monitor. The stupid bitch could have said something.

She handed me two sheets of company headed paper. It was from one of my customers. Probably a cancellation.

'Thank you,' I told her, in a sharp, annoyed tone.

She walked off, swinging her odd-shaped figure and hips, from side to side. I pulled a face behind her back.

Taking time to read what she gave me, I leaned back in my chair and the biggest of grins appeared on my face. I punched the air, and let out a quiet 'yes'. No one saw me.

This was a change for the better. This was something I could rub in Tom's face. At last a huge order. Over half a million pounds worth of business and I had the purchase order to prove it.

My mind ran through the possibilities, what preparation should I perform to win more business. Maybe going out with Emily or my family did the trick. Freeing my mind of work, not thinking about it and being totally relaxed. Then getting it could just be plain old luck. Whatever it was, I was bloody grateful.

Pushing aside what I was doing, I made the necessary calls to our admin team to organise the contract. Sent the purchase order to finance to the invoices raised. Inputted the data into my forecast and pipeline our CRM package. Lastly but certainly most importantly, I called the customer to thank him for placing the business with Eiron.

At lunchtime, Shaun had arrived, looking like he'd been beaten up over the weekend. He looked rough.

We decided to go to the Café Bar that was a five-minute drive from the office. Although I didn't notice, Errol had also come back from wherever he'd been. He tagged along.

I drove and the bar was quiet for a Monday. Something must be happening and I was the last one to know.

'So, tell me Justin, what are your figures like for the first quarter? Going make it or miss it?' Errol asked me as we took our seats, at a window table.

Shaun had a routine smile, which he altered to make his face expressionless. I glanced at him, and then back to Errol.

'Let me see,' I began my little build-up. 'According to my latest calculations, it does give me an outside chance of meeting my target for the first quarter.'

The waiter came over and asked for our drinks order. Errol stared at me. A look that wondered whether I was bullshitting him. He could check the forecast and look at the 'wins' column. I was 100% positive he would, as soon as we got back from lunch.

'When did you ever get near your Q1 number?' Shaun asked with good deal of surprise in his voice.

I could see Errol sitting forward in anticipation of my answer. Glaring at Shaun, he got the message. It was a question he shouldn't have asked, not in front of Errol.

'Come on, Just, we're waiting,' Errol quietly stated, tapping his fingers on the Formica-topped table.

'Okay, my secret's out…' I paused and Errol took the bait by leaping in.

'So you're not going to make Q1? Is that what you're saying?'

Shaun's eyes flicked between Errol and I like an avid spectator watching tennis.

'If I could be allowed to finish,' I jumped back in.

'Of course, you can. Go ahead.' Errol sat back. Shaun folded his arms.

'As of today I am about forty grand off my Q1 number.' Errol sat forward, interlocking both his hands and tilting his head at an angle.

'The Bottomly deal?' Errol queried.

'That's the one. Over half a mil.' Errol was nodding his head now.

'Shit, you jammy bastard,' Shaun called out and immediately held his hand over his mouth. 'Well done, mate, I'm happy for ya.'

'Thanks Shaun, things are looking up.'

'Well done, Just, always had faith. Always,' Errol said as his voice faded.

Our drinks were served a few minutes later, followed by our food. Homemade cheeseburger with Swiss cheese and a spicy salsa dip. And of course fries.

We discussed what other opportunities we had, Shaun and I with Errol. How we seriously, genuinely thought Q2 would end up. My list of opportunities looked okay. Needed more though. However, I had at least one biggie in there. If that closed, I would be sorted.

When we talked about our weekends, Errol wanted to know where I'd gone.

'I went to Jennifer's in Birmingham, with Emily. We both needed a boost.'

'Anything good happen?'

Shaun was watching tennis again.

'Not sure about good, but most certainly interesting.' I smiled and Errol reciprocated, thinking it would be nothing exciting.

'What kind of interesting? Funny, nice, found a girlfriend?' Errol stopped there when my smile grew bigger. I said nothing and finished my last mouthful of cheeseburger.

Shaun grabbed at my arm, with an animated grin on his face.

'Wooh, who's got a new girlfriend then?' he jibed.

'Let's not get ahead ourselves here, she's just a friend, someone I know that I met in Birmingham.'

This left Errol absolutely confused. His brain was working overtime. Turning over like an idle engine.

'Errol, look, don't worry, I'll save you the trouble of trying to fathom out who she is. Remember, we've only met this once and Emily and Jennifer were there. I just think she's quite nice. Good fun to be with, you—'

'For God's sake, man, tell us will ya?' Shaun cried with anxiety.

'Mary Leadbetter. That's who she is.'

Errol's face was a picture. An absolute Rembrandt. He shook his head, in surprise, disgust, bewilderment, I wasn't sure. And to be honest I didn't care.

'Wow! You certainly know how to pick 'em. Shit, Just, Mary Leadbetter, in Birmingham?' Errol's voice strained to push the words out.

'Yep, that's right. Her dad lives there now. Emily and her are good friends. The rest is history.'

'Well you just be careful with her. You know how I feel about her.'

'Yes I do, Errol. And I can probably understand why you're biased.'

'Maybe so, however, watch what you tell her. It may not stay private. I'm looking out for you, that's all,' was Errol's paternal comment.

Self-preservation became Errol's main concern. For his own well-being and maybe for any potential extracurricular shenanigans he could be getting up to. So much for looking out for his protégé, when his own shit could be exposed by my new female acquaintance. Errol was all grown up and would have to manage whatever the fallout would be, assuming there was any.

I knew Errol well enough to notice the signs. The fact he attempted to 'warn me off' seeing Mary, only piqued my interest in what Errol may have going on in the background. A selfish unwavering streak Errol had. Not a bad facet within the world of sales and management, where that sort of bullet of an attribute could be required, when you need to load your gun. Although his behaviour and response was somewhat extravagant for the situation, I know he had cause to keep a beady eye on my mentor and manager's private life. Just for my own personal satisfaction.

At least Shaun congratulated me on my sort of discovery into the female ranks. Possibly. I still had to warn him, we were just going to be friends.

Quietly excitable, with my emotions fluctuating, my recourse was to keep a lid on it all. Especially around my teammates. I had to develop my own cloaking skills, to withhold a particular way of being. Maybe poker would help, create that poker face to truly conceal my deepest, innermost feelings.

I commenced my training when speaking to Shaun. To his surprise I explained in no uncertain terms that were plenty more fish in the sea. Winking at me with his right eye, he concurred and agreed with my sentiments wholeheartedly.

30

Back at the office, Errol took no time in searching out that what I'd told him over lunch was true and bona fide.

Once that check had been completed, Errol disseminated an email which told all of sales about my huge win. The mail read:

To all Sales

Recently you may made have heard various rumours about one of our salespeople, from the Nottingham office. That person has proved and continues to do so, the reason why we all here. That is to sell. Make money for Eiron and for ourselves.

It is with great pleasure to announce then, that Justin Whalley had closed one of the largest deals this quarter. This win has taken many months of hard work, negotiation, and presentations to the board to finally succeed where our competitors have failed.

Can I ask all of you to look at this as an example of dedication, hard work and a 'will to win', supported by a positive attitude.

I'm sure this is something we can all learn from.

Regards
Errol Hughes
Regional Sales Manager (North)
Eiron Plc

It was as of a surprise to me, and more so to Tom, when he read it. The groan of disquiet could be easily heard across the office. Tom was in a foul mood.

A few of the internal sales girls came over to my desk and congratulated me on my win. Little did they know I had no idea it was going to come off. I took the plaudits, nonetheless.

By the end of the week I had just scraped past by Q1 goal by fifteen thousand pounds. So did everyone in my team, which made Errol shine like a real star. Walter Baker certainly thought so. The other regional managers were not getting any similar treatment from Walter.

The Southern and London regional managers were on written warnings for non-performance of their team. I sat back with a small smile on my face as I read Walter's email, listing each of the salespersons' results for Q1. It was his way of psychologically stimulating the troops. The worst offenders had their names highlighted in red. If that didn't do the trick then nothing would.

By five in the afternoon on the Friday, I had a fresh memory of Mary Leadbetter in my head.

Errol called me into his office at just gone five thirty for a chat, as everyone else was disappearing home for the weekend.

'Come in, Just.' Errol welcomed me into his office, as he looked over me, from top to bottom.

Fridays were casual days and sometimes my choice of designer jeans caught the eye. I tried to look a little different. I never knew whether it had the desired effect.

'Thanks.'

Errol closed the door behind him. As the door was closing I glimpsed a very curious Tom Greenfield-Crown, peering anxiously into Errol's office. Gosh, this must have gnawed at him. He would be bursting to find some way to intervene, to hear what we were going to discuss. His look of total despondency summed up how he must have felt.

'So er, how's the woman-finding thing going?' Errol asked cautiously.

'Why, what have you heard?' My tone was effusive, vibrant.

'Oh, nothing much really, just wanted to hear if you'd made any in roads, you know the stuff I mean.' Errol sat on his desk, looking directly into my weary, yet apprehensive eyes.

'So basically you want to know if I'm seeing Mary. Does that sum it up?'

'Yes,' Errol nodded, with a worried expression displayed on his face.

'Look Errol, we're friends, yes, but, I can see who I like, agreed?'

'Agreed.'

'So, yes, is the answer, and I'm seeing her this weekend too, if that's okay by you?'

Errol smiled and shrugged his shoulders.

'You're a big man, Just. I'm sure you can take whatever she throws at you.' It was a veiled warning to me. I ignored it. I liked Mary.

'Errol, thanks for your advice, and if anything happens I'll let you know.' I turned toward the door and reached for the handle. I turned and looked back so Errol could see my face.

'You never know, I may ask you to be best man.' I left the office laughing, smiling like a man who'd just won the lottery. Without looking back to see Errol's' expression, I walked down the four flights of stairs and out into the car park.

My car started first time and I drove all the home with a strange, inane smile, permanently stuck to my face.

31

The following day whilst in a happy mood, Emily came over to see me in the evening.

She reminded me, when we were talking about our youth, of something that I always wanted to do. Be on camera.

I also thought it would be good idea to use my old school video recorder I had to tell women about me. Emily wholeheartedly agreed. Sad as it sounded, Emily reinforced the edict that I needed experience and Mary was becoming more of a friend than a potential lover. Or someone who I could possibly treat with some contempt and leave after a one-nighter.

After a few brandies I set up my video, with Emily's help. In the lounge, I sat on my TV armchair. Emily stood behind the tripod and camera.

She pressed the play button and the time seem to fly. It was rare for me to get drunk, and I had no reason to get up early.

'You were great, Just, Hollywood will be calling.' Emily slurred her words. I was no better.

'Here come the Oscars!' I shouted 'And the best actor is…' I performed a drum roll in a beat-box style. 'Justin Ignacious Whalleee…'

We both laughed until our stomachs were hurting.

Once we'd returned to a sensible state, Emily stood up gingerly to make for the hallway to call a cab. I don't know what she said, or if the person on the other end understood, but sometime later, a taxi arrived.

Five minutes later, as the drink stifled me, controlled my every movement, the realisation paralysed me, that I was alone again. I wanted to call off my date with Mary tomorrow, but had no power of inclination to do it. It wouldn't be a coherent enough message to communicate with anyone or anything.

My paternal side awakened from the deep regions of by brain, to advise me to go to bed to sleep off my alcohol-induced state. Somehow, my heart concurred and I couldn't fight my eyes from closing, or my head from drumming. Sleep seemed the ideal resolution.

*

After seeing Mary on Sunday evening, my happy state had melted away. She told me how Emily wasn't coping that well and was putting on a very courageous show. It dulled the night for me and made our relationship more friends than lovers, just as I'd originally been thinking and feeling.

That was a plus for the night, to have a female friend in general, with Mary explaining the situation about my sister Emily to me. Things that only women can feel and men could never fully understand. Understandable, in my eyes, considering what she had endured, suffered, experienced.

The loss of Emily's first child had affected her mentally. There was physical damage, where she would probably have to try other forms of reproduction. Thinking, listening to Mary tell me about my sister, was sobering news indeed. I thought I had problems.

I thanked Mary as we left a wine bar in the city centre by holding her, hugging her in a brotherly embrace. I kissed her on her cheek and stared gratefully into her dull blue eyes. She smiled back and we linked arms walking towards the taxi rank.

My thoughts were catacombed inside my head. Immoveable, rock solid, visions of Emily suffering not only when it happened, but right now.

Once home, although time crept by ten in the evening, I picked up my receiver and made contact by calling Emily.

The phone rang and rang and I began to feel guilty as she could be asleep. Eventually the receiver was picked up at the other end.

'Hello?' a gruff, incoherent voice said.

'Em, is that you?' I asked foolishly, my nerves jangling a bit.

'Who is... Oh, is that you, Just?'

'Yeah, sorry sis, did I wake you?'

'No, no, not really, just having a power nap...' She chuckled whilst yawning immediately after.

Leaving a nervous pause to sit, Emily filled the void.

'What's wrong, Just, why did you call?'

'I just, er, wanted, to er, make sure that you're okay, that's all...' Any sentimental stuff like this, was not my strongest or best asset.

'Have you been talking to Mary?'

Not wanting to get Mary into any trouble, I tried and failed to think of a quick retort.

'You have, haven't you?' Emily sighed a huge sigh. I had to jump in.

'She was only try to help and so am I. I'm worried, she's worried.'

Emily bounced back quickly, cutting me off.

'I'm fine, okay. What happened to me happens to lots of women, who get over it every single day.'

She was being strong. Projecting this confidence and togetherness that was frightening me.

'Well what about having another child?' I asked her.

Emily probably had tears in her eyes and I felt guilty. What a ridiculous statement.

'Sorry, Em, I'm sorry, I didn't think, if you couldn't, you know, have...' I was rambling and she curtailed her sobbing to interject.

'I can have them, however it will probably have to go through IVF.'

Now it was my turn to release a huge sigh. Without noticing, tears were building up in my eyes, however, I could not afford for Emily to recognise or notice me being weak, I had to be strong for her. I also didn't know what to say.

She left the receiver for a second or two to get some tissue. I'd steadied my own tears and heart rate to offer my help.

'Em, look, if you ever decide to try again, you know, I'll support whatever you do, okay?' My voice was steady, balanced, with no inflections.

'Thanks, Just, and please don't say anything to Mark or Oliver, Jennifer knows the story.'

'Whatever you want, Em, whatever's best for you.'

'You're a star, Just.' I could hear her little snivels as she controlled her tears and I imagined her wiping her nose, which would have gone red by now.

'What did Jennifer say about your chances of having children and that?' She seemed to be coping a bit better, although it could not have been easy talking to me. We did get on well. Always had done.

'She was brilliant about it. Told me a little secret to that no one else knows, not even Dad.' I was intrigued.

'Go on.' I sat on the floor in my hallway, the receiver stuck to my left ear and head leaning against the hallway wall.

'She told me that Ben was born after three attempts at IVF.'

'No way!'

'That's nearly what I said. I was a bit stronger.' She must have been smiling, I could hear and feel it down the line.

'How come she told you that?'

'I think she wanted to let me know that it wasn't over for me having children. I'm young, and will have ample time to start the treatments if I wanted to. She's offered to pay for it too.'

'I know I can't, you know, understand the pain you go through or the desperation any women must suffer who want a child and cannot have one. I can only offer my money to help with the treatments too.'

'Justin, you've done enough already. Plus, you and Jennifer will be the first two to know if I ever want to try for another baby.'

She was smiling now; her infectious fervour was back. My guilt at the outset dissipated into a fundamental reason for calling my sister and staying on the phone for nearly an hour. Emily didn't seem to mind. I know I certainly didn't.

We discussed our dad briefly. I hated talking about him. Where he might be and what he was doing. I changed the subject.

Emily then questioned me about Mary Leadbetter. Being coy, I told her very little, informing her that she could get the full unabridged version from Mary herself. I made the comment: 'You know how women love to talk.'

Emily laughed, replying, 'You cheeky little shit – just you wait 'til I speak to her.'

We both laughed. I'd relaxed and so had Emily. I was ever so glad that I called.

'I'll speak to you in the week, maybe,' I told her.

'Okay, speak to you soon, Just. Thanks for the call.'

'Anytime, sis.'

We closed the call. I heard her line die.

Standing up, I rubbed my legs and back, which were numb. It was time for bed and another week of battling, selling, hitting targets and pleasing Walter Baker. Yippee.

32

By the middle of the following week, business had returned to its usual pace of a tango dance. Slow, slow, quick!

Things never seem to change. Everything comes in spurts. No steady stream of business.

On Friday we would be listening to a videoed broadcast from the EMEA Managing Director, who was based in Stockholm. Another exciting episode describing how Q1 went for all the EMEA countries.

Following on from that, we'd have to submit our forecasts for Q2. Errol and Walter would be paying very close attention to them. Shaun and I would be creative and add additional customer opportunities that looked genuine enough on paper. No one ever checked. Yet the personification of perfect and honest forecasting was brown-noser, Tom. I, however, was convinced not everything about Tom was honest.

My list of customers did grow in the first quarter. I'd also lost a few to the competition. The smaller suppliers always won on price. We sold on quality, excellence and our brand name. It worked for the customer who had the budgets to fit the cost of our solutions.

To my surprise Errol asked me if he could come round to my house on Wednesday evening. Said he wanted to have a man-to-man chat. Whatever that meant. I agreed and he agreed to bring a film over and a few cans. We hadn't done that in years.

*

Unfortunately for me I didn't feel like drinking. I'd had quite a bit over the last few weeks and tried minimise how much alcohol I ingested. Errol, however, had no such sentiments; he guzzled five out of the six cans. Sensibly he walked to my house and planned to call a taxi on the way home.

Annoyingly our conversations focussed around Mary Leadbetter once again. It was as though I was in a reoccurring nightmare with the voice being constantly played in my head. Errol really had it in for her. I could probably guess why.

The film was a thriller. A not too bad one at that. It was an old film from the sixties, but I enjoyed it, in between defending my relationship with Mary.

Errol relaxed on my sofa, somewhat worse for wear, thanking me for inviting him over.

'That's okay, boss, any time of the week except Sundays.' My attempt at humour seemed to have the desired effect.

'Oh, shit, look at the time, Just, got to go. Customers to see, money to make and Walter to please.' I had to laugh privately at the last part of Errol's reply.

'I'll call you a taxi. Can't have Walter blaming me for allowing you to be late in the morning, or for falling asleep during the day,' I quipped. Errol smiled and sat upward, shaking his head and then holding it with his hands.

'Headache,' I called out as I ventured into the hallway to use the phone.

'Got any aspirin?' Errol asked, and I heard him laugh as I spoke to the taxi firm.

Returning to the lounge, Errol was on his knees, removing the ejecting video tape from the recorder and putting it in its case.

He stood up facing a shelf I had with my selection of videos and asked to borrow one. Nonchalantly, I waved him off and said he could, as I walked into the kitchen with six empty cans to dispose of.

'Thanks, Just. How long will the taxi be?'

'Should be about five minutes,' I shouted back from the kitchen. My bin needed emptying. The damn thing was permanently full.

'Oh, here it is.' I heard a car engine rattling outside.

I met Errol in the lounge and told him I'd see him on Friday, as I had a customer meeting tomorrow in Carlisle. It would a bloody long drive and hopefully worthwhile.

'See you Friday, Just. Don't be late.' Errol burped and hiccupped almost simultaneously. I chuckled. So did he. 'Pardon me.'

'Oh, don't mind me, Errol, I've seen you do worse.'

'Whatever,' he responded.

'See you, Errol. Friday morning, yeah?'

He raised his free hand after opening the door to signal his response. He closed the door and I moved into the lounge and stood by the window, to see him enter the taxi and it drive away.

Yawning veraciously, it was time enough to go to bed. So I did.

33

My scenic drive to Carlisle was one of the only good aspects of my visit. Plaintive beauty, panoramic views, winding roads through woods, rocks and forestry, made the journey a perfect remedy following a bad day.

Returning home, there was a message on the answerphone from my brother Mark, saying he wanted to come up and see me tomorrow night. That was a strange, out-of-the-blue type of request, but I definitely would welcome the company.

My body decided to acquiesce under the energy deprivation it had suffered during my four-hundred-mile round trip.

Friday morning I awoke refreshed and ready.

When I arrived at work, no one else from my team was in. Errol seemed busy in his office, already on the phone at eight fifteen.

As time passed, Shaun and Tom strolled in. As did all the internal sales and field sales account execs.

'Morning, Tom.' I was effusive in my tone and facial expression.

'Yeah, same to you, Whalley.'

'Oh, got out on the wrong side this morning, have we?' I teased.

'Piss off, Whalley, and mind this!' He pointed to his nose with his index finger.

I was grinning by this time and Shaun was doing the same behind his monitor.

Tom gave us both a filthy look. It was a good way to start the day.

'Hey Justin,' Shaun called out, 'are you still going for that promotion, you know, the one…?' Shaun's voice trailed off as Tom's head popped up as though he a coiled spring attached to it.

'Erm, not sure. Need to speak to Errol and Walter about the money side of things. We're still in negotiation about the transfer fee.' Tom refused to take the bait. He mumbled some expletives under his breath, cursing Eiron and Walter Baker.

By nine forty-five, Errol had come out onto the sales floor and reminded everyone to be downstairs for the EMEA director's Q1 address. He'd given Tom, as he was deemed the most technical person, the task of setting up the television and video units.

At nine fifty-five I received a call from my customer in Carlisle. Shit, I hated walking in late for a room full of salespeople. Errol would see me about it as well.

As best as I could I curtailed the customer's conversation, in my most diplomatic of call-handling styles. It was an important call, that lasted nearly fifteen minutes.

Recording the call in my notebook, I linked it to my 'call database' I kept. I placed my extension on voicemail and switched off my mobile phone.

As quick as I could I ran down the flights of stairs to the second-floor 'Masters Room'. From the small rectangular-shaped window, I could see all the lights were off and the flicker of the television screen, bouncing around the room.

Quietly I opened the door, slid my body inside and closed the door behind me. The door let me in via the rear, so scanned as best I could through my specs to find a seat at the back of the room. My backside nearly touched the seat when my name was called out.

'Whalley.'

Standing erect, I looked ahead of me. It was Tom. Everyone was laughing. I mean really laughing. My name couldn't be that funny.

'Yeah, yeah, sorry I'm late, customer called, and unless I'm mistaken, they come first.' My retort was confident, maybe a little aggressive.

'That's fine, Justin. We complement you on your dedication, as did the management. However I wonder if the management would compliment you on your Oscar-winning performance?'

Looking at Tom in frustration, and remembering there were over thirty salespeople laughing at me, I stood facing Tom with my arms folded. Asking him without saying another word, what the hell he was going on about.

'Okay, Justin, let me show you what I mean.'

Tom pressed the play button. I don't know where Errol was, but he obviously left Tom in charge.

The videoed images played out on the television screen. My heart, legs, arms and whole body melted into the deepest embarrassment. Right then and there I could have passed out. Fainted, feigned illness, anything to claim absolution from what everyone had seen and was being repeated in front of my own eyes. The video that Emily did, the one I thought was a good idea to do, was being aired to a captive excited, feverish audience.

After a few minutes of me telling everyone how desperate I was find a girlfriend and what my special interest and hobbies were, in order to possibly attract a woman, Tom, spared me any further vilification.

'So, Mr Whalley, in your defence, what do you have to say?' My hearing was excellent, yet I barely heard what Tom asked me over the riotous and justified chaos I had caused in the 'Masters Room'.

Without saying a word I turned swiftly and left the same way I came in. Passing Errol in corridor, he asked me if the video airing had already finished. I ignored him and carried on upstairs.

Immediately I went to my desk. Packed my laptop, notebooks, stationery away and left the building. Holding back tears of anger, frustration and utter shamefulness, I drove uncharacteristically like a mad man all the way home. My brain continued to percolate how my personal video could have got into the office. Then it hit me as I pulled up outside my house in Wollaton. Errol bloody Hughes. Shit! Too little too late. The damage had been done.

34

By the time Mark had arrived, it was nearly nine in the evening. I'd done my shopping and purchased over twenty pounds worth of alcohol. It seemed to be my only friend and it never made fun of me.

Before settling Mark in, and getting one of the spare rooms ready, I mentioned briefly what had happened. I could see him trying desperately to withhold a laugh that probably was begging to be let out. He succeeded in withstanding the pressures making my pain ease, by not succumbing to the compulsive reaction that I would expect most people to perform.

'Justin, I'm your brother, yeah. I spoke to Emily and Jennifer. I'm here to help you from a man's point of view. Okay, granted, my relationship isn't the best at the moment, but I can still give you a few ideas. Whaddya say?'

'We'll sort something out in the morning, I'm off to bed. Shattered, you know how it is.'

'Ummm.'

In the morning Mark and I visited the gym for a quick circuit. Something I should have done more often, to release all my pent-up emotions and stress. We ate a healthy lunch and talked about his relationship. Where he thought it'd gone wrong. I didn't throw in, however, that his partner had tried and failed to get me into bed with her. That might have altered his views somewhat.

Aside from her failed attempt at entrapment with me, Sarah was a very fanciable woman. In another life, maybe I would have acquiesced and pleasured myself with Sarah and suffered the consequences later, whatever they may have been. Who knows, the pain may have been worth the gain.

Fleeting glimpses of what it would have been like, sleeping with Sarah, flashed through me. I knew it was wrong, morally, in any realm to desire another woman, that was already 'spoken for'.

Not just any woman. My potential sister-in-law. My subconscious had to deliver some rational thought process to keep me focussed and on the straight and narrow.

Then Mark came up with what seemed an odd, suggestion.

'Do you read books, Justin?'

'Of course I do.' I was taken aback. What was he trying to say?

'No, what I mean is, do you ever go to the library?'

'Oh, I see what you mean.' We both had grins on our faces and Mark raised his eyebrows in quick succession.

'Okay, a visit to the library it is.' A little journey into the unknown might help put behind me the ghosts in my past. I was looking forward to it.

Once we were there, Mark suggested I look for books on women, and how to attract and keep them. I gave him a harsh look, although he softened his comment by saying he was only trying to help. Any help would be beneficial. That was something I had to accept.

We separated and look down different aisles on the second floor. To my absolute amazement I saw Victoria Shepard. My mouth developed a bitter taste when from behind her, the smarmy body of Tom Greenfield-Crown appeared. I quickly moved out of vision for either of them. What was she doing in Nottingham? A plethora of teasing questions commenced their journey into my brain.

Moving around the opposite of the aisle that they stood in, I tried to listen to their conversation. At first I couldn't hear much as they were whispering. Getting closer I did hear this.

'You go over to the computer books, I'll catch you up, Tom.' I made out Victoria's smooth, soft voice.

Looking around me, an old man watched me cautiously. I smiled an innocent smile to hopefully placate him. I had too much on my mind to be bothered what he thought. Slowly but surely I progressed to the end of the aisle I was in.

I moved to my left, still looking around to see everything and anyone. Pushing my head into view of Victoria's aisle, I took my first quick look. It was her. She was stooping down looking at some books. Pulling my head back, I took a deep inhalation of air and nonchalantly strolled into the aisle.

'They say that you can judge a woman by what she reads.' That was my opening gambit.

Victoria Shepard almost fell backward.

'Justin. Oh hiya, Justin.' Victoria's face turned red. She had no reason to, other than being caught with Tom. It was obvious that they were seeing each other, and he was a married man. I had no inclination to inform his wife. I had enough problems. However, my petty, vindictive side nagged at me to do something to get that little shit back. He needed to feel some pain. A virtual knife in the stomach or in the back would suit me, if I had my way.

Then I realised why Victoria was embarrassed. She was looking a books on plastic surgery. Breast reductions and the like.

Turning round, a couple were sniggering at my comment and Victoria's choice of books. She stood up and looked up at me. He attitude no longer receptive of my unexpected welcome.

'Well you know what they say, Justin, "You can always judge a man by how he smells."'

I was speechless. What a thing to say. She was pissed at me. Again.

'Look Vicky, I probably startled you. You okay?'

'Fine thanks.' Her reply was frosty, cold like the weather outside.

'So how come you're in Nottingham then?'

'None of your business.'

'Whoa, I was only being friendly, that's all, gee wizz.'

The hostility toward me would have come from being with Tom. Maybe I should tell his friggin' wife. Give him something to worry about. And his young son.

'Oh well, I'll see you around sometime, Victoria. Give my regards to Tom.' I walked away, leaving that comment ringing in her ears. She had to know that I had seen them. They'd tried to keep it quiet because of Tom's marital status, that much was clear for me to see. It would have been interesting if Errol had seen them together.

I located Mark, who asked me what was wrong. I said it was nothing and he didn't press me any further.

As we were leaving, oddly enough with some books on DIY and cars, I turned to see Victoria and Tom heading for the exit. As soon as he knew I was looking at them, he put his arm around her and smiled at me. The cheating bastard had balls to wink on his way out. My blood was boiling. Mark watched and understood what had pissed me off a few moments ago. He didn't need to ask.

The temptation to bring down this Casanova had increased tenfold. As the minutes went by, and as Mark and I followed them for a while, my mind spun into all types of vicious, acrimonious thoughts and ideas that resurfaced. What to do and how to do it.

'Just, I think we should let them go. Our car is that way.' Mark held my right arm and I agreed.

I had to calm down, I had to work with this prick. I had to beat him as well at everything. Work and at play.

When we'd got home, I thanked Mark for restraining me. He told me that Jennifer would be coming up in the week to stay with Emily.

When I asked if anything was wrong with her, he said he didn't know. But that got me worried. I hoped if there were anything the matter, it wouldn't be anything serious.

35

Determination had to be my game plan. I would not give up or acquiesce. No way would I abdicate my responsibility to gain the well needed experience I so desperately sought.

The damaging scene with Victoria Shepard, did hurt, yet that was a long-term strategy. My strategy involved Tom, more than Victoria. He was in the way and had to be eventually and surreptitiously removed.

Mark left me alone again and went back to Birmingham, after a phone call from Sarah. He had every reason go as Lucy was ill. When Mark left me on Sunday morning, like in a train station, another train arrived in the form of Jennifer and Emily. They turned up later that afternoon on my doorstep.

'Bloody hell, what are you two doing here?' My voice was higher than it should have been, due to the surprise. They both laughed out loud.

I ushered them inside quickly, before any of my nosey neighbours had the opportunity to twitch their curtains.

'So, why are you two here, now?' I repeated my question.

'We're here to cheer you up, number one. Secondly, we're here to tell you that Emily has a new man in her life,' Jennifer revealed. Emily nudged her, and raised her eyebrows at her older half-sister. I obviously wasn't supposed to find out.

We were in the lounge and Emily slumped into one of the armchairs.

'Em, don't worry about it. As long as he makes you happy, I'm happy for you. Okay?' I attempted to quash any reticence she may have had about me knowing.

'Thanks, Just. It's a newish thing, didn't want the whole world to know, that's all,' she answered with a slight frown. Jennifer defended herself.

'He's your brother, not just anyone. Now it's his turn.' Jennifer could not help a smile playing on her lips as she finished her statement.

'So when you said you came to cheer me up, what did you have in mind?'

I waited for their response. I'd tried the library, a place for learning, yet what I saw was opportunity, pain and a cheating husband. Wine bars and night clubs were always going to be hit and miss, depending on what I wanted at that time. They did always provide a regular litany of possibles and hopefuls who could fall under my debonair spell.

'Bingo!' Jennifer shouted.

'What?'

'Bingo. You know, the game where they call out, "Two fat ladies, eighty-eight."'

I sarcastically cast my spectacled eyes at my two sisters, who quickly got my humour. They stared back and Emily and Jennifer responded.

'Cheeky bastard!' We all laughed.

'But bingo, that's, that's, do you want to find an OAP for a girlfriend?'

They were both still giggling, more so after I commented on what was deemed a place for older women to fritter away the last few pound coins on a whim.

'Justin, it's not like that anymore. You're coming with us, and there's no turning back, so get your coat, we're going to have our dinner out at a pub, then on to bingo.' Jennifer put her finger to lips. She didn't want me to say any more.

On the way to the bingo hall from the pub, I asked Jennifer and

Emily what they would do with my scenario. I explained that I'd always 'had a thing' for this woman. Explaining carefully that I knew she was seeing a married man. And whether I should say something to his wife or him.

'Everyone sees this differently, Justin, some would not say anything, as often, it is best not to get involved. Especially for the wrong reasons. Then again, if you feel strongly enough about it, and her, speak to him, warn him off. If he doesn't stop then tell the wife. Do they have any children?' Jennifer asked after her piece of advice.

'Yep. A little boy I think.'

'It's up to you. However, get your evidence absolutely clear, before you do anything. Many relationships have been broken up on supposition and hearsay. Don't make that mistake, just because he is seeing the woman you want. The situation is bigger than everyone realises. Remember that.'

'Cheers, Jen.'

'Remember too,' Emily piped up, 'his wife may already suspect something and may even know. They may have one of those 'open marriages', where she does what she likes and so does he. So telling her might not have the effect you want.'

My heart sank when I heard that. Of course it could be true. Tom's wife from what I'd heard was a free-spirited woman. Shit!

'Justin, stop thinking about Victoria. We're here.' I gave Emily a quizzical look. So much for trying to hide the names of the innocent.

In an enormously wide and high-ceilinged room, we took our seats after paying three pounds fifty to play. That was the first shock for me. The second was the women that were in there. Damn, they were some younger than me. However, there were some old enough to be my grandmother.

Emily and Jennifer explained how it worked. The game was easier to play these days due to technology, but the bingo hall we played was somewhere in between.

We sat at a small rectangular table and had our bingo cards in front of us. As we'd had lunch I didn't want any more drinks. The humming of chatter filled the room. The excitement and anticipation oozed out of every pore in every person sat pensively waiting for the numbers to be called. I could see clearly in Emily's face. She was into this.

So were other women. Into me. On a table across from us, two women, one clearly in her late forties or fifties, the other a lot younger, constantly stared in my direction. They whispered in an earnest fashion. Emily noticed and was not impressed.

The first game started, and the thin, puny-looking bingo caller, with a light blue jacket on and black trousers, raised the mic to his crooked mouth.

All eyes were down, hoping, hearts beating in keen, anticipated readiness. Each person had a little stamping implement (which was basically a pen with bit of coloured felt tip stuck on the end), to mark each number as they were called out, assuming they had that number.

Looking around, the noise that had reverberated around the huge hall, fell to a whisper of glasses clanging and, oohs and aahs for the near misses.

In the first game I crossed five numbers. Emily had four and so did Jennifer. I was beginning to enjoy this. Those women continued to smile at me. I reciprocated accordingly, to Emily's disgust. Jennifer smirked as she sipped her tomato juice.

In the break that ensued between the first and second game, the older woman came over to the table. Emily had gone to the ladies' with Jennifer.

'I take it this is your first time?'

'Yes actually. I'm still a virgin.' Damn, I was quick today. She laughed hard, which made me embarrassed. People would have been watching, including what could be this woman's oldest daughter.

'Ooh you are funny as well as handsome,' she replied in a forced ladylike voice.

'Thank you. And you are?' My confidence was coming from somewhere.

'Tracey.'

'Oh, I see. So tell me, who's the young girl with you?' Her face noticeably drooped. Her flashy, hearty smile, began to fade slowly, as she thought about the answer. She stood holding onto the chair that Emily sat in, looking down at me.

'Oh her, aw, she's just a friend from work?'

Her eyes moved to the left. She was lying. Not a bad try though.

'Great. Well my sisters are on their way back, I might see you after, yeah?'

Her smile returned. Bright and effervescent.

Emily asked what the woman wanted, a concerned tone and expression displayed in her voice and on her face.

'She thought she knew me from somewhere, that's all,' I calmly replied.

'Bullshit. She's a known slapper. Got four kids. Three different fathers. All different races too by all accounts. Talk about being easy.'

'I get the point, Em. Geez, I was only having polite conversation.'

'Well, her conversations end up being with the CSA, 'cause all the fathers have buggered off.'

I raised both palms of my hands up in surrender. Emily apologised. The thought of her looking out for me was reassuring though.

The thin man on stage spoke his words precisely.

'Eyes down.' We did what we were told.

Each number that was called gave us all heartache with worry. A feverish atmosphere pervaded the entire hall. Things were getting close. I had stamped off all but three of my numbers. Emily covered her card. Jennifer's face gave it away she was nowhere close. The sound of someone shouting house was a weird dream of mine. Maybe I could shout it if I could got three more numbers.

Jennifer mumbled that it was taking part, not the winning that made the game exciting. In the next breath she whispered, 'I've done it, I got a full house.'

'Well shout it out then,' I told her. What a lucky night.

Emily looked at Jennifer. Emily returned her gaze, looking bemused as to how Jennifer had the full house. I still couldn't believe it.

'Aren't you going shout it, Jen? There's two grand up for grabs.' I pressed her to do it. Then she spun things around.

'I can't be bothered, you do it if you want.'

'Can I?' I opened my eyes wide and my mouth followed suit. This was my moment.

Snatching Jennifer's card I held it aloft and yelled, 'House!'

'We have a winner. The man in the black polo-neck sweater and leather jacket.'

The hall erupted when I stood and made my way to the stage. Tracey and her 'friend' applauded as though their lives depended on my winning.

I reached the stage and the thin man announced that he would now check all the numbers on my card. Looking over the hundreds of eyes leering up at me, it reminded me of my speech at the sales conference. This was piss easy.

Holding Jennifer's card in my hand the bingo caller called out the first number.

It wasn't on the card. Nor was the second, or the third and so on. The beaming smile and air of confidence not only died, it was cremated. Over a hundred people, mostly women, watched in amazement and astonishment as I stood on the stage, with a card with two correct numbers on. Jennifer had played the ultimate trick on me. At that moment there was no room for laughter.

The bingo caller whispered what I'd already realised.

'You've been had, son.'

No shit.

Over in the corner of the hall by the exit doors were Jennifer and Emily, wiping tears away from their eyes. There weren't the only ones. Tracey the floozy and her 'friend' watched me step down and walk, excruciatingly, back to me table. They too were doubled over in fits of giggles.

I walked by their table and leant over to Tracey.

'Say hi to all your four kids. I take it you can speak at least five different languages!'

Before she could muster a response I was off, heading for the door.

Both my sisters apologised profusely all way back to my house. I told them in no uncertain terms did I didn't want any company tonight. They said I was being sour and that I couldn't take a joke. That was a humiliation. One of the highest order. I wanted to do that to Tom. Something like that, where Victoria would see. That might swing things in my favour.

Haunted by this endless cloud of doom that followed me everywhere, was becoming tiring, annoying and mildly incapacitating. Whichever cartoon character I represented I couldn't remember, however there was a few that seemed to carry the same fate as I.

Jennifer dropped me off and went back to Emily's.

I completed my night of disappointments, when I found my brandy bottle empty. I could have burst into tears right there. Instead I went to bed.

36

I'd completed two customer meetings. I was late for both them.

The occurrences at the weekend left me wondering if anyone cared about my predicament, or me. On Wednesday, Errol asked me how I was. Instinctively he guessed not everything was right with me. Maybe it was because I had stopped smiling and rarely spoke to anyone.

He sat me down in his office, and once again, Tom became nervous. He had tried unsuccessfully to speak to me about what Mark and I witnessed at the library. That led me to believe that his salacious behaviour would not be a welcome bit of news for his free-spirited wife. He gave his game away far too easily. He should have projected an air of confidence and arrogance, pushing me not to say anything. I'd got to him.

Errol advised me to concentrate on my work and let the girlfriend thing happen on its own. Admittedly I had been trying far too hard to find one. Anyone. Just for practice's sake. Increase my knowledge, develop some experience which would all help me in the long journey of a loving relationship.

Exiting Errol's office I directed my eyesight immediately toward Tom's desk. He was on the phone, but turned to face me. He watched me sit at my desk and pack my things away. I heard him attempt several times to rush the call, in order to close it. Nevertheless, he was too late. As I drove out of the car park, I looked up to see a forlorn, vulnerable expression displayed on Tom's round face. It made me feel all warm and gloating inside.

Using my work mobile phone, I contacted someone who could

give me a lift. Mary Leadbetter. I had that intention, but I wouldn't reveal that to Errol.

Mary without any pressure or coercion from me agreed to meet in the city centre after she finished work. She giggled when I told her she was the only person who could cheer me up. I suspect she heard the depression in my voice.

At ten minutes after five, Mary approached me and hugged me. It was the best tonic I'd received in a long time. Her smile was bright, warm and energetic.

'Gonna buy me a drink or what?' she asked, grinning from ear to ear.

We ventured into 'The Bar' that was part of a large cinema complex. I ordered a white wine and soda for Mary and started with a brandy and Coke.

Politely Mary listened to me ramble on about my problems. She quietly sipped her drinks and I finished my first three far too quickly.

Then Mary pointed out that two women were staring at me. I began to wonder if I was an alien or something. It seemed to be a regular thing. I turned to look at them, and they were gorgeous, and I recognised one of the faces.

'Bloody hell, it's er, what's 'er name, Nikki Weaver. Shit, ooops, sorry Mary.' I held my hand up to her to apologise.

Nikki stood up and I waved for her to come over.

'They work for Eiron, well at least the one in the blue faded jeans does,' I explained to Mary, in case she was wondering how I knew this woman.

'Hello, Nikki, what are you doing in Nottingham?'

Nikki and her shorter, auburn-haired friend sat down at our table. Mary was intrigued.

'I'm up here a few days every week now with a customer on site.'

'Great, good. Oh by the way, this is Mary, a very good friend of mine.'

They shook hands and Nikki introduced Chelsea, her younger sister. Damn, she looked good. A bit like the woman off a beer advert on television.

'Can I get you ladies a drink?' My offer was genuine and gentlemanly.

'No, I'm okay,' Nikki replied.

'I'll have one if you don't mind,' Chelsea perked up. 'A Bacardi and Coke please.'

'Coming right up.'

I panicked just for split second, wondering what the atmosphere would like between Mary and two women she'd just met.

When I returned they were all laughing. Probably about me. Mary must have given the abridged version and they found it hilarious.

'What all you girlies laughing at then?' I asked in trepidation.

They went quiet.

'Oh, I get it, Mary's told you about me, hasn't she?' I turned to Mary, giving her a false hard stare.

'She hasn't actually, but we'd like to know if you don't mind telling us,' Chelsea requested.

Mary interjected.

'We were laughing because Nikki told us about an incident at your sales conference…'

I laughed to cover it up. My phoenix decide to rise once again. It was coming back more times that a Rocky film.

'Yeah, that was the best moment of the whole event. It was great. Everyone loved it.' I played to it, so no one could go any further.

Switching the subject cleverly, I asked Chelsea where she worked and what was like to have Nikki as a sister.

That kept us occupied for another half-hour or so.

At nine thirty, we left the bar and walked to the Boston Bean. Mary had to go home, so I thanked her for her support and hugged her before she left. Nikki and Chelsea said they'd come in for one drink. I had already had one too many.

We stood at the bar and I noticed an awful-looking woman standing next to me. My nostrils were filled with a viciously diabolical odour of perfume.

'Damn, that stuff would unblock my drains. Got any left, love?' She glared at me and Nikki nudged me to be quiet.

'Whoa, look at the dress, I've seen better at the local circus, ha ha!' The woman stormed off into a corner. We took our drinks and sat down near the bar. As I sat down there was a tap on my right shoulder. Rotating on my stool I saw a fist heading towards me. My drunken stupor saved me as I fell off the stool and the punch missed me. My specs somehow stayed attached to my ears. It was her boyfriend or husband attempting a Hagler-style punch.

'Come here, you little bastard, I'm gone kick the living shit out of ya,' his voice gruff with anger.

He leaned over me to kick me when without warning I heard this big man yelp in pain. His legs buckled and he fell to my level on the floor. In a flash sitting on his back, with arms pulled behind, was Nikki Weaver.

'Say you're sorry, say you're sorry!' she shouted. The barman, who at first looked decidedly worried, had a quirky grin on his face. The big man mumbled something in reply. His girlfriend could only watch helplessly as Nikki Weaver ushered him to his feet.

'Say it so we can hear it,' Nikki repeated forcefully.

The angry man holding his head in shame and bewilderment eventually spoke up.

'Sorry. It was my mistake and I didn't mean any harm.'

Nikki pushed him towards his girlfriend, who displayed an expression of utter embarrassment, coupled with seething anger at his overreaction.

'You okay, Justin?'

'Umm.' I could not muster anything else.

Nikki and Chelsea took me home.

WORK HARD, PLAY HARD

37

Now the tide was turning. My only fear was pondering on whether I was aboard the HMS Titanic. Hopefully I was not.

The night after I was taken home by the Weaver sisters, Chelsea and I began seeing each other, to Nikki's approval. Apparently Chelsea wanted some regular male company, so we decided to give it go. And boy oh boy, was I pleased.

A cute, bubbly, vibrant woman that had the sexiest laugh I'd ever heard. She didn't look half bad in jeans either.

Each time we went out, she revealed a little more of herself to me. A cautious girl, unlike her sister.

The days became worthwhile. I looked forward to rushing home from work or phoning her. My emotions at times personified a man in love. That couldn't be me. No way.

Her hair hung loosely around her small shoulders. No cosmetics whatsoever, a natural beauty, with attitude to match. I had to stop myself from just simply staring at her. Thankfully Chelsea did not mind one bit.

Our visits to the cinema and bars made me proud; at last I was holding down a relationship, that started after I was drunk. And I thought drink was to be the ruin of me. It must have been the Florence Nightingale effect. Whatever it was, it worked. And I was a happy man.

In the office, Shaun congratulated me on my new status.

'About bloody time too, son. What kept ya?'

'Waiting for the right train to come along. You see, there's not enough patience in the world these days…' was my witty retort.

'We should do a foursome, yeah, that'd be great. Ask your lovely lass if she wants to meet the Irish George Clooney, with a fantastic tan, and the brains to match.' Now that was funny.

'I'll see. We're going through the "getting to know you better" stage. Maybe in a few weeks.' I nodded to show Shaun that I thought it was a good idea.

It didn't last long before Errol tapped me on my shoulder and asked me when he was going to meet her.

'Want a coffee?'

'Okay.'

Downstairs in the canteen, Errol quietly attempted to eke out information on my girlfriend.

'Errol, I think it's best if I er, you know let you meet her. I can guarantee you'll like her. But don't steal her from me. Agreed.'

'Agreed.' He was smiling, as he understood my comment had a compliment hidden inside it.

The coffee was tasteless, yet the warm liquid quenched a building thirst.

'We'll all meet up one day, you and Elisa, Shaun and whoever he's with, how does that sound?' I proposed something to see how serious Errol was about meeting Chelsea. I still refused to tell anyone what she was called.

'Yep. That's a deal. You say the word and we'll be there.'

'Good stuff.'

Back at my desk I noticed Shaun had gone but that prat of a graduate sales trainee was sat in his chair. I threw him a scant glance and continued preparing my monthly forecast.

As with everything that had happened in my life, anything wonderful was ultimately followed by something not so good.

In the four weeks since we'd been seeing each other, Chelsea let me slowly but surely into her world. Part of that world was something I just did not consider. I should have.

At her house in Basford, not too far from the city of Nottingham, a two-bed semi, she allowed me in. It was a Saturday and in effect a one month anniversary.

'Justin,' she said in a soft voice, 'I want you to meet someone.' She held my hand and led me into her large lounge.

There playing on the floor with some toys was a little boy. Maybe five or six years old.

'Hello,' he said quickly.

I then knew what would come next. My heart rate increased, my hands clammy and moist.

Chelsea took a deep breath.

'Is he yours?' I stole her answer with my question.

'Yeah he is,' she said softly. Her eyes searching mine for my reaction. I'm not sure what she was reading in them. Possibly shock and horror.

'Wow, he's cute, just like his mum, hey.' I didn't know what else to say.

Chelsea smiled coyly, still looking for me to say something like, 'Why didn't you tell me sooner?' I could not say anything like that. At least not yet and not in front of the boy.

She moved toward him and sat down beside him, as he played with some multi-coloured plastic building blocks.

'So how old is he?' I kept my voice calm, lucid.

'He'll be six in September. Started school earlier this year.' She looked back up at me, and I decided to take a seat.

We talked and joined in with Robert. Helping him build a castle-shaped structure. Chelsea watched me with her son, get on well. Every minute my heart was pumping ten times faster. As much as I was enjoying this, I also wanted to get out and get some air, take this all in.

I accepted a hot drink and some home-made cake. Chelsea mastered the art of cooking and baking very well indeed. She was also fantastic in bed. I know I needed to 'play the field' but she was holding me longer than I expected. And now this.

At the end of the afternoon, I told Chelsea that I had to go. She smiled and winked at me, which made any decision I was going make even more difficult.

We kissed, a passionate kiss. He soft tender lips interlocking with mine. Her arms gripping my body firm, a hold that said 'don't let go'. My response reciprocated her feelings. They flowed out of me naturally, without any prompting. That told me something. Whatever I did, it was not going to be easy.

'I'll speak to you tomorrow, although I'm out all day, remember.' I reminded Chelsea of my plans for Sunday.

'I remember. See you soon.'

She walked me to her front door, where she kissed me quickly on my lips. My heart skipped a beat.

38

After a day of ambiguous and conflicting scenarios that cluttered my mind, I called on Errol for some reassurances.

'Hey, you okay, Just?' Errol asked as I entered his four-bedroom house.

'Coping, I think.'

Errol directed me into his lounge, where I sat down, exhaling with a heavy sigh.

'That bad, is it?' Errol guessed as much, by my actions as well as my tired maligned expression. 'A drink?' he asked.

I nodded.

Upstairs Elisa attempted to sing a Stevie Wonder song, Lately, whilst in the shower or bath.

Errol re-entered the lounge with a strong cup of coffee. Not what I was expecting, but probably prudent. I did drive over.

He sat opposite in an armchair that had an automatic foot rest that flipped up when you leaned backward.

'So tell me, Mr Whalley, what seems to be bothering you.' Errol made an excellent mimic of a psychologist, and their voice.

'I'll get straight to it. Chelsea has a son. He's nearly six and he's as cute as she is. Problem is, I only found this out yesterday.'

Errol pulled his lips downward. He drummed his right hand fingers on the arm of his chair.

'I see, so your girlfriend of about four weeks has just told you that she has a child. Nothing wrong in that.'

I looked at Errol with my brow furrowed. 'Nothing wrong. Damn it, Errol, this is serious. Why didn't she say anything before?'

'Justin, the answer is simple.' Errol leaned forward in his armchair. 'If you had a child and you met someone, would that be your first topic of conversation?'

I shook my head.

'Damn right. Course it wouldn't. Also any woman that has a child will want to check you over first, before letting you anywhere near their child. That's why it's taken so long. And believe me, four weeks is quick. She must trust you and of course, she might be falling for you.'

I looked upward at the ceiling for some absolution. Only a swirling Artex pattern greeted me. Sitting in my leather jacket, thick jeans and walking shoes, I looked back at Errol for answers.

'I know you can't say what to do, but how am I going to cope with the fact that she has another man's child?'

I leaned forward, sitting now on the edge of Errol's large sofa.

'It is all part of the relationship. Instead of two there is three. If you wanted kids, then there you go, you've just bypassed about ten years on having children. And one more thing.' I put down my cup of coffee on a coaster, interlocking my hands together. 'Whatever thoughts you have about Victoria Shepard, get rid of them. Put them away, burn them. Don't allow her to confuse your chance of happiness.'

How the hell did he know that? At the back of my mind I was subconsciously pontificating about my faint hopes with Victoria Shepard. Errol was right. I was being naïve, stupid and foolish.

'Errol, you're a star. I'll call her tomorrow and tell what I'm going to do. I've wanted a family and a woman of my own. Now I have it all in one. Mustn't throw that away.'

'That's the spirit, Just. It's yours for the taking. However, be warned. It won't be easy. Remember the maths. Two instead of one. The needs and desires of both will be completely different. You have a tough task ahead, Just, I won't kid you. If it's what you want bad enough, you'll make it work. Millions have.'

'I won't forget. Thanks again. I'd better be off. Early start in the morning. Can't have you saying I was late in again!!' We laughed, and it helped release some of my pent-up tension.

Ten minutes later I arrived home.

Knowing it, feeling it, my life was about change, more dramatically than ever before. It was what I wanted. I had the opportunity to grab with both hands. There was only one decision to make. So I made the call.

39

Maybe because I had more responsibility, my work ethic, followed by justified results, made me a new man. In my eyes, and in those of Eiron's management.

I'm positive that my arch enemy Tom Greenfield-Crown would wholeheartedly disagree. He was still smarting over the possibility of a revelation that I could make to his dear, loving wife.

Q2, began and continued to go well for me. For the second time since I'd started at Eiron, I was well ahead of my quarter two target. Errol thanked me several times during the next week on my results and customer visits.

It was Thursday and Chelsea and her son were coming to my house for tea. I had babysat for Robert twice this week whilst Chelsea went out to her mother's and then out with her sister Nikki. The days were getting longer and harder.

In the office Shaun called me whilst I was driving, heading home from my third customer visit.

'Justin, just a quickie.'

'Yeah, what's up, Shaun?' My voice reverberated around the car. Echoing and crackling over the wind-driven noise.

'That slimy bastard Tom, has been in to see Errol about not getting put on the rota for promotion.'

'Who cares? They've probably found out what he's like. Good luck to him.' I hoped Shaun could hear me loud and clear.

'That's not all though.' Shaun's tone registered concern.

'Can't be anything serious.' I was confident. Assured.

'It's about you and Chelsea.' That did hold my attention. What could Tom know about me and Chelsea?

After a pause, I responded.

'So?'

'He's been letting everyone know you're seeing someone with a kid. Making out you couldn't find anyone else. I'd tell his friggin' wife about his extra-marital shenanigans. Screw the bastard to the wall!' Shaun was pissed off. He wanted payback ever since Tom screwed him out of a deal when Shaun first started. Shaun lost out on two thousand pounds.

'You know what, Shaun. I don't give a shit what Tom has being saying. He can't touch me and he knows it. I'm gonna make him sweat it out.'

'Good for you. But listen, I think he's into something else too. Something that can get him into real trouble. However, I'm waiting for some hard evidence to come through.'

When Shaun explained what he meant, he couldn't believe it when I mentioned that I had the same suspicions. Tom was in more trouble than he could imagine from all sorts of angles.

'Shaun, thanks for the call. Must go. Got to get the fish fingers on for my little step-son.' I laughed a relaxed, happy laugh that came from someone who was content with life.

'You take care now, Justin.' Shaun closed the call.

After a fraught night with Chelsea and Robert, who misbehaved for the first time since I'd met him, I went to work on Friday only to receive some not-so-good news.

All the salespeople in every office were raging. Walter Baker sent an email to all of us saying:

To All Sales

As always during the year we need to reassess our financial position and our results as a group. It is my unfortunate duty to inform you that your targets and goals will be increased by between ten and fifteen percent.

Secondly there will be restrictions on expenses, company cars with any money to be spent being personally reviewed and signed off by me.

This is necessary to keep the company on a safe financial footing globally. Other areas and geographies are not doing as well as we are, nevertheless, in the end we are all one company.

This I agree is not the way we should be doing things, yet it is necessary. As soon as this ban is lifted, I will let you all know.

All the above stands until further notice.

Regards
Walter Baker
UK Managing Sales Director

The cacophony of groans could be heard, like a flock of seagulls squawking on a beach. It was justified. Just when I thought I was ahead of my targets, the increase would make me just about level for Q2.

Errol followed Walter with his version, telling us all to make every customer visit count. Be aggressive and ensure that we forecast accurately every single time.

From now on we would have weekly conference calls, for all our external and internal sales teams, to go through our list of opportunities. The spotlight would be on everyone and every deal. Nothing would be missed. And there was I thinking, for one brief moment, that work was going well. I couldn't have been more wrong.

Learning to be flexible was one of the attractions of working in sales. Yet some of the sales guys were ready to hand in their notice.

Len Ferris mouthed off, as he did, saying he would walk out.

In an emergency sales meeting that afternoon, Errol told him he could walk if he wanted to.

'Look Len, since I've known you, you've said a lot but never acted on it. It's about time you did something constructive.' Errol's face was serious, eyes fixed, body language annoyed.

In front of fourteen people who were in, Len looked around and had nowhere to go.

'Your answer, Len?' Errol would not let go. The insidious nob-head was stumped.

'I'll see you after the meeting. You may as well go and pack your things and wait for me to call you.'

There was a whisper-like quietness pervading the Elijah McCoy room. All eyes peered at Len as he slowly and with tail firmly between his legs, trudged aimlessly out of the room.

Finally and ultimately Len's tenure at Eiron ceased in the manner I expected it to. No surprises there. All bark and definitely no bite. Mutterings followed, which concurred with my own cynical view of the now infamous Len Ferris. The man who exposed himself verbally, brazenly announcing his infidelity with his wife's best friend and work colleague. Len viewed his indiscretion as cathartic. A stress reliever. Now an employment release by the hand of Errol Hughes, who for a rare moment had no spare quarter for Len's typical cantankerous behaviour.

Regardless of the momentous incident with Len, Errol continued the meeting, which was a meeting to comfort us, give us reassurance, that this was only a blip.

A proactive move to protect the whole of Eiron. Not many salespeople believed it. We sold stories every day for a living. We'd recognise one a mile away.

Once I convinced myself I hadn't been working for the security services, as some clandestine version of MI5 or 6, I could deal with and handle the pitch by Errol.

Taking everything on board, I accepted what was going on and was glad to have a job I liked and a woman I believed I was falling in love with. Errol once told me, if I always think about her, and want to be with her when I'm at work or anywhere else, that is the beginning of it. Admittedly I was getting scared. I was also in uncharted territory.

40

I remember my mother telling Mark once that love was blind. To this day it was something I felt ambiguous about believing.

Chelsea and Robert stayed over at my house for a few nights. The difficulties occurred when Chelsea left me in charge of Robert. He played up something rotten. Kids, this kid was a clever little sod. And my patience ebbed away slowly, and I began to ponder about my self-control.

I had heard so many horror stories about getting into a relationship with a single mother. As an open-minded person, my views always erred on the side of giving the parent the benefit of the doubt. Yet here I was in the middle of it. Here I was enjoying, for the most part, all the three 'golden nuggets' I wished for. I listed them in my head, as Robert slept and Chelsea visited her girlfriends.

1. A job – I had that, going okay.
2. Girlfriend/wife – maybe. Lovely, bright, sexy, fun to be with. Falling in love? Maybe, not sure, but I want to keep on seeing her.
3. A child/children – not necessarily this child, a child or children of my own.

Unbelievable. Sitting on my sofa, staring aimlessly at the television set, my mind chewing over what I had right here inside my home. Was this really happening? In some way I hoped it was, and in another I hoped it was just a dream. Going from having nothing twenty months ago when I was unemployed, my halitosis was at its worse and my problems with the death of my mother, continued to linger in my head. How times had changed for the better.

Pinching my cheeks to carry out my reality check wasn't enough. Understanding the complexities of any relationship, if you have one. Then building it. Keeping it going. Managing a decent job, whatever category that falls under, minimising the chances of losing it. Working alongside some great people and some that test my personality, my moral fibre, the things I believe in or hold dear. Never easy and certainly a daily grind that erodes, or can, my very essence. One of those facets came to the forefront a short time later that night.

The sound of keys in the door, jerked me to attention. It was Chelsea. She'd arrived home after 1am. Her son soundly asleep, me the adult you'd say not very impressed.

Compartmentalising that incident, allowed me to refresh my thoughts, not to overreact in a negative way. Our relationship ticked along sufficiently, so there was no need to rock the boat. Certainly not at this hour. Those thoughts, whatever they were, had to coexist with the real issue. Work and what the hell was happening. Who really knew?

When I arrived at the office the following morning, there was uproar once again. Errol was at the nerve centre in a meeting room on the other side of the atrium.

Four other salespeople had handed in their notice, following Walter's email. Errol's saving package of a confidence meeting obviously didn't do the job. The old jackass Len Ferris had already signed his own death warrant; it seemed others were following him.

The furore started when I read an email from Errol, stating that the remaining field sales personnel would have to manage the accounts that would be left behind. This meant more work, increased goals, for the same money. Things were not going so well.

I watched Errol's face as he stormed out of the 'Socrates room'.

He was pissed off. Angry. It was his team that was being decimated because of the other geographies doing so poorly. The one successful area was being punished. Everyone knew it. Yet it was either shut up or put up. Errol used a phrase which I remembered when no one wanted to do something, even though it meant them gaining something worthwhile. 'Everybody wants to go to the party, but no one wants to stay and clean up'. How true that was.

Shaun and I waited for Tom to come in to gauge his reaction. We found out from Errol that he was in the Birmingham office. I didn't need any guesses.

'What do think, Just? Stay. Go. Run. Hide?' Shaun asked.

'I'm gonna ride out the storm, see what happens on the other side. You never know, this could be to our advantage.' Shaun threw me a confused look.

'What?'

'Look. Okay for now, it's shit. I'll agree with anyone on that. But just think in three or four months' time we could be senior execs or even managers. Think of the people who have handed in their notice. Who's next in line?' I gave Shaun my reassurance speech.

He sat in his chair and I stood by his desk, seeing his reaction metamorphose. Shaun began to smile.

'I see what you mean, Mr Whalley. We better get on with it, don't complain, bring in the numbers and voila!' I'd never heard any French uttered from Shaun before. I was impressed.

'Yeah, let's do that, support Errol and put ourselves in the frame,' I replied.

Shaun gave me the thumbs-up as I walked over to my desk.

Secretly I hid my true feeling from Shaun. Nevertheless, I'm sure Errol had his fill of everyone shouting, moaning and complaining about our latest situation. It was a huge disappointment. All round.

More work, more accounts, less support, and no more money. In fact probably less as our goals would increase.

Looking up from my laptop, Errol's body came into view.

'Justin, can I see you a minute please?' His voice was that of a man under pressure. His tone was cold, direct, emotionless.

Sat in his office was a woman. A friggin' gorgeous one. She was Walter's secretarial replacement due to maternity leave. Errol asked me to show her around. He wanted her out of his office.

The task was generally a boring one. However, today's task had custard on it. My favourite. A dainty lady, prim and proper in my eyes. With a professional courteous smile I led her out of the Errol's office.

I took her to admin and then into the sales area. I explained it was usually busier than it looked. Shaun spun around and once his large searching eyes happened upon her, he displayed the biggest of Irish smiles. He stood and approached us walking over.

'Hello, and who's this wonderful woman?' Shaun asked, still smiling from ear to ear. Then without warning he took his hand out of his right pocket and tossed his keys at her feet.

'Oh sorry, I'm sorry, please forgive my rudeness, where I come from it's how we ask girls out!'

Bloody Shaun. I should have reprimanded him. Instead I joined in the chorus of laughter. At least the secretary thought it was funny. It lightened the day a little. Even more so when I took her to the canteen for lunch, to Shaun's dismay and frustration.

We spoke in generalities about where she'd worked before. Usually at smaller companies, with very little processes or chances for advancement or improvement. She seemed normal, whatever that meant, yet serious in terms of her career.

Glancing at her left hand, I searched for a ring, which was naughty of me, since I had my Chelsea at home. A quick reprimand of my naughtiness put my thoughts back to the level-headed area they should be at.

Once my touring duties were over, I sat at my desk for the rest of the afternoon, making numerous phone calls to all my new customers. I called Chelsea and told her I wouldn't be home until late and explained briefly what had happened. In some respects I was glad to be at work. Yet again, I understood the next few months would be a trying and a tiring time. Late finishes, early starts and long days.

This was made certain when Errol emailed everyone late in the day that there was a hiring freeze on and anyone that had handed in their notice would not be replaced. It was fantastic news at the end of an otherwise perfect day. I wish.

41

After another tumultuous night with Robert, attempting to get him to go to bed was followed by a beautiful and stress-relieving night of passion with Chelsea. I understood why she wanted to get Robert off to bed so eagerly.

I hoped I was getting really good at this stuff. Chelsea seemed to enjoy herself tremendously. I had to cover her mouth a couple times, frightened in the knowledge that Robert would hear us and wander in to see Mummy copulating with boyfriend Justin. I was learning whether the noise, that crescendo Chelsea peaked at, amounted to genuine pleasure and satisfaction. Hopefully she did so automatically, rather than just to make me feel as if I'd done the job right. Although I thoroughly enjoyed myself, there was just a little bit missing. Something that I couldn't explain. Maybe that spark that other people talk about.

To this day I truly couldn't fathom what that could be, or what it might feel or look like. Our harmonious sexual session seemed to deliver a damn good vision of this illusive facet. Like love, I suppose. Invisible, transparent, yet as tangible as a hard, cold stone wall. Ignoring any ambiguity I had exposed my happy thoughts to, it was time to focus on another day, in the world of sales. A unique world run by jumped-up, privileged characters like Walter Baker.

Chelsea left for school with Robert in tow from my house with a huge, pleasing grin. Confirmation of a good night's work, I began to feel. Not being conceited, I must have done something right.

When she'd gone I began to prepare in five minutes what I should have done last night, for the four customer meetings I had planned.

On my call planning sheet I wrote them out, checking my diary for the correct meeting start times.

1. First to Leeds up the M1 for a ten thirty meeting. Good opportunity.
2. Second meeting – Huddersfield. Healthcare customer. Bring special pricing and documents for public sector customers. Twelve thirty start.
3. Third meeting – Harrogate, North Yorkshire. Retail company, Networks opportunity. Seeing MD, FD, IT Director and Network Manager. **Two thirty** start – DON'T BE LATE!
4. Fourth meeting – Back down M1 to Sheffield. Small company, but growing good future potential. Four fifteen start.
5. Back to the Birmingham office to meet Shaun for drink after work. (May need it!)

The day flew by. My third meeting was the best. I had all or most of the answers they wanted. Our pricing seemed okay, but they would let us know after a board meeting discussion the following week. Getting there fifteen minutes early was a bonus, as it gave me more time to get to my last appointment.

As part of our new dictatorship regime, we had to send in our notes of what happened at each meeting to Errol. What we were looking to sell into the customer. When they were likely to buy. And more importantly, whether they had the budget to spend.

Walter operated everything with the closest of inspections. There was no more work done on the golf course or in a pub. Expenses had be trimmed. Kept to a minimum.

On arriving into the Birmingham office following my manic drive from Sheffield, my eyes searched the sales floor. It was desolated.

Like a ghost town. Peeping into Walter's office, I saw no one there. Either this was a very good sign and all the field sales personnel had appointments, or everyone had buggered off, leaving me on my own as the only sales man in Eiron Plc. A chilling prospect.

Turning to leave as I'd come in, my mobile chirped inside my top jacket pocket.

'Hi, Shaun. Where are you?'

'In the bleedin' car park, waiting for you. I'm gaspin' for a beer. Hurry up, mate.'

'Sorry. Be there in a sec.'

Typical Shaun, always ready for a few beers.

I followed Shaun's Audi for a few miles, turning here and there. I did wonder where the hell we were going. On Lichfield Road, in Sutton Coldfield, he pulled into the large hotel car park.

At the bar, Shaun bought the first round of drinks. Two pints of lager. We sat over in a quiet corner of the busying hotel bar. Locals and patrons from all over, mulled around sipping wine, bottled beers and talking about topics in the news or what the chef might cook for their dinner.

I sat looking into Shaun's usually exuberant eyes. The liveliness had waned.

'You alright, Shaun? You don't seem yourself.' I sipped my pint.

'I'm thinkin' of going back to Dublin.'

I almost spat my mouthful of lager all over our circular table. A quick flash in my memory resurfaced of me and a certain girl and rice.

Staying quiet without responding to Shaun's shock statement, he looked forlorn into his pint and took a gulp.

'Is it because of… you know, all this latest stuff.' I tried to assume what his reasons were.

'Mostly. Yeah. Plus, I'm missing my home. I know I've been here for years, but it's not the same. And believe it or not,' Shaun took another two gulps, 'I might even want to settle down.'

I raised my eyebrows and pointed at Shaun.

'Now I know I'm dreaming. You, settle down? You're too young anyway.' My ears heard the words, my brain refused to accept them.

'Justin, don't say anything to anyone, not to Errol, or anyone.' Shaun seemed almost despondent.

'So you've thought about this for some time?'

'Yeah. I'm looking at the end of Q3 to move maybe. If I can get transfer to Dublin, or anywhere else, it would suit me fine.'

'I'll miss you, you know. No more laughs or jokes or stories about your women.' Shaun managed a wry smile.

'Enough about my women, what about Victoria Shepard? Still interested?' Shaun reverted the conversation me.

'Nope. Not interested in a page-three-type woman.' That made Shaun gasp.

'What makes you call her that?'

'Don't tell me you of all people haven't noticed her assets. Come one, they're bloody huge. And they're nice!'

We both laughed. The locals must have been wondering what was going on.

'You filthy-minded beast, Justin. You wait 'til I see Vicky Shepard and tell her what you've said,' Shaun jokingly threatened.

'Go ahead, you might as well tell Tom, he'll tell the whole world.'

'That's the reason he's goes about with her. That's it, I remember,' Shaun spouted excitedly.

I looked at him, shrugging my shoulders as to why Tom was seeing Vicky Shepard. I thought it was obvious and Shaun backed up my innermost thoughts.

'Her tits, that's why,' Shaun said a little too loud. I kept my head straight, only looking at Shaun. 'Yeah, his wife's as flat as an ironing board. Probably can't believe how much he's got to hold onto. Ooh, just imagine seeing those. Oh yes.' Shaun was back on form.

'Now, now, calm down. I'm sure Tom would be happy to describe them for you, you filthy animal.' Shaun just chuckled at my last comment and downed the remainder of his lager.

He ordered another and I ordered a soft drink.

We settled down to talking about more serious matters. Whether I should go to Tom's wife and tell her. Shaun explained that Tom had a very good job once and held senior positions. He was about the same age as Len Ferris, didn't look a day over thirty. Shaun revealed how the company he'd worked for was embezzled by a director and the company had to close. He'd been there over ten years. So coming to Eiron was a job to fill to the void, but he'd been there ever since.

'I think he's bitter about what happened, because the director was supposed to be his best friend. Apparently this director was Tom's best man at his wedding. Tom lost a big house, money, two cars they had. So you can see why he's always miserable and creeping around management. I feel sorry for the man.' Shaun nodded his head slowly as though he meant it.

'I don't. His problems have nothing to do with why he dislikes me. Everyone has a history, some good, some not so good. He's old enough to move on.'

'True.'

I had no sympathy for Tom Greenfield-Crown. The cheating bastard deserved everything he got. One day in the not too distant future I might just make sure that happened. He'd have something else to lose.

If he did lose it, all of his undoing would be derived from his own rapacious desire to take what he shouldn't. Somehow Tom felt entitled, that he could substantiate his methods as a replacement, for that which had been taken away. When the timing was right, I could intervene, impinge upon his duplicitous fraternising, whilst observing him squirm at the result. Umm, it was tempting.

'Okay Shaun, I'm off. It's six forty-five and there's a footie match on. Let me know first if you do anything about leaving. I'm warning you.'

Shaun smiled and we both got up and left as the pub steadily welcomed in more customers.

ALL GOOD THINGS…

42

I never believed in coincidences until the following day.

We'd stayed over in Birmingham separately. Jennifer had forced me to stay at hers. She wouldn't hear of me staying over in a hotel, when she lived so nearby.

Shaun, myself and Tom were in the Birmingham office for a day's training in the morning, on a new quoting tool that Eiron's development team had created.

As we all gathered slowly for the ten o'clock start, Shaun and I overhead some of the other field saleswomen talking about Victoria and Tom.

Our heads both spun around when one the women said that Tom's wife was in a hotel bar last night and heard his name mentioned. Shaun and I tried to shift ourselves over to hear more, but the trainer shouted for everyone to take their seats. We both had worried looks on our faces.

Tom sat beside Victoria who gave me a sharp look. Shaun told me not to worry and to leave them to it.

The trainer droned on and about how beneficial the tool would be. How we could quote for customer request right then and there on the customer's site. If I was paying my usual full attention, I'm sure whatever he was saying was useful.

Errol came in late, slipping onto the back row of theatre-style seats. I turned around and nodded at him. He raised his right hand to acknowledge me.

At the interval, which could not have come sooner, I made an effort to go over to Victoria.

'You okay, Vicky? Everything going well?' Tom's eyes followed me like a hawk.

'Yeah, fine. Thanks for asking. What about you?'

'Could be better, as always, but yeah, I'm getting there,' I replied with a rueful smile.

Then I had to say the words. I'd held them back for too long. The trio of me, Tom and Victoria stood quietly near the wall of the large reception area of the Birmingham office.

'This may not be any of my business but—' Tom interjected right there.

'That's right, it's not. Don't say another word, alright?' he told me firmly.

'Let me finish,' I bounced back. Victoria watched my face and knew I was not to be trifled with. She also looked a little worried. She must have heard the rumours.

'Look, Vicky. You know I like you. However, I'm not doing this because of that, believe me or not, it's up to you.'

Then she jumped in. It was as if the penny had dropped. A few of the Birmingham sales girls were looking at us.

That day of reckoning, I had told myself it would be in the near future. So maybe I was right, just not too specific. As delectable as Victoria was, I was disappointed she couldn't decipher the real Tom Greenfield-Crown. Gathered the necessary evidence, each component to determine what, or really who she was seeing. Like the waves of the sea building momentum, Tom was the beach and the surf was up.

Victoria turned to face Tom. Her piercing green eyes bore into him.

'Shit, you're married and it's true. Aren't you?' She raised her voice slightly, emphasising her last two words.

Tom was taken aback. Her words, not mine. Wow, she said it, not me. Served the bastard right.

I walked off and left them to it. *Get out of that one,* I thought, *you degenerate son-of-a-bitch.*

Shaun sauntered across towards me. Grinning.

'You told her, didn't you?'

Without replying immediately, I shook my head. Shaun raised his hands in surprise. Then I told him.

'She guessed.'

'Bloody hell. Yeah, that makes sense. You know what we heard this morning.' I nodded my head to agree.

As we headed back into the meeting room, which was to the left of the reception area, Tom and Victoria pushed by us, Tom following a pissed off Victoria. That brought a smile to our faces. My smile, however, was tinged with sadness. She should have known.

Halfway through the next section, we could hear some sort of commotion. Voices being raised from reception. Errol signalled the trainer to say he would go and ask whoever it was to keep the noise down. He left the room and we carried on.

Three minutes later Errol popped his head around the door of the room and asked for Tom to come out. Shaun and I were intrigued. So was everyone else.

Tom left the room with Vicky's eyes following him every step of the way. Errol closed the door again. I stepped out after him, as though to use the toilet.

At reception I witnessed the very lifelike sight of Tom's wife. Oh shit.

She started yelling.

'You bastard, how could you do this to our son? You cheating bastard! Well don't bother coming back home, you can take these.' She had thrown a suitcase full of Tom's clothes all over the reception floor.

I looked up and the first floor had as many people as I could count, standing over the atrium viewing the ongoing scene.

'Whoever this Victoria is, you can keep the bitch. She's probably not the first of your whores!' Tom's wife was sobbing, uncontrollable, distraught.

She calmed a little and Errol turned to see me behind him.

'Get Vicky out of that room and up the stairs around the back.'

'Okay. Done.'

I rotated to go back when there coming towards me was Vicky. Damn.

Tom was trying to apologise, yet he had no recourse with his incoherent and potentially violent wife.

Errol raised his hands to his head when he saw Victoria behind me.

He moved swiftly to try and remove the match from igniting the fire. It was too late. Tom lit the fuse.

Frustrated by not getting through to his wife, he saw Victoria and lost concentration.

'Vicky, go back in...' That's all he had to say.

Tom's wife pushed us, reached out and punched Victoria across her face. Victoria yelped in pain and headed for the linoleum floor with a thump.

I could hear the gasps everywhere. Without warning Tom and I, for the first time, grabbed his wife by an arm each and marched her into another of the meeting rooms.

Errol ran to Vicky's attention.

The receptionist pulled out the first aid kit.

I left Tom and his wife in the Tower room alone.

Back at reception, Errol shouted to everyone watching, that it was over and to get back to work. I'd never seen anything like it.

Neither had Walter Baker, who had a bird's-eye view from behind the smoked-glass-encased reception desk.

'Errol, Justin, I want a report on this and tell that Tom fella to see me after he's finished patching up his marital affairs!'

Errol nodded. I stood there like a statue not sure what to do or say. Errol touched my arm and we ventured back toward our training room.

'Okay – not one word to anyone. Not even Shaun for now. Agreed?' Errol was as serious as I'd ever seen him.

'Agreed.'

We sat through our training until lunch. I was guaranteed that Shaun would ask what happened. I didn't tell him. Although, I was sure this 'front pager' event, meant he'd learn soon enough.

Errol explained to the trainer that we would not be going back in.

We told Walter everything and his new temporary secretary took down copious notes. I noticed Errol's eyes rolling over her curvaceous body. She noticed and I caught her, but she got off on it. One of those women. Loved the attention, yet wouldn't let a man near her.

When we left the room, she gave Errol a come-on smile. Errol loved it and duly reciprocated. I raised my eyebrows and walked out ahead of him.

Downstairs, with his life latterly in tatters and all over the Eiron floor, sat a beleaguered Tom Greenfield-Crown. In reception, Errol called to Tom; the call disturbed his ruinous reverie, and Tom looked up at Errol.

'Time to see your uncle.' I shot Errol a quizzical look.

Uncle. The shit-stirring bastard. I wondered if Walter had called Tom's wife to tell her about the affair, or at least to confirm it. Something had gone on, and I wasn't sure what. This was news of the highest order. Blurted out like everyone already knew this was the case.

Errol gave me a short version of the family history. How Walter's two wives had cheated on him and how he hated anyone who did it.

Errol said it as though he agreed entirely. That was rich coming from Errol. However, pardon me and the phrase, but that was the pot calling the kettle black.

Now I understood why Tom got the job in the first place and he didn't automatically get promoted. His fraternising with Victoria Shepard. Her card could be marked because of this, if Walter decided to be vindictive, which came easy to him.

I would love to be a fly on the wall when they met. What would Walter say to his nephew, Mr Greenfield-Crown?

43

The next few weeks passed quietly. We all did our best under the immense pressure we that pervaded.

I knew I wouldn't make my Q2 goal. Shaun was more concerned about going back home. His decision to settle down seemed a timely move after Tom's humiliation.

My evenings and weekends were routine and getting on top of me. Sex with Chelsea solved a lot of angst in me, but it wasn't the long-term solution. Her brat of a son, really began to get to me. Yet I had no release.

Shaun buggered off to Dublin for a nearly a week. Errol never seemed to be home. Elisa was getting pissed off. So was I when he started to ask me to cover for him. I reminded him of Tom, although Errol reminded me of two 'life rules' that his father told him.

No. 2 – DON'T GET CAUGHT.

No. 1 - DON'T BOAST and you won't get caught.

Errol's mood was invincible, confident. I hated lying for him. And maybe I confused the lines between integrity and honesty. Blurry, completely.

Luckily I had one outlet. A stable source of normality, laughter, a vortex of good company and relaxation. Mary Leadbetter.

I called, we met, and we had a great time.

'Don't feel embarrassed to ever call me, Justin. Whether I'm seeing someone or not. I hope you and I can always do this. I like doing this with you. No strings, just a chance for both of us to feel better.'

'You took all the words out of my mouth!' I jested.

On our way home, we met up with Emily and Shaun. That did

worry me. Shaun and Emily. She had a new boyfriend and wouldn't say who. It got me thinking.

'So where have you guys been?' I asked with trepidation, nervous at the sight of Shaun with my sister.

'Just a for a few bevvies down at the local ur...' He was trying to concoct a story, but was obviously flustered my seeing him.

'It doesn't matter, Shaun. I get the gist.'

Shaun looked sheepish. So did Emily.

We decided to all get a taxi home together. As the taxi drove us toward Wollaton, I noticed what looked like the temporary secretary at work. She was with a black guy. It was Errol. They walked up towards a group of maisonettes. I hoped no one else saw them.

'Shit, that's Errol and that fit temp. The lucky bastard,' Shaun called out. Emily elbowed him in his ribs. Mary didn't say a word. I shook my head.

Mary declared in a cold, firm voice to the taxi driver to stop around the corner. I hoped she wouldn't intervene. There was no way of covering up Errol's alleged infidelity. The proof was incidental so far. He could be as I was with Mary. She would have none of that.

The ramifications for Errol were immeasurable. Elisa would show no dispensation whatsoever.

We all got out and paid the taxi driver. I felt awful, effectively spying on my boss and best friend. The situation was now out of my fiefdom. Errol was on his own and in the lap of the gods.

Ten minutes passed.

'Justin, come with me, we're going in.' Mary's voice and tone demanded I go without resistance. Should I man up and refuse, even though it was the correct moral call? I needed some steel, or a contingency plan for this sort of delinquent behaviour, once again. Invariably, I, Justin Whalley, bowed to the greater sense of what was deemed proper. Weak, some would say. Nevertheless, Errol brought whatever was about to occur on himself. A grown man, broad shoulders and an unwavering passion for clandestine fraternising, now was ready to be exposed as a double agent of sorts.

The light which had being turned on, displayed two shadows. Then the curtains were drawn. We approached a front door, in wood, which had been varnished. An outside light shone onto the door.

Listening carefully, I heard the all too familiar sounds of groaning. Not in pain, sheer deep, longing ecstasy. The evidence moved from circumstantial to firm when the temp cried out Errol's name, time after time. He was indeed a lucky bastard. Even for ten or fifteen minutes. Would it be worth it? At that moment, I would be the wrong man to ask.

Mary rapped on the door. And again.

The girl shouted to ask who it was.

'It's Errol's girlfriend, that's who.'

There must have been mass panic inside as an object fell to the floor and smashed. I can only imagine the connotations ricocheting around Errol's pleasured mind, fracturing that passionate moment into a thousand pieces. Following swiftly, like a whirlwind in his path, would be the utter, vitriolic abuse he'd have to endure from his fiancée Elisa. That would only be the beginning of a series of arduous, pernicious episodes, promptly delivered by a rifle in the hands of Elisa.

We left the scene as Mary pulled me away to follow her. She'd done what she came to do.

'You'd better tell him to tell Elisa what he's been doing. You've got a week. That's long enough. If you don't I will.' Mary was forthright and direct.

My heart sagged. My head throbbed. Errol, my best friend and manager. Versus a new friendship that was now being tested. I despised confrontations.

We walked Mary home and then Emily, Shaun and I pondered on what to do about Errol.

When I got home, my answerphone light was flashing. Errol left a message, for me to cover for him. To say he was staying over at mine. Goodness knows whether he dared to go back home tonight. Knowing Errol he'd have a story ready. Smooth and plausible. No stuttering. He would never falter in his response. No wavering in his conjured story.

Errol with some fortune and grace from the unforgiving Mary Leadbetter, now occupied the requisite time to conjure the counteracting message he would need for Elisa. Somehow from all the occasions and history I had with Errol, my usual high confidence rating reduced somewhat. It just didn't feel quite right. Whatever ingenious scheme Errol had brewing over the proceeding twenty-four hours, wouldn't cut it. This was one almighty intricate bomb, that the master of diffusion, I believe, would not be able to stop exploding.

After such a long, hectic, fretful or fruitful night, depending where you were standing, I told Shaun he could sleep in my spare room or I could call a taxi. Once I detailed my home situation, that my partner and girlfriend Chelsea and Robert were there, he asked for the taxi option.

Initially I didn't know what to think of his decision. I could have been oversensitive, with everything that was happening everywhere. At work, at home and now with Errol. It reminded me of fireworks. All shooting in different directions. You never know if you need to duck, or get hit. Or simply sit back and enjoy the splendour of them. Their colours. Their sounds. The spectacular sparkling nature of them.

Anyway, Shaun and I agreed that we would talk in the morning about Errol and what to do about it. In my book, that grace that

Mary had seen fit to emancipate Errol would not be long enough. With that in mind, Mary would never extend that period once it had been set. And why should she?

44

We both had customer meetings the following morning. Shaun's meeting, however, was further away and he wouldn't be back until late in the afternoon. We spoke mobile to mobile.

'I called Errol first thing this morning, no reply from his mobile,' I told Shaun.

'Who knows where he is. I just hope we can get to him in time. Do you think Mary will tell Elisa?' Shaun asked.

'Maybe. She's pissed. And she's loyal to Elisa. Worse still,' Shaun interrupted me, hearing the inflection in my voice drop.

'What? What's worse?' I could hear the motorway noise reverberating in background.

'You didn't know?'

'Know what?' Shaun's tone raised a few octaves, into a higher pitch.

'Mary and Errol hate each other. She's never trusted him, ever since Errol and Elisa were together. I suppose her long-term view has been proved correct.'

'Shit.'

'Exactly.'

Shaun said nothing for a second whilst the news sunk into his simple, straight forward mind.

'You still in shock?' I asked.

'No. No, I'm not, I'm just thinkin' maybe Errol will be. No way out, I think. Or maybe…' His voice trailed off. Now it was my turn to pursue Shaun's line of thinking, for his revelation or idea.

'Yeah. Maybe…'

'What time are you getting back to the office today?' Shaun asked, as the cacophonous sound of an emergency services vehicle or more than one echoed loudly in the background. Goodness knows where he was driving.

'Before you I suspect. Why?' I was intrigued and cautious.

'Why don't you speak to this girl? This temp. See if you can get her to make up a story and then tell Errol the same one, so it matches.'

'Okay. I'll have a word, if she's in our office. Don't know what good it'll do, but Errol better not forget this, if it works.'

Shaun chuckled a little laugh. We knew deep down Errol would fry for this. His only chance of valediction would be if Mary hadn't been there. I suppose once again, it was my fault in some indirect way. Somehow I had developed a chronic knack for being in the middle of these situations. I felt like a cartoon character that has a single nimbus cloud following overhead. Every now and then it pisses on me. Hopefully one day it might go away.

*

Back in the office, not long after I had set up my laptop, I saw her come out of Errol's office. Although I hadn't seen Errol's car in the car park. Standing up, I walked over to his office and looked in. Tom was in there and so was Errol and the Human Resources manager. I'd wait to get the full SP on that one.

I tapped the temp on her right shoulder. She turned to me, her face lit up. Her smouldering eyes fixed on mine. I had to pinch myself to get out of the split-second trance.

'We better have a word.' Her expression disappeared.

In a quiet area which surrounded the atrium, we talked briefly about the other night. It didn't take much to get Sally to admit to what had happened. She listed the events of how long her relationship had been going on for. 'How did he do it?' I kept asking myself. She was far too young and model like to be fraternising with a mid-thirty-year-old man such as Errol Hughes. I, of course, I was insanely jealous.

Sally apologised several times and I stopped her from shedding too many tears. We had to keep this under wraps as much as we could.

I sent her back to her station and desperately wanted to fill Errol in. Who cares what happened to Tom? He deserved everything he got. A forty-two-year-old man with a lovely woman like Vicky Shepard, who also should have known better. She should have guessed he was married or at least asked. She disappointed me.

When I returned to my desk, I couldn't believe who was sitting at Tom's. I swallowed hard and sat down.

'Hiya. Fancy you being here today.' I wasn't sure what my salutation meant, but I said it anyway.

'I like to get around, you know me,' Vicky Shepard responded. I couldn't say what I really thought.

'I had heard.' She gave me a filthy look. I smiled. She didn't speak to me again.

At ten minutes after five Tom emerged with the HR manager and Errol, who look tired, and for the first time ever, slightly dishevelled. They all shook hands which worried me. It looked too formal. The worry was plain to witness on Vicky's face. If she was here as his supporter, then I was terribly disappointed.

Without waiting to view the unfolding scene, I packed my things away and left. Before going I tapped on Errol's office door and popped my head around.

'I'll call you later or whenever you're free, on your mobile. Leave it on. Okay?'

Errol didn't look up at me.

'Okay. I might not be available tonight, but give me a try anyway. I'll speak soon. Cheers.'

I closed his door and left the office. As I did, I looked at Tom's face. His eyes were puffy, and red. Bags sat underneath them, as though he'd had very little or no sleep. His face looked emaciated, as though he hadn't been eating. Maybe he was living and sleeping rough. His wife had kicked him out.

He looked ten times worse than Errol. What the hell was going on? Someone had to find out. I had Chelsea and Robert to consider too. This was more important.

45

To my utter surprise Errol answered his mobile when I called him at around nine in the evening.

'Yo, it's Justin.'

'Yeah. Okay, haven't got much time, Just. What did you want to tell me?' Errol's response was slightly terse and unexpected.

'Oh, nothing much really.' I sighed in a matter-of-fact way to show I didn't really care. 'Just to say that Mary Leadbetter knows you're screwing around with the Sally the temp. Oh, and by the way so do I, and Shaun. Mary's given us a few days' grace to tell you to call it off. If you don't she's itching to pull that trigger she has her finger on aimed at you.'

Errol's silence meant he understood the ramifications of Mary telling his long-time partner and correctly, his fiancée Elisa, of his infidelity. I deliberately waited for Errol to respond.

'Yeah, thanks Just.' Errol cleared his throat. 'She's a fantastic girl. We've got so much in common. I don't know if I can stop seeing her.' His voice softened and sounded needy. Bloody hell, Errol the master of women Hughes had fallen for a younger woman. Hook, line and sinker.

'I take it you're not speaking about your Elisa, are you?' I couldn't resist being flippant.

Errol stuttered a with a sound between a cough and a forced laugh, that didn't quite come out as either.

'So you're in love with the leggy Sally. Can't blame you, mate, but you'd better sort out Elisa and fast. That's if you don't want to give Mary the pleasure,' I told Errol.

'It was always one the cards, Just. I'll tell her tonight. Get it over with. I'm looking at renting an apartment near the city centre anyway. May as well make the move.'

'Shit, you've got this all planned out.' It seemed Errol used that grace period effectively to concoct his next move. Agile, flexible and able to shift direction as a chameleon changes colour to adapt to its environment. Maybe that should be Errol's new name.

'I didn't mean to, Just, however I always remind myself to keep a spare.'

'What?'

'A back-up plan. If anything goes wrong have something to fall back on.'

'I see.'

Errol wrapped up our conversation after explaining how he felt about Sally. The differences between her and Elisa. Elisa would be heartbroken. Mary would be glad. I didn't know how to feel. On the fence, I suppose. Somewhere in the middle, between confrontation and turning the other cheek. I liked Elisa. However, who said life is a bowl of cherries?

Errol wouldn't disclose any information about Tom and the meeting they had. He jokingly said it was 'classified'.

We said our goodbyes and an ambiguous thought spun in my head in all different directions, about what Errol had told me.

Sitting in my TV armchair, I waited for Chelsea to come home. Luckily Robert had gone to bed without any bribery from me. I, too, had some difficult discussions to have with Chelsea. I just had to find that prodigious 'right time' to talk to her. I hoped it would be soon.

It was ten minutes after eleven when I was abruptly awoken by the front door slamming.

'Hiya Chelsea.' She flashed that amazing smile of hers at me.

'Hellooo Justin. Have you been waiting up for me? What have you been waiting for?' She grinned wickedly and opened up her arms. She was consummately drunk. I could smell her from across the lounge.

'Aren't you gonna hug your girlfriend?' She threw off her coat and shook her breasts like a lap dancer would on stage (I presumed).

'Wow. You must have had a good night. You er… ready for bed?' I raised my eyebrows in quick succession. She knew what that meant.

'Okay, Mr Whalley, let me run upstairs and get myself ready. I hope you've got the energy for a long night.' Now she raised her eyebrows and ran upstairs.

I attempted to follow her, but was halted by the phone ringing in the hallway.

'Hello?' I was apprehensive of answering due to the lateness of the call. My energy levels were being recharged.

'Justin?' a shaky female voice said.

'Yeah. Oh, Mary, what's wrong?' I said cautiously, yet deep down I knew what the call was about.

'That bastard, that fucking bastard's dumped Elisa for some young slut. Elisa's here on my sofa crying her eyes out. I hope he drops dead, Justin. He's a wicked, wicked man.'

What could I say?

'Look, Mary, I cannot say how sorry I am. Really. I mean it. I know this is no comfort, and maybe she's better off without him.'

Mary controlled her breathing, by taking deep breaths. Elisa's audible sobbing could easily be heard echoing in the background. My stomach churned, with the fact that I had known about my best friend's indiscretion. I could do nothing to stop the wheels of social relationships and interaction from turning. I also felt guilty for not doing enough or anything to postpone or prevent this from happening.

'Do you want me to come over?' It was the only on-the-spot-reaction answer I could muster.

'Only if it's not too much trouble. Elisa would like it too. I know it's going to be difficult, but do it for me?' Mary's voice pleaded to my chivalrous side. She'd been there for me and now it was time to reciprocate. Do the decent, honourable thing. So I did.

46

Following my Mary Nightingale visit to see the beleaguered Elisa and the furious, yet concerned Mary, I had very little to say to Errol whenever our paths crossed at work. Only if I needed to know about any work-related matters would I speak to him. It was the first real strain on our relationship. A test or multiple attributes in any relationship. Like his with Elisa or even now with the sumptuous Sally. Who knew what would occur next?

I was not an angel, however, Errol Hughes had led Elisa along the path for over a decade. A merry dance of a waltz gliding foot to foot with your partner. Giving the genuine impression of closeness, a bond of love shared between two people. Conversely Errol had a Paso Doble, in the background, that issued the fire, heat and the anger.

Again I pondered, stirring on whether Elisa paid enough attention to the real signs. Who am I to say? Yet like Victoria she too possibly had some inkling, just a nugget of a second shooter hiding in the bushes. If this is what the 'blind' side of love is, I hope I don't get it.

Retrospect allows me to see what I could have done better or changed. For Elisa's sake. For her wellbeing and mental health, could she have made the move to someone else, sooner?

*

Three days and the weekend had gone by and Tom was nowhere to be seen. I asked Errol to get in contact with his wife. He told me HR had already done that, as anyone ill for more than two days, gets a return-to-work interview.

Tom's wife couldn't tell HR where he was as she'd thrown him out nearly two weeks ago. She told them she didn't care where he was. So I tried my route of information.

'Vicky, is that you? It's Justin.'

'Yeah, what do you want?' She was abrupt, just because it was me.

'Give me a straight answer and don't infer anything by what I'm about to ask.' I was firm back.

'What is it?'

'Have you seen or heard from Tom?'

'Piss off, you Whalley!'

I responded with a false laugh. Then I gave it to her.

'Shut the fuck up, Vicky. Tom has gone missing and no one knows where he is. So once again, have you seen or heard from him recently!' I looked around the office to check if anyone heard my caustic language.

I could hear Vicky gasp with astonishment. I was mortified by what I'd said, but there was no time to piss around.

Questioning once again my motives for playing Columbo on the asshole that made my work life a misery, created some type of paradox in me. Why was I of all people doing this? I shouldn't care less about that man. Yet something judicious inside me, set my moral high standards into engagement mode.

'No, no I haven't. I'm sorry Justin, I'm worried about him, not the way you think. The bastard cheated on me and his wife. I think he might do something stupid.'

'What do you mean?'

'I think he was into drugs. Cocaine or heroin, I'm not sure. I only saw him high once. He could get violent. Especially if he'd being drinking as well. Whiskey mostly.' Vicky's voice began to crack as she revealed painful, secretive personal details about Tom.

Shaun and I always suspected something like this. Vicky Shepard had just proved us right. We hoped we wouldn't be.

When I finished talking to Vicky, I promised I would keep her up to date. She told me she would drive up to Nottingham and work from our office for the next week, until we had information on Tom. Was that an exculpatory move on Vicky's part? Or simply a concerned work colleague, who had once known the subject on a personal, sensitive level. I wasn't the real Columbo, for surmising Vicky's true reasons, so maybe I should remind myself who I really am.

I called Errol and told him the latest, advising him to call the police, for various reasons.

Errol agreed and got onto it immediately.

Three hours later, just prior to going home, Errol came out of his office ashen faced. Shaun who had arrived an hour earlier watched Errol come over to the sales floor. He asked everyone to gather around. It wasn't going to be good news. I saw it in Errol's eyes. I felt it in my gut.

'People, I have some very sad news. Most of you here know Tom Greenfield-Crown. Unfortunately he is no longer with us. He died in a car crash three days ago. His body was found in a ditch near the Trent embankments. Please do not reveal this to anyone else outside this office. I will let you know more when I have it.'

It was what I expected and more terrible than I could have ever imagined.

47

The next few hours passed by as though we were all in a parallel universe. The strangest feelings absorbed by mind.

Victoria Shepard wept on my shoulder for nearly an hour in one of the meeting rooms. I couldn't console her. She was uncontrollably crying, sobbing streams of tears, which flooded her mascara and clown-like face. I had run out of tissues and my jacket was soaked. I held her tightly and she nuzzled her head into my chest.

Shaun tapped on the door and I signalled him to enter. Vicky didn't look up.

'Errol wants to see you both. And by the way, I'm genuinely sorry. If there's anything I can do, just say the word.'

'Thanks,' I whispered in return.

Shaun displayed a look of bewilderment that I'd never witnessed before. As much as he and I didn't favour Tom, his untimely death made us think. It made me think.

Exoneration. What a topic. From everything he'd done. Wilfully, willingly, deceitful to those close to him. Maybe even to his dreaded uncle, Mr Walter Baker. What a circle of shit that now pervaded. This superseded by a biggest of margins, the 'wife throwing his clothes into our office reception floor' debacle into perspective. Tom Greenfield-Crown had his exoneration. A final one. For himself, although not from his crimes. Yet I sensed cautiously, there'd be more recriminations to follow, considering what Shaun and I believed and Victoria understood.

'Vicky, do you feel up to seeing Errol? He may have some news about Tom,' I asked her quietly.

She pulled her head away and wiped away her drying tears. I used my index finger to push her hair out of her face and behind her ears. She flashed a brief, but weak smile to say thanks.

'Why the hell am I crying over a man that treated me with such contempt? I shouldn't be crying over him. And I'm not. It's her and their little boy.'

I held both her arms and looked her in the eyes.

'You cry if you want. You don't have explain why to me or anyone else. Everyone's in shock. It's the last thing we all expected. Do you want to speak to Errol?'

'Yes. I will. Will you come in with me?'

'Of course.'

As we walked through the open-plan office following the path that took us on the outer rims of where all the desks were located, everyone stood in transient silence looking at us. Mainly at Victoria Shepard. If anyone did not know about her affair with Tom, then they did now. Errol was at his door and beckoned us in.

'Take a seat,' Errol told us in a serene tone of voice. 'I won't drag this out and won't be easy for anyone to hear. Walter is devastated and has asked me to pass on this information. However I must ask, and this is very important, that what I'm about to tell must not leave this room.'

Vicky looked across at me. I returned her look with one of in trepidation. Errol continued. He was calm, professional, doing his best to cover his innermost emotions.

'The police have informed Walter that Tom died of a heart attack.'

Vicky and I both audibly gasped. Errol raised his right hand, to show that there was more.

'Yeah, exactly what I thought. Anyway, that wasn't it. They tested his blood, and performed a toxicology scan or something it's called, to check if he'd been drinking. He had. Four times over the limit.'

That last sentence made my blood rise in temperature. I shook my head and Errol, I hoped, would understand why. Tom's death was becoming harder to forgive.

'And that's not the worst part,' Errol continued. 'From the tests they did they found significant traces of cocaine. Yep, that's right. It seems the concoction of drink and drugs killed him. He overdosed. The heart attack story was just that, a story. In reality his heart did stop working, so technically we're not lying, not that it matters.'

'Shaun and I suspected he was mixed up in something like that.'

Vicky threw me a sharp look. Errol watched in utter surprise. He had no idea. I presumed Walter didn't either.

'Didn't you tell anyone or say anything to him?' Errol asked, bemused by me keeping it a secret.

I looked at Vicky, who hung her head in shame. Errol noticed and slumped back into his chair.

'Bloody hell. How many other people knew about this?'

'Don't shoot the messenger, Errol, I suspected. Shaun and I had no proof whatsoever.'

'Yes, that's true, I guessed he did, but I thought, he could… er, control it… Plus I didn't understand what kind of drugs he was taking.' Victoria stuttered an embarrassed reply.

'Well whatever the history is, it's just that now, history. As cruel as this sounds, life goes on. If he died because of his addiction, then there's nothing anyone could have done to stop him. I just hope his wife manages okay.'

Errol suggested that Vicky go home. He told me after Vicky left the room, that the police were looking into where the drugs came from as they found a half a kilo in Tom's car. The drug piece worried me for more than one reason.

The office was decimated when I returned to my desk. I found a Post-it note stuck to my screen from Victoria.

Thanks for today, I'm staying in a hotel, not sure where, but call me on my mobile. Would love to talk. Love Vicky xx.

I exhaled heavily as a million thoughts flashed through my mind – again. I took the note and placed it in my right jacket pocket. Before logging off my computer I created a new email and sent it to 'office-nots-all', and 'office-birm-all' so that it would go to everyone in the Birmingham and Nottingham offices.

All

By now you will have learned of the tragic death of our colleague Tom Greenfield-Crown. As a mark of respect, and to support his wife and young son, I'm asking everyone who knew him to send a small donation which I will collect and pass on.
 Any donation will be appreciated and I will find out if some of us will be allowed to attend the funeral. As sad as this situation is, Tom would want us to be successful. Let's do it for him and continue to work and succeed when and where we can.
 Thanks for listening.

Kind regards
Justin Whalley.

I hit the send button and watched the email disappear.
 That was me Justin Whalley taking up the baton for Eiron. For his traumatised uncle and my ultimate boss Walter Baker. Expressing

leadership skills in communication to wider sales and employee pool. No time, however, for congratulating myself. People were here hurting in the same way I could imagine. Certainly empathise with. So many ambiguous, mind-splitting views arrived at my mental door, and I had no reason to let them in. Remaining focussed, dispassionate to some degree, earned me the right to send that email, that needed doing. I'm hoping, when the moment arrives, these situations will be remembered for the correct reasons.

As I packed away my laptop, I saw Errol leave the building with Sally. No hope of getting back with Elisa. It worried me that after so long with one person, a relationship could just so easily disintegrate. Tom's death did nothing to interrupt Errol's love life. That's the way it should be. Life does go on and Tom was no angel to himself or anyone he supposedly loved.

The taste of disdain still remained at the back of my throat over what Errol had done. Vicky was my main concern. I couldn't imagine what she and more so Tom's wife and son must be going through. Well, I had an idea and I didn't want to ever feel like it again. If it could be avoided. The peace and quiet of the office programmed my memory to go and see my mum. Something that always benefited me, in terms of advice, solemnity and clear-headedness that one requires when the world of your close ones turns upside down.

Working out where I could stop to buy some flowers, I plotted my route home. I also reserved some time to call Victoria.

After what took place earlier, our exposure to the shocking news that informed us about the road to perdition that Tom decide to drive down, I could only ask myself, what more could I do? Duty had to follow, however, so as per my current high moral standing my first call was to Chelsea, to let her know I would be late home tonight.

48

To my utter surprise Victoria sounded like a different person when I called her. Although her voice trembled in parts, she was mostly getting back to her normal sprightly self. She told me she was going to do her best to forget Tom, yet understood realistically it would not be a simple task.

I congratulated her and I could hear her smiling on the other end of the phone. It made my evening.

That night I was distant from Chelsea. She sensed something was wrong and kept asking me. When I finally acquiesced and informed her of what happened at work, she wanted to cuddle me even more. It wasn't what I wanted. I felt awful, disingenuous even, however I needed to think about things on my own. Have a clear head. My guilt increased when I heard Chelsea crying next to me in bed. My emotional rollercoaster's wheels were ready to fly off, throwing me into the air completely out of control. Somehow, I needed strength from within to master all the loose ends that required tying off.

The next two days zipped by. To my utter astonishment, the collection for Tom was building momentum. I counted, with Shaun's help, up to four hundred and twenty-two pounds and eighteen pence. Cheques had arrived in the post, with donations ranging from fifty pence to twenty pounds.

Errol circulated an email informing everyone of the date and time of the funeral. He mentioned that he had spoken to Tom's wife and how she thanked Eiron for their support and for sorting out Tom's death benefits. Anyone who wanted to go to the funeral had to notify their line manager, in order to ensure the phones were covered with enough staff.

There were, however, the dissidents who believed Tom should not be honoured. He was a selfish womaniser who deserved what came to him. His just desserts. Those voters against, were the exception.

On Friday at 11am, on a lukewarm drizzling day, a funeral hearse parked inside the local two-thirds-full cemetery. I viewed the scene of everyone person dressed in black or navy standing over the graveside as the priest read out some words of comfort and remembrance of Tom's life. His wife and young son stood bravely without cover from any umbrellas as the windswept the drizzle back and forth across the graveside.

As the coffin was lowered into the grave, Tom's wife broke down in tears. Walter walked over and supported her. He held his grand-nephew's hand and stooped down to talk to him.

Everyone's eyes locked onto Walter Baker. I didn't think I'd ever see him display any emotion. This was the first time.

Walter encouraged Tom's wife and son to collect some earth and toss it onto the coffin. Brave lad, I thought, barely six years old. And so was Victoria, for staying away. She wanted to spare Tom's wife any further embarrassment and of course their son.

Shaun and I approached Tom's wife after the crowd had begun to dissipate, to pass on our condolences. I did feel somewhat like a hypocrite because I never really liked Tom, and the manner or reason for what he did was self-inflicted. He did deserve what he got, however, those he left behind didn't. How do you split loyalties like that? I didn't have the answer, so played the concerned work colleague, as did Shaun.

She smiled, I think at us, and thanked us politely for coming. My hunch was that she didn't seem all that upset about her cheating husband dying, particularly the way he left this mortal coil.

It wasn't until after the crowds had gone that Shaun told me, that the police had originally questioned Tom's wife. As they were separated, they thought she may have played a role in his death. I told Shaun that would be ridiculous. He agreed. Nevertheless, the police were following up all leads.

As we walked back to our cars, Shaun told me he was definitely leaving to move back to Dublin. It was sad news on top of what was happening around me. I couldn't blame him.

I joked and said it would give me somewhere to go and maybe find a lovely Irish woman to settle down with. Shaun said I'd have no problem, as he'd set me up with one of his cousins. I responded by saying I wasn't sure if he could find someone of a high enough calibre. He told me to piss off.

We ventured our separate ways, with my mind flicking back and forth over Tom's wife and her son. Vicky sat alone in some hotel probably crying or bored shitless. Chelsea at work and her precocious little Robert, who was slowly becoming a thorn in my side. Shaun soon to skulk off back to Dublin. And Errol rolling around with the leggy and the sexual 'one look and you're turned on' Sally. Who said my life wasn't exciting?

49

The excitement got a bit too much when Emily called me, leaving a frantic message on my answerphone:

"Justin, can you come to the police station on Mansfield Road? They want to question me about some guy you worked with called Tom." She snivelled for a second and her breathing was short and laboured.

"Come as soon as you get the message. I've no one else to call." The phone died.

I couldn't catch my breath. What the hell could Emily have in connection with Tom's death?

Without stopping to tell Chelsea where I was going, I shouted that I had to leave in a hurried urgent voice.

'What about your din…' Her words faded as I slammed the door behind and ran to my car.

Chelsea had tried in vain to open me up about Tom's death. It wasn't that particular niggle that was bothering me. Her frustration was obvious and I apologised to her, but there was more than her and Robert on my mind and now this.

The early evening traffic was lighter than I expected. I pushed my Jaguar XF through the lights that were turning red. Swept around traffic islands without hesitation. Horns tooted and blasted at me, although I ignored them all. Once onto Mansfield road I slowed a little and drove down the hill towards the city centre. Following a one-way system and avoiding the road works for the tram system, I pulled into a space across the road from the station. Looking towards the police station, I saw Emily coming out in tears.

Once it was clear, I got out of the car can ran across the road. She saw me and immediately began sobbing loudly.

'What's happened, Em? Speak to me, what have you done?'

She shook her head without saying a word.

'What did they want with you? And why has it got anything to do with Tom's death?'

She calmed herself a little after a coughing fit. I pulled a handkerchief out of my trouser pocket and gave it to her.

'Can we get in the car first?'

'Okay.'

Two policemen watched us cross the road and get into the car. I wondered if they thought I was her boyfriend or partner. I sped away and drove back to Emily's house.

Once I'd put the kettle on and sorted out two clean cups from her newly fitted kitchen, we sat down in the living room.

'Come on, now Em, what's going on?'

She took a deep breath.

'You're not going to like this, Just, but I, er, you know I smoke every now and then.' She paused.

'Yeah, go on.' My mind was racing now with endless possibilities.

'It wasn't just cigarettes…'

'Shit, Emily, are you saying you're into drugs!' I sounded like my mum or dad.

'Only cannabis or some ecstasy for when I'm out partying.'

'You silly, silly girl. Do you know what that shit does to you? One tablet can kill you or at least fuck your brain up!' I got to my feet with hands on hips, pacing the room. The kettle had boiled, but I was in no mood for tea. I scratched my head, considering what led my lovely 'innocent' sister down this particular spiralling staircase.

'So, okay you're a druggie,' she glared at me, 'so how the hell does this tie you with Tom's death?'

'We used the same dealer.'

'Great.' She dropped her head as though there was more to come. I felt like walking out and leaving her to 'party'. The memory of our weekend in Birmingham flashed before me. More evidential weight placed on my sister's illegal actions and friends it looked like. To consummate the illegality there was the night out in Nottingham. It began to add up. Two plus two. Always equals the same.

'And what did the police say? Are you under arrest? Do they think you're involved?'

'No, okay! No, they don't. I'm sorry I ever got mixed up with him.' I turned around to face her.

'You were seeing this dealer. A drug fucking dealer. For chrissakes!' I walked into the kitchen and gripped one of the chairs that surrounded a small circular table. This was not happening. There was no way I could let Jenny know or Mark know. I tried to calm down and searched for a proper drink in her cupboards. There was some old Jamaican rum left. I poured two glasses, laced one glass with orange juice and brought them into the room.

'Look, I'm sorry for shouting, peace offering.' I handed her the glass of rum, neat.

We clinked glasses and I sat beside her on the sofa.

'Why, Em?'

Her eyes looked forlornly at me. Begging forgiveness.

'He was cute, sexy, fun to be with. Made me laugh. Always had loads of money on him. Dressed nicely, polite, you know, probably too good to be true. And he was,' Emily lamented.

'Hey, it's not your fault. I'm glad you're not too deeply involved with this guy. I hope.'

'No bloody way. The drug squad are putting him under surveillance.

They say he's one of East Midlands' kingpins in the drug world. Apparently he gets a girlfriend like me, so he seems legit. Gets them to move in with him, or them with him. Treats them well, showering them with presents and them he has them on the hook. And if you take drugs, he'll have you doped up to the eyeballs.'

'That's a close shave, sis, very close.'

'Did you ever see Tom buy stuff?'

'Yeah, once or twice. He was well hooked up. Always had loads of cash on him. Bought half a kilo the other week, probably before he crashed.'

I sat in my sister's living room, listening to the stunts that this dealer pulled. How Tom needed the drugs to get by. Ironically it never showed at work. Whatever skills Tom had, he was a master at concealing his real personality. From everyone, especially his wife and little boy. And how did he keep it under control when he was seeing Victoria? She had an inkling, yet didn't know what to do? Or didn't want to? That's another conundrum for another day.

We finished our rum and I told Emily I would call her every day if it was necessary. I promised I would not reveal anything to our family, especially Jenny, who would be absolutely distraught.

'Look, if you want a man, I can find you one,' I told her as she walked me to my car.

'You, find me a boyfriend? Bloody hell, how things have changed.' She laughed the way she used to. Some of the fear of being questioned by the police had gone for now. A residue remained although I felt safe leaving her alone.

'I'll prime the suspect and see what he says. Would be a good man to have as brother-in-law.'

'You're serious?'

'Why not? You helped me.' I was grinning by now, but Emily

knew why I made the gesture.

'I see, you don't trust me anymore, you want to pick this guy so that you can check him out.'

'Oh shit, you've got me. I'm just looking out for you, sis, that's all.'

'Whatever.'

She waved me off and thanked me for coming to her rescue.

The sweet-tasting rum had dulled my reactions slightly, coupled with the lack of sleep I'd been getting. And I hated drinking and getting in my car to drive, even short distances.

Doing anything in the dark was never a good idea. The last thing I needed was a bruised knee from walking into the kitchen table. After I had switched on the hallway light and then the kitchen lights, I noticed a note stuck to the fridge-freezer. The house was shrouded in total darkness and I did wonder if Chelsea and Robert were in bed. They weren't. the note read:

Gone to my mother's, taken Robert. We'll talk whenever you're ready. You obviously don't need me around at the moment. Still love you loads. Chelsea xx"

Could I blame her? From the circumstantial evidence against my sister, connecting to Tom's death. Cohesively the triangle was completed by this dealer boyfriend of Emily's. You cannot make this shit up. It was all happening to me, Justin Whalley.

All I ever wanted were some simple, everyday acquaintances, from work or from play. Minimal circumspect behaviour, followed by some intermingling with the opposite sex, to keep my wheels turning.

Now this note complemented the whole day once again. Not in a pleasant, harmonic way. Just the opposite. Lightning seemed to strike, no, was in fact becoming my nemesis. Soon I'd be imbued with electro powers like one of the X-Men or another Marvel superhero character.

With my right hand, I crumpled the note and tossed it in the general direction of the bin. It was only nine twenty in the evening and my bed was calling me. The light on the answerphone was flashing. I had two messages. Whoever they were, they would have to wait until the morning. My immediate goal was for a good night's sleep. If that would be possible.

50

That gratifying slumber supported my efforts to recover from the grim reality that pervaded. Lying in my comfortable bed, there were fleeting moments of happier, calmer times. When my world and those in it, rotated as it should on its axis. No spinning off in obscure directions. Just a steady rotation, not too fast or too slow.

However, the ingredients that brought me to where I was mentally returned, unbidden. That fleeting glimpse of a 'utopian' world, was just that. Like Xanadu from a film my mum used to tell me about and had seen snippets of on a re-run.

With little immediate urgency, which there should have been, I pushed, urged my body to move. Rising out of bed to commence my daily process, I lurched from my bed to the bathroom. Once completed, the next steps followed, getting ready for work in suitable attire befitting a man of man standing.

Enjoying a fairly healthy breakfast of muesli, with warm milk, washed down with a small glass of orange juice with the bits in. Teeth brushed with my new battery-powered brush, completed with a swig of minty mouthwash. That was still required. And always ensured I had some minty chewing gum as a backup.

It wasn't until I was ready to leave for work, that I decided to listen to the messages on my home phone from last night. The ones I could not be arsed with, due to the ever suffocating tiredness that beseeched me.

The first message made me stop and listen intently. It was Victoria, asking me to come to the hotel. She sounded lucid, and confident. No hint of tremors in her voice or any wavering. I apologised quietly to her.

The second message was from Emily. She thanked me again for my help. I was expecting Chelsea to leave a message, but she didn't.

Instead, on my way from my customer meeting, which I hadn't prepared for and no one was checking on, my curiosity coupled with a secret desire to see Vicky Shepard, clouded my thinking.

My brief meeting resulted in Eiron losing another account. Our price was too high and the IT manger was a miserable tosser. Good riddance. There were plenty more customers who had money to spend, didn't wreak of BO, and had half a business brain. I stopped the meeting and left after only twenty minutes to his amazement. He tried to beat me down on price, telling me: 'There's no point continuing if you cannot agree to drop your price.'

When my reply came, it was a firm riposte.

'Eiron firmly believe that our price gives you not only the best value for money, and one of the top three companies in regards to quality for the last three years. We firmly believe in the motto – "you get what you pay for".'

He didn't like that one bit. The IT manager's face contorted with anger and disdain. I couldn't care less. The arsehole was obviously trying to make a name for himself in front of the Purchasing Director and the Finance Director. He was shot down by my missile.

Their faces were a picture to behold as I put my paperwork away in my slim briefcase. The FD sat up, wondering whether it was a sales trick of some sort. I confirmed it was wasn't when I told them, 'Gentlemen, thanks for your time today, however as you can see we will have to agree to disagree and leave things as they stand. I trust you will find another supplier who can beat our price. Whether they can match Eiron's quality of service is another matter. I'll leave the decisions up to you. Thanks.'

Without offering to shake anyone's hand I left the room in total silence.

Once in the car I drove from Cheshire back to Nottingham. On the way I stopped to purchase some flowers. Peonies, they were called. Beautiful, full-bodied flowers, in a dusty shade of pink.

Before heading to Vicky's hotel, I made a stop at the cemetery. I laid the flowers at my mother's headstone and asked her to help me sort out my life. I checked that no one was around me or in earshot. Crouched facing my mother's grave, brought a still calmness I'd never felt anywhere else. As though my dearly departed mother was reaching out to me as some apparition. A spirit, a beacon of advice, of comfort in my troubled, turbulent times.

Only now at this juncture, the pain of my mother's passing reached out to me, following Tom's death. A great loss of life, due to someone's ineptitude. Their lack of humanity. Their ultimate selfishness, thinking only of themselves, regardless of whether it was intended or not. Every now and then, there were moments that pervaded, briefly, of what happened to my mother. They disappear, as though it never occurred.

When I think I'm getting through the fog, incidents like Tom's catapult it into the foreground. It was something else to deal with. Handle in my own unique way.

In closing off my visit, I performed a short prayer. Bowing my head, I prayed silently. As I rose to my feet, moving away in the direction of the exit, still looking around me, as though I was being followed.

Ten minutes later I knocked on Victoria's hotel door. When I had called from the car, I asked her to order lunch for two. She seemed happy to hear from me.

Inside, we sat around a small table tucking into omelette and chips, with a limp-looking side salad.

'I really appreciate you coming to see me. I haven't seen anyone, in what seems like weeks,' Vicky told me.

'What about you and work? When will you go back?'

'Walter wants me back ASAP. The numbers aren't looking good again and he needs as many feet on the street as possible.'

'That sounds like Walter. Getting back to his old self. You going back to your Birmingham patch?'

'I've asked Walter for a transfer.'

The omelette was delicious. I took my time to savour the taste and to fill a large empty gap in my stomach.

'Where to? Or should I not ask?'

'To the East Midlands region. There is an area that Walter wants to focus on in the Derbyshire-Cheshire borders. I may even take on some of your accounts.'

That was news. Again, moves were afoot behind your back. Information only leaked out, as we were hardly told directly. Maybe Errol knew but didn't tell me, to spite me. That was an option.

'Well, whatever happens, I'd be glad to have you working alongside me.'

'Me too.'

We finished our meals and talked for hours. This was relaxing. Both our mobiles were switched off, and I'm sure there'd be hell to pay, although every now and then I had to live dangerously, so what the heck?

I'd never seen her laugh so freely before. Maybe it was nervous energy following Tom's death and her central role in the whole debacle. Whatever it was, I was there for her, keeping her company, and it allowed me to talk to someone about something other than my problems.

'You'd better call in or go home at least, Justin, it's after six.'

'Shit. That's your fault, you shouldn't be so easy to talk to.' She smiled, as we sat next to each other on a sofa that rested against the radiator in the large room. We had fleetingly watched afternoon television, which was dire. The conversation and company was far more to my liking.

'Okay, I'd better go. Remember to buy the local paper and I will help you find some accommodation. Tell you where all the dodgy areas are, and where to avoid. And er, I suppose you'd best contact Walter or Errol, and confirm that you're going back to work and where…' I smiled and she reciprocated.

'You're good friend to have, Mr Whalley. Thanks again.'

'My pleasure. Anytime.'

My heart palpitations started realising my now immediate situation. I knew Chelsea might now be at home and wondering where I'd been. I refused to switch my mobile on, knowing full well that there'd be too many messages to listen to. They could wait. All of them could.

Bracing myself for a possible onslaught, I drove precariously slow all the way back to my house in Wollaton. Victoria Shepard was back on my mind. I shouldn't let her creep back in. Chelsea and other key incidents had kept me busy. Kept my mind off Victoria Shepard. However, I was glad she'd called me a friend. If nothing else, that's what I wanted to be for her and to her. My journey home was saturated with those conflicting thoughts.

51

For the next three days I visited Vicky without fail. Chelsea and I spent only a few fleeting minutes with each other over that period of time. I had capitulated under Vicky's spell of friendship and warming company. Chelsea asked me to baby-sit on the fourth night. It was a sign of my dedication to our creaking relationship. Giving her her due, she never shouted once, or yelled at me, asking me where I was. Coming home late. Always looking tired. Speaking only when necessary. Remaining distant from her. Chelsea was handling it well.

I couldn't remember the last time we made love, or kissed in any passionate way. My mind just could not focus on those things. The impetus or motivation was nowhere to be found.

There was palpable concern on Chelsea's behalf, when she learned that my time 'working late', was actually being spent with another woman. I had two guesses as to who leaked the information. That night Chelsea told me, via a note, that she was going out and Robert needing looking after.

When I arrived home from work, Chelsea glared at me. A look of hatred, betrayal and abhorrence. She brushed by me in the hallway.

'I'll be back late so don't wait up.'

'What about…?' The door slammed and curtailed my full response.

Upstairs I heard Robert playing a video game that Chelsea must have bribed him with.

This was last thing I needed. The last two weeks had been long for all the reasons I didn't care to think about. With very little sleep in that time, what I longed for was a few days off. My figures at work were okay. Q3 ticked along, but wasn't brilliant. Losing customers and deals didn't often help. Walter increased the pressure on every salesperson. Q3 (which was July to September) ended up being a slow quarter every year. Your key contacts were all on holiday with *their* children. It became a regular nightmare to set meetings up, get deals closed, especially when they were ready to say yes; the signatory would bugger off on holiday, leaving you 'pissing in the wind'. It made perfect sense to go on holiday at the same time. I however, had no inclination to, or anyone I wanted to spend two whole weeks with.

My house needed a few jobs doing, and after the last few weeks some private, personal time alone would do me good, just to sleep.

Once I'd finished my dinner and sorted out Robert's, I sat half asleep in front of the television. Robert continued to irritate me by repeatedly switching channels.

'Look, Robert, leave it on the cartoons, I thought you wanted to watch them.'

The annoying flicker of the forever changing channels was giving me a headache, and of course destroying any chance of a quick power nap.

'No, I want to play with it. Mum always lets me.'

'Well your mum's not here now, and she's left me in charge, okay? So give me the remote control.'

'No, I had it first.' He screwed up his little face, hugging the controller.

'Robert, I won't ask again. Give me the remote control.' I gave him a harsh stare and held out my hand to receive it.

Instead of getting the remote, Robert decided to leap to his feet and run out of the room. I gave chase. I leapt over the sofa and attempted to rugby tackle a six-year-old boy. I missed, falling flat on my face, my chin hitting the floor and the pain that resulted coursed through me. My spectacles careered across the floor. I searched, grabbed them and followed. I quickly scanned to check if they'd cracked, they hadn't.

'Little shit. Robert, come here now,' I yelled at him, as he flew upstairs.

'No, it's mine, it's mine. You can't tell me to give it you, cause you're not my daddy.'

Now where did that come from? Did Chelsea take him to meet the biological father, or had she met someone else who she's called Robert's birth dad?

My notoriously long patience, had run its course. My blood was boiling. I wasn't thinking straight.

I stomped up the stairs where Robert watch me advance towards him, threateningly so. Like the ogre in the fairy tale stories. Fe Fi Fo Fum and all that.

'For the last time, Robert, give me the bloody remote control and then you can go to bed. You spoilt little brat.' The word released themselves with ease and without any means of being curtailed or stopped.

His little face turned bright red as I snatched the controller from him in a flash. He began to cry and in his anger he lashed out and kicked me, saying, 'I hate you, I hate you.'

I flipped and grabbed him by his hooded top.

'Don't you ever, ever say that to me again, you got it? Okay!' My voice sounded like it came through a foghorn. Rasping, menacing, to a six-year-old. I released him quickly and his crying had stopped immediately. He was in shock. He stood staring at me, hands by his sides, waiting for me to hit him, I suppose. Only then did I realise what I'd done.

It was crucial that Chelsea didn't find out about this, but I didn't have a clue how.

'Robert, I'm sorry, I didn't mean to shout at you. Look, you can have the remote, watch whatever you like. Yeah?' He started crying again, weeping, sobbing.

'Look, don't cry, I'm your friend, it's Justin, mum's special friend. Tell you what, shall we get some sweets? Yeah, let's get some popcorn and watch Shrek – your favourite film.' It wasn't working.

'Do you want to go to bed instead and for Justin to read you a story?'

'No!' Robert ran off to his bedroom, in my bloody house. Oh shit.

I sat on the top stairs, thinking about the repercussions of what had transpired. I'd be in the dock, standing accused, of what I wouldn't dare to think about.

An hour or two had passed and I checked on Robert; he was sleeping soundly in his clothes. Hopefully he'd have forgotten what happened. A new day for a six-year-old, became my only solace. A hopeful recompense for my diabolical behaviour and actions. No justifications on this one, whichever way I spun it. Carefully I covered him with a cartoon character patterned duvet, observing his small chest rise and fall. I stood there for minute hoping against all hope that I'd never do what I did to Robert to one of my own children, should I ever have any. I sighed heavily and closed the door behind me. Doing what I could to think positive and erase those fresh despicable memories, I concluded I needed sleep too. Maybe tonight of all nights, I'd sleep well, as strange as it sounds.

Fortunately, my diary for the following day allowed me to stay in bed a little longer than normal. I had a meeting at two in the afternoon, and took the opportunity to lie in. That proved to be a mistake. It was 10.30am, when I trudged downstairs in my dressing gown, after washing my face. The house was inordinately quiet.

Chelsea had obviously slept in the third bedroom or with Robert. Her side of my bed was cold.

'Chelsea, Robert, anyone here?'

Then my question was half answered. In the hallway were three suitcases, packed. The memory of last night returned with veracious vengeance. As I entered the kitchen, Chelsea sat with Robert on her lap, cuddling him.

She gave me that stare again. The one she gave me last night before she left.

'How could you?' That's all she said, shaking her head continually.

'If I can give my side of the story—' Chelsea cut me off.

'Not interested. You're lucky I'm not going to press charges and get the police or social services involved.' I looked back at her in astonishment. What the hell had he told her? Whatever it was, she was not going to listen to my defence.

'What the hell for?' I was angry, when I knew I shouldn't be.

'I don't have to say another word to you, thank goodness. I hope you're happy with that other woman you've been seeing. I hope you burn in hell, not before you get run over by a bus!'

I heard the cacophonous sound of a car horn outside the house. It was a taxi. Without uttering another word, Chelsea and Robert left my house, with the driver helping her with the suitcases. The car drove away and my day had got off to the best start possible. Not.

I knew right then and there, that I could not spend time, not now, mulling over what had happened. I had a job to do, a customer to see and business was scarce. There was no time for emotions. What occurred had be compartmentalised, viewed dispassionately, for my own mental well-being. It was probably the best way forward. Yet, my mind was full, cluttered with embarrassing, and unforgivable thoughts, about what had happened. Time passed by and I had to leave to get to the meeting within an hour.

Once I'd arranged my briefcase with the necessary paperwork, laptop, I located my mobile phone and tried four times to record a message. In the end I left the last message recorded and it erased the previous one.

It was time to leave. Concentrate on IT services, the big deal at the end of the rainbow. 'Money to be made, big bonuses to be paid.' That was my little motto, adopted by our team. Locking my house and driving away towards the motorway, only two things filled the void in my head.

52

Notwithstanding the previous twenty-four hours, my meeting and the way it went, preserved my thinking, that I was in fact sane. Somehow all the right words, about Total Cost of Ownership, and how to reduce it were uttered. How to increase their return on the investment they needed to make. The savings and efficiency Eiron's IT services and systems would deliver, all sounded, smooth, believable and at the best value price to the customer.

From some dark nether region, this spouting of sales talk would have won any award going. If I could have recorded myself and then played it back every time I need inspiration, this was it. My confidence was at its highest. The meeting and the way it went offered me the olive branch I was seeking, to eradicate the memories of last night and this morning. It was working a treat.

My buoyancy allowed me to return to the office, instead of heading to an empty, quiet home. En route, my mobile chirped and flashing up was the Nottingham office number.

'Justin Whalley speaking, how can I be of help?'

'Justin, it's Walter.'

Bollocks. Just when I was in the mood for a spat with one of the team or Shaun, Walter's on the line. My voice immediately altered to that of a trained sales professional.

'Walter.'

'Where are you now, Justin?'

'On my way from a customer meeting, heading into the office.'

'Good, can you come and see me and Errol in his office when you arrive please, thanks.'

Walter cut the conversation there. I had no opportunity to confirm why he wanted to see me. Something had happened and I'm sure I'd find out as soon as I got there.

Forty minutes later, I dropped my briefcase on my desk and scanned the office floor. All eyes in the unusually busy office arrowed at me.

'What, have I won the lottery and I don't know about it?' I announced to everyone watching.

Some laughed, others looked away in embarrassment.

No Shaun, no ally to ask what the lay of the land was. Anyway there wasn't the time.

'Oh, Justin you're here, can we see you now?' Errol asked as he stood by the door of his office.

'Yeah, be there in a sec.' My heart began to thump. I glanced around again, and all eyes locked onto me like a computer-guided missile. They watched make the short trip, weaving through desks, to get to Errol's glass encased office.

As soon as I entered I noticed a tape recorder, sitting on the small round table that Errol and Walter sat around.

'Take a seat, Justin,' Walter requested.

I sat, crossed my legs and waited, looking at both men, in their eyes.

'Let me start by saying, you have nothing to worry about. Business is slow, but as you know it's Q3 which is traditionally slow, so there's nothing to worry about on that score.'

I was wondering where this was going. A typical Walter 'build up to the moment' pre-talk. *Get on with it*, I told myself.

'As you know, a small but vital part of any salesman's role is interfacing with Eiron's most important asset. Our customers.'

'I agree.' I said it to speed him up.

'So when we interface with customers, this is done through many different forms.' Walter stopped in mid-flow, as someone tapped on the door. I swung my chair around to see a slim, slightly balding Human Resources manager enter Errol's office.

'Oh sorry, Justin, you know Edwards from HR.'

He nodded and smiled at me. I nodded back to be civil.

'Edwards is here because I wanted this to be official and ensure all the correct steps are taken.'

'Right. Okay, can we get on with this then?' I urged Walter.

Edwards pulled up a chair.

Walter pulled the tape recorder closer.

'Of course we can. And this is no time to be flippant. Remember that. I'd like you to listen to this and tell me first, who it is and second, what is wrong with it.'

Walter pressed play button and Errol's face almost broke into a smile. It was a voice mail recorded message:

"Hello, you're through to the voicemail of Justin Whalley of Eiron Enterprise Services Division. I'm unavailable right to speak to you, oh fuckin' hell, this bastard phone's is shite, ugh." Walter turned the recorder off.

Errol couldn't control his smile which became outright laughter. Edwards reversed his smirk when Walter searched his face for a reaction. Now I knew why they all stared at me when I entered.

The scenario would have been for someone to call my mobile, hear my voicemail message and play it back on loudspeaker so everyone heard it.

'As you can imagine, Justin, the situation where three or four of our major customers had called your mobile this afternoon, what do you think there reaction would be?'

'One of humour, or a genuine error being made, nothing more.'

Errol stopped laughing. Walter was deadly serious.

'Umm. I see. Well I don't see it that way. It was unprofessional and I will not have anyone bring this company down, in any way shape or form. Please note that I'm giving you a formal verbal warning, in front of two witnesses, HR and your line manager.'

'Is that it then? Can I go now?'

Errol's face registered surprise at my reaction. The asshole in charge had no importance in my immediate thinking. I just wanted to leave and fast. Walter sat back in his chair, disappointment displayed on his face.

'Edwards, is everything in order?' Walter asked for verification on the procedure.

'Yes it is. A note will be made on his record regarding this meeting.'

'Justin, you are free to leave now.'

'Thanks.' I said it in a matter-of-fact manner, which Walter didn't like.

Immediately back at my desk, I collected my things without, a word to anyone. No one was smiling anymore. No mumbling comments in the background. I was leaving, Victoria entered.

I said nothing to her and she gave me a look, of 'what's up with you?' She watched me get into me car and slam my door shut. She jumped.

With a wheel spin, my Jaguar XF sped out of the car park and within minutes I was on the ring road in Nottingham, heading for Wollaton. No idea what I would do when I got home. To think that far ahead became farcical.

*

At four forty-five, my home enshrouded in silence, I sat staring into open space. The plain beige-coloured walls helped me concentrate. Good thing I didn't go for the paisley colour scheme. At a time like this I would call Mary for a motivational drink and a bag of chips, loaded with salt and vinegar. Instead my heart wanted me to call Vicky Shepard. So I did.

The extension at the Nottingham office rang three times before I heard a female voice answer.

'Hello, Vicky Shepard speaking.'

'Hi Vicky, it's Justin.' My voice sounded as though the office was devoid of anyone there.

'Oh, you're speaking to me now are you?'

'I'm sorry about before, bad timing and all that. Just came out of a meeting with—' Vicky finished my sentence.

'Walter Baker?'

'How did you...' I heard her chuckle on the other end of the phone. 'Okay, maybe it was just a little bit funny, but Walter didn't think so. Gave me a grilling about how unprofessional I was, and "it wasn't the way to represent Eiron".'

'So you're pissed off then, I take it.'

'Too bloody right, couldn't wait to get out.'

'So how can little ol' me help the eponymous Justin Whalley.'

'By er, you know, er, going out for drink with me. No strings, mind you, just like we'd done over the few weeks, you know as friends, or not as friends, either way it doesn't matter to me, yeah, whaddya say, Vick?'

After rambling on, I distinctly heard laughing sounds in the background. Sniggering, muffled by hands over mouths. Then I heard Vicky chuckling too.

'Vicky who else is there?' Then uproar, in the background as the booming sounds of what must have the whole office heard me ask Vicky out.

When the noise had died down, I remained quiet for a moment longer.

'Justin, are you still there?' She still had me on load speaker. She asked another three times before I spoke.

'I'll take that as a no, then, shall I? See you round. Maybe.' I disconnected the call.

Why did I bother? Flippin' Vicky Shepard. After all the comfort and support I gave her after Tom's passing. Mary Leadbetter floated into my mind. I'd see her and of course Elisa. Errol's ex.

When I contacted Mary on her mobile, she told me she was still at work, however if I came around in thirty minutes, she'd be there. Mary mentioned that Elisa would love to see me, which I did find strange. No stranger to all the pile of horseshit I had ready and available to spread on my patch.

My time at Mary's house made me decide once and for all, that as lovely as Mary was as a friend, deep down, I would need more than that, if I was to ever have any hopes of a marriage and two-point-five children.

Whilst we were there, Errol called Elisa twice, which surprised me all the more. What left me aghast was the fact that they spoke, civilly. Probably for the first time in weeks. Mary watched in anxious apprehension. Hoping that Elisa would not fall for the infamous Errol Hughes charm and succumb to his will. That didn't happen.

I thanked Mary and Elisa for their company and stopped by at Emily's on the way home, as I promised to check on her status as often as I could.

Arriving to my empty two-bedroom home, was a depressing sight. Thankfully I was knackered and at least I could sleep without having to think too much about my shitty day. Roll on tomorrow.

FOOLS

53

Two days had gone by and I had called in ill on both days. Made up some bullshit excuse about a reoccurring bad knee that I had. Thinking of the excuse made me realise that I hadn't been to the gym in months. That was another source of fine specimen women. Lean, fit, healthy, all good points from the viewpoint of bearing children.

Instead of going, I sat in my lovely, warm house wallowing in own luscious self-pity. And a sweet-tasting hip flask of brandy. Errol called several times to check up on me. Probably guessing I made up the story. So what? He couldn't prove it. I was self-certified for the first five days anyway. So screw Eiron.

The French brandy tasted beautiful, and after two hip flasks, I listened to radio drone on in the background. It was only sound in the house.

The show talked about finding a partner and gave callers the option to send a message of love to someone they fancied. The radio station would set them up on a blind date, then the couple would report back, assuming they hadn't killed each other before that.

I had nothing to lose. And it was still early. Well, I didn't really know what time it was.

'Hello, it's caller number seven, what's your name and what can Doctor Matchlove do for you?' The disc jockey's voice was nasal, and slightly whining. I envisaged he had the perfect face for radio, that's why he was so good at his job.

'Well, I'm, Fred. Fred Jones,' my words, slightly slurred.

'So Fred, what's on your mind?'

'Drink. Ha ha! Yep, drink and a love of a big bosomed woman, umm umm...'

Dr Matchlove cleared his throat.

'Wouldn't we all,' he responded, giving out a brief nervous laugh.

'So, who would you like Dr Matchlove to seek out for you, Fred?'

'Well, she should be gorgeous. Short.' I burped. 'Oops. Sorry.'

'That's okay. Continue please.'

'Yeah, she's got a flippin' pair of you-know-whats, lovely eyes, umm, yeah those eyes, smells like lilies or something, and nice hair, always shiny...' My voice began to fade.

'Fred. Fred, you still with us, pal?'

'Oh, yep, still fighting fit, heh heh.'

'Okay, right. Does this woman have a name?'

'Uh?'

'Her name, the woman of your dreams. What is she called?' The DJ spelled it out for me in childlike fashion.

'She's a Shepard, ha ha, like a sheep woman. Yeah, Vicky Big Tits Shepard, oh yeah, I can see myself sucking—'

'Anyway, thanks to Fred there for his request and we'll get back to him next year some time maybe. Okay, it's time for Ten CC and 'I'm Not In Love', back in three.'

The rest of my conversation disappeared as Dr Matchlove swiftly and dutifully curtailed my call with precision. Cheeky shit. I listened to melodic tones and sounds of the song as it smoothly mellowed me out. It was one of my favourites. Maybe Vicky put a request in for me. She knew I'd be listening to 94.4 FM. That must have been a dream. The request by Vicky was.

Slumped on the sofa, I awoke with a rasping headache. I'm sure it was Saturday and the time – four thirty-two in the morning. Damn. I slumped back into the comfy sofa and returned to the forty winks I must have been enjoying.

At ten thirty, half awake, I dressed myself following a hot, well needed shower. Hair gelled, aftershave on, mints in my pocket. I had nowhere to go.

Running downstairs, a random feverish excitement enlivened me as my doorbell chimed. It was Errol.

'Want some company?'

'Yeah, come on in.'

Errol knew me frighteningly well. He'd brought a bottle of water and some over indulgence tablets. I took them gratefully.

'So how's the knee?'

'Which one?' I responded. We paused and then both howled with laughter.

'So how's the sexist woman that ever walked into Eiron?' I winced with vengeful jealousy and envy every time I thought what I could do to Sally if I ever had the chance. I felt like a sexual deviant, yet I didn't care. It was natural and I wasn't harming anyone.

'She's doing fine.'

'A woman like that. And just fine? Bloody hell mate, if you're not too sure, I could er…'

'Okay, okay, I'm sure you could. What about you? And what about Miss Shepard? Still chasing her?'

'Maybe. She'll come round in time.'

Errol smiled wildly as he watched me cross my fingers. 'You know, since she's transferred to the Notts office, I don't think she's quite got over the whole Tom thing. You never know, mate, I'd persevere with that one. I think she's putting on a brave face.'

'Cheers, thanks for the inside track.'

'Anytime.'

'You fancy going to the gym later?' The question just popped into my head.

'Why not? Got some stress to release.'

'Me too. Tell you what, I'll get packed and we'll go to yours… Er, where are you staying?' I'd completely forgot he'd moved out of his house. So had Elisa. It seemed rather strange.

'I'm in a rented flat, over in the city. Quite nice, it's new and clean, bit pricey though. It'll do for now.'

'Great, that's settled. Switch on the TV and check the early kick-off score. Arsenal v Man U.'

'Oh yes, that's another three points to United,' Errol boasted as I leapt up my stairs in twos.

The rest of my Saturday was relaxing and went well. Errol and I eased slowly back into our previous routine. Only this time he wasn't with Elisa.

54

The end of every quarter was a frenetic time. Special deals were cut and signed off by Walter and other managers to bring in the numbers. My sales numbers were on the up, and with a final push I would over-achieve my target thus far.

On the Monday morning, after the weekend with Errol, I covered three meetings. All in the West Midlands, so distance was not an issue. Surprisingly traffic treated me well, with no jams or major hold-ups to speak of.

To alleviate any possible pressure from Errol or Walter, only one of the three customers I visited needed to place an order before September 30th. The quantity and size of any of those deals, would push me over my already increased goal. Shaun, on the other hand, was flailing and some way behind. Only then, when we talked on our mobile towards end of Monday, did I realise he had confirmed his decision to return home. It was beginning to make sense.

Returning to the office at four thirty-five, proved my dedication to the cause. Deliberately I strolled by Errol's office, walking slowly so he'd see me and hopefully check his watch. A bit of brownnosing never did anyone any harm. Not wanting to mimic Tom's footsteps exactly. However, he became a master at it, so he left me with at least one decent tip, from a career point of view.

Firing up my laptop and searching through over twenty emails, took valuable time. The Monday night football match was on between Newcastle United and Chelsea. That brought a quick memory flash, that I erased expediently.

Entering the office at ten minutes after five was a short-ish woman, with glasses similar to mine, only thinner, and more oval in shape. Poker-straight, light blonde, shoulder-length hair, facial makeup, nails painted, and couldn't resist a quick look at her figure. One area in particular. A few eyebrows were raised when she approached Errol's office. I ignored whoever she was and continued to pursue my goal of getting home on time.

Whilst deleting any 'junk' emails, I contacted Shaun and invited him over for a few beers and an opportunity to watch a good match.

Before I knew what time it was, most of the internal salespeople had left. So it was time for me to follow suit. Errol shouted goodbye as he left his office and strolled out towards to the lifts. The woman who had gone in, stood adjacent to Errol's office on her mobile phone. Hurriedly I closed my laptop down, doing so without looking as though I was in a rush. She started to make her way along the path around the desk, and towards the lifts on the fourth floor.

Clearing my throat, I directed myself to trail her with my briefcase and laptop bag in tow. We stood juxtaposed, waiting for the lift to arrive. The humming sounds increased as the lift approached. The doors slid open, and she stepped in, and promptly terminated her phone call.

I smiled at her as she turned to face the lift doors. Then my nostrils accepted an odour of familiarity. She hung her head down, slightly as though she did not want her face to be seen. Then the odour that had registered allowed me to register the face. It was the eyes. Those enigmatic sparklers. Vibrant and alive green eyes.

The doors slid shut and the lift announced what floor we were on.

Moving closer, she looked up at me.

'Victoria, is that you?'

She peeled her spectacles away from her exquisitely made-up face. She nodded her head and burst into tears.

Immediately I dropped my bags and we hugged each other.

'It's okay, Vicky, I'm here now. Shush, don't cry, Justin's here.'

Damn. I hated it when Errol was right.

She replaced her glasses after drying her tears, and ruining her perfectly applied mascara.

'Bet you I look a right mess. No one would fancy me now, would they?' she blabbed.

'I would.'

'Would you? Really. I mean really fancy, even if I look like a clown right now?'

She attempted a half smile, out of courage. It almost worked.

I stood looking at her, holding her now by both her shoulders.

'Since that day at the sales conference I've thought about nothing but you. Well not all the time, you understand I had to work as well.'

Now she smiled healthily, snivelling less and less.

The lift doors had opened, without either of us realising.

'Fancying coming back to mine for a few beers and the footie match?'

'Yeah, on one condition.' She smiled again, warmly, shaking her head at my suggestion.

'Name it.'

'As long as I can wash this ridiculous muck off my face. I don't know how women wear this stuff.'

'You look far better without it.' I looked into her eyes hopefully showing genuine desire and concern.

'Anyway, the deal is on. I'll even get you a clean flannel and a bar of soap,' I told her.

She nudged me to get of out of the lift. We walked slowly back to my car.

'Thanks, Just. I'll follow you, yeah?'

'Okay. I'll go slow, yeah?'

'Piss off, Whalley.' She skulked back to her car. She was getting back to normal. That melancholy Victoria Shepard I had known and fancied.

We needed to talk. There were so many fundamental topics to discuss. Her absolution from the Tom Gate affair. Her moving from Birmingham to Nottingham. And the issue I didn't want to consider, Victoria and me. Consciously, I wanted there to be something. Subconsciously, and realistically, I favoured a seventy-thirty against me and Victoria being an item.

Yet the one aspect of this year that I had observed and learned, painfully sometimes, was that the unexpected will happen. On this occasion, I hoped for the latter.

Driving home, an uncontained smile appeared on my face. Thankfully no one was watching. Yet I had one more phone call to make to Shaun. There had to be a change of plans. I'm sure he would understand, more than most.

55

Whilst the beer flowed and the football match played out in the background, I found myself staring at Victoria, in a hypnotic state. She surreptitiously ignored me, watching the football, shouting, oohs and aahs. Shouting out, 'That was never offside, ref!' I couldn't believe what I was hearing.

We sat on my sofa, with Victoria curled up next to me, slurping her beer. I came to the conclusion she was acting as though she was another bloke, or least that's what she thought we did, when we swooned over football. It made me relax anyway.

Only the light emitted from the television set lit the room. The beam of light shot out in a V shape, encompassing the sofa and the two of us in a bright flickering light. I removed my spectacles, which I only really needed for driving and for watching TV, although the flickering screen irritated my eyes sometimes and it felt easier to watch without them.

Victoria looked up at me at half time and smiled.

'What are we going to do when the match has finished?' she asked with a cheeky grin.

'Do you want me to answer that?' I replied, taking the final gulp of my third can of lager. Internally controlling my emotions had to be the number one priority. Mesmerised by having Victoria in my house, on my sofa next to me, supping beer and watching football, well I must have been dreaming. A cruel vindictive joke, a last-gasp screw you, sent from the grave by Tom Greenfield-Crown. Again, I overthought things and pontificated over potential scenarios, that were at best unlikely to ever happen.

Victoria sat up to face me, a can in her hand.

'It's up to you, Whalley. I'll wait for your reply by email in the morning. Don't forget to put a read receipt on it, just to check that I've read it.' She grinned and then began to laugh. My heart was beating fast, my hands steady from the drink. At least I hoped they were.

'Yeah, yeah, I'll send you one now shall I?' I joked. 'Okay, you can either: A, stay here, in the spare room.' I dropped my head slightly and looked at her with raised eyebrows. 'Or B, I can drop you to your hotel, which I shouldn't do because I'm over the limit. Or C, I'll call a taxi. Any preferred choice?'

This answer was important to me. Even though it was put in a non-threatening way. I understood that Victoria was still confused, angry, bitter, and I had to move slow, however I still wanted to know how far she'd come. Secondly, how far at this present time could I go, circumventing treading over any 'moral lines' that always seem to be there?

She drank from the can and leaned forward, her clean cosmetic-free face inches from mine. How I could just for a moment be impetuous. Pull her toward me and plant a full kiss on those soft, feather-like lips. Like a horse ready for a full pelt, my reins were yanked, restricting any false movement, in the wrong direction.

'Well…' She paused. 'I've been thinking about you ever since your performance at the sales conference. I'll never forget that,' she told me in a whispery voice. She stared straight into my dancing eyes.

'I never realised what smouldering eyes you had, Justin, without those specs on.' She was deadly serious, and I didn't know whether to smile, say thanks or what.

Instead, my response was for a large, lengthy burp to race out of my mouth and cover her soft tender face with alcohol breath. Lovely.

'Ooh, Justin.' Victoria recoiled in disgust. 'You could have warned me.' So much for unilaterally nuking the soft, tender moment.

'Sorry Vicky, it's a mating call of the umigaggy birds of the Caribbean, and it's also a sign that the male bird really fancies the female bird.' What the hell was I going on about?

Luckily Vicky saw the humour in my outrageous and obviously false tale about some rare birds.

She pulled closer again, for a second attempt. Bravely, I thought. And it also displayed her truest intentions? I was hopeful. Patiently hopeful.

'Look, Justin.' She was serious now. Her tone had altered, her expression, more solemn looking. She held my left hand. 'I've never forgotten you. But I never wanted to see anyone from work. And I didn't like being chased. Tom came out of the blue. He was cute, kind, made me laugh, believe or not. It was totally unexpected, that's why it happened.'

'So did you really fancy him, maybe love him?' I asked cautiously.

'Sort of. Fancied him at first. We started as friends, went for a few drinks and the rest is history. He was company, yet I still thought of you every now and then.'

Then bravery and courage surged from within me to ask the next question. It would be the straw to break the camel's back. I had to know.

'That's nice. I guess you know that I always talked and thought about you. So when you were seeing Tom, was it really because you liked him?'

Shit; her face contorted, she moved back away from me. I prepared myself for the blast. It didn't come.

Victoria cupped her hands and covered her face. I moved closer to her.

'I'm sorry, Vicky, I shouldn't have asked that, I'm...'

'Ah ha, fooled you!'

'You little shit.' My heart was racing. Dancing like a Paso Doble dancer in Argentina. She was laughing uncontrollably. 'You had me there, I'd thought I'd upset you.' I tried to interrupt her laughter, but she was enjoying it too much. Whatever expression my face displayed gave Victoria enough reason to hold her stomach, as she doubled over in a continued laughing fit.

When she'd calmed down, she switched her emotion back to a sombre one.

'Look Justin, I did fancy you.' She moved closer to me, she retook my hand. 'Tom was a stop-gap, okay? That's the honest truth. In fact, I liked him more than I thought I would, although deep down, we were poles apart. It never would have worked. And every time he'd some to see me in Birmingham, I wanted ask him about you, and couldn't. I had to seem as though I would never go near you, Tom hated you something rotten. I couldn't let him believe that I had any feelings for you.'

'Why not?' I asked gently.

'I, er, I couldn't, it would have made things complicated. The right time or opportunity never arose and when it did, you were seeing someone. Guess you couldn't wait for vivacious Victoria!' She smiled innocently.

'No, I couldn't. Men have needs.' I raised my eyebrows in quick succession.

'Naughty.'

'Sorry.'

We looked at each other, holding hands on my Ikea sofa, like teenagers.

She moved forward and we hugged each other. I rubbed her back, and endured the warmth of her body against mine. It was a wonderful and comforting feeling. We pulled away and I watched her fluorescent green eyes sparkle again.

'Thanks,' I told her.

'For what?'

'For being here. For being you. For being beautiful.'

She looked down, in an embarrassed manner. I moved closer, and lifted up her chin with my right hand.

'No need to be embarrassed, Vicky. You are everything this man would ever need and much, much more.'

She gestured with her two fingers, putting them in her mouth, feigning as though she was about to throw up.

'Ugh, sickly sweet. Where did you read that from? A fag packet?' she retorted.

'No. It's just how I feel.'

Her expression metamorphosed from that of derision, to apologetic.

'I'm sorry, Justin, I didn't mean to—'

'Ha, ha, got you back!'

She picked up one of the cushions and hurled it at me, striking me on my head.

'You sicko, I felt for you then. Hope you're not gonna be like this when we live together.'

The room went quiet, with the exception of the football match in the background. We'd missed most of the second half.

'Yeah, okay, very funny. No need to be nasty,' I told her, not believing her last few words.

'Okay, let's set the record straight,' Vicky started. I'd recovered from the cushion incident and sat up next her. We both leant back into the sofa, looking directly at each other.

'If anyone asks we're an item, okay? Boyfriend and girlfriend.

Remember this, however; it is the early stages and things could change. I'm going to stay in the hotel for now and we'll see how things go. Eiron are picking up the tab until I find somewhere suitable. After a period of 'probation",' she made those inverted speak marks gestures with her fingers, 'we will review our position.' I smiled and winked at her when she said that. She gave me a harsh look. 'And then take things from there. How does that sound?'

'Where do I sign?'

'Right here.' She pulled me close and kissed me full on the lips. I responded gently, not forcing the issue. She put her arms over my head and pushed me closer, as we became more animated and passionate in our kissing. We separated, and I exhaled heavily. Smiling, I admit, from ear to ear.

'Wow! You're fantastic kisser. Ugh, I feel all dizzy now.' I slumped into a horizontal position on the sofa, as though I'd passed out.

'You'd better get up now, 'cause I'm going. You better call me a taxi.'

I shot upward and got to my feet within seconds.

'Yes ma'am.'

I ran to the hallway and called the local taxi firm for a cab. When I returned Vicky had her coat on and her bags from work ready to go.

'Thank you again, Vicky. I won't ask when we'll see each other again, apart from at work, so I'll wait for you to call, or email me.'

She liked that last part.

We stood in the middle of my living room kissing, in small bursts, until the hooting of a car horn outside destroyed my growing and building pleasure. I'm sure the neighbours wouldn't be too pleased with me as it was nearly ten thirty in the evening.

I stood by the door after kissing her goodnight, watching her closely as she entered the taxi and sat in the rear. She waved and I waved back with my heart fluttering, nerves shaking, and with the biggest hard-on I could recall and do nothing with. Well maybe…

I closed the door and looked at the cans in the living room. They'd have to wait until the morning. There was something else I had to do before going to bed.

56

Victoria had two days' holiday, so I didn't see her at work. Errol called me the following morning to say that Nikki Walters had been in contact with him, revealing what had happened with her sister Chelsea. He said it was none of his business but we could go for a drink after work. I told him I'd think about it.

In the office, neatly stacked on my desk, I searched through my post. I opened a piece of mail from one of the companies I'd been selling to. They sent in the first part of a purchase order for the first stage of a rollout and migration project. Excellent timing.

I looked across at Shaun's desk and he sat there on the phone arranging an appointment with a customer. My good news was tainted with the fact that he wasn't doing so well. That was sales. Peaks and troughs and everything in between. We were good friends, and I couldn't do the selling for him. He understood that intrinsically. Maybe in fifty years' time when we're all cloned it won't matter. We'd create another version of the bestselling person who made their target no matter what. Not sure what would happen to the person being 'cloned' though… frightful thought.

'Hey Shaun, look what's come in.'

'You jammy bastard, where does that put you against you numbers?'

'Hold on, let me consult my personal self-calculating, bonus Excel spreadsheet.' Shaun waited, then came over to my desk. 'There we have it. One hundred and two percent. How about that?'

'Well done that, man. You couldn't pass some of that winning streak over, could ya?'

'What do you need?'

'A fucking miracle.'

'Okay. I'll see what I can do,' I jested with Shaun.

'No, you're okay, Just. I've got one or two big things in the pipeline.'

'Who is she, and does she know about it!' Shaun laughed raucously with the rest of the office looking at us, wondering what was so funny.

Feeling somewhat guilty and without seeming obvious I invited Shaun to come for a drink with Errol and I. I did this as I had cancelled our previous arrangements, for beer and football in favour of a night in with Vicky Shepard.

'Yeah, sure. Staying local or going into town?' Shaun questioned.

'Not sure. I'll let you know. I'll be in the office all day anyway. Admin day,' I explained as I took off my glasses and rubbed my weary eyes.

The remainder of the day passed without incident. It was a first and it worried me unduly as well. It probably meant something ten times worse would happen.

At ten minutes after six, Shaun, Errol and I strolled up the Corner House complex in the city centre, from a multi-storey car park.

It had been a lovely warm day, at least in the late seventies in Fahrenheit I think. We were suited up, but all with our top buttons undone on our shirts. Ties festooned themselves loosely around our necks. A smooth, cooling breeze engulfed us as we approached 'The Bar'.

I paid for the first round, buying two bottled beers for Shaun and Errol, and a J2O orange and passionfruit juice drink for me. A Mediterranean-looking young man served us. Dark hair, tanned skin and the patter to flatter most women. I witnessed one or two ogling the barman, which of course he soaked up with ease and liberating pleasure.

Sitting down near the window seat, clientele looked as we did. Workers coming in for a stress-relieving drink after a hard day's graft.

We lifted up our bottles and glass and clinked 'cheers'.

'So Errol, my man,' I started, eager to learn more, and Shaun nudged me under the table to dig for the information. 'You and Sally…' He stopped me right there.

'Chaps, you can be the first to know and hopefully the last. Don't say this to anyone else.' Errol's usually calm, poised exterior, displayed tension, nerves even.

'I've decided to call it a day with Sally.' Shaun and I looked at each other. Surprised and somewhat shocked. 'I was greedy, saw an opportunity, and I didn't realise what I had. Thought the grass was greener, you know. And it isn't.' He spoke the last few words in staccato mode.

'Shit, Errol, what, why did you…?' I could not form a sensible sentence to ask what I wanted to.

'It doesn't matter now, Just. I'm going to move back into my home. Whether Elisa will move back, I don't know. I'm expecting that she won't.'

'Bad luck, my man. I hope it all works out for you, Errol.' Shaun added his view on the revelation.

'Elisa might have you back if she sees it as a one-off fling, rather than a long, drawn-out, tawdry affair. That's if you want her back and she'll have you, of course.'

'Umm. Indeed.' Errol swigged his bottled Belgian lager and glanced ruefully out of the window at the passing trade.

'Whoa, okay, Shaun, who are you settling with these days? Anyone we know?' I smiled to try and lighten the situation.

Shaun watched me sip my drink and looked across at Errol before replying.

'You may remember her actually. That girl from the South African branch. Thelma.' Thankfully I swallowed my mouthful of juice, otherwise I was positive it would have being coming up the other way.

'Flippin' hell!' My voice was louder than it should have been. Heads turned in our direction.

'Sorry,' I apologised, and smiled nervously at everyone looking.

'What's wrong with her, Just? Why the shock?' Errol asked.

'Oh nothing, it's just that she's in South Africa and Shaun's going to be in Dublin.' As soon as the word Dublin left my mouth I flashed a look at Shaun, hoping he'd already told Errol about his impending move.

They both laughed, seeing my pained expression.

'It's okay, Just, Shaun's told me all about it. That's one reason why Vicky Shepard was allowed to move up here.'

I nodded my head as though I had full knowledge of what was happening.

'So Thelma, eh. How did you, how did you to manage to...?' Shaun could see that I wasn't going to let go. Errol was quite happy to sit and listen.

'She's moving with me to Ireland. Strange as it sounds, she has relatives there. Distant mind you, but still family, nonetheless. And before you ask, yes, she's been in the UK for about a two months. She was transferring to somewhere quieter, and it coincided with my move. Happy now?'

'Not really, but that will do for now,' I retorted, raising my glass to Shaun.

'Well, do you guys want to hear about me?' I asked them excitedly.

'No, not really,' Errol and Shaun said simultaneously.

'I'm going to say it anyway,' I told them, sitting forward in my comfy, leather armchair. 'Victoria and I are an item. Yes, that's right, boyfriend and girlfriend. How about that, eh?'

There was silence on our table as Errol looked at Shaun and they both in a synchronised manner shrugged their shoulders, as if to say, 'So what?'

Then they started to laugh. They had me.

'Congratulations, Just. It goes to show perseverance is the name of the game. You showed tenacity, dedication, a persistence that does you proud. Attributes a salesperson should have.' Errol gave his expert opinion on my news.

'About bloody time too,' Shaun quipped. 'I was worried I was gonna have to find you a woman... thank goodness for that.'

We finished our drinks and Errol ventured to the bar to buy another round. I spoke to Shaun, telling him I hoped everything would work out work-wise and personally for him. He only had another week or so to pack his things up. Errol returned to the table with the same three drinks.

'So how long have you and Vicky been an official item?' Errol asked, knocking back his beer.

'About thirty-six hours.'

'Oh, I see. So no chance of you know what then?'

'No. We're taking things slowly. Carefully. We want this to last.' Errol's expression changed. He almost looked angry for a second.

'I'm sorry, I didn't mean to...'

'Don't worry, Justin, everything I've done is my fault. All down to me. No one else. It's up to me to change. It's not going to be easy.' Just then, two women in their twenties with athletic bodies and revealing clothes walked by. Errol took a glance. One of them looked back at him and smiled. They walked along, giggling between themselves.

'See what I mean, fellas? There's too many fit, lovely, gorgeous women. I can't have them all or be with them all. I guess I'll just have to put my mind to the task, realising that I can only have one and settle with her.'

'Do you mean Elisa?' Shaun asked, looking directly at Errol. He said nothing for moment or two. Casting tentative looks at Shaun and at me.

'Yeah. I do.'

'You going to fight for her?' I asked Errol.

'Looks like I'll have to.'

'If it's worth fighting…' I left the sentence hanging.

We finished our drinks and didn't notice how noisy and busy the 'The Bar' had become. Flanked both sides by woman and men in suits, mainly white-collar workers, no manual labour employees in here. Mind you, at the prices they charged, I was surprised it was this full.

We walked to the multi-storey car park where we'd left our respective cars. Shaun told us he didn't want a big party or any send-off. He wanted to leave quietly and without any fuss. Errol and I agreed.

Going our separate ways, I walked with Errol back to his car, mentioning that he had nothing to lose by calling Elisa. He said he might, but not straight away. I hoped that they'd get back together. Whether she could forgive him was another matter.

57

Strangely enough, Victoria and I met each other every night. A routine was beginning to develop. Each night at seven thirty, we alternated between her hotel and my house.

On the house front, she'd seen and visited four properties that showed some promise. One stood out in particular, not because it was keenly priced, but the decor and the fact that it was a fully furnished flat, suited Victoria ideally.

Each night we'd discuss what we liked or disliked about the people we worked with. When we began talking about who was having affairs with who, we both stopped immediately. Then we switched topics without hesitation or resistance from either of us.

My heart fluttered as the anticipation of the end-of-night kiss wished away the few hours we spent in each other's company. Waiting, yearning for that moment when our lips would caress each other. The indescribable emotion of sheer joy. The tingling sensation that rippled through my body. The control that Victoria showed, when she'd tell me to relax.

That night I attempted the tongue sandwich, the French Kiss as I knew it, which made her pull away and wag her finger at me. She then winked, saying quietly that she liked it. The little tease.

Without pressing her, she allowed me to help her get over Tom's demise and her illicit affair with a married man. Hopefully just being with her on a regular basis would do the job. Or at least most of it.

On the Friday night after work, on our one-week anniversary, I took her to a small Mexican restaurant.

Nothing fancy, nothing overstated, just a quiet simple meal, between, 'steady' boyfriend and girlfriend. Somehow Victoria managed to look effervescent. Radiant after a day on the road and closing a huge half-a-million-pound deal.

We sat in a corner and I ordered champagne, my and our only extravagance for the evening.

'Would madam like to raise her glass?' I asked, beaming like the Cheshire Cat in Alice.

My eyes felt as though they were dancing in their sockets. I hope Victoria wouldn't become dizzy because of my giddy excitement.

As I watched her eyes sparkle and her skin glisten, the swan scenario I'd forgotten, floated across my mind. My heart increased its tempo, as we clinked glasses.

'To us,' I said.

'To Victoria and Justin Whalley.' I covered my mouth in time to block any champagne that was about to project itself in Vicky's direction.

'Oh sorry, didn't mean to make you choke, Mr Whalley,' she told me, grinning mischievously.

I quickly scanned the half-filled restaurant to check if anyone witnessed my potential guffaw. It didn't seem as though anyone did. They were too interested in their partners or the wonderfully smelling food.

'You caught me off-guard, Vicky, hope you didn't mean that. That's way too fast, even for me.'

'So you're saying you wouldn't marry me. You're just using me for sex.'

'No, no. Shush!' The table adjacent must have heard. The mid-fifty-something couple didn't know where to look. Victoria continued to laugh, unabated.

'Well are you?' She pinged another question at me. I sipped two mouthfuls of my fizzy wine and loosened my tie.

'Am I what?'

'Just using my for my luscious body?'

'I might be. It's a good enough body, so why not?'

'I see. What I'm telling you, is that I'm only using you because you've a big—' I stopped her right there.

'Glass. Like another?' I held up the champagne bottle, and Victoria laughed, pointing at me. She obviously loved to see me go red. It was bloody hot and the air conditioning could not have been working.

'I'm sorry, I'll calm down and we'll order, shall we, before I get us thrown out.' Victoria finally relented. The couple adjacent smiled nervously at me as I looked in their direction, following the waiter coming over to take our order.

The food did taste as good as it smelt. Victoria could eat. All three courses tucked inside a not too badly tuned body.

She watched me eat and I watched her. Every forkful or spoonful of food. It never dawned on me before, but I couldn't take my eyes off her. Every now and then, I woke myself from reverie to hopefully find no one looking or realising how smitten I must have looked. To be honest I didn't care anymore. I fancied Victoria Shepard, and everyone should know about it.

'Would you like a coffee or a shot of brandy to finish off?' the waiter asked in a half Mexican, or South American style accent. An attempt at least at authenticity.

'Darling, would you?' I asked, sounding as pompous as I could.

'Not for me, dear, it give me an awful headache,' Victoria responded in like manner.

'Just the bill for us, please. Thank you,' I told him, looking at Vicky and not the waiter. He turned on his heels and disappeared as surreptitiously as he'd arrived.

Paying wasn't a problem, although seeing how much it was, did make me take a gulp of air. My credit card was crying before it hit the table. I gave the waiter a ten-pound tip. What the hell.

On route home, in the back of a taxi, we agreed to stay over at my house. She had left some clothes the last night she'd come round, in preparation for tonight. I hoped I had everything I needed to.

In the interests of equality and the fact that Victoria was already hard to say no to, she paid for the taxi. She insisted.

Once inside, we shed our clothes. It was after midnight and we were both genuinely tired. I watched Victoria undress to her bra and G-string. Wow. I was embarrassingly erect with seconds. My poor boxers moved like a greyhound out of its trap. Vicky looked over at me in the bedroom and sniggered.

'Where do you think you're going with that thing? It's not coming near me.'

I was about to reply, when she anticipated what it might be.

'I'd…'

'Don't say it. Don't say anything about you know what. Just calm it down and I'll let you sleep with me. Beside me. Okay. No funny business or else.'

'Whatever you say, master,' I replied in a paltry kung fu master voice, with my hands clasped together and the bowing motion to boot.

I followed her into bed, after ensuring all the lights in house were off. She got into bed only after she'd dressed herself in one of my t-shirts.

Snuggling up behind her in bed, her odour of DKNY perfume filled my nostrils, which were at the nape of her neck. I placed my arms around just under her breasts, and her hand held mine firm. That was the red light.

'Night Justin, thanks for a lovely evening.'

'Thanks. Happy anniversary.'

She turned to face me and we kissed each other. Rolling back into position, we fell asleep. Victoria first, then me.

58

We were all on a relative high when next week arrived. Every day Victoria, Shaun and myself met after work for a quick drink and chat about our Q4 figures and forecasts.

Shaun had not a care in the world and had his things packed and ready to fly.

It was Tuesday and following a customer meeting in the morning, I received a call from Errol asking me to come back to the office. He sounded a tad too ominous.

Early in the afternoon, all the available sales personnel, sat in 'St. George's' room, waiting for some announcement to be delivered by Errol.

We sat tentatively waiting for what Walter had dreamed up for Q4.

Errol stood pensively waiting for everyone to settle. In his hand he held an A4 pad. He used his free left hand and asked everyone to be seated and be quiet.

'People, we know from time to time the company has to make new rules, change our plan of attack to cope with this every progressive and aggressive market. We need good numbers to survive and the UK it seems is bucking the trend. However…' and this is when we expected the bombshell.

'With immediate effect, all sales will have to report to me by phone with their location every day.' There was a huge sigh. 'Secondly, you must have a genuine reason for seeing a customer. You will be required to fill out one of these.' Errol held up a new pre-call visit form. The sound of mumbling increased. Errol looked embarrassed.

'There will be a goal of a least eight meetings per week. The more customers we see the more business we'll get. As you know, it's a numbers game.' The groaning grew louder. Errol asked everyone to calm down.

'I'm taking the opportunity to announce to new senior managers who have been brought in to win Eiron more business. They are here to ensure we have a successful Q4. John Breedon, Tactical Sales Director, and Andrew Wisemore, Marketing Guru.' Everyone laughed at that point. Then we all wanted to know what the hell a 'Guru' and a 'Tactical' director was.

Victoria leaned across and whispered in my ear.

'Those bastards never have any women in senior positions. Don't tell me there's not one qualified lady who could have filled those roles, and do a better job.'

'I agree. Walter's from the old school. Wouldn't think it was right to have a woman have such responsibility, except at home of course.'

Victoria gave me a hard stare and I recoiled immediately. I hope she didn't think that was my view of women. Walter on the other hand selected those from the same gene pool. My flashback memory about cloning was only too true and alive right now.

Errol continued.

'I'm sure you have more questions, to which I'm afraid I don't or won't have the answers for. As you know I'm the messenger of bad news, so please don't try and shoot me.' Errol's request did seem genuine.

Europe was having a poor run of not making money. It was affecting the UK and the US. Because EMEA accounted for forty percent of the global revenue, its poor performance was having a knock-on effect. I didn't like the smell of the whole announcement. There was more behind it, and Errol either didn't know, or couldn't say. I'd put my money, as a non-betting man, that it was the latter.

A now disconsolate, disillusioned sales force ventured home or went for several alcoholic drinks to vent their frustration and anger at what had happened. Everyone would be under the microscope. There'd be nowhere to hide.

The micro-management that Walter had introduced was on top of all the multiple reports, forecast data, and admin that we had to perform.

Returning to my desk, closely followed by Victoria, I sat and worked out how much of our time would be spent reporting rather than selling. I was not surprised by the results. Showing it to Victoria, she agreed and shook her head in bemusement.

If Eiron wanted to make more sales, they were going the wrong way about it. That was only my acclimated view based on my years in the business. I was sure, however, that I was not the only one that harboured those opinions.

On our way back to my house, Vicky asked me if I thought Walter was deliberately sexist. I told her he grew up in a different era, and a lot of men do still think a woman's place is in the home. Unfortunately, a lot of them are in high-ranking positions in large companies. However, I reassured her that generally things are a lot better. Or at least getting better. Marginally I would admit and certainly nowhere near quick enough.

I quoted a prime example of a woman that is a CEO of the second largest global IT company in the world, it put a little smile on her face. I just hoped it didn't give her any delusions of grandeur.

We stopped off on the way home to buy Shaun a small gift and a leaving card. Errol had already purchased the customary large card for all the salespeople to sign and record a brief witticism of some sort.

Vicky chose the gift, something that we thought represented Shaun O'Dwyer.

I chose the card; I was sure he'd see the funny side of things.

Once at home I called Errol so we could arrange a drink with Shaun. A last-ditch opportunity to try and get him to stay. Errol hinted that he would not be replaced. That made my theory about something else going on, ring true. Whatever the secretive overtures were, I could not allow them to affect me or my performance.

Victoria and I agreed that Errol would contact Shaun, so he could make our meeting sound official, even though it would be after work. It had to sound as legitimate as possible, however I'm positive Shaun would recognise our translucent scheme. I did understand, however, that in all truth, Shaun O'Dwyer wouldn't care less.

59

We sat in the 'Loft' bar at ten minutes to six, sipping on a white Chenin Blanc dry wine. The day had been like the rest recently. More disparaging news about how the salespeople were to operate. How we should be following the new procedures in order for Eiron as a whole to succeed.

The noose was tightening. Errol was under increasing pressure to squeeze even more business out of the UK. I could see that the pressure made him angry, incapacitated, with the tightening of the rope they gave him. Minimal wiggle room, to be flexible, all points of the Eiron machine, tracked and monitored. Walter at the helm, at the controls, steering, guiding the UK as it led the way. This achievement presented by the diligence and never-say-die attitude of the UK team, meant they were having to cover for failures in other countries.

'So what would it take for you to stay and fight with us, Shaunie boy?' Errol asked cheekily.

'A million euros and buxom blonde!' he retorted.

We all laughed. The bar was half full with a mixture of people standing and sitting.

'So there's no way back for you, eh?' I asked.

'I'm afraid not, boys. I've got my apartment. I've got Thelma waiting in the wings.' Shaun winked at us both. Errol and I smiled back. 'Yep, so er, I think I'm sorted.'

'We'll miss you, Shaun. All of us will. Especially the women,' I praised him. Shaun took in his stride. Errol nodded his head to agree.

'Okay, chaps. I propose a toast. Raise your glass, to one of best young salesmen we've had at Eiron. It's been a pleasure and a joy working with you, and I hope everything works out for you in Dublin. Keep in touch and the very best of luck.' Errol was practising for Shaun's leaving speech in the office.

After clinking glasses and saying, 'Hear, hear,' I checked the room to see if anyone was staring at us. They weren't.

The noise in the bar increased as I returned with another bottle of white wine to our small round table. I loosened my navy-blue tie and adjusted my specs. Pouring each of us another glass, Errol told us how his plan to get Elisa back seemed to be having some positive effects.

'She called me the other day and asked if I could help choose a new sofa,' Errol began to reveal.

'So what happened?' I eagerly intercepted.

'We spent several hours looking around and then spent a few more having lunch. It felt good. It felt like old times.' Errol's voice fell in pitch. There was solemnity in his voice. It sounded genuine, not orchestrated or canned.

'Hey Errol, be patient and it will happen in time, my friend. Just keep on trying, never give up.' Shaun's astute and paternal-sounding advice surprised me. But he'd begun to change too. Maybe it was only me that still lived in some sordid dream world. However, hopefully I no longer required that. Victoria Shepard provided more than enough in that department.

Shaun explained to Errol that he'd be leaving at the end of next week. All his accounts would be spread out amongst those remaining salespeople. Victoria had already taken over some of them. It meant both of us would have a lot more accounts to manage, but no extra resources. It didn't sound like fun.

'So I'm not going to be replaced?' Shaun asked Errol, to see what the official answer was.

'You've heard the rumours too, have you?' Errol took two sips of his wine. 'That's true, but do not tell anyone yet. Walter wants this kept under wraps. It's another way of Eiron saving money. If the real truth leaks out, I'm finished.'

Shaun and I looked at Errol and realised what a predicament he was in. I wouldn't be surprised if Errol began looking elsewhere for another job.

'Anyway, forget all that stuff, how's you and the voluptuous Vicky?' Errol pointed the attention on me.

'What can I say? Couldn't be better. I'm getting there slowly and she's teaching me well.' I raised my eyebrows and smiled.

'You dirty ol' bastard, Whalley. Always knew you'd land on your feet somehow,' Shaun jested.

'You know the strange thing is, everything changed after Tom died. When she found out he was married, that clinched things I feel. I was there to comfort her, in her hour of need.'

'Yeah right. I know what kind of comfort you mean,' Shaun replied.

'Absolutely,' Errol added.

I shrugged my shoulders to feign ignorance. Yes, now I consider the timeline, with Victoria. The powerful recriminations since that embarrassing debacle with Tom's wife in the office. The revelations about his drug use, which we suspected, then confirmed, in his own iniquitous manner. Right time, right place, with some prior selfish desire to be with Victoria added up. Numbers are never wrong.

I hadn't laboured on the other possibility, if Tom Green-Crown was still around now. In existence. Would Victoria and I be together? Who knows? These transcendent thoughts are like smoke, here now and disappearing in a flash. Living in the moment, I had to remind myself. Focus on my true inclinations from the start. On my work goals. My life goal, utilising the experience and support from those around me.

We drank our wine and went our separate ways, telling Shaun we'd see him next week before he left the Eiron zoo. He repeated his wish not to have a big leaving booze-up. We told him this was it, just the three of us. I don't think he believed us.

As we exited the Loft onto Mansfield Road my mobile chirped with the original James Bond theme tune. Errol and Shaun turned away from me looking embarrassed.

'Hello darlin', you okay?' It was Vicky.

She asked me to get some milk and bread on my way home.

'Okay, I will. Anything else?'

'No, just yourself, that's all.'

I laughed nervously.

'See you soon.'

'Love you.'

'Love you too.'

Errol and Shaun, stood beside me, simulating putting their fingers down their throats to throw up.

'Piss off,' was my response. 'I'll see you chaps next week,' I called out as I moved away from them.

Ha, I thought, *they'd carry out the same performance with their respective other halves.* In a blithe, liberal happy state, I had the inner strength, comfort that fortified me against those types of bullets. Like a shield. An invisible suit of armour, which I hoped would become my unbidden superhero superpower.

Nonchalantly striding to my car, I approached it, depressed my key-fob, watching my latches shoot upward. Once inside my car, I drove to the supermarket, looking forward to going home to the comforting arms of Victoria Shepard.

60

On Monday morning, Errol seemed determined to get Shaun out for one last drink, before he left. He approached me and Victoria to ask if we could come up with a secretive scheme to get Shaun to the Boston Bean bar at lunchtime. Hopefully the element of surprise would do it.

Errol returned to his office to have a meeting with Walter and two other senior management members. I understood that Edwards from HR would also be an attendee. Another clandestine meetings of the minds, I suspected. Gosh, the elocutionary standards must be extremely high inside those four walls. Coupled with inflated eminence, ego, subterfuge and goodness knows what else that they want to throw into the mix.

Ignoring whatever rhetoric tosh in the meeting room, I asked Victoria to ask Shaun out to lunch and ask him to pay. I told her to use her feminine charms and skill to get him to go. In the meantime I would inform the remainder of the internal sales teams, and of the account managers who were there, to go to Boston Bean for about twelve thirty.

Leaving Victoria to it, I continued to contact every one of my customers, as per another new mandate cast down from Walter the great. Latching onto any and every opportunity for Eiron to sell our various offerings, I made the necessary appointments.

My task was doubled as I offered to do Victoria's customers as well, whilst she used her delectableness on Shaun.

One customer I had been working on for six months, told me they were ready to make a decision on a big deal, that would blow my annual target.

Not trying to get to excited, I arranged to see him on Thursday morning. He wanted some final assurances and I'm sure I would give them to him, with Errol and Walter's blessing. This would be it for me. A massive bonus, increased kudos and I'd be one of the few people who would have made their new increased targets.

At nearly noon, the plan was set. Shaun had agreed to take Victoria to lunch. It was her leaving opportunity. All the salespeople had signed the card, which Shaun would receive on his last day.

Victoria had told Shaun that Errol was too busy in meetings, and I had to join Errol once Walter and his cronies were gone. She explained that he did not need to be involved as he was leaving. Shaun agreed, not seeming to be bothered.

Deliberately I disappeared as Shaun gave Victoria the nudge to go to the bar for lunch.

Errol and I drove on ahead, leaving out the rear entrance. The others followed us, immediately after Victoria took Shaun slowly around the long way, taking the lift from the fourth floor. Maybe this secretive spy stuff from Walter was rubbing off on us. Stupidly for a fleeting moment, I pondered on us all having the necessary adeptness, sharp awareness, and patter to become real spies. The inanity of these ideas were not lost on me. Oh well, I regained my status in reality unflinchingly, to remain conscientious for the task in play.

Minutes later we'd parked up, with most of us sharing cars. In the Boston Bean, there were four tables put together in a corner, which we immediately went over and sat in.

We waited until we saw Victoria's white cotton blouse appear through the doors. Her shades holding her hair back on top on her head. Following her, was that man himself, Shaun O' Dwyer, who didn't have a clue. She cleverly directed him to the bar to order some drinks. He turned to his left and we all started to sing happy birthday.

He pointed at me and Errol.

'You just wait, Hughes and Whalley, I won't forget this.' He started laughing, as did everyone there, including the bar staff.

'You getting the drinks in then?' I shouted from the corner.

Shaun showed me his middle finger. There was a chorus of oohs.

Shaun purchased drinks, as everyone shouted up their choice. Vicky carried some of them over, Shaun carried the remaining drinks on a tray. Errol and I went over to order food.

As Shaun walked away from the bar he tripped on a leg from a bar stool. The tray shot into the air. Shaun headed towards the wooden floor. A white wine and soda careered off the tray, the wine catching Victoria's blouse and soaking it on her left side. Her bra was as visible as in a wet T-shirt competition.

A pint of lager hurtled to floor, the plastic glass bounced in front of Errol's legs, the lager soaking his trousers and expensive designer shoes. The second pint somersaulted in the air, spilling its contents over my cheap suit jacket but my favourite white shirt. Painfully, some of it caught a couple sitting peacefully to my right. The woman screamed, a little dramatically. Anyone would think her husband was being murdered. It would have been better if she was. Her husband, shouted out a string of curses and expletives.

The last drink a glass of red wine, seemed to be tossed the highest. Its trajectory on the way down headed towards the bar staff. The quick thinking of the young barman, reached out and grabbed the glass, as though he was concocting a cocktail. However, the contents still managed to shower him over his ultra-clean green and white uniform. He yelled out as the wine shot into his face and eyes. The female bar woman ran to his aid.

The tray cascaded as if from the heavens. Shaun lay prostrate on the hard, cold, wooden floor, watching the silver tray hurtle towards him. Without being able to move, the tray landed flat on top of his midriff. Shaun yelled. 'You bastards!'

No one knew whether to laugh or to cry. A state of shock and total silence ensued.

I helped Shaun to his feet, checking if he was okay to walk. Errol bemoaned the drink spilt over his suit.

The husband couldn't attack Shaun, clearly it was accident. Errol offered to pay for any dry cleaning as compensation. He gave the man his name and the Eiron's telephone number.

The barman raised his hand to say it was okay. He asked Shaun if he would like a job working there. That broke the ice a little.

We agreed to finish off our drinks – those that had them – and eat elsewhere. It had to be for the best. Needless to say, none of us would be venturing back there. Well, maybe not for another six months or so. Hopefully no one would recognise us.

Driving back to the office, I felt sorry for Shaun, yet at the same time, relieved. Relieved that something like that incident, does happen to other people and not just me. My paranoia was going away slowly. Things were changing for the better.

I had Victoria. A good job. Good circle of friends, male and female. And no more Laurel and Hardy stuff has happened to me. More to the point, it ***did*** happen to someone else.

61

The following morning, after Victoria showed me how loving she could be, we both had customer meetings miles apart.

I ventured north east to Hull of all places, whereas Victoria journeyed to her meeting in suburban Staffordshire.

After that night it made me decide to ask my family to come up and meet her. Jenny couldn't wait. Emily had already spoken to Vicky. Mark and Oliver, who were both planning to move out of the family home (about time too in my book), were not sure if they could make it. I hoped none of them informed my father about the visit. His presence would only inflame the acrimony I felt toward him. As affable as I was, Victoria was the most important thing that had happened to me. There was no way I would allow him to trample over this occasion, even if it was informal.

My father had been a fugitive, like the Harrison Ford film. Nowhere near as exciting mind you, however, nonetheless on the run. From his fatherly duties. My mother displayed no recriminations for his unacceptable behaviour. A stalwart, patient and far too lenient towards her husband of over twenty years.

The realisation that he absconded from some of the most basic facets of family life. Cooking a meal that your family could actually eat. Maintaining discipline routine of school, homework, answering questions you had. My memories juxtaposed themselves against a faded backdrop of those frustrating times.

Although being the youngest boy, my outlook, my view from 'my window' allowed no emancipation from what I witnessed. In order to remain utterly focussed, I compartmentalise blocks of the past. No inclination to let what are now trivialities from my history, hobble me from moving forward in a positive manner.

Nevertheless, whatever happened, my main concern was for Victoria's wellbeing. At the back of my mind, it did matter somewhat that my brothers and sisters liked her. My worst-case scenario meant with only Emily living near me, I would only see her every day on the off-chance that anything despicable occurred. I had to remain quietly confident. Effusive.

Errol contacted me on my return, whilst in the car, to ask me how my meeting went. I informed him that the meeting went well and we would have a decision by the end of the week. The deal wouldn't be fundamental to me reaching my annual target. Every deal, however, helped me towards it.

Errol sounded laconic when he called, so something else had happened back at the ranch. It was easy to decipher his frustration, which for the last few days had not abated.

Settling into my seat at my desk, just after lunch, I learned why Errol's attitude radiated utter annoyance.

Another email pinged into everyone's mailbox, from our infamous Managing Director Walter Baker. Another meeting had been arranged for Thursday after work. The mail stressed the importance of everyone attending. A registry of names would be called and everyone would have to sign by their names on a clipboard as they entered the meeting room.

Walter outlined his justification for having the meeting after work. There was no ambiguity in his email at all. He clearly explained the need to get everyone as much selling time as possible. This had to eclipse anything else. He also referred to the importance to all salespeople of each and every deal, large or small.

I sat reading this lengthy email, thinking about Victoria, who'd not been selling much since her transfer to Nottingham. She did bring one two decent sized bits of business.

In another time, if the company was doing exceedingly well, it may have been overlooked. Not now. The microscope pointed at each of us.

All the pre-call sheets we would complete. The post-visit forms that needed our input. Then they'd be sent to Errol or any of the other managers and kept on file. Our forecast and pipeline spreadsheets would be rigorously scrutinised. Questions being fired at us, from every angle, about when deals would close. How much more can we get out of the customer? There'd be no dispensation if a customer cancelled their contracts. Early in the year I had a two hundred and fifty grand cancellation. Luckily I made it back up with a big deal. Now no one could take that chance.

Scanning the fourth floor, solemn faces could be seen everywhere. Heavy sighs engulfed the room as everyone expected Thursday's meeting to announce redundancies. That was the rumour-mill churning. Usually there was some truth in it. It was typical salespeople speculation. Wild theories abounded. This link back to the secret service kept returning with a vengeance. Recovering adroitly from these ridiculous thoughts, I told myself I'd rather wait and see.

Errol was nowhere to be seen. Neither was Shaun. Victoria had another meeting this afternoon. For her sake I hoped she could close something, however small. Perception was nine tenths in sales.

I spent the remainder of the afternoon making notes on all the possible deals that would close in the next month or so. Calculated how much they would add up to, and worked out whether I could pass some over to Victoria, to protect her. Once my calculations were completed, I smiled to myself, quickly checking no one was watching. *She should be okay,* I thought to myself. My only stumbling block could be Errol. I needed to run it by him first, to see if he could pull it off.

Driving home in total silence, my mind wondered why Vicky hadn't moved in fully. I wasn't sure whether to wait, or to ask her outright. My reverie was punctured by my mobile phone ringing. Using the hands-free kit, I answered the phone. I was glad I did.

62

That night, following my phone call, I brought home a bottle of wine. I would have purchased champagne, however the threadbare corner store didn't stock any Bollinger.

With my demeanour in check, trying to control my raging excitement, I phoned Victoria at her hotel. I told her to come over immediately. She didn't ask why, yet she responded promptly to my request.

Somehow she read my mind. When she arrived she was carrying a bottle of champagne. How the hell did she guess? I never bothered to find out.

'Did you do it then?' she asked, beaming with that fantastic sexy smile of hers.

'Yep, I did. Customer called me to say the purchase order will be with me tomorrow.' I, too, was beaming from ear to ear.

Vicky showed me the bottle and raised her eyebrows, shaking it.

'Go on then, open, Mr Salesman!'

I popped open the champagne cork, and we simultaneously 'whooped' together as the fizzy wine spayed over the kitchen floor. For once I couldn't care less.

Victoria hugged me and took my face in her warm hands. She pulled me close and gave me a sensual long kiss. Who needed champagne to get this feeling?

Drinking from two flutes, we clinked glasses and toasted my excellent selling skills and good fortune. I removed my spectacles which had globules of champagne all over them.

'You know what this means, Vicky…' I began, doing my utmost

to let the adrenalin fade.

'What?'

'I'm now one hundred and twenty percent of my annual target. It also means I may be able to help you.' She gave me a quizzical look.

She stood staring at me and said nothing for a while. Then:

'You have the most beautiful and piercing blue eyes. Did you know that?'

I smiled, chuckled with a mouthful of champagne, not knowing how to respond to that.

'You should wear contacts. Then again, I don't want other women looking at you,' she told me, sipping away.

'Thanks, I mean for the compliment. I didn't expect that. It was nice of you.'

'It's my pleasure, Mr Whalley. Now what else would be your pleasure…?' she asked as she approached me and flung her arms around me. She kissed me softly, tenderly, then whispered in my left ear, 'Wanna go upstairs?'

'Well, er, why not?' She rubbed up close to me and I was already ready.

Without asking again, we made our way to the bedroom and it was only ten minutes after six in the evening.

The television was on, otherwise my house was quiet, apart from the groans and moans emanating from Victoria. Damn, I was getting good at this, if the sounds were anything to go by.

We lay in bed naked, holding each other tight.

'I really love you, Justin Whalley.' Although I may have known, hearing it, made my heart leap. My stomach churn, knees felt weak, trembling.

'I love you too, Victoria Shepard. Why don't we show everyone how much we love each other by you moving in. Permanently.'

She didn't respond immediately, which made me worry initially.

'I thought you would never ask.' She turned to face me in bed. She kissed my forehead and then my lips, then my chin. I wondered where she was going to stop. She did right there.

'I'll get my things tomorrow, if that's not too soon.'

'I'll help you of course, with everything and anything you need.' I was smiling at her as I reached over with my left hand and pinched her firm bottom.

'Ouch! Stop that!' We both laughed. I moved in and curtailed her laughter by kissing her gently at first. Then the situation heated up, quite nicely. She rolled me over, and sat on top of me. I must have had the biggest of smiles of my face, when the front door bell rang twice in succession.

'Shit. Oh bloody hell, shit, bollocks!' Victoria gave me a strange glaring look. I'd forgot she didn't like to hear me curse or use expletives.

'What the hell is it?' She asked, with a strained expression.

'I forgot.'

'Forgot what, Justin?'

'I invited my family to meet you.'

'You what?'

'I know, I'm sorry. Forgive me?' I held my hands up after leaping off the bed and putting on my boxer shorts.

'Oh, Justin. I need a shower. What about makeup, clothes, oh!' She slumped back into bed. The doorbell rang and rang two more times.

By now I had slipped on a pair of jeans and a t-shirt with a slogan 'only a handsome man would wear this'.

'Look, I'll say you're in the shower, you know, make some excuse, saying you wanted to look your best and all that stuff.'

'Okay.' She pointed her index finger at me as a warning for any future occasions such as this.

Running downstairs, I forgot I didn't have any socks on, or my glasses.

I reached the front door and calmed myself a little. Took two deep gulps of air, allowing them to settle. Reaching out with my left hand I opened my front door.

'Hello, people. Apologies for the wait.'

Jennifer walked in first, followed by Emily, who had an innocuous smile on her face. Oliver shook my hand. Mark patted me on my shoulder. Behind him was my irreverent father. Donald.

'Hiya, son.'

'You'd better come in too then, I suppose.'

They took seats in the living room and I asked if they wanted drinks. My dad asked for orange juice, everyone else had some form of alcohol.

'So Just, what's with the champagne?' Jennifer's eagle eyes didn't miss a trick.

'Closed a huge deal. Made my numbers for the year. You never know, this could mean a promotion!' I teased her, but I couldn't fool her.

'Where's this lovely lady of yours?' Oliver asked.

'Oh she's making herself even more beautiful than she already is. Believe me, she's a real stunner.' Emily looked at me and winked.

Oliver, Mark and I ventured into the kitchen and organised ordering pizzas for dinner. I also wanted to ask them why Dad had come along.

Oliver explained that Jennifer felt it was time I made up with Dad, since Mum died. They told me I couldn't hold it against him forever. I supposed they were right, but it didn't take the pain or the memory away.

In many ways I deliberated on my maturity by withholding inane grudges. Parts of history or actions, or words that I was better leaving in the past. How would I manage being a father, with all the new-found stresses that that would invariably deliver? I had to locate a new strategy to begin tinkering with my own processes. Build a pragmatic program so I, Justin Whalley, could operate at all levels in ultimately a harsh environment.

Victoria made her way downstairs and into the kitchen, where I introduced her to my two older brothers. They shook hands and said they were glad to meet her. Mark gave her a close inspection, which made her look uncomfortable. Mind you, I knew what he was looking at. As I ushered Victoria out of the kitchen Oliver and Mark winked me and gave me the 'thumbs up' sign.

In the living room, I introduced Vicky to Jennifer first, Emily and then Donald.

'I've been so excited to meet you. Justin's never stopped talking about you.'

'Jenny, please, don't embarrass me.'

'I'm not, am I Victoria?'

'No, you're not. He's easily embarrassed, that's one of the reason I love your brother. He's a wonderful man.'

I didn't know whether to laugh, cry, hug her, or simply disappear from the room.

It was becoming something of an inauguration for me. No ambivalence from Victoria. Consummate, confident, without stuttering her words, her aura imbued me with a quintessential blanket of pure comfort. This burgeoning live act, that I was party to, caught me a little off guard. Negating any hesitation on my part, I had to draw on skills of cloaking, like the Star Trek baddies had, to minimise my truest feelings. Certainly whilst I was holding an audience of my nearest and dearest.

Thankfully the evening went smoothly enough. The lads, apart from my dad, went out to collect the pizzas. In the car Mark was frantic to ask me something.

'Look, Just, what were you doing when we arrived, eh? Or shouldn't I ask?' he asked me, grinning, in the passenger seat. Oliver took it all in, smirking in the back. He wanted to know too. They obviously don't get out enough.

'No, you shouldn't ask,' I replied, keeping my vision focussed straight ahead.

So I hit back in an clandestine yet blunt way.

'You and Sarah divorced yet? Or just separated?'

Oliver's smirk disappeared in a flash. Mark's smile evaporated like cigarette smoke in a stiff breeze.

'We're trying to work it out. Having counselling. For the children's sake, we're trying not to fight or make things acrimonious.'

'How are my nieces?'

'They're fine. Enjoying school. Always asking for Uncle Justin. "When can we visit him again?"'

'And what about you, Oliver? How's the job?'

'Not bad. Still getting paid. Can't grumble.'

'Moved out of Dad's yet?'

My Jaguar XF hummed along, as we neared the pizza takeaway restaurant.

'Yep. Got an apartment, not too far away. I move out in a few weeks. Can't wait, to be honest.'

I couldn't be bothered to ask why.

With four different types of pizza everyone had something to enjoy. We brought back some chicken wings for Dad, who said he was too old to eat pizza. It was young people's food.

Victoria and Emily and Jennifer seemed to be gelling well. I couldn't separate them. My dad observed this, although I got the distinct impression he wasn't sure about my Victoria. It was strange irony that his opinion was the one I couldn't care less about. It didn't have any currency of any value.

By ten forty-five in the evening, Donald requested to Oliver if he could be taken home. It was late and a mid-week night.

Jenny thanked me for the invite and my hospitality. As did Mark, Oliver and Emily. My dad muttered something at the end of the evening. I had selective deafness to whatever he said.

'Thanks, chaps. I'll come down to see you soon, Jenny, with Emily again.'

'Yes, you must do. I'm going to hold you to that.'

'It's a deal then.' I turned to look at Victoria for confirmation. She nodded her agreement.

We waved them off, as Oliver pulled away from the drive and the Merc cruised off into the warm, dark night.

'Whoa, thank goodness that's over.' I yawned, stretching every muscle and sinew.

'Your sisters are lovely. Emily's fun.'

'I thought you'd get on with her.'

'Not sure about your pervy brothers though.'

I laughed and she punched in my arm, making it numb.

'I'll get you for that.'

Making a quick check that the front door was locked and bolted, I chased after Vicky. That was my last expression of energy for the rest of the night. I was supremely knackered.

63

We'd heard it too many times during this financial year. The all too familiar story of how the 'other half' of Eiron had not performed as forecasted. Walter's meeting had a certain air of conspicuousness to it. Nothing new there.

Sales executives and account managers and internal sales gathered in the large Apollo meeting room, in the Nottingham office.

I nodded to a few sales guys who I knew and worked with when I had first started at Eiron. A few others gave me that knowing glint of an expression which told me they remembered. Remembered me from the sales conference some ten and half months ago. Damn, I wish I could be held in such high esteem for the right reasons.

As the masses descended on the Apollo room, Errol and Walter entered. Both had stern, mannequin-like straight faces. I was positive neither man played poker. But they would have been able to carry it off if they had to.

Five minutes later, the rumbling cacophony of conversations simmered down. There was a podium set up for Walter to approach. The smell of fear and trepidation entered my nostrils. Vicky sat beside me attempting to look calm. She wasn't.

Nerves were on edge. This would possibly eclipse any other announcement that Walter had given this year. He waited for complete silence. Behind Walter were three seats. His PA Fiona Watson sat in one, armed with a note pad. I assumed for any questions, and maybe who asked them. The names would probably be taken, so that Walter could punish them at a later date.

Errol sat beside her, doing his utmost to look erudite and radiate confidence to his salesforce.

Beside Errol sat one of the new directors, Andrew Wisemore. Why he was there, I could not fathom out.

Vicky and I looked at each other briefly, then turned our attention to our illustrious leader.

'Hello and welcome everyone. You all know why I'm here today. You will have been informed by all your sales managers about Eiron's global financial position. Let me first of all say, that no one in sales, I'll repeat that, no one sales has anything to worry about. If there is one thing Eiron needs it's good salespeople. Salespeople who can bring in the revenue. You all have my word on that.'

I shook my head immediately. Glancing around the room, everyone else smelt a huge stinking rat. He was in front us.

'I have to be brutal now, because there is no other way to say this. Job cuts will have to be made. As I've said, this will not be in sales. The number passed down to me by the EMEA director and our CEO in the US, is a relatively small number. This will be cascaded throughout all groups and divisions of Eiron, except sales.'

Walter attempted to bamboozle us with technical financial jargon. How Eiron had to report to the shareholders. The share price had fallen steadily to an all-time low, which made them nervous. The large and major shareholders were worried that they would not make any tangible returns on their Eiron investment. It was a fair argument, however I, and Vicky, and lot of the other salespeople sensed that there was always job preservation to consider.

This meant that people in Walter's position made sure that their jobs were immune from any potential threat. A protection system only offered to those inimitable special few. I considered if Walter's thoughts would ever spin to everyone else's future at Eiron. Then a pulsating, jolting nugget shot itself across me. Errol. Would he survive?

Middle management in many large companies like Eiron became an easy way to curtail the wage bill. Pay them off, take out that level of management and reorganise. Maybe he knew deep down, that was why he seemed more nervous than usual.

'So to wrap things up. The back office functions, HR, Payroll etc., will lose some bodies. As will our delivery capability and our consultants in all our specialist areas. Overall, including the USA, Eiron will attempt to lay off over seventeen hundred employees by the end of this month. Packages are in place and we have initiated an "early release" program for anyone over fifty years old. This is being sent out today and they have two days to inform their line manager and Human Resources of their decision.'

That last comment brought moans of derision. Two days to decide on your future is not enough. Walter responded.

'Two days may seem like a tight deadline, however the company is at risk. Let me remind you all of that. Everyone who is not performing, may do well to ask for the package that is on offer. The company must survive. The quicker we act, we give ourselves more of a fighting chance.' Walter was deadly serious when he uttered those words.

As I had envisaged, Eiron's predicament was circumspect to say the least. Their contingency plan. Making people redundant.

When he'd finished Errol approached the podium.

'Some of the details in regards to Eiron's overall plans will be discussed with each salesperson and their immediate managers. Deals where you had consultants involved or engineers, who may no longer be working for Eiron, these specifics will need to be discussed with myself or your manager. Once again, the essence is on speed. You all need to go through your list of opportunities and get back to us ASAP.'

Errol moved away from the podium and sat back down. More rumbles in the packed room. I couldn't see one spare seat. I turned to look behind me; some salespeople were standing up.

Walter returned to the podium and asked everyone to get to work, keeping their heads down, bringing in absolutely everything they could, regardless of how small.

Everyone filed out, talking animatedly about Walter's announcement.

'What do you think I should do, Just? Should I look for another job?' Vicky asked me, with hint of worry in her smooth voice.

'You know what, Walter had to say that stuff about underperformers. It was said so no one in sales would dare take anything for granted. We'll all work our butts off 'til Christmas and he'll still make his inflated bonus. Jammy bastard.'

'Yeah, that may be the case for him. What about my figures? I'm at seventy-four percent. I'm way behind.'

'Look, Vicky, I have a little plan to boost you numbers up, okay? Errol is aware and hopefully he can carry it off for us. I won't let them get rid of you that easy.' I smiled confidently at her. Vicky finally responded in kind.

As the car park emptied, with the other salespeople going home or returning to the Birmingham office, Errol worried me. He wasn't the same person. The strain was beginning to show.

Somehow, Vicky and I returned to desks to see Shaun sitting at an empty desk. He had one more day officially. He, too, had concerns about his role in Dublin and wondered if one would still be there.

'Youse been to that meeting with Mr Baker?'

'Yeah, not good news though,' I answered, whilst taking my seat.

'Yeah I know. Thelma's told me. Half the South African workforce have been given their notices. It started on Monday.'

'What? On Monday?' Vicky's voice reached an unusually higher pitch.

'Yep. Some countries are way ahead. Some have made all the cutbacks they need to make already. They badly need to stop losing money.' Shaun seemed frighteningly well informed.

Vicky and I sat talking to Shaun, whilst sporadically sorting out the information that Walter had asked us to glean.

At five thirty every person left on the dot. As for Vicky, Shaun and I, when we exited the building, Errol was still in a meeting with Walter and Andrew Wisemore. Something was not right at all.

STORMY WEATHER

64

Without warning, like a thief in the night, Shaun slipped out without coming in the following day. Everyone suffered from a hangover from Walter's pitch. What that did was allow everyone the opportunity to jump off the sinking ship.

Phone calls were being made to other IT partners and companies who were doing better than Eiron.

Shaun had taken an early flight to South Africa to meet Thelma. He did say he didn't want any fuss and under the present circumstances, it wouldn't have got any.

Errol turned himself into a virtual ghost. He was nowhere to be seen on Friday. His location a mystery with not a clue for me or anyone to track him down.

Victoria had three customer meetings – a positive sign in the least, displaying the correct work ethic required at this sensitive company juncture.

Two of those were mine. Looking at my calendar, I had meetings booked in for the next four weeks, running to mid-December. That would cover me until Christmas.

Looking across the office, hardly anyone, execs or account managers, were in the office. I could not ascertain or speculate as to whether they were busy with Eiron prospects or out at interviews. Most likely the latter.

Sales is a job for the survival of the fittest, the smartest, the cleverest and who you know in the industry. All of these ingredients coupled with a splice of luck, thrown in for good measure. Who you knew within the IT/telecoms industry was, however, the 'golden key'.

It was something I needed to develop and develop quickly. I was always told, 'Whatever you do, build up a network of people to know you, trust you, and will support whenever you might need it.' That statement couldn't be more prudent or validated at this time.

I made several calls to chase up business that was outstanding. Sent multiple emails, with attachments for quotes, responses to requests for information (RFIs), all morning.

Vicky called me to say that she thought there was some opportunity in her first two visits. I reinforced that sentiment by telling her she was better than she thought. She could do this job and do it very well. I could hear her smiling down the phone and she uttered her words in a vibrant, excited way. Prior to curtailing our call I informed her that we'd go out for a meal at the weekend, after such shitty week. She concurred wholeheartedly.

Lunch was a lonely affair. A chicken salad sandwich on rye bread. A packet of bacon-flavoured crisps, a bottle of strawberry enhanced water, plus a Danish pastry. Sitting at my desk, tucking in, the sales section on the fourth floor was deathly quiet. The abandoned ship, called *The Eiron Titanic*. How apt would that be at this moment in the company's affluent history? Not so much of that now, it seemed.

The rest of my day represented a mass exodus, with no one having any intention of returning.

I left early, with still no sign of Errol all day. I had to call him. Something more was behind this restructuring.

Meeting Victoria at home, she informed me that the last meeting was a waste of time. The customer was 'in bed' with his current supplier and wouldn't move, regardless of any deal we could offer him.

Sitting at the kitchen table sampling Victoria's 'chicken and bacon surprise', she sat staring at me eating.

'Anything wrong?' I asked.

'What's up? You looked worried about something.'

'Do I?'

'Don't play with me, Whalley, spit it out.' I actually wanted to. Her 'chicken and bacon surprise', was surprisingly awful and bland.

'Okay, okay. I'm worried about Errol. I've tried three times to contact him at home and his mobile seems to be switched off. I've tried Elisa's – no reply there either.' I pushed my plate aside, only having consumed half the amount. I had my excuse ready.

My legitimacy surrounding Errol's disappearance displayed itself for Victoria to witness. I never doubted that she would question my motives about my manager and long-term friend. She didn't, instead she provided me with a possible solution, to a troubling and niggly angst that had built up in me.

'What about calling… what's her name?' Vicky snapped her fingers a few times in succession. 'That's it, Mary Leadbetter.'

'You know something, you're not just a pretty face.' I stroked her cheek and left the table.

Victoria smiled back, raising her eyebrows. Then her vision angled downward at my plate. I was gone, heading for the telephone in my bedroom.

65

We had a fantastic weekend. Went to the cinema on Sunday. On Saturday out for a meal in a lovely, quiet, traditional Italian restaurant, run by Italians.

However, all that enjoyment and excitement was tempered by not being able to get hold of Elisa or Errol. Mary hadn't seen or heard from Elisa either. Hysterically, Mary had visions and wild theories about Errol kidnapping Elisa. At one stage she suggested Errol may even do something vicious or despicable and dump her body somewhere. I quickly and curtly reminded Mary, that this was Errol, not some homicidal maniac.

For the next week I swapped some of my meetings to give them to Victoria. Everyone who did turn up for work, claimed to have other things lined up or in the pipeline.

Eiron's financial position was all over the news and in the broadsheets. Another large deal closed for me, when I opened my post to see a purchase order for three hundred and two thousand pounds. However, the customer contacted me, once he had seen the business news.

I reassured him that Eiron were still committed to delivering services and products to all its customers. This news would not make it any easier for any company to buy from us. Particularly the larger corporations.

On Thursday of that week I received a postcard from Shaun. It was from South Africa. He said things could not be better, due to the shake-up that Eiron S.A. had been under. He said that they would be leaving for Dublin at the weekend. 'Wish you were here' is how he ended his message.

Victoria closed two deals. Not massive by any stretch of the imagination, yet worthwhile. As Walter said, every deal counts, regardless of size. It made her feel a whole lot better.

On that day, Errol was back in the office, although I was out on customer site, explaining what was happening to Eiron's financial state. Vicky called me to tell me he was in. I asked her to confirm if he would be in on Friday. He gave her an evasive answer. Said he wasn't sure. It depends on how things go.

I thought last week was shitty, however this was getting ridiculous. Merging on incompetence from our supreme leaders.

A percentage of the workforce in the Midlands had looked for and probably had other job roles lined up. A few had already handed in their notices. This was what Walter would have counted on to reduce the head count, negating the standard HR process that would have to follow. Crucially it also meant any potential redundancy fees were drastically reduced, with only the usual monthly wage bill to be met. The perfect scenario.

Friday morning arrived and Vicky and I had worked hard this week. She made and visited some of her own appointments. I made six out of the targeted eight per week, which was a stupefying number to achieve. No one to my knowledge ever did eight meetings in one week. Myself and two other guys held the record with seven.

Errol was nowhere to be seen. He had his mobile switched off again. What the hell?

I'm sure he had been made redundant and his phone had been handed in. If he had, it was typical of Walter's supposed leadership. No manager for the Midlands. No one had been informed. No one knew what was going on. The next thing for Eiron to lose would be their customer base.

On the way home, Vicky followed me in her car. We had house work to do all weekend. My mobile chirped and it was Walter Baker.

'Justin, I've seen you have Monday afternoon free. Can I ask you to not to eat anything at lunchtime?' At first I wondered what the hell he was on about. 'I would like to take you to lunch on Monday, along with Errol. I'll meet you at the office first. Okay?'

'Walter, what about…?' He hung up, the miserable bastard.

He didn't want me to ask about Errol. Maybe that was it. Errol was going or had 'unofficially' gone. I would be the next in line. I didn't want to arouse any excitement in Victoria, so I was determined not to say anything about the whole sordid malaise that had ensnared the company.

My doubts about how this happened and who to fundamentally target, left me pondering on far too many possibilities. Walter's lack of real clarity in his decisions, his leadership, if you can call it that, dumbfounded little ol' me. Nothing he did impinged on his personal career, his feelings as a person or an employee. Maybe that was somewhat harsh, yet his demeanour, his outwardly predominating manner, showed his complete dispassion for his teams.

Thinking on, I, Justin Whalley, could be completely and utterly talking out my backside. Having worked with this man, been showered by his management style of the 'sloping shoulder', I could only manage to be perfunctory about him. Again, I had to muster the inner strength required to set aside these ideas, thoughts of potential negativity that would pull me under, with a buoy to save me.

Retaining and achieving my PMA (positive mental attitude), I focussed on the points; with everyone else leaving it left gaps that would still need to be filled. This could emancipate me from the doldrums of just being an account manager. I calmed myself and drove safely home, with Victoria in tow. That weekend I would ensure she didn't have a clue what was happening.

66

Emily, Victoria and I had Sunday lunch together, out in the tranquil countryside of Derbyshire. Somewhere off the A6, as the road meanders heading towards Buxton and across the Peak District.

It was a small, original stone-brick public house, which served an astonishing amount of food, with plenty of choice on their menu.

Victoria and Emily talked liberally, as though they had been friends for years. I was more happy for Emily, than Victoria. Following her deviation into drugs, losing a baby, going out regularly and drinking heavily, I was glad there was someone she could talk to. She needed people like Mary and hopefully Victoria to support her and keep her away from the things that ultimately could bring her serious harm.

I sat there listening to them. Watching them laugh unabated at each other's experiences with men. Every now and then I'd throw a comment in, which they counteracted with their own cutting response. I was warned to be careful, as I was paying for the meal.

The weather was cold yet little or no breeze kept the temperature at a bearable near-winter chill. We were a few weeks from Christmas and of course Victoria and Emily discussed what presents to get their nearest and dearest.

Emily returned with us, and stayed for dinner, that evening. She loved my car. Its heated seats. The electric front seats with memory. I calmly explained it was a company car of sorts, for which I paid a monthly fee. Victoria smiled. She drove a German executive car, about the same size as my Jaguar XF.

Going to bed, I kept up my normal pretence. Normal behaviour, keeping in mind my meeting with Walter and Errol tomorrow.

Deliberately I did not contact Errol. I didn't want to let him know, and maybe he didn't anyway. In addition Errol probably had the sense and inclination to keep his mobile switched off. Any callers would be greeted by his dulcet tones, revealing his voicemail message about not being available. I proposed Errol wouldn't have performed erroneously as I did, with my voicemail debacle. There was a level of professionalism I expected and was delivered in the main by Errol.

To cap things off, I fully understood any message left on his voicemail system would not be returned. Incommunicado, I think they call it. Errol was almost like one of my favourite films – the Scarlet Pimpernel.

As I lay in bed wide awake, eyes rolling, my beautiful, serene Victoria breathed heavily in a rhythmic whimpering manner. My heightened adrenalin that I desperately attempted to repudiate, pumped around me, keeping me alert. Sharp. Electrified.

With a building growth in sheer exhaustion and at the umpteenth, uncounted attempt my eyes eventually closed and I finally drifted off to sleep.

67

Getting to work early, had to be one of my key priorities for Monday morning. To catch up on any deals, close them and make a few more appointments for December or possibly January.

Errol arrived in the office at about eleven thirty. No suit on. No tie. A pair of combat-style trousers, long-sleeved printed top, Nike trainers and a baseball cap. Was I right? Had our manager been laid off? Had Walter not informed anyone? Or was this the new way of doing things? Everyone had to piece it together like one of these murder mystery weekends. Conjecture, rumour and gossip was the order of the day in Eiron. If it was, then it stunk. It would be typical of Walter. As our leader for the UK, in my humble opinion, he should be doing a lot more to safeguard one of the few successful territories for Eiron globally.

He said nothing to anyone and headed for his office. The door closed. I stood up to have a look. As I did so, I realised the few people still in the office followed suit.

Errol sat at his desk and made some phone calls. The few of us looked at each other and shrugged shoulders, wondering what was happening. I sat down to read emails of four sales guys who had handed in their notice. They had found other employment. How times had altered from when I had first begun my career at Eiron. You never understood fully what the company was like or would be. What the people would genuinely like as you went through your tenure. No crystal balls allowed, so no peeking at any possible futures.

Leaning back, scratching my head, my eyes locked onto the huge frame of Walter Baker. His jaded blond hair, looked freshly washed and combed. I peered into his ice-blue eyes, which stared back at me, as he came over to stand by my desk. It was only then that my nostrils absorbed the odour of nicotine. After all this time, I just realised that Walter was a smoker.

'You ready, Whalley?' His voice was deep and booming.

'Ready when you are, Walter.' My response was confident, assured. I intended to make my response sounded confident, without being cocky, or worse still, facetious.

'I'll get Errol. We'll go in your car.'

'No problem, I'll be downstairs in the car park. Do I need to bring anything with me?' I asked just in case.

'No. Just yourself will do.' He offered an insincere, paltry smile.

Without hesitating I closed down my laptop. Took the stairs to car park, to clean up my car. There were petrol receipts, sweet wrappers all over. Luckily I had a new air freshener in the car. Victoria's idea.

Minutes later Errol came out to the car with Walter adjacent to him. They got in and we drove off.

'Boston Bean, Just. I've booked us a table.' Errol finally spoke.

'Or what about a little country pub somewhere within a fifteen-to-twenty-minute drive?' Walter suggested. It also meant Errol no longer had any power. I couldn't understand why he was there either.

Walter won, and we ended up out of the city centre along Mansfield Road. We took the A614 for about a mile then turned off. I knew a place we could go to.

Sitting down, we ordered our food and drinks from the extensive bar menu. The public house hummed with the cacophonous noise of a myriad of conversations. Sitting in a corner, we sipped fizzy drinks. No alcohol.

'So Justin, I guess you've been wondering why I've asked you here today,' Walter opened up. Errol looked across at him pensively.

'You could say that.'

'As you know Eiron's financial state is not good. Our reputation is taking a battering in the marketplace. As you have found out, customers are wanting us to prove that we will still be around in six months' time, before they'll buy anything from us.'

I nodded to show my understanding of the situation. Walter took two gulps of his drink and continued. He had no tie on, but a dark pin-stripe navy suit, with a chambray buttoned-down collar shirt.

'At the time I informed all the salespeople last week about the "human" losses, the information I gave everyone was correct.' Errol threw me a worrying look, but kept quiet. Saying absolutely nothing.

'What has happened is that, the board have asked for every employee to be assessed. For their skills, experience, what they can offer Eiron. This work has now been completed.'

'Okay. So how is it that this wasn't mentioned before, Walter, why now?' I had to ask.

'Fair question. You're one of the first to be told. You have to understand, that some people have already left the company, no doubt lots are planning to. What Eiron don't need is to be left without experienced salespeople.' Then Errol leapt in, surprisingly.

'You see, Justin, part of the process to reduce costs, also it finds out who Eiron want to keep. So on the flip side, when things upturn, Eiron has the right people to pull them back to where they were. Do you understand what I'm trying to say?'

I watched Errol's stern, conscientious expression.

'Maybe, however I'm not totally sure. Please explain.' I genuinely had an idea, yet I needed it explaining to me. Clearly and concisely.

A waiter came over to our table with our food. It smelt tempting and looked delicious. He left the table as calmly and as efficiently as he'd approached.

We began tucking in, whilst in between mouthfuls Errol explained.

'You must have been quietly wondering why I'm here, for instance.'

'Yes I had. Not just today, however. You've been acting weird for the last week or two.' Walter ate without looking at me. He flashed Errol a quick, cursory glance.

'So you had noticed. I'll tell you why.' Errol paused to swallow a mouthful of his chicken burger with cheese and bacon. He swigged his drink to wash it down.

'The reason is, Justin, and there's no easy way to reveal this. Apart from the back office staff that were been made redundant, one of the higher costs for Eiron is salespeople and their large wages. A list over time had been created, which links in with what Walter told you when we first got here.'

'I see.' My heart began to thunder. Thump inside my ribcage. It felt as though Lennox Lewis was practising inside me. Taking a few calm sips of my drink, I looked for a response from Walter. Nothing.

The noise in the pub increased, as more lunch-timers entered.

'To be direct, Justin, your name is on that list.'

A pregnant pause ensued. I continued to eat as though I hadn't heard what Errol said. Walter stopped eating and looked up. Waiting, I presume, for my reaction. My world spun on its axis, in total utter bewilderment. Parallel universe, yes, that's gotta be it.

The lunch now made sense. In public. No opportunity to make or cause a scene. Errol was there for moral support. I think. I still wasn't sure. It was up to me to respond. Puncture the silence that engulfed our little world of Eiron.

'So what exactly are you saying?' I put my knife and fork on my plate. Put my elbows on the table and interlocked my hands under my chin, leaning forward a little.

Fixing my bespectacled gaze on Walter, his eyes shifted uneasily in his round sockets. The yellow-bellied bastard had suckered me and brought Errol to defend him or at least defuse me.

'It's like this, Justin. The reason I'm in these clothes is because I resigned. Do you know the reason for my resignation?' I shook my head, flicking my vision now between Walter and Errol as though watching a game of tennis.

'Because your name was on the list. When I was told that I had to let you go, I told Walter I'd rather resign than lose one of best salespeople.' That was news. Errol a martyr, umm, I wasn't convinced, yet I had to believe what he was telling me. All the evidence suggested that he had been made redundant. No laptop, mobile not working, it did seem that he had put me first.

'Thank you, Errol. Nevertheless, it does not save me or my job. What you're telling me now is that sales have always been affected.' Then I turned my direct focus onto Walter. 'However, you categorically told us that sales would not be affected, several times. Stressing, as I understand, the importance of selling that supports the company.' I hoped my voice did not travel or increase to much in volume.

'It's one of those things.' That's all Walter could muster.

I sighed, shook my head and finished off my lunch, which was tasty. Scant consolation, if any.

We sat in silence again for another few minutes before I spoke.

'So what happens now? A month's notice. I claim "the package", you talked about, assuming it's still available. Get paid holiday pay and anything else that I'm owed.'

'Yes, that's correct.' Walter sat forward, responding in an assertive tone. 'No one likes doing this, Justin, believe me. I'll make sure you get everything that's due to you.'

'I should bloody well hope so too.'

'I'll go and pay for this, shall I?' Walter offered. Errol and I said nothing. We watched him escape from my fury that was building by the minute, by leaving the table.

'So what are you doing about work?' I asked Errol.

'Nothing so far. I'm on three months' guardian leave. I'm using them as holiday. I haven't had a break from working for over ten years. I intend to make the most of it. Look, if you need any help getting another job, just call, okay?' Errol looked genuinely pissed off for me. I knew there would nothing he could have done.

Pragmatically it would have been a numbers game. A cull to get the workforce to a specific number that would also minimise costs whichever way they could. I imagined due to my short tenure at Eiron my 'redundancy package' calculation, amounted to less than others. Usually, companies like Eiron put aside a set fee for compensation in these matters of employment release. If by some mystical stroke of luck they can keep that budget in check or reduce, then, it's a gold star for them.

Conversely I may be completely way off the mark. Whatever method or strategy they deployed, was again a thing of pure obscurity.

By now I didn't have the energy to argue the toss. My evidence was strong. Assured, as I had delivered figures that meant I had exceeded my targets. One of the only few salespeople. A contradiction in terms was my tenure at Eiron, compared to others. In that meeting Walter talked about keeping good salespeople. Bullshit, obviously. I can only think I was earning or about to get paid too much. How could success be treated as a liability? I had joined a company for fools. And I, Justin Whalley, was the biggest one of them. My mother always had a saying – 'the higher a monkey climbs, the more he is exposed'. Well I felt like I had a monkey on my back. Walter fucking Baker. I attempted to calm myself and think things through, whilst Walter paid for our lunch.

It was palpably clear that the decision had already been made. Errol informed me that four other salesmen would be given the same news today. Some of them by email. How cold would that be? If it was any consolation, the fact that I had lunch bought, and the UK Managing Director came down to see me, was something. I suppose.

For the first time, I thought about telling Victoria. How would she take the news? It sounded as though her job was safe. Errol said 'salesmen'.

He left the table to use the gents'. I sat there alone, trying to remain calm, but couldn't. Walter the lying bastard Baker, had screwed me. Good and proper.

All along I was promised to be promoted or for greater things. I did my numbers, smashed my increased targets. Yet there was no logic to the selection process. It would have been Walter's 'names out of a hat' process.

My adrenalin kicked in again. The more I thought about this huge six-foot-five weasel only made things worse. He conned me and all the other hard-working salespeople. The little shithead and saved himself and sacrificed everyone else. Even willing to let Errol resign, so he'd look good in front of the EMEA directors and the US CEO. The tosser had to feel some pain. I couldn't work out how to give him some.

Errol returned to the table, standing.

'Ready to go?'

'S'pose so. Might as well start looking on the internet for jobs and joining agencies,' I told Errol solemnly.

'Look, I mean what I said. Give me a call, send your resume and I'll have a word with one or two resellers. You never know. Think about it first. Let this sink in, yeah?' That was Errol's penny's worth of advice.

Walter signalled us over to leave. Walter's embarrassed expression was clear to see. Secretly he must be enjoying this. Or maybe I was just angry, and pissed off at what Eiron had done to me.

Walking out of the pub I felt anesthetised, numbed by it all. Walter must be frightened of what I'd do. He obviously had no inclination to tell me by himself. Errol was used as the calming factor. Potentially as protection too. Mind you, I couldn't see Walter and Errol being best buddies out of work.

Walter sat in the passenger seat and Errol buckled up in the back. It was fifteen minutes after two in the afternoon.

68

Errol, sitting in the rear of the car, noticed me glance at him in my mirror. He attempted a half smile. I didn't respond.

The warm day was now overcast and threatened to rain. Dark nimbus clouds circled menacingly overhead.

If Walter Baker wanted to see what was like living on the edge, facing customers day in day out, I was about to show him what risks salespeople encountered every single day.

Increasing my speed down the meandering 'B' road, Walter looked head on. Traffic was heavier than I expected and far too slow. I assumed there was a tractor up ahead, slowing the traffic. I hit the brakes to reduce my speed, throwing Walter and Errol forward abruptly. Then the heavens opened. Commencing bucketloads of rain, in a flurry.

'Steady on, Just, we're in no hurry.' Errol looked frantically at me.

'We'll see about that, shall we?'

I watched Walter's face turn whiter as I pulled out on the narrow opposing lane. My front-wheel-drive Jaguar XF, its eighteen-inch, low-profile tyres fighting to find grip, as my wheels spun in desperation.

I depressed the sport button on the automatic gear lever, listening to revs race to over four thousand RPM.

'Justin, pull back in right now!'

I just laughed and pressed harder on the accelerator. We overtook one car, then two, then three, there was at least another six cars to go, oh, and the ten-mile-an-hour tractor.

The rain lashed down hard. My wipers were on the fastest speed. Up ahead, in the distance, through the thick ever increasing spray was a articulated lorry heading directly for us.

'Justin, Justin! What the fuck are you doing?' Walter was squealing. My heart was racing. Beating exponentially.

Errol sat back in total silence. Holding on for dear life.

The rain crashed against the windscreen. It seemed as though someone had a bucket full of water above the car.

I pressed harder on the accelerator, increasing to speed to eighty-five miles an hour. The opposing lorry began to flash his headlights, as we overtook car number six and seven. Just three more to go.

'Yeeha! Don't you just love this adrenalin rush! It's what I do every time I see a customer and when they tell me I wouldn't get the contract. Sort of flushes out all the negative energy. Don't you feel that way too, Walter?'

'Stop this fucking car right now!' Walter screamed at me. He dare not try and interfere, for fear of a worse outcome.

Now the artic began blowing his horn, vehemently. I removed my specs, to barely make out the driver waving his arms frantically. I was now driving with just my right hand.

'Oh shit, Justin! You'd better cut in. Do it now!!' Errol yelled from the back.

The lorry began to brake. I floored the car and glanced over to my left. The car was halfway past the tractor when I swerved in front, skidding wildly, in a snake-like pattern, as I fought to keep the car from sliding down the embankment.

'Justin!!' Errol and Walter screamed.

The car reverberated with their in-tandem voices.

The car swung this way and that, as the rear snaked viciously. Errol's body shifted with the movement of the car. Thank goodness he was wearing his seat belt.

I calmly put back my spectacles with my left hand. Grinning

wickedly as they slipped over my ears. Driving an automatic with power steering made it easier to control with one hand.

The cacophony of car horns could be heard, particularly the one from the lorry driver. In the rain, I glimpsed some sort of hand gesture out of his window. I just smiled.

'What the hell are you smiling at? You could have easily killed us. You want locking up, Whalley! You were obviously born into the right family.'

'What the fuck did you just say? You weaselling little prick. I ought to drive this thing right in front of an oncoming car, making sure they hit your side. You're lucky I didn't kill you. You're a pathetic excuse for a director, Walter. Just to let you know, not one salesperson could bear to work for you. If you were on fire, no one would piss on you. Slimly arsehole.' I mumbled the last few words.

After a deep breath and rolling his head from side to side, Errol leaned forward.

'Just. Get us back safely, then you'd better go home and cool off. Do what you have to, but I'd suggest you don't come in again. I'll collect what's yours, and leave everything else to the company.'

'Whatever. Couldn't give a shit now. Pussies! Wankers!' I looked at Walter, who was cowering in the passenger seat. His knuckles white as a hospital sheet.

The next ten minutes followed in perfect silence. I hoped Walter would not hyperventilate, as his breathing became rapid and short. In any case I didn't care. And why the heck should I?

69

Walter and Errol both stepped out of the car gingerly. Shaking with my capricious driving behaviour. The car park at the office was nearly empty. It was Friday afternoon.

Walter slammed the door shut; my car shuddered under the vibrations. I watched them both in my rear-view mirror as I sped off, wheels screeching from the car park. I was still fuming.

Now for the for the ominous part. Telling Victoria. She had only recently moved in. Now we'd have one less wage coming in to pay the bills. And I had quite a few of them.

My two-bedroom house in Wollaton cost over three hundred thousand. I would also have to pay for my car. The car allowance Eiron gave would stop immediately. Another area where they could save money.

Driving home, I slowed down, and tried to calm myself. Ambiguous thoughts permeated my mind, sending me dizzy. How unjustified this all was. What kind of hierarchy did Eiron have? What were they thinking? Or weren't they? There could be no dispensation by me, for the despicable actions that they took. I wanted to know who the other three sales guys were, that also received the same shocking and unexpected news.

Arriving home early, Vicky's car was nowhere to be seen. My phone had been switched off all afternoon. The sun beamed down rays of warmth, through random gaps in the white fluffy clouds. My temperature had dropped, as my adrenalin subsided.

Sitting in the lounge after polishing off a vodka and orange, the fact of my redundancy hadn't begun to truly sink in. What I did with Walter and Errol in car surprised me. It wasn't me driving. Someone else, something else, was in there. On the flipside, I was glad I did it. Shook up the cowardly little shit. Gave Weaselly Walter a genuine taste of really living on the edge. Taking risks and accepting the consequences later.

My reverie was unceremoniously interrupted by my front door slamming shut.

'Justin, are you there lover?' Victoria called out from the hallway.

'In here, Vicky. The lounge.'

She entered with a beaming smile and a both arms full. One with her briefcase and laptop bag over her right shoulder. The left hand, she had a bunch of flowers.

'Aren't you gonna help me with this? Or are you just going to watch me struggle?' She gave me her warm, sexy smile, which for a split second, made me forget what I needed to tell her.

'Sorry, Vicky, of course I will help.' I hoped she didn't recognise any tone of solemnity in my voice.

I allowed Vicky to sit down in the lounge. She sat stretched out on the sofa, with legs on my lap. I rubbed her sweaty feet, massaged them to a degree. She moaned in a thankful way, saying it relieved some of tension and aching. My that was my next career move. Be a masseuse. All those women… ummm, maybe.

I turned to her, looking at my lover of the last few months.

'Vicky, something happened today. I won't be easy, to explain it but I'll tell it to you straight.' She looked concerned immediately.

'What is it, Justin?'

'Walter made me redundant. Today, just now. This afternoon. The son-of-a-bitch took me to lunch to fire me. Brought Errol along for backup, just in case.' Victoria sat there, covering her mouth in disbelief. She reached over, after the initial shock had subsided, to hug me.

'Don't worry, Just, we'll manage. We'll show that prick.' She was as angry as me. I hadn't told her the best part yet.

'That's not all, Vicky. I think he'll get rid of me ASAP. Errol will have to back him up.' Vicky pulled away from me, as if my halitosis had returned. It had been a problem previously.

'Justin. What did you do? Did you tell him to—' I interjected.

'No. Well not in so many words. It was what I did that will make him not want me to hang around.' I sat adjacent to Victoria, holding both her hands in mine.

The house was deathly quiet. No TV or radio on in the background. The central heating was also on mute, no clanking or knocking sounds.

'Justin.' She raised her voice. 'What did you do?' she asked again in staccato fashion.

'I nearly killed him. Walter and Errol, oh and maybe me.'

'What the hell for? Are you bloody crazy? What would I do without you, Justin? Did you think about that!' So much for the good part. Vicky blasted me for being irresponsible. And for making things worse with Walter. She pointed out that he could mess me around with my last wage packet and bonuses that were owed. I would need every penny and a reference. Oh dear. I didn't think ahead. Now Walter would have veritable reasons for dishing his own style of reciprocity with impunity.

I buried my head in my hands and apologised.

'I was fuming, Vicky. You had to be there. That smarmy bastard enjoyed doing it. I'd been promised promotion, and that's why I thought he was paying for lunch. With everyone else going, I was certain to be promoted. That weasel couldn't give me one reason why

I was selected. I mean, I've done my number for this year, how many other people could say that? Fuckin' place is a joke. Len Ferris knew what he was talking about. Now I know exactly what he means.'

'Look, Just, we'll cope. You'll get something else and forget Eiron.'

'I bloody hope so.' She hugged me again and I felt sorry, angry, confused, for me and Vicky.

Later on as Vicky made dinner, my brain commenced thinking with some form of clarity. Had my stunt put her job at risk? Where would we be then? Screwed.

Unusually for me, I had been self-centred, displayed utter selfishness, without considering any wider plans or effects. My only desired hope, lay with Walter knowing I wouldn't be returning, so he'd forget about me, leaving me alone.

After a dinner of chicken stir-fry, which was delicious, I stood in the shower, allowing the water to reinvigorate me. Washing away all the shit that had passed over me today. For my sake as well as Vicky's I had to think clearly. Formulate a strategy of moving on.

Once dry and freshly coated in a masculine-smelling body cream, I ventured back downstairs.

In the kitchen, I hugged Vicky from behind, kissing her on her neck. She giggled a little.

'What would I do without you, Vicky, eh?'

'Be down the pub getting rat-arsed, probably.'

'You know me too well.'

'Why don't you give Errol a call?'

'Not a good idea,' I told her, pulling away.

'Oh. Oh, okay. If you say so.'

'I do.'

There was no way I'd could call Errol, not yet anyway. I wanted to ask him about Elisa, as a diversionary tactic in order to learn about

Walter's position. The procedure for redundancy was to have an exit interview, where I would hand in my mobile, laptop and any other company equipment. I wanted Errol's confirmation.

Victoria sat on top of me on the sofa and playfully opened her blouse. I knew what was coming next. And I couldn't resist.

70

By the time I had arrived at work for my exit interview, everyone knew what had happened. About my demise and fall from grace to a fall of shame.

Apparently, Walter took a few days to recover from my rally-style driving session. Maybe that could be my new career. I wondered what qualifications I would need to enrol.

Walking over to my section, I said hello to a few of the salespeople I had worked with for just over two years.

They apathetically apologised about my being made expendable. I accepted their condolences sceptically. However, I smiled and hoped my expressions were genuine enough to convince them, that I was truly thankful for their pity. I had no recourse to expend the vital emotional energy to care whether it worked or not.

After my brief tour around the fourth floor, I directed my attention to Errol's office. He had called me to arrange this date and time for the exit interview.

To my surprise, he told me he had been asked to take up a position in EMEA. I knew that most managers, when faced with redundancy from their position, had the opportunity to seek roles elsewhere within the organisation. He reluctantly told me that he'd accepted it, only after I had pushed him several times. I couldn't quibble. I would have mirrored his conscientious decision. So much for resigning, when that carrot is dangled in front of you. How much of a resignation Errol delivered, I suspect I'll never truly learn.

Another facet I'd have to absorb, understand, index it away for another time.

I approached what was Errol's office for the last time. Looking through the glass-encased office, my brain registered another surprise. There was Errol, large as life, sitting in his office. Suited and booted. Facing him, the arsehole, Walter chicken-shit Baker. At a small round table in front of Errol's desk, was the HR manager.

Tapping lightly on the door, I felt all eyes on the fourth floor bore into me. Vivid memories of my speech at the sales conference whizzed through my mind in a flash. It was no time for the swan scenario. I had to be calm, focused and professional to the end.

Errol beckoned me in.

'Come in, Justin, come in.'

I replied with a false weak smile, aiming it at Walter and the HR manager.

Walter stealthily diverted his vision from mine. He directed his sight to the ceiling, the floor, the pictures on the wall. It made think even less of him. *Man up,* I told myself.

Errol and Walter moved to the small table that the HR manager sat at.

Errol then gave me a strange look. Then he sniffed. I then remembered that I'd been drinking over the last few days. Had a skinful last night, hadn't shaved and probably didn't look too sexy at all.

My casual chambray shirt, looked frayed at the cuffs. My expensive torn designers jeans only served to make me look anything but expensive.

'I take it you've not taken this too well?' The HR manager spoke in a nasal tone.

'What's it to you?' My reply was implacable, my tone accusatory. The room fell into a library like silence.

'Okay, can we get on with this then?' I asked assertively. I received stern looks from Walter and the HR manager. Errol gave me a softer look, to say calm down.

'Have you got all the company equipment, as required by your terms of employment?' the HR manager asked.

'It's all stacked neatly on top of my old desk, just across the office. Hope that's okay.' My facetiousness increased.

The HR manager glared at me through his thick-rimmed spectacles. I glared back through my thin ones.

He slid a paper form, which he wanted me to sign. It was a document which I agreed to, that stated that all the company's equipment had been handed back. It was in good order, with no damage.

Eyeing over each word in the standard templated document, I annoyingly took my time. Anything now to be petty, childish underneath, on display however was a professional person, reading an important document, that required fastidious attention.

Drawing my eye line to the bottom of the page, there were sections detailing where to sign and date the document. Below those were two dotted lines entitled: witness 1 and witness 2.

'Thank you,' he said after I signed it.

'Now can you also sign this too, please.' He grinned when he said please.

'Absolutely.'

I took this form, repeating my concentrated reading, another step to antagonise the prat sitting directly opposite me. I nodded my head every now and then, to make my reading seem genuine. It was inconsequential what the document said. Looking up at all of them for a second or two, I then signed the document. It was more a like a doctor's scribble. Unreadable.

'Mr Whalley, once again thank you. Now that is it, unless you have any final questions.'

That word, 'final'. The bastard had to rub it in.

'Yes, I do have a final question. And I would like Walter to give me a genuine and not a bullshit answer.' I leaned forward. Walter looked at me and for the first time since I'd entered Errol's office.

'Then ask it,' Errol interjected firmly. We stared hard at each other for a few seconds. I looked away, back at Walter.

'How, or should I say, what process was used for me and the other salespeople, for us to be chosen, to be made redundant?'

Walter leaned back. I could see him thinking about the answer. Trying to conjure something up.

'You said you wanted the truth.' Walter finally spoke, in an even monotone voice.

'Yes I did. I have nothing else,' I answered back.

'Well here it is. We asked several salespeople some time ago, if we had to make redundancies, who would they choose. Do you want to know something, Justin?' Walter paused and sat on the edge of his seat. 'To my surprise, your name came up a number of times.'

Now I leaned back in my chair. My stomach began to gurgle. I wasn't hungry. It was the low punch that Walter had just dealt me. Errol nodded his head to confirm he was telling me the truth.

'We kept that data, along with other managers who had to put names forward. Strange as it may seem, the sales team is vitally important. Maybe more than one successful individual, or a few. And Mr Whalley,' Walter sat forward further, and leaned on the table to steady himself, looking at me eye-to-eye, 'do you know who voted for you?' He waited for me to say something. I didn't. I couldn't. My heart was thumping. My head pounding.

'Yes, that's right, your very own Victoria!'

'Bullshit. You can't get back at me, Walter, just because I made you shit your pants!' My voice rose an octave or two.

'Well you'd better believe it, Whalley. Ask Errol if I'm bullshitting you. Ask him!' For the first time Walter shouted. Lost his cool.

'He's telling the truth, Justin. I'm sorry.' Errol's words rolled out of his mouth as small knives. All of them, stabbing me all over.

My mind was a motorway. Too many lanes, junctions, to keep control of. Too many things to think about. Far too many scenarios.

I sat there staring vacantly into space. Completely alone.

'Justin. Justin!' Errol called out, and snapped me out of my trance.

'I can't believe she would do that to me. She wouldn't.' I was rambling.

'She did, and she wasn't the only one,' Walter decided to inform me.

'I think we should call this meeting to an end now. Thank you again, Justin. Can you leave the premises and sign out at reception?' The HR manager followed protocol to the letter. Now it was my turn to tremble and shake with fear as Walter did when he stepped out of my Formula One car. How the bloody table had rotated on me. Throwing stones and glass houses is a mantra my mother always meted out. How I wished at that very moment that I had paid so much more keen attention to it.

Standing up, I had to grab hold of my chair. My legs had no strength to support me. Turning to see the three faces watch me, genuine surprise registered when they saw what the news had done to me.

'Just, will you be alright driving home?' Errol asked with some concern in his voice.

I sighed heavily, then nodded to say yes.

Leaving the office, I carefully looked around me. I wondered if they heard the raised voices. I shouldn't have cared or have any concern. I was still in a daze. My head cluttered with conspiratorial thoughts.

Moving swiftly and keeping my head poker straight, I headed for the stairs. Ran down them. Into the corridor that led to the reception area. I smiled at the middle-aged, and attractive-looking receptionist and signed out.

Sitting in my car, I took one last look at the edifice-looking office. Eiron Plc was the name on the front of the building. I looked for a while, then started up my Jaguar XF.

Driving home, I could think of nothing else, other than talking to Victoria. It was going to be a long day. Probably the second longest of my life.

71

Sitting at home staring aimlessly at the television set, I sipped my fifth brandy and Coke. I burped, looking around to see if anyone was there. There wasn't. Maybe I was going mad. The state I was in, I could have been, and didn't have the deference to know if I was.

Strolling over to my kitchen, I removed my spectacles and rubbed my weary eyes. I looked at the glass of brandy and Coke, and wanted another. Reaching up to the cupboard for the brandy bottle, an odour emitting from armpits entered my nostrils. It wasn't pleasant.

Once I poured my glass, one quarter high, I added some Coke from the integrated fridge. The Coke fizzed, and I watched this in a heady daze.

Shuffling back into the lounge, I heard a key in the door.

'Hiya Justin, are you there?' It was my luscious Victoria. 'I've got some news,' she said excitedly.

'Oh yeah, can't wait.' I burped loudly. 'In here, darling,' I called back in a high-pitched voice.

Vicky walked in the lounge and her eyes immediately focused on my glass. She looked into my eyes and her smile vanished.

'You've been drinking again! What have I told you?'

I smiled in a tipsy stupor, annoying her even more.

She huffed for a while then sat down beside me on the sofa.

'So how did the exit thingy go?'

'Oh, that.' The gas from the Coke did not agree. I burped several times in succession. 'Pardon me. Oh yes, Eiron Plc, the world leader in bullshit, that's bull, with a capital I.T. on the end.' I began to laugh falsely.

'Justin. Just tell me what happened, or I'm out of here.'

'You may as well be.' She glared hard at me. Sitting more erect on the sofa. Her brow furrowed. It was the first time I'd seen that happen.

'What the hell do you mean by that, Whalley?'

I sipped the remainder of my sweet-tasting beverage and yearned for more.

'Vicky, Vicky, Vicky. What can I say? You think you know someone, and what do they do? They stab you right there.' I showed a stabbing motion in my back, with my right arm. 'When you least expect, they rise up and knock you down.' Victoria folded her arms in frustration. She hadn't a clue what I was going on about.

'Justin, say what's happened, I'm in no mood for pissing riddles!' Her patience had almost expired. So had the good mood she came in with.

'Okay. Here it is.' I turned to face her dead on. Her face directly opposite mine. 'Apparently when Walter asked the sales force who they would put as a possible casualty of any redundancy, you put my name on the list. How's that, for a lovely clean bullet to the heart, eh? Good enough for you?'

Victoria was in shock. Her face tightened. The realisation of what she'd done was clear to see. She unfolded her arms, stood up and walked around the room. Her left hand rubbing her chin, thinking.

I re-entered the kitchen and poured myself another B&C. I drained the brandy bottle, throwing it in the bin from where I stood. On entering the lounge, Victoria sat in the armchair biting at her nails.

'Truth hurts. Can't remember doing it. Well I thought I knew you. Loved you too.' I sat down on the large sofa. She looked back with solemnity in her expression. I was fuming. How could she?

'No, I don't remember.'

'Liar. You're a pissing good liar, Vicky. I got this info from Errol and Walter, and bloody HR!'

'So what? It wasn't my fault they got rid of you. That's down to Walter and HR, nothing to do with me.'

'Nothing to do with you! That's a politician's answer. You didn't fucking help my case though, did you?' I didn't realise how loud I had become. And abusive.

Victoria looked at me in absolute horror at my tirade.

'Well you can fuck off too, then. And don't expect me to help you out or find you another job.'

'I don't need your friggin' help anyway. I've had a belly full of it. And look where it's got me!!'

'You bastard!!' Victoria shouted back and ran upstairs in tears.

'Stupid bitch,' I mumbled.

I talked to myself for an hour at least maybe longer. Trying to calm myself down. My heart was racing, head thumping from the brandy.

Disillusionment ensued, exacerbated by my copious amounts of smooth, sweet-tasting brandy. No quantity large or otherwise would emancipate me from this rabbit hole of shit I was neck deep in.

Then Victoria's bullet from the past pierced my armour, knocking me clean off my already unbalanced feet. The sordid incidents from the deposing lunch, to my exit interview, to the revelation about Victoria wreaked havoc on my supposed stable status, as it was.

My body lacked any source of energy. Feeling as though I'd been smothered with chloroform, I decided to curl up on the sofa and drift off. Umm, comfort at last.

72

Waking up in the dark, initially scared the shit out of me. It took a minute or so, to try and fathom out what was happening.

Stretching and yawning, I straightened up as my eyes became accustomed to the eerie, silent darkness. My eyes were hurting and so did my head. I needed some paracetamol.

Switching the lights on, I viewed the living room clock. Damn, it was eleven in the evening. Still not thinking with any clarity, I tidied the sofa cushions and carried my glass into the kitchen. I put my spectacles back on, and that eased the pressure on my visual acuities.

The house did seem too quiet. Then my memory played its part, as it refreshed me with what happened a few hours ago. A reboot if you like, knitting the relevant elements of a memory together. Rubbing my head in frustration, I knew I had to apologise.

Turning off the lights downstairs, I stumbled languorously up to my bedroom. I could have done with a shower. Man, did I not smell rosy at all.

I used the toilet first, then removed my shirt and trousers, dumping them in the linen basket in corner of my 'family sized' bathroom.

'Vicky,' I whispered as I pushed open our bedroom door. 'Vicky, I'm sorry.'

I approached the bed in the dark, ready to remove my specs. Then I noticed her side seemed too flat.

'Vicky,' I called out. I pulled the sheets back. No one was there. 'Oh shit!'

Slumping onto the bed, I silently cursed myself. I reached for the lamp on the bedside table and flicked it on. Immediately in front of me on the table, was a note.

My heart missed beats. Oxygen emitted from me as though I'd been punched in the stomach. I felt light-headed.

Carefully and slowly I opened the folded piece of paper.

From Vicky.

Justin, I'm so sorry we fought. And yes I did put your name forward, but only after Tom had died. I was mixed up and they caught me at a bad time. They obviously hadn't changed the list since then. You surprised me today, with the way you spoke to me.

A tear ran down my cheek, as I sat on the edge of my lonely bed reading Victoria's note.

I didn't think you were like that. Anyway, if you're reading this, you'll know that I'm not there. I won't say where I've gone for now, and I might contact you soon. I will see how I feel once things settle. We'll see how things go.

More tears streamed down my face, which I wiped away with the tip of the duvet cover.

Don't think I don't love you, because I do, however you hurt me today, more than you know. And, I'm not sure now if I should tell you my news. Some good news it would have been. However one thing I'll tell you, please, please do not try and find me. You have to promise me that.

I made a silent promise to, quickly, and I was eager to read on.

There's no easy way to write this down, other than to say that you're going to be a father!

I had my emotions under control until I read that part. Now who was the arsehole? Me. Yes, Jonathan Augustus Whalley, first-class, premier-league idiot and screw-up artist.

Don't worry about anything. I'm only a few weeks gone. I will let you know how things are going. I just need some space right now. I am genuinely sorry.

Still love you loads.
Vicky
xxx

There was too much to take in. Losing Victoria, even temporarily, was difficult to accept. And now becoming a father, gosh, this was a huge, gigantic step. The step I'd always wanted to take. Yet not like this. Maybe my dream of a loving, always happy relationship was just that, a dream.

Trying to make sense of what I had engineered, became Mission Impossible, and I, Justin Whalley, was no Ethan Hunt. With no special tools, equipment to save me or super-spy friends with special skills, I was supremely on my own. And with no one else at fault, only me. No chance to cast accusatory slants at anybody else, to at a minimum, misdirect anyone who bothered to be around.

Drying my tears, and attempting to calm my whole body from trembling violently, the only person I could call right now was Errol. So yes, maybe one friend, and I hoped he was available and ready to display his special set of 'friendship' that I required.

In an utter state of depression and justifiable angst, I rang Errol and five minutes to midnight. The phone rang several times with no answer. That was his mobile phone. My second attempt tried his original home number where he may have moved back in with Elisa.

That number rang and rang. No answer.

I put the receiver back in its cradle and re-read Victoria's letter once more. Slower this time. Interrogating each word, its meaning in the context of her gut wrenching note.

I was searching for something. A ray of hope, a glimmer of an opportunity to get Victoria back.

Folding the letter neatly, I placed it under my pillow.

Switching the lamp off, I slid under the duvet, buried my head in my hands, curled up in a foetal position and cried myself to sleep.

73

I must have slept forever. At least that's what it felt like. My head throbbed rhythmically, as though someone was playing the drums from a heavy metal song.

At first I thought it was my head that was banging. It wasn't. It was my front door.

'Hang on, will you?' I shouted, using every muscle and sinew and bit of strength I had.

Someone continued to veraciously bang my front door. Moving gingerly, I made my way out of the bedroom, looking at myself in my clothes, which I had slept in. Without my spectacles I stumbled towards the stairs. To avoid falling down them, I slid on my bottom over each step, feeling my way down with my right hand.

Then I heard a voice calling my name through the letterbox. My tired and overworked brain, tried to decipher the voice. Slowly it came to me, as I yawned for umpteenth time. It was a man's voice. It was Errol's.

'Justin, are you in there? It's Errol,' I heard him shout repeatedly.

'Hold on, I'm coming,' I called back.

Standing up at the bottom of the stairs, I pulled myself as erect as I could.

Bright light crept into the house. I decided to check the time, as my normality began to resurface. It was one thirty in the afternoon.

On opening the door, Errol stood with a worried look on his face. And frustrated.

'I hope I didn't keep you waiting, boss. Sorry about that,' was my opening gambit.

Errol said nothing and barged his way in.

I closed the door and followed him into my kitchen.

'What have you done, Just? Victoria gone. Left you. You've been drinking, and damn, you need a shower. And a helping hand. So er, you run along and get yourself cleaned up. I'll make breakfast, or brunch or whatever.'

'You're an arsehole, you know that.'

'But a very good and kind one. Get in the shower,' Errol ordered me.

Still in some sort of a daze I obeyed and acquiesced, devoid of any fighting or resisting tendency.

Twenty minutes later, I felt like a different man. Only superficially, yet better nonetheless.

Errol made me sausages, scrambled eggs, baked beans, toast and a large mug of black coffee. He placed two paracetamol on a napkin and a glass of water beside them. I took them first, before devouring my lunch and breakfast in one.

He stood watching me eat. I gave him something to occupy his time.

'Here, read this.'

Errol took a seat and sat opposite me at my kitchen table and took the letter Vicky had written me.

As I chomped through my food, I watched Errol's eyes roll over each word. Observed him rubbing his chin. Shaking his head. Leaning back and sitting forward in his chair.

Errol looked at me as he tapped the letter on the table.

'Justin Whalley, a father. Who'd have thought it?' Errol opened up. 'Any ideas how it happened?' I smiled painfully. That hurt returned. The hurt from last night. 'What happened, Just? Why did she leave you?'

'We had a fight over my redundancy.' As soon as I said those words, a flicker of recognition appeared in Errol's eyes. He knew immediately what I was driving at. He must have known too.

'You knew about my name being on the list, didn't you?'

Errol looked directly in my eyes. I could see clearly now, with my specs on.

'Of course I did. You would have guessed that already. Remember Justin, I put my resignation in based on not being able to save you. I was the only one who fought for your position at Eiron. So did Shaun before he left. For some reason, most of the other salespeople didn't care that much. If you want my opinion...'

'Whatever,' I interrupted Errol.

'Look, on the flipside, they wanted you out because you were the best. Alright. It might be little consolation now, but when you go for another job, you can prove that you were the best. And for one thing I'll give you a glowing reference. If that's not positive, then I don't know what is.'

Errol was quite firm and forthright in his speech. And of course he was right. A small glow of satisfaction did pass through, knowing that the other salespeople were frightened of my ability.

I slurped my coffee, emitting an audible thankful sigh.

'You know something, Errol, I'm happy that I did myself proud. Okay, maybe not with the Walter driving incident. Apart from that, I feel I did okay. Made my numbers, with possibility of future advancement. Yet here I am, at home, pissed, no job, no girlfriend, no baby. Isn't life a piece of shit?' I laughed in crazy sort of way, putting it on, as though I was acting. Errol watched me, unmoved, not eclipsed at all by my acting.

'I know you're hurting. You feel angry, bitter resentment over everything. The best way to get through this, is to do something about it. Don't cry over the spilt milk. Get on and mop it up. The quicker you do it, the easier things will be. Leave it too long, you'll be in rut that you'll have no way of getting out of. Think about it.'

Errol's words of advice. Ummm, maybe he was right. Those special skills were probably there all time. Secretly, quietly I knew they were. Mr Errol Hughes with powers of deduction, clear thinking, coupled with simple steps to put me back on my feet.

We decided, or Errol did, for me to go the gym, to work off my angst and pent-up frustrations. I agreed only after being badgered continuously by Errol.

He told me Elisa had accepted him back on her terms. He wouldn't go into what those were.

Errol spent the remainder of day with me. The gym did help with relieving some physical stresses. Errol played the psychiatrist for the mental support.

At just after ten in the evening Errol called Elisa to come and pick him up. That must be one the conditions, she had to know exactly where he was going. The only way to do that was to take him there herself. Maybe my life wasn't that bad after all.

I waved goodbye to Errol and thanked him with a big manly hug, before he could leave. Elisa waved from inside her car and I smiled and waved back. The car sped off into the distance and I was all alone again, with my thoughts.

Closing the door behind me, it was time for an early night. My house echoed around me. It missed the warmth of a woman. Victoria, to be exact. So did I. For the second night running and without resistance, I cried myself to sleep.

74

It was a few days from Christmas. The last few days had melted by. I'd only been out once for bottles of rum, a few two-litre bottles of Coke, lemonade and orange juice.

I purchased some food, nothing healthy, and lived like a hermit.

Every single day since Errol had gone, I pondered on what I did to deserve where I was now. What was the single most devastating act, that I performed which led people to despise me so much. Right down to my own girlfriend. Day after day of soul-searching, I could not prescribe an answer.

Emily left several messages on my home answerphone, asking me if I was going to Jenny's for Christmas dinner and staying over. Jenny left three messages. My brothers didn't ring, but that was no surprise. The messages became more and more frantic, when I didn't reply. The only thing I could do was sleep, eat a little and sleep some more.

My house began to reek and could not remember the last time I had a bath or shower. No way could anyone come round, or would I let them in.

On Christmas Eve, Emily drove all the way from Birmingham to come up see me. She told me so on the answerphone. I didn't open the door. Jenny swore she wouldn't speak to me again. Emily felt the same. She told me if she could get over her ectopic pregnancy, and her drugs involvement, I could get over my problems.

Maybe she was right. Maybe they all were. Nevertheless, apathy was a better and easier solution. I loved wallowing in my own self-pity. Someone would help me eventually.

On Christmas Day I awoke at midday. The sun was out, my

clothes were crumpled. I'd slept in them again.

Downstairs on the mat behind the front door, were several cards, some posted, some pushed through the letterbox.

Amongst the envelopes was a postcard. It was from Dublin.

Happy crimbo Just! Hope you're having a fantastic time. Must come over here with me and you know who (he he!) , I'm havin' a ball. Anyway, take care mate, give my undying love to everyone at Eiron in Nottingham.
I'm havin' a Murphy's and a traditional Irish Christmas dinner!!
Cheers

Shaun & Thelma.
Xxx!!

He'd obviously not heard. And why should he have?

Sitting at the kitchen table I looked through over ten Christmas card envelopes. At the bottom was another postcard. The post mark showed it as Monaco.

It was from, Errol, Elisa and Mary Leadbetter. Mary wrote the card.

Justin Whalley. We'd have invited you here, but you wouldn't have come. The weather, company and the resort is fantastic. (I have missed not seeing you – as a friend of course) – so get off your arse and get back to the Justin Whalley I know and love! Promise me, or I'll never speak to you again..
Anyway, have the best crimbo you can,

Love from your <u>FRIENDS!</u>
Mary, Elisa and Errol

That was the wakeup call I needed. I read every card that was sent or posted to me. Four of the cards were from my family. And then there was one from Victoria Shepard.

It didn't say much, which at first left me despondent. However, it was a small weak signal, to show that something, might still be there between us.

It read:

Missing you, Just. Want to see you again, but not sure. My mum says, I should talk to you for the sake of our baby. I do miss you.

Happy Christmas
Love Vicky
Xxxx

By four in the afternoon, I had showered and cleaned up my house. I returned five phone calls to my family, wishing them a belated happy Christmas. I apologised for not buying any presents. Emily said she was on her way to see me and wouldn't stay over at Jenny's. I expected her about six thirty.

Whilst watching a James Bond film on television, the doorbell rang right on cue.

'Well done, Em,' I said out loud as I looked at the time.

I opened the door and nearly passed out. It was Emily, but behind her, stood an attractive looking Victoria Shepard.

'Hello Justin. You've got your sister to thank for this,' she said in a whisper-like voice.

I moved forward and hugged Emily as tears rolled down my cheeks. Victoria smiled coyly as I opened my tearful eyes to see her in full view.

'I'm sorry, I never thought—' Vicky stopped me.

'Sssh. Not another word, Justin. Let's go in, eh?'

Emily and Vicky walked into the house and I closed the door behind them.

My opportunity for a new slate. A clean start had arrived. I know life is full of clichés and irony, yet I could not turn down the best present that I, Justin Whalley, had ever been gifted.

Now I, for the first time, knew what was inside. I couldn't wait to open it.

ABOUT THE AUTHOR

I was born in Birmingham on the same day as my mother. I have enjoyed writing since I was ten years old. My stories were often read out to the class in English at school. Since then I have continued to write for the enjoyment of it, whether it was lyrics for songs, poems. I attempt to dedicate time to writing full-length manuscripts (hopefully for publication). I'd welcome the opportunity one day to be able to write screenplays and scripts for movies and/or television.

Currently I have started the follow up to *Company of Fools* – entitled 'Journey into History', with most of the same characters. I have a self-published book of poetry on Amazon (eBook *Poems for the Festive Season*), and I have written a thriller trilogy entitled *Crime of the Century,* set in the year 2000 and I hope to issue this series too for submission at some stage.

Additionally I have ideas for several books, including a Young Adult series, which I have begun writing called: 'Pentagon Pirate Gang; The Secret of the Orchard' and some stories for younger children, mainly poetry based.

Thank You.

Printed in Poland
by Amazon Fulfillment
Poland Sp. z o.o., Wrocław